CHASING
YESTERDAY

—— A NOVEL ——

OTHER BOOKS BY
RACHEL ANN NUNES

HUNTINGTON FAMILY
Winter Fire
No Longer Strangers

ARIANA SERIES
Ariana: The Making of a Queen
Ariana: A Gift Most Precious
Ariana: A New Beginning
Ariana: A Glimpse of Eternity
This Time Forever
Ties That Bind
Twice in a Lifetime

ROMANTIC SUSPENSE
A Bid for Love
Framed for Love
Love on the Run

OTHER NOVELS
A Greater Love
To Love and to Promise
Tomorrow and Always
Bridge to Forever
This Very Moment
A Heartbeat Away
Where I Belong
In Your Place

PICTURE BOOKS
Daughter of a King
The Secret of the King

CHASING YESTERDAY

A NOVEL

RACHEL ANN NUNES

DESERET BOOK

SALT LAKE CITY, UTAH

To my editor, Suzanne Brady,
I dedicate the penultimate novel
in the Huntington family saga.
You're the best!

Once again I'm indebted to so many
talented Deseret Book employees.
Your willingness to go
the extra mile is appreciated.
Thanks for everything.

© 2006 Rachel Ann Nunes

Library of Congress Cataloging-in-Publication Data
Nunes, Rachel Ann, 1966–
   Chasing yesterday / Rachel Ann Nunes.
     p.   cm.
   ISBN 1-59038-542-X (pbk.)
   1. Stepsisters—Fiction. I. Title.
   PS3564.U468C47 2006
   813'.54—dc22   2005028231

Printed in the United States of America   54459
Malloy Lithographing Inc., Ann Arbor, MI

10   9   8   7   6   5   4   3   2   1

Chapter One

Tyler Huntington stared into the flushed face of his editor, Chantel Hull. Hands on her hips, she tossed her shoulder length brown hair. "Face it, Tyler, you blew it," she growled with more than her customary Friday morning irritation.

Hands on hips, Tyler thought. *Not good. Not good at all.* No doubt about it, Chantel was seriously upset.

"We need a more sympathetic voice," Chantel continued. She wore black dress pants, a white fitted blouse, and suede high heels that put her at Tyler's eye level. She didn't look like a mother of four and grand-mother of one—probably because she was always too busy working to eat.

"I'm sympathetic," he protested.

"Telling parents it's their fault for not being stricter when their kid messes up might have some basis in truth, but it does nothing for their grief—or for the public good. You were supposed to report, not wage a diatribe against lenient parents. That's not good journalism. You should know that."

He let his face show surprise. "What do you mean it's not good

1

journalism? Papers sell better because of a certain kind of story. We all know that. It might be sensational, but I got attention, didn't I?"

"The *wrong* kind of attention. I won't stand for reporters using stories for their own agendas."

"Even if I'm right?" He tried not to make the words challenging, but he wasn't backing down, either. "I stand by what I wrote: parents *are* too lenient."

Chantel snorted, hands still on her hips. "That's a rather procrustean attitude. I don't know what hole you've been living in, but one size certainly doesn't fit all in child rearing. For crying out loud, you're only twenty-four and a year out of college. What were you trying to prove?"

He adjusted his black-framed glasses to buy a few seconds. "Okay, so I might have been a bit rash." He hated to admit it, but he would if it meant keeping the peace. He felt a sudden strong urge to see and talk with Savvy Hergarter, who had once been his closest friend. She would understand what he'd been trying to do. She would offer encouragement and give him the insight to help him pinpoint the exact blend of emotion and objectivity he had struggled—and obviously failed—to achieve in his last article. He was glad she was coming home today. Maybe that's why he kept thinking about her.

"Rash?" Chantel's voice rose an octave. Another not-so-good sign. Her finger came between them as though she wanted to shake it at him. "Tyler, you accused a prominent and favored politician of emotionally neglecting his daughter—and in an election year, no less." A hardness glinted in her hazel eyes, something he hadn't noticed the other three thousand times she'd yelled at him. Yelling wasn't necessarily bad when it came from Chantel, but that steely look was something new.

"I'll retract. I'll make an apology. I'll write something more favorable."

She shook her head. "There aren't enough apologies or excuses left in the whole world. He's threatening to sue."

With a sickening twist in his stomach, Tyler realized the situation was far more serious than he'd thought. For a year he'd interned at the paper, working every free moment, and then after finishing college a year ago, he'd been hired full-time by the *Deseret Morning News*. Now his diligence and all the overtime had been for nothing.

"I'll write you a recommendation," Chantel said, not quite meeting his eyes. "You're a talented guy. I'm sure you'll find another paper. Maybe at the *Trib*. Or maybe you'll want to go out of state. You might find more sensational journalism in, say, New York or California. Though I hope you'll stay away from badgering popular politicians."

We're the ones who make them popular! he wanted to yell. It wasn't exactly true, but at least partially. By getting their names in the newspaper, politicians received free publicity. He swallowed hard, feeling something that resembled sand scratching at his throat. "Please, Chantel."

Her face was impassive. "I'm sorry, Tyler. You'll need to get your things now."

It was too late. He had used up all his chances at the paper.

Chantel walked with him to the small cubby he had worked in for the past year. He moved slowly, as though in a dream, taking down the year-old photographs of his family, the more recent one of his friend, Savvy, standing with him at a restaurant after she'd returned from her mission, the small wallet-sized pictures of his seven nieces and nephews, and the glamor shot LaNae had had taken at some mall.

LaNae Fugal.

For the first time he thought of his girlfriend and how this would affect their plans. LaNae was hinting at marriage, and to be honest, he was leaning that way himself. Since his older brother Mitch had been married last September, after waiting a year for his fiancée, Cory, a new member of the Church, to obtain a temple recommend, Tyler was the only Huntington sibling who hadn't taken the marital plunge. His mother was on his case about hurrying up—one of the few things she and LaNae seemed to have in common.

That LaNae wouldn't be excited about his new circumstances was putting it mildly. She worked in Orem at Utah Valley State College as a guidance counselor, but she was always talking about how happy she would be to quit once they got married and started a family.

Chantel allowed Tyler to delete or forward his personal files from his computer, though he didn't keep anything there except a few e-mails. His gaze fell on the notes he'd taken during the early morning press conference called by the governor, loose pages waiting to be typed up before press time. Someone else would do the story now. He left the notes next to the keyboard.

Theo Brewer, the aging editor of the sports page, appeared at his elbow with a slightly dusty cardboard box, the kind that had once held ten reams of copy paper. Tyler had always liked Theo, though he'd refused an offer to transfer to Theo's department because he didn't enjoy sports. Now he wondered if that offer might be still available. He opened his mouth to ask, but another steely glare from Chantel lodged the plea in his throat. It was just as well. He had enough pride left that he didn't want her to see him beg. Besides, sports was a last resort, and he wasn't that desperate—yet.

"I'm going to miss you around here," Theo said, proffering the box.

"Thanks." Tyler dumped his personal belongings inside. Pens, four pencils, a half-eaten box of Milk Duds, three pads of paper, the pictures, his personal paperclip holder, two books on journalism, his spare Book of Mormon, several paper files crammed with story ideas he'd collected over the past few years, a few quarters and dimes, four music CDs, a new pad of Post-it notes, and a *Star Wars* novel. That was it. That small box represented his whole life at the paper. He suddenly wished there'd been time to accumulate more, that he'd moved up enough to have space for accumulation.

"Won't have anyone to bounce my crazy ideas off," Theo said, giving Chantel a pointed glance. Theo had a lot of ideas about everything—mostly strange ones about politics and conspiracies, but none of that ever interfered with his passion and expertise in editing or writing his sports columns. "I'll walk him out," Theo added.

Nodding, Chantel gave Tyler a last conciliatory glance. "I'll send your letter of recommendation. Good luck."

The walk out to the parking lot was long. Tyler felt the stares of his fellow reporters as an almost physical touch. Most were sympathetic, except for that of a round-faced intern who regarded his passage with poorly concealed glee. With Tyler gone, there would be room for another full-time employee. Tyler forgave him, remembering how it was to want to be a reporter so bad that it ate into every waking thought or sleeping dream.

To tell the truth, he still felt that way.

And he was right, darn it all! How did a politician think he could run a city if he couldn't control his own child?

"Give it a while," Theo said as they stepped outside. The turgid clouds overhead were dark and dangerous-looking, a late summer storm on its way. "This thing with the politician, it'll blow over. When it does, I'll request you in my department."

Tyler forced a grin. Theo knew of his dislike for sports; they had talked about it often enough during their debates on the mysteries of life and pro wrestling. But their disagreements hadn't hindered their relationship in the least. "Thanks, Theo."

"Unless you have a job by then. I've no doubt you'll find something. I've got faith in you."

Tyler started for the new green Jeep Cherokee that had replaced his battered green pickup when he'd been hired. He'd had no worries about making the payments then, and the gas mileage was better than with his old truck. Now he wasn't so sure the decision had been a good one.

"Uh, Tyler."

Tyler turned back to face Theo, who had stopped on the sidewalk in front of the door. "Look," he said. "I feel kind of responsible. I shouldn't have talked to you the way I did the other day."

Tyler let his breath out, without realizing he'd been holding it. He had wondered if Theo would bring that up. Their discussion about inept and lazy parents had been much deeper and more pointed than anything Tyler had written in his article. "It has nothing to do with you. You were right, I was right. If parents aren't responsible, who will be?"

"Maybe it's not my place to judge."

Tyler cradled the cardboard box to his chest. It didn't matter now if the dust rubbed off on his blue dress shirt. "You've raised six children, all of them upstanding citizens."

Theo rubbed his jaw with his mottled, age-spotted hand. For a moment his blue eyes looked haggard and sad. "Well, in retrospect I think that had more to do with their mother than it ever had to do with me."

Tyler dipped his head. He'd met Theo's wife, and she was impressive. "I wrote the article," he said. "I'm responsible. Don't worry. I'm young. I have time to find my niche, as you have yours."

Theo nodded, the lines around his eyes relaxing, making him appear younger than he had a minute before. He extended a hand. "Well, good luck. Call me if you need something or if you ever want to talk."

Tyler shook his hand, smiling widely. He held the smile until Theo was back inside the building. Then with a loud sigh, he walked heavily toward his Jeep, shivering at the cooling breeze that ran up his back and around his neck. The breeze reminded him of Savvy and how for one of her advanced astronomy classes two years ago she'd had to go up into the mountains and look at the stars through a telescope. She'd invited him along, and he'd accepted because he enjoyed watching her work. She came alive when she talked about or studied the sky. That night, as they shared a picnic under the stars, they had come up with a plot for a science fiction novel—a really terrible plot, but one that made them laugh hysterically.

He hadn't thought of that night in a long time, not since he'd finally come to terms with Savvy going on a mission. Yes, he could admit now that he'd been against her going. The idea of not having her around to bounce his ideas off had been unfathomable. Who else would endure all those foreign films or his latest sci-fi plot? Who else would offer counsel for his latest romance? What would he do without her?

Savvy had been in his life forever—well, that wasn't really true. It just felt that way. Actually, Savvy and his sister Amanda had been friends long before Tyler met her. Though Savvy was four and a half years younger than Amanda, she'd been mature for her age, and the two women had become fast friends in their singles ward, almost as close as sisters. With the intent of making her a real sister, Amanda had set Savvy up with Mitch, Tyler's older brother, but the two hadn't hit it off romantically. Amanda had tried again with Tyler after his mission to Bolivia.

Tyler had loved being with Savvy from the very first minute, and they dated for six months. But eventually they became just friends, dating others but always staying in close touch. His upset reaction at the time Savvy announced her mission plans still puzzled him. He'd been hurt and angry. He'd felt his heart breaking. Why? There was no explanation.

When he tried to tell her how he felt, Savvy admitted to harboring feelings for him that ran deeper than friendship. He had been stunned with the revelation and began to wonder if he really did love her; but after a few months, he decided that he simply missed her friendship. If he hadn't dated the first year she was gone, it didn't mean anything. He'd only been concentrating on his studies. Of course, they'd kept in touch with many letters, and though it wasn't quite the same as having her around, it was enough.

Before he knew it, she was home and gone again within a few months, back to her beloved mission area near San Francisco—Berkeley, to be exact. She transferred her college credits to the University of California at Berkeley, where she planned to finish her education and then teach. Tyler still missed her—more than he would admit.

Reaching the Jeep, Tyler saw his reflection in the window. He looked thinner than he remembered, and his sandy blond hair needed cutting. He'd have to tell LaNae. She liked cutting it for him, though she really didn't do as good a job as the girl with the black spiky hair at Collar Cuts. His face was pale—or was that only in contrast to the grim, roiling clouds above his head? His green eyes disturbed him most of all. They were scared. Not angry, not offended, but scared and depressed. Glaring at his reflection, Tyler opened the door and slid inside, setting his box on the passenger seat.

Glancing at the dash clock, he saw it was well after ten. In less than two hours Savvy would be home for a visit. Her sister had called to let him know she was picking her up at the airport and that the family would be gathering at their parents' home in American Fork to welcome her. Tyler was planning to stop by, but it was too early to head there now.

He passed Sandy without getting off at the freeway exit for home. He was living in his brother's house and paying the mortgage while Mitch, his wife, Cory, and their three-year-old daughter, EmJay, were in the Australian outback, snapping pictures and writing facts about exotic animals for a children's book and documentary they were putting together.

As the first drops of rain splattered on the windshield, Tyler pulled into the visitors' parking lot at UVSC. He put several coins in the meter and dashed down the sidewalk, feeling the raindrops on his head. They were colder than he expected for August.

He walked into the counseling center, past all the cubbies that resembled all the other crowded cubbies in the world, until he reached LaNae's desk. She wasn't there, so he sat down to wait, noting that her computer had been idle long enough for the screen saver to come on—a series of geometric shapes skittering across a black background.

His eyes fell on a picture of him and LaNae together. She was of average height and thin—something he'd always loved about her. Her makeup wasn't thick but it was noticeable, and her blonde hair, cut short and sassy, had darker streaks underneath. Her face was narrow, her jaw slightly too small for perfect balance, though no one ever noticed after seeing her warm, wide smile. Her eyes were a pale blue. Tyler puzzled about that for a moment. Why had he always thought they were more the deeper color of the sky on a hot summer day? In all, she was a striking woman, and he felt a rush of what might be a hint of pride.

"Tyler!"

He looked up to see LaNae coming toward him. Standing slowly, he tried to discern what was different about her voice. Must have something to do with the man at her side. The stranger was tall and big like a football player. He wore canvas pants and a button-down shirt with short sleeves, and his hair was spiky on top but in a reserved sort of way. The same look Tyler himself usually sported when his hair wasn't too long.

LaNae looked as beautiful as ever, dressed in an olive flowered skirt and a matching short-sleeved sweater. Her ankles were attractive in dressy, high-heeled pumps. "This is a surprise," she said. She touched his arm, but she didn't give him a hug or kiss as she normally did. Of course, this was her workplace; he certainly wouldn't be hugging and kissing her in front of his co-workers at the paper, either.

His former co-workers, that is.

Tyler looked from LaNae to the football jock, expecting an introduction, but the guy thumbed over his shoulder. "I'll see you later," he said. "I've got someone coming for a consultation."

Tyler waited until he was out of earshot. "He works here?"

"Yeah, that's Rob. He's new."

As an unreasonable jealousy surged through him, LaNae grabbed his hand and sat down, pulling him into the chair opposite hers. "I'm glad you're here. I've been wanting to talk to you. Did you come to take me to lunch?" He'd surprised her like that occasionally, when he'd been able to get away from the paper.

"Well, uh, actually . . ." He trailed off, not wanting to admit that he planned to spend the afternoon with Savvy and her family. Though he assured LaNae repeatedly that they were just friends, old friends, she didn't like Savvy.

LaNae's eyes narrowed. "Well, if not that, then why did you come? And why is your shirt so dirty?"

"I lost my job." There. That bit, at least, was out in the open.

Her eyes widened as she gave a little gasp. "What . . . why? Was it that article you were telling me about?" Her tone went from surprised to sympathetic to accusing faster than Tyler could have thought possible. Sitting tall in her chair, she put her hands on her hips. Tyler nearly groaned. Why did women do that?

"I was right," he said stubbornly. "The least you can do is be sympathetic. That's why I came here, you know. Looking for comfort. It's not like I won't get another job."

LaNae clucked her tongue, reaching out to take his hand. "I am sorry, Tyler, and I know you'll find another job, but I sometimes wish you'd consider the consequences before you act. I was just thinking we should make some solid plans about our future. But this puts a hold on everything. You know how my dad feels about you being able to support me."

He knew. No job meant no official engagement. Why didn't he feel more sorry?

"Don't worry about it," he said. "Things will work out."

He was a hard worker—there had to be something available. Maybe at the *Salt Lake Tribune,* as Chantel had suggested. Or perhaps in another state. Take California, for instance. When he'd talked to Savvy on the phone last month, she'd mentioned that some Berkeley students were picketing against gay rights. There were several clashes, and after a little research, he'd written up a story about it for his newspaper that had gone over really well. If he freelanced a few articles like that, he could begin to make a reputation for himself. In fact, maybe he'd drive to California next week and feel out the area.

"Let's go to lunch and talk about it," LaNae said. "We can even go by the *Daily Herald* to see if they have an opening."

Tyler shook his head. "I'm not ready to work for a smaller paper—at least not yet. I'd rather try the *Trib* first. Besides, now's not exactly a good time. I've got plans." He swallowed hard before adding, "Savvy's coming home for a visit today. I thought I'd stop by and say hi."

LaNae dropped his hand as though it had suddenly burned her. "You didn't tell me she was coming home."

He shrugged. "I only found out myself a few days ago. Her sister called."

"I don't see why you have to go see her." Her jaw clenched as though she hated voicing the words.

"We're old friends—of course I want to see her." Though if he were truthful, Savvy might not exactly welcome his presence. She hadn't told him herself that she was coming.

"Can I go with you?"

Tyler was beginning to feel sick. He really, really didn't want LaNae to go, but he knew that feeling was wrong. LaNae was the woman he was thinking about spending eternity with, and she should be his first concern. "You can. Of course, you can," he found himself saying. "But I don't know exactly when the plane is coming in or what the plan is for lunch. I was going to swing by the house and say hi, that's all. I don't know if I could have you back here on time. Honestly, it's not a big deal."

She didn't reply, but her face was rigid, and Tyler wanted to kick himself. Why did he have to hurt her? He didn't want to.

After a few moments, she spoke. "You don't want me to go, do you?" Her perception was one of the things he had always loved about her—until now.

"It was rather awkward the last time," he admitted. "With her family and all."

LaNae had shown up uninvited for Savvy's homecoming dinner at Tony Roma's. Tyler remembered how Savvy's vibrant smile had frozen on her face. Her blue, blue eyes met his. "Your girlfriend?" she'd asked. He thought he saw a disappointment there, something so deep and filled with hurt that it made him want to take her into his arms. Or to deny his relationship with LaNae. Anything to make Savvy smile again. Yet how he could feel that way, or why he should imagine such hurt in her eyes was beyond his understanding. After all, they were just friends, and LaNae really was his girlfriend. He had to admit to that.

"We've been dating over three weeks," LaNae had replied, grabbing Tyler's arm possessively. "He's a keeper."

Savvy had nodded and turned back to the conversation with her family. For the rest of the meal, she was gracious to him and LaNae, but there was an impassable wall between them. Later she didn't return his calls. He'd become involved with a big story at work and before he knew it, she'd gone back to California. There had been no opportunity to talk, to find out what had gone so dreadfully wrong between them. When he'd finally called her in California, she'd talked to him, though distantly. They'd even exchanged a few letters, but things were definitely awkward between them. He hoped to repair that today.

"I told you a hundred times I was sorry for showing up like that," LaNae said. "I didn't know it would turn out so awful. Are you still holding that against me?"

"No, of course not. But Savvy doesn't even know I'm coming. I didn't want to make a big deal out of it."

"Go, then," LaNae retorted, folding her slender arms over her stomach. "Do what you want."

Tyler knew LaNae was touchy about Savvy, but he'd never expected this vehemence. She was generally sweet and understanding. What was going on? Had he missed something? "Honestly," he tried again, "it's not a big deal."

LaNae turned in her chair and typed something on her computer. The lazy motion of the geometric cubes vanished, replaced by a Windows icon.

"LaNae?"

No reply.

Women! They could be so infuriating.

He stood up to leave, retreat seeming the best solution. "Let's talk later, okay? What about tonight?" She still didn't look up, so he walked away.

Outside, it was still raining, though lightly, and the breeze blew the drops into his face. Halfway to the Jeep, he stopped and turned around. He couldn't leave things like that with LaNae. Better to have her come with him and risk making things worse between him and Savvy. At the very least, he should try to talk to LaNae—providing she didn't call security and have him thrown out. He'd seen her do that once with an unruly student.

Yes, that was the responsible thing to do. He darted back inside the building. Removing his glasses, he cleaned them on his shirttails and then tucked the shirt back in. He tried to brush the dust from the box off his chest, but it clung like a scum on the top of a stagnant pond.

Great.

LaNae wasn't at her desk, but Tyler refused to be daunted. He thought about asking a co-worker but instead went down the aisles himself. At the last cubicle, one seemingly more isolated than the others, he saw LaNae with her new friend Rob. She had tears on her cheeks, and Rob's arm was around her comfortingly. Without seeing Tyler, they walked through a back door and disappeared.

I blew it, he thought, staring down at the dirt on his shirt. The numb feeling he'd had since being fired intensified. What kind of man loses his job and alienates his girlfriend all in one day?

I need to talk to Savvy. Yes. That was it. She'd understand. She'd help him figure out what to do, how to smooth things over with LaNae. Savvy had always been there for him when he needed her.

As he walked to his Jeep, he pulled out his cell phone, scrolled through his contacts, and called Savvy's younger sister, Camille. Of Savvy's four siblings, the soft-spoken Camille was his favorite.

"Hi, Tyler," she said, picking up on the second ring. "I was just going to call you."

Rain dripped down his head and into his ear. "Are you at the airport? Has her plane come in?"

"No, I'm still in American Fork. We were about to leave for the airport when Savvy called. I know how much you were looking forward to seeing her, but she's not coming home. Something very serious has happened."

Chapter Two

Savvy Hergarter was stuffing last-minute items into her suitcase when the doorbell rang, reverberating through the small apartment. Probably Chris, ready to take her and Miranda to the airport. She'd finished up her summer finals, worked her last shift at the planetarium, and was flying home to visit for nearly twelve days before returning for school—this time to finish her remaining two classes and co-teach a beginning class to freshmen. After this semester, she'd begin her master's.

She was eager to see her family. Four months had passed since she'd left Utah, and missing them had grown to a sharp ache in her chest. Camille had written about a boy she was dating, and Savvy couldn't believe her twenty-year-old sister was seriously considering marriage. She hoped the others hadn't changed too much in her absence. Rosalie would begin college in September, and the twins, Gabriel and Forest, were fourteen now and would start ninth grade next week.

"The door is probably for you," said Miranda Guercio, her short, small-boned, dark-skinned roommate who was heading home to Texas—for good. She was speaking Spanish at the moment, but Savvy hardly noticed. Spanish had become an integral part of her life on her mission, and she loved practicing with Miranda every chance she had.

"Yeah, he's early. I'm almost finished, but I need to get my makeup from the bathroom." Savvy surveyed her freshly made bed, looking neat and welcoming compared to Miranda's bare mattress. "I just wish you—" Savvy broke off and let out a long sigh.

Miranda smiled, her dark eyes gleaming. "Don't worry. We'll write. Or at least e-mail."

Savvy nodded, returning her friend's smile with a sad one of her own. Writing wasn't the same thing. She should know. She'd written to Tyler for the past two years and still didn't know what he wanted from her. Before she'd left on her mission, he'd told her his heart was breaking. "You already broke mine a long time ago," she'd replied. She wished now that she'd never told him that truth.

At the time she'd hoped he was finally growing up. That at last he would understand what was important in life and realize they were meant for each other. But it was she who had been wrong. He might have grown up while she was serving a mission, but they hadn't been meant for each other after all. That was the real reason she'd left Utah to study at Berkeley. Or at least the compelling reason. Yes, she'd run away.

The thought shook her deeply. How after all these months could she still think of him so much? It wasn't as if he was the only man in her life. Chris Davis—stable, loyal, brilliant, handsome Chris—was here for her now. He was safe. She didn't need or want Tyler.

Shaking off the melancholy, she flipped her straight blonde hair over her shoulder and bent down to pick up a suitcase. "These are heavy," she said. "It's going to take two trips."

"I'll be there in a minute," Miranda said as Savvy headed into the hall.

The aroma of the waffle breakfast they had eaten earlier that morning still lingered in the air, complete with the scent of sweet maple syrup. Savvy had indulged more than usual, but she had done well at maintaining her weight over the past months and a few pancakes shouldn't set her back that far. Regardless, she would never look like the tiny Miranda. Savvy would always be curvaceous, and she had long ago come to terms with the fact that her body was meant to carry an extra few pounds. It hadn't seemed to make a difference in her relationships—she'd received eight serious proposals of marriage during her early years at BYU. Unfortunately, none of them had come from Tyler. Why she'd been so cursed to be in love with him was something she'd spent late nights wondering.

All that was now in the past. Savvy was ready to finish her degree in astronomy and go on with her life. She was almost sure that going on meant having Chris in her future. Chris was a guy in her ward, a returned missionary, now working on a master's degree in astrophysics at Berkeley. They'd met at the summer ward barbecue where he had been flipping burgers. Upon hearing that Savvy was studying astronomy at Berkeley, he had launched into a discussion on spiral galaxies that had fascinated her. A week later, he'd helped her get a job at the planetarium.

Since then they'd spent many hours together talking about their shared interest in the complex workings of the heavens. Unbeknownst to him, his excitement had reawakened her deep love and fascination for astronomy, feelings that had suffered during her preoccupation with Tyler. Suddenly she couldn't wait to open her textbooks again, to study the stars, to dream about space. To her great relief, even math regained its place of honor in her life. She now understood that whatever the impetus, transferring to Berkeley had been the right thing to do.

The doorbell rang for the second time as Savvy entered the small living room. Dropping her suitcase to the ground, she went to the door, smiling widely in anticipation of seeing Chris. Her smile faltered as she looked instead upon a scrawny teenage girl clutching a bulging backpack that looked ready to burst at any moment. The girl wore sandals, frayed shorts that barely covered her behind, and a red tube-top that left her shoulders and stomach bare, revealing the glint of a belly button ring. Her shoulder-length hair, bleached white and poorly cut in layers, was pushed to the side to reveal a wide forehead and an ear that sported multiple piercings. Her skin was pale, almost translucent, odd for summer in California. Black eyeliner and shadow emphasized bright blue eyes that were strangely familiar.

"Can I help you?" Savvy asked, darting a quick glance up and down the outside porch that linked all of the second-story apartments, searching for signs of a companion or maybe a parent. Nothing. Down below in the street there was no car at the curb, no adult waiting.

"I'm looking for someone," the girl said. "I hope she still lives here, because if not, I don't know what I'm gonna do."

"Do you want Miranda? She's my roommate."

"I'm looking for my sister." The girl's eyes held a sense of desperation that evoked Savvy's sympathy. "I've been on a bus all day and night, and then I hitched a ride from the station. She has to be here. If she's gone back to her family, I don't think they would be happy to see me."

Savvy arched a brow. "But wouldn't her family be your family?"

"It's not like that." The girl's frustration was growing. She stared at Savvy intently, as though trying to see inside her head.

"Tell me her name," Savvy said gently. "I'll try to help you." She was almost certain the girl had the wrong address. This child didn't look like she could be related to Miranda.

"Her name's Savannah—Savannah Hergarter." The girl lifted her chin as though getting ready for rejection. Her left shoulder jerked twice in a sort of violent half shrug. "I gotta find her."

Savvy's breath caught in her throat. *It can't be,* she thought. *My sisters are Camille and Rosalie.* Yet even as the thoughts rushed through her brain, she knew it was possible. This girl *could* be her sister—her half sister. Aloud she managed to say, "I'm Savvy Hergarter."

Relief filled the girl's face as she let her backpack down on the porch. "I should have known. You look like him in the eyes."

His eyes. The girl's eyes.

"I look like my mother," Savvy rejoined.

The girl smirked, her desperation vanishing completely. Bending over, she took a photograph from an outer pocket of her backpack and handed it to Savvy.

There it was, a picture similar to one Savvy had in her own album back home. A tiny girl, nearly two years old, was walking hand in hand with a man she barely recognized: her father. Not Jesse Hergarter, the man who had married her divorced mother and later adopted her, but her birth father, her mother's first husband. A huge roller coaster spanned the sky in back of the man and child. She didn't remember the day, but her mother had told her it was the first and last time her father had come to see her after the divorce.

In an instant, Savvy was transported back to her childhood. Not to the day in the picture but to a day years later when she'd stumbled across a similar picture lying loose at the back of an old photo album. "Who is he?" she'd asked.

Her mother had explained how her birth father had come to take her to Lagoon, the local amusement park. He'd brought his new wife, who had been trying without success to have a baby of her own. When Savvy pressed for more information, her mother had told her that her father's new wife was hoping to share custody of Savvy.

"But you didn't want to share custody?" Savvy shivered at the possibility. She couldn't imagine living with that stranger in the photo. No matter how tall or attractive, he simply couldn't be her daddy. Jesse was her daddy, and she loved only him.

Her mother had pulled her close. "Oh, Savvy, it's hard to explain, but I'll try. Derek—your father—had fallen away from the Church, and neither he nor his wife was interested in any of our values. I was scared about your future. I was willing to let him spend time with you but not willing to let you go live with him for extended periods. You were a tiny baby when we divorced, so you didn't even know who he was."

"What happened?"

"After coming to see you, Derek had a change of heart." Her

mother paused, her eyes tearful. "He saw how much Jesse loved you and decided that you really did belong with us. At the same time his wife became pregnant. She was really sick and even hospitalized at one point. She decided not to pursue custody and encouraged Derek to let Jesse adopt you. We were very grateful."

As far as Savvy knew, her birth father had never tried to contact her again. Mostly she'd been glad because she loved Jesse—her real father, as she called him—so much, but sometimes when she was feeling sad, she wondered what was wrong with her that her birth father had not wanted to see her. Logically, she knew those feelings were unfounded— what could have been wrong with a two-year-old? Still, the idea remained.

That's all behind me now, Savvy thought. Or was it? That past was in fact staring her in the face.

"He's Derek Roathe," the girl said, snatching back the picture as though afraid Savvy would want to keep it. "He's my father. Your father, too."

Savvy was having a hard time breathing. *In, out,* she told herself. *In, out.*

Behind the girl, Chris's navy convertible rolled up to the curb. "My ride," Savvy said. "I've got to catch a plane." She would be glad to escape this encounter, to think about it from a distance.

At her words, the girl on the porch lost all appearance of calm. "No! I've come so far! The least you can do is talk to me!"

She was right. Underneath the shock, Savvy was experiencing a potent curiosity. Did the girl have siblings? She was certainly too young to be the baby her father's new wife had been expecting all those years ago. How many children did her father have? Where were they? Where was he? And why had he never asked to see her?

Savvy shook that last question from her mind. She certainly didn't care to know why he'd kept away. He was nothing to her life. Nothing but a donated cell. Jesse was the man who'd been there for her. He was the man who'd gone on campouts, taught her to fish, baptized her, and read her stories for hours at night. He loved her, and she wouldn't have any other father for anything in the whole world.

"Please." The girl's black-rimmed eyes were full of tears, her hands balled in fists at her sides.

Savvy blinked the tears from her own eyes. "Of course," she said softly. "I'll take a later plane." It would be expensive, but what choice did she have? "Please, go on in and wait for me on the couch. I'll need to tell him"—she motioned at Chris who was coming up the stairs—"that I'm not going. Then we'll find some place to talk." She took two steps past the girl before asking, "What's your name, anyway?"

"Lexi."

Savvy nodded and reached to help her with her backpack, but the girl quickly bent and slung it over her shoulder. As she stepped inside, Savvy noticed they were a similar height, though she suspected Lexi would grow taller. Evidently, the girl had taken after their father in height while Savvy had received her mother's genes.

"Ready to go?" Chris had reached the top of the stairs and smiled at her, one hand on the black cast iron railing. Dressed today in baggy brown knee-length shorts, a T-shirt, and sandals, he looked younger than the graduate student he was. He was tall and big-boned, and his dark brown hair and gray eyes gave him a rather exotic look. Those gray eyes had studied the stars; they were patient eyes that could stare into a telescope and wait for hours to document some rare phenomenon. If his forehead was a bit narrow and his nose slightly pointed, these were made up for by the full lips, chiseled face, and wide shoulders. His height definitely made Savvy feel small and protected.

"I was, but there's been a change." Savvy glanced back through the open door, where she could see Lexi slumped on the couch.

Chris's brow creased with concern. "What happened? Are you sick? You look pale."

"I—I'm fine. It's . . . well . . . you're not going to believe this, but that girl in there seems to be my half sister."

Chris glanced inside the apartment, his eyes wide. "What can I do?"

She shook her head. "Nothing. But I can't leave. I have to talk to her."

"You'll have to pay extra to change your flight."

"I know." She was stressed about it, but what was money in the face of this child's obvious need? For despite Lexi's air of bravado and the heavy makeup, Savvy could see that she was only a child—one who needed her.

Chris searched Savvy's face. "Are you sure? Look, you could talk on the way to the airport, and then I could drop her somewhere. I know how much this trip means to you."

Savvy stifled irritation, though she knew he was only trying to help. "I'll probably need more time to find out why she's here and what she wants."

What does she want? The thought made Savvy abruptly suspicious. Had her birth father sent her? Could Lexi hurt Savvy's mother in some way? Savvy didn't think it possible, but she knew there were tender places inside her mother's heart that still ached from her early failure. Or rather, from her first husband's betrayals.

"Savvy? What's going on?" Miranda came out to the door, her eyes darting between the couch and Savvy's face.

Shaking off her somber thoughts, Savvy went inside the apartment. "This is Lexi," she said. "She—she says she's my sister."

"I *am* her sister." Lexi's chin rose a notch, as if daring them to disagree.

Savvy nodded. "I was adopted by my stepfather as a child," she explained. "It's seems my birth father is Lexi's father as well."

Miranda's mouth rounded to an O. Though Savvy had told Chris briefly about her adoption, the subject had never come up between her and Miranda in the four months they had shared the apartment. "Should I call a taxi?" Miranda asked, glancing at the apple clock hanging on the wall that led into their tiny kitchen. "I can't miss my flight."

"Look, you go on ahead. Chris will still take you. Won't you?"

Savvy looked at Chris, and he nodded. "After Lexi and I talk, I'll decide what to do."

"I'll come back, then," Chris said. His gaze rested sternly on Lexi, as though worried for Savvy's safety. Savvy herself felt a tremor of unease, though more because of the child's sudden arrival than anything else. How would Savvy explain this delay to her parents? Especially to her mother? The last thing she wanted to do was to drag Derek back into her mother's life.

Miranda hugged Savvy. "Good luck," she whispered. "And don't worry, I'll take good care of your handsome guy here."

Chris wasn't exactly her guy, but not for lack of his trying. Savvy grinned. "Thanks." Over Miranda's shoulder, she saw Lexi watching her intently with an unreadable look in those wide blue eyes.

Within minutes, Chris and Miranda had left for the airport. Savvy sat down by Lexi, biting her lip as she wondered what to say. The girl's eyes *were* familiar, Savvy saw. They did strongly resemble hers. The resemblance wasn't just in the color—Savvy's mother had that same sky-colored hue—but rather in the wide-set, oval shape. Savvy's other four siblings had darker, rounder eyes like Jesse.

"So," Savvy prompted. "What brings you here?"

Lexi scooted to the far edge of the couch, as far away from Savvy as possible, pushing her backpack along with her. "I found your address, and I came." Her eyes were guarded now, and Savvy wondered why.

"How did you get the address?"

Lexi hesitated a fraction of a second. "My brother."

"Your brother?" Savvy asked. Her heartbeat quickened. Was he perhaps another long-lost sibling?

"He's my half brother actually." Lexi studied her for a minute. "I know what you're thinking. You want to know if he's your brother too. Well, he is. He's older than me. Twenty. That's three years younger than you, right?"

"Yeah. So how old are you?"

"Sixteen."

Savvy doubted she was that old. She looked closer to twelve.

"How did your brother get my address?" Savvy couldn't help the question as the analytical part of her sensed something that didn't quite add up.

Lexi shrugged. "I think he wrote to your mom a couple months ago."

Savvy couldn't believe her mother wouldn't have mentioned it, though she could hardly call Lexi a liar so early in their relationship. "That still doesn't explain why you're here."

"I wanted to meet you."

Savvy cocked her head. "Don't get me wrong. Now that the surprise has worn off a bit, I'm really glad to meet you. But why didn't you call? Or write a letter? And why now after all this time?"

Lexi's shoulder twitched. "The time is right, that's all."

"I could have come to see you. Spared you coming here on that bus. And you certainly shouldn't be hitchhiking. That can be dangerous."

"I was careful."

"Do you live here in Berkeley?"

"No." Lexi's eyes dropped to her lap, where she rubbed her right thumb against the nail of her left.

"California?"

"No."

"Where are you from?"

Lexi shook her head, still not looking at Savvy. "I'm not going back," she said tightly. "I'm not. And you can't make me."

Understanding dawned. Lexi hadn't come just to meet Savvy. She was running away. The unease Savvy had felt earlier swept up her spine in a rush. She inched closer to the girl, "Look at me, Lexi." She fell silent until Lexi's gaze rose reluctantly. "Why did you run away?"

Her shoulder jerked twice. "I can't stand to be with him anymore."

"With who? Your brother?"

"No. He doesn't live there."

"Then who?"

"My father. Our father." Before it slid back to her lap, Lexi's gaze held a silent agony that burned into Savvy's heart.

She swallowed hard. "Did he hurt you?"

Lexi didn't reply.

"What about your mother?"

No answer.

"Lexi, where's your mother?"

Lexi's jaw worked. "I'm not going back."

"Fine," Savvy said, sensing that she wasn't going to receive any answers for the moment. "We'll work something out. Do you have ID? We can get the next flight back to Utah and go from there, okay? I promise I'll help you."

"I don't have ID." At last Lexi looked up, and Savvy was relieved that her eyes no longer held that unspeakable pain.

"Oh." Savvy wondered what she should do now. Her car, an old red Subaru, was on its last tread, and she didn't trust it for the long ride to Utah. Would she have to give up her visit altogether? Maybe she could rent a car, though her bank account was running uncomfortably low. Driving wouldn't be as fast as flying, but it might give them a chance to get to know one another.

Then again, Lexi was a minor, and Savvy knew she had to think long and hard about taking her across state lines. What if she was lying about not being from California? What if Savvy was accused of kidnapping? Still, whatever had driven Lexi to seek her out didn't seem to be idle curiosity about a half sibling she had never seen. There was something more. Savvy felt her entire being alive with that surety. But what exactly was Lexi's true reason?

"What if you give me your parents' phone number?" she said. "Then I can call and let them know you're okay. I'll ask for permission for you to visit. Maybe we can get your ID from them and fly to Utah together."

Lexi was shaking her head violently. "No. No. He won't." Her lower lip trembled, and her face looked ready to crumple. "He won't let me miss school."

"Your school started already?"

"This week."

Hmm, that was a week earlier than her brother's school in Utah. Savvy wondered if she could use that information somehow to pinpoint the school Lexi attended, but she discarded the idea quickly. Of all the thousands of schools in America, many of them likely began that same week. "I can talk to him," she tried again.

"No!" Lexi folded her arms across her stomach and glared. Her shoulder ticked.

Savvy sighed. "Well, I'd better call my parents and let them know I'm not coming." She knew they'd want to give her money to rent a car, and despite her desire to be self-sufficient, she found herself leaning toward accepting any offer they might make. She felt completely off balance. Here she was with barely enough funds to pay for her own necessities, and now she had a child to deal with. Not just any child, but a sister she'd never met. They shared some of the same DNA; they were linked.

Did that mean anything? Savvy thought of shy Camille and the outgoing Rosalie. Savvy loved her sisters more than almost anything in the world. Was there room for Lexi? Did she want to make room?

Worse, what secrets did this child hide? Savvy shivered, though the room felt too warm. None of this really mattered. Like it or not, for the moment, Lexi was here to stay.

Chapter Three

Tyler stopped on the sidewalk in front of UVSC, clutching his cell phone tightly with whitened fingers. The rain came down more quickly now with the fury of a summer storm. He couldn't believe it. Strike one, his job. Strike two, LaNae. Strike three, Savvy. This August Friday would go down as being the worst in history.

"What's happened?" he demanded, his imagination building up all sorts of frightening images of car accidents or random shootings.

"Don't worry. It's not anything bad," Camille said, her voice fading in and out as though her cell phone would cut them off at any moment. "I mean, it's sort of bad and sort of good, but it's still a shock. Dad's on the phone with her now. They're trying to decide what to do."

Relief spread through him as he realized Savvy was all right. *At least well enough to talk on the phone,* he thought. Yet his relief was followed immediately by new fears. Why wasn't Savvy returning home? What could be both good and bad that would prevent her from making her plane? Had she found a boyfriend and was running off to get married?

"So what is it?" he said more forcefully.

"It's her half sister."

"What?"

"Well, you know how my mom was married before and how my dad adopted Savvy after they got married."

"Yeah." He knew that, of course, but it wasn't a huge part of Savvy's life. At least not that he could ever tell. Once when it had come up, she'd asked him if he thought he would ever have been able to give up a child. He'd been surprised by the question and unable to answer to her satisfaction. If he'd learned anything as a reporter, it was that just when you thought you had all the answers, something new came to the surface that changed everything. Was this one of those times in Savvy's life?

"Well," Camille went on after letting that sink in, "a girl appeared on her doorstep this morning and said she was there to see her sister. She had a picture of Savvy and her birth father and everything."

"So now what?"

"They're still talking. Seems to be some problem about the plane. Savvy wants to rent a car, but Dad's set against it for some reason. Look, I'll go see what's happening and call you back."

"Can I stop by? It's pretty much on my way home."

"Sure. It's been crazy here since practically the whole family came over to surprise her, but they've all started leaving now. I'd be glad to have you come over. In fact, I have some news to tell you."

"What?"

She giggled. "No way. I want to tell you in person."

"Okay. See you in a bit."

Tyler spent the entire twenty-five-minute drive to American Fork thinking of Savvy and how she must be feeling. *I should be there for her,* he thought. *At least by phone if nothing else.* But would she even confide in him? After the past six months, he doubted it.

He parked at Savvy's parents' house and jumped from the Jeep, banging his ankle on the side of the curb. "Ow!" he muttered. At least the rain had finally abated, and the bright yellow sun was peeking from behind the clouds.

Camille ushered him inside the big house, her brown eyes smiling. "Good, you're here," she said, giving him a token hug. Of all the siblings, Camille most closely resembled Savvy, though the resemblance was mainly in her height, build, and the shape of her face. She was slightly plump, and the top of her head came only to his chin. Her long dark hair fell in layers over her shoulders. Today she wore a green suit dress that emphasized her dark coloring.

"You look great," he said, meaning it.

Camille shrugged, though she looked pleased. "Thanks. Hey, what's that on your shirt?"

"I was carrying a dusty box. So, what have they decided?"

"In just a minute. Look, before we go into the family room with the others, I want to tell you something."

Belatedly, Tyler remembered her news. "That's right. What is it?" There was something in her expression that he couldn't quite pinpoint.

"I met a guy!"

Tyler grinned. "That's wonderful."

"It is," she said, her face radiant. "He's so great!"

Tyler couldn't help the protective urge welling in his chest. Camille had tagged along too many times to count on his outings with Savvy, and since he was the youngest of his siblings, she was the closest thing he had to a little sister.

What about Savvy? came a thought. She was younger, too. Tyler frowned. Maybe so, but she had never really been like a sister. Savvy was a friend.

"Congratulations!" he said to Camille, reaching out to squeeze her arm. "I'll want to meet him, of course. You know, put him through a few tests to make sure he's right for you."

Camille ducked her head and giggled, looking more like a high schooler than someone with two years of college under her belt. Love did strange things to people. Tyler felt a twinge of envy. Seeing Camille in love made him feel old. According to his mother, he should have been married years ago. If he had, he could have been a father by now.

A father—him? Well, he couldn't do any worse than certain politicians he could name—had named. He heaved an inner sigh.

"So about Savvy," he began.

Camille's smile faded as she gazed past him to the large family portrait that graced their entryway. "It's hard imagining her having another sister. I mean, the adoption and our religious beliefs aside, that girl is as much Savvy's sister as I am. Blood-wise, I mean."

Tyler blinked at the idea. He'd never given much thought to the fact that Camille and Rosalie were Savvy's half sisters. "You can't take our beliefs from the deal," he said. "Savvy belongs to your mom, and your mom is sealed to your dad. Period."

"I know that, but she doesn't—the girl, I mean. I don't think she's a member. So what does it matter to her?"

Camille was right. To this girl, Savvy was family, at least close enough to search for. "So what's going to happen?"

Camille shook her head. "I don't know. Apparently, the girl doesn't have any ID, so she can't buy a plane ticket. She's a minor anyway, and that complicates things. She says she's sixteen, but she won't tell Savvy where she lives or anything."

"Savvy'll have to report her to the police."

Camille's brow rose. "That's what my dad says, but Savvy won't. She says that something's wrong at Lexi's house—that's the girl's name. Savvy doesn't want to send her back until she knows more."

"She could get into big trouble. Maybe even for kidnapping."

"My dad's lawyer doesn't think so. Not yet, anyway. Maybe she'll come around in a few days so we can find her family."

"If they want to be found."

Camille frowned. "What does that mean?"

Tyler sighed. "I guess I'm too suspicious. I mean, why did she appear after all these years? Hasn't she heard of a post office or a phone?"

"You sound just like my dad." Camille rolled her eyes. "If I didn't know him better, I'd say he was jealous that Savvy's birth father might come into her life."

"How'd this girl find Savvy anyway? You'd think she'd come here, if anywhere."

"Well, the girl says her brother wrote to Mom, and Mom gave him Savvy's address in case he wanted to write. But Mom says that's not true. She did get a letter from someone last month saying he was an old college friend of Savvy's. Mom gave him her phone number—not her address, though. Mom thinks maybe the letter was actually from the brother and that somehow they found out Savvy's address using her phone number."

"So there's a brother, too." Tyler wondered how he would feel to suddenly have two more siblings. Confused, probably.

"We *think* there's a brother." Camille shrugged, making a face. "Who knows if there is. It all sounds sort of fishy, if you ask me."

Tyler had the same feeling. "What do you think this girl wants?"

"Savvy thinks she wants to live with her. You know, leave her home altogether." Camille shook her head. "I guess we'll have to wait and see. Come on, maybe they've decided something. All they've done so far is talk."

Tyler followed Camille through the kitchen and into the adjoining family room. He saw not only Savvy's immediate family but also Savvy's aunt and uncle and their adult son Tanner.

"If Damon and I weren't going to Japan tomorrow," Savvy's father, Jesse Hergarter, was saying, "I'd fly down and drive her back myself. I don't like the idea of her renting a car and coming back alone."

"She's an adult," said Savvy's aunt. "And very capable. If that's what she wants to do, you'll have to let her." The woman looked apologetically at her sister, Brionney Hergarter.

Brionney shook her head. With her golden hair and blue eyes, Savvy's mother was a striking woman that reminded Tyler a great deal of Savvy, though Savvy's hair was longer and her waist significantly smaller. "She'll listen to us if we tell her our concerns. Of course, she's capable, but it's just too far to drive with a stranger. This girl could be everything Savvy thinks she is—or it could be, well, a scam."

Tanner, Savvy's cousin, arose from a brown leather sofa opposite a fireplace. He rubbed the dark five o'clock shadow that covered the lower part of his face. "I wish I could go, but Heather's too close to her due date. I can't forget that our first child came two weeks early."

"There's nothing for it," Brionney said. "I'll go. I've been wanting to meet that guy she's been dating anyway. I'll just have to miss the boys' concert." This remark was met by affronted stares from her dark-headed twins. "Come on, boys," their mother added. "It's not like I haven't heard you both banging on those drums all summer."

Tyler was having a hard time focusing. Savvy was dating someone? She hadn't mentioned it last month when he'd talked to her on the phone. Why hadn't she said something? But he knew why, and it made him sad. This gulf between them was mostly of his making.

Savvy's youngest sister, Rosalie, jumped up from the couch, her short, light brown hair curling outward from her face. "There's no way Savvy'll want any of you to come. She's an adult, for crying out loud. You need to trust her opinion about this girl. And as for her boyfriend, if she decides he's for real, she'll bring him home!" Rolling her eyes, she stomped from the room in disgust.

"I'll go." Tyler was surprised to hear his own voice, sounding loud in the sudden silence.

Everyone turned in his direction. Brionney smiled a greeting and walked toward him across the carpet. "Hi, Tyler. It's so nice to see you. I've missed having you around." She gave him a warm hug.

Tyler felt the tips of his ears turning red. Good thing LaNae hadn't cut his hair yet, so his ears were still hidden. Savvy's mom had a way of making him feel self-conscious, not only because she was beautiful but because he felt as though she could see thoughts in his head that he himself was not yet aware of. This was a talent she shared with Savvy. "It's nice to see you, too," he said, pushing up his glasses.

"We appreciate the offer." Jesse closed the gap between them and shook Tyler's hand. "But we'll work something out."

"I want to." Tyler surprised himself by how true his statement was.

Brionney hesitated. "What about your job?"

"Actually, I was thinking about heading down there anyway for work in the near future," he said vaguely. "I could go early."

"How long would you be there?"

"Just a few days." A few days would give him enough time to put out some feelers, maybe write an article or two. That he could help Savvy was beside the point. "I've been thinking about checking out newspapers there. Maybe put in a resume or two."

Camille gaped at him. "You'd leave Utah?"

He shrugged, glad Rosalie had left the room. She would have somehow wormed the whole truth from him. *Like Savvy,* he thought. Savvy would guess in a minute that he'd lost his job. He flexed his hands.

"Just let her know I'm coming," he said. "Or ask her if it's okay."

"We'll call her in a bit," Brionney said. "She was making lunch. But I'm sure she'll look forward to spending time with you."

Tyler hoped so.

Jesse looked thoughtful. "Would you be flying down or driving?"

"I think I'd rather drive. I may stop off at a newspaper in Vegas."

"Are you sure? To get to Berkeley, it'll take ten hours or so—and that's driving straight through."

"Yeah, I'm sure."

"Okay," Brionney said with a smile, "but we're paying for gas. Don't give me any argument. Jesse?"

Nodding in agreement, Jesse pulled out his wallet and forced a few bills into Tyler's unwilling hands.

"I'd go with you," Camille said, "but I don't want to leave right now." Her secret smile told him clearly that she wanted to stay because of the guy she was dating. "What about your girlfriend. Will she mind?"

Tyler blinked in consternation. He'd completely forgotten about LaNae! What was wrong with him? He hated how wishy-washy his

33

feelings seemed to be. Maybe his brother was right when he wondered aloud if Tyler would ever grow up.

I am an adult, he thought. *I'll show all of them.* Still, he couldn't help thinking how much easier his life would be if he wasn't the youngest in his family. Aloud, he mumbled something about being sure it'd be okay with LaNae and was glad when Camille didn't question him further.

After saying good-bye to the Hergarters, Tyler sat alone in his Jeep, studying the dissipating clouds through his windshield while debating whether to tell his family of his trip. Then again, there was really no choice. He couldn't simply disappear for a few days. His mother would likely call the police and organize a neighborhood search party, complete with dogs and high-powered flashlights. No, better to come clean, though maybe he should leave out the part about submitting resumes. Having lost Mitch to exotic places for up to half the year, his mother wasn't going to be happy contemplating losing Tyler as well.

Sighing loudly, Tyler turned on his engine, deciding to drive to his oldest sister's house. Since his other siblings, Amanda and Mitch, were only a year apart in school and had been involved in many of the same activities, he and Kerrianne had spent a lot of time together by default. She was one of the kindest, wisest people he had ever known.

Of course, she was different now, since her husband, Adam, had died. Tyler had been on his mission when the news had come about Adam's car accident, nearly four years ago. When he returned from Bolivia, Kerrianne was still mourning, and to him it seemed that she'd never quite been her old self again. She was distracted easily and no longer radiated contentment. He missed that contentment in her more than anything else.

But would she want to be her old self? Certainly, Adam's death had affected her life in many ways, and she had grown because of the trials. Maybe it was okay not to return to normal after someone you loved died. What was normal anyway?

His Jeep traced the path to Kerrianne's Pleasant Grove home as though it knew the way. She lived in the modest, two-story house with vaulted ceilings, a well-kept yard, and a porch with white railings that she and Adam had bought together. Tyler's two nephews, Benjamin and Caleb, were playing outside in the driveway that had sunk slightly, which had caused the rain to gather in a huge puddle in the middle.

Six-year-old Benjamin came running to the curb. His brother, younger by two years, stumbled after him down the gentle slope of the front yard. Both boys resembled their mother, with narrow faces, blue eyes, and dark blond hair.

"Uncle Tyler, Uncle Tyler!" Benjamin shouted.

"Do me an airplane, Uncle Tyler!" Caleb pleaded as Tyler climbed from the Jeep. "An airplane. Please?"

"Me too, me too!"

Tyler grinned, squatting on the sidewalk that was already drying from the bright sun that had emerged overhead. After catching the boys in a warm embrace, he tucked an arm around each child's stomach and stood, twirling them around. The boys giggled, extending their arms and flapping them like birds.

"Hey," he teased, "airplanes don't flap their wings." That made the boys giggle and wave harder. He let them down on their bare feet on the concrete and began tickling them.

"Stop! Stop!" little Caleb shouted after a few minutes of wild giggling.

Pulling the boys close, Tyler hugged them again.

"Hi, Mom." Benjamin waved. Tyler looked over to where his sister had come onto the front porch to watch them.

"Uncle Tyler's here," Caleb added.

"I see that," Kerrianne called. "Looks like the sun chased away the clouds."

"That means we can play!" shouted Benjamin, heading again for the puddle. Laughing, Caleb ran after him.

Skirting the water, Tyler made his way up to the porch. "Where's Misty?" Tyler asked Kerrianne.

"Next door, playing with her friend."

Kerrianne watched the boys for a minute, smiling at their joyful splashing. "I have to get that fixed. The cement is starting to flake."

"Aw, they love it so much."

She smiled. "Exactly. Oh well, I guess I'm raising kids, not cement." She laughed, and the laughter changed her thin face and somber blue eyes, making them come alive. She'd cut her long hair since the last time he'd seen her, and now the dark blonde locks layered around her face and curved gently at the back of her graceful neck. She looked well, though her face today was slightly wan and she was definitely too thin. *As thin as LaNae,* he thought, though he had never considered LaNae too thin before. Kerrianne wore baggy sweatpants and an oversized man's T-shirt that must have belonged to Adam.

"What brings you here?" she asked. "I'm a mess. I've been cleaning."

He sighed. "I'm not sure where to start."

"Let's go out on the deck and talk." She glanced over at her children. "If you want lemonade, come around back in a few minutes."

"Yay!" shouted the boys in unison.

Tyler followed Kerrianne through the small entryway, across the kitchen, and out to the back patio. "Have a seat," she said. "I'll be back in a moment."

Tyler settled on one of the deck chairs, looking out over the yard. The grass needed trimming again, though he'd cut it at the first of the week. If he was longer than expected in California, he'd have to ask his dad to drop by. Though the yard wasn't large, the fruit trees, garden area, flowerbeds, and the grass were too much for one person all the time. Adam's life insurance and social security death benefits made it possible for Kerrianne to stay home with the children, but it wasn't enough to waste on hiring someone to care for the yard. He and his family made sure they helped Kerrianne several times a month.

When his sister returned, she was carrying a glass pitcher of pink lemonade, two tall glass cups, and two small plastic ones. "I hate drinking lemonade from a plastic cup," she said, setting everything down on the green wrought-iron table. She poured the lemonade. "Do you want raspberries?"

Tyler smiled to himself. Only Kerrianne would have raspberries on hand to put in lemonade. She had always been the epitome of the perfect hostess, homemaker, wife, and mother—until things had fallen apart with Adam's death. Tyler guessed that in the face of such loss, raspberries didn't mean much. Still, he was glad to see that some of her old self was shining through.

"I'd love some," he said, sipping his lemonade.

She disappeared for less than a minute, returning with a bowl of fresh raspberries, chilled and slightly blended. For a moment, they sipped their raspberry lemonade in companionable silence. The sun shone down on them, feeling warm despite the light breeze that refused to leave them in peace. Tyler wondered what kind of weather they were having in California. Was it hot? Or were they having a summer storm?

Kerrianne eyed his shirt. "Did the boys get you dirty?"

"No."

"I know that look—what happened?" She set her glass on the table.

"I'm going to California," he said, glad he could tell her about that instead of his job. He quickly outlined the situation with Savvy.

"Hmmm." Kerrianne's eyes narrowed. "And you can just take off work like that?"

Tyler shrugged. "It's not a problem." He didn't want to tell her about his job until he had some idea of what the future held for him.

"You're not going to believe this, but for the past two days, I've been praying for an answer to a problem, and I think you're it."

He blinked. This was a vein of conversation he hadn't expected. "What do you mean?"

"Well, Adam's mother called a few weeks ago and wanted to know if there was any way I could take the kids down to visit her in Pleasant Hill for a few days—that's thirty minutes west of Berkeley. It's her birthday, and they're her only grandchildren, but she hasn't seen them for a year. Since the attack on the World Trade Center, she's petrified of flying, and her health really isn't good enough for her to drive all that way. I was thinking of taking the children, but I was worried about the expense of plane tickets. Driving would be less expensive, but going that far alone with three children didn't sound very appealing."

"You want to come with me?"

"Yeah, I think I do."

"What about Misty and Benjamin? Don't they have school?"

Kerrianne gave him a smile. "Not till the middle of next week. Besides, they can miss a few days if they need to."

Tyler couldn't think of any reason to refuse Kerrianne's request. LaNae would certainly feel better about Kerrianne going—that is, if he could get her to talk to him. And Savvy? Well, she and Kerrianne enjoyed each other's company, and the kids probably liked her better than they liked him. "Okay, but don't worry about gas," he said with a grin. "Savvy's dad forced me to take some money. He has to leave for Japan tomorrow, and he's really happy Savvy won't be driving home alone."

His two nephews picked that moment to come running around the side of the house. Spying the lemonade on the table, Benjamin called to his brother who was six paces behind him, "It's time, it's time!" They raced up the two steps of the deck and came to an abrupt halt before the table. Kerrianne passed them each a blue plastic cup, the kind with a straw. Tyler had always loved those cups as a child, and he grinned as the boys slurped up their lemonade.

Feeling better than he had all day, he pulled out his cell phone and tried to call LaNae. Surely they could work things out. She answered, but when he began to speak, she hung up on him.

So much for his good day.

Chapter Four

Savvy sat on a wooden bench beneath a huge palm tree in the backyard of her apartment building. Lexi stood a few feet away, nervously flipping a red, water-filled plastic ball in her hands. The ball was attached by a thick string to a ring she'd put on her finger, recalling to Savvy's mind a yo-yo, though the plastic string didn't roll up but stretched and rebounded unpredictably.

The scent of oranges perfumed the air, and wild birds chirped from the tall shade tree nearer the building. The grass was a deep green in the fading light, as were the vines that crept along the white-painted concrete wall lining the back property line. When she'd first moved to California, the palms and orange trees had been foreign to her, though now they were familiar, comforting. The vegetation was so different in Utah. In a few months, fall would arrive with her palette of colors, and the majestic mountains hovering overhead, a constant protective presence, would be preparing for their cold, white sleep. Not so in California, where the grass and bushes were green all year long.

A piercing longing caught Savvy's breath, and for a moment, she yearned to be home with her family. If not for Lexi, she would have been with them now.

But she's also family. Or was she? Didn't the fact that Savvy's birth father had given Savvy up mean there should be no lasting connection? Didn't Savvy's adoption mean never looking back?

Yet here was Lexi, and according to her, Savvy had a new brother as well.

"What's his name?" Savvy asked.

Lexi glanced at her, blinking at the question. She looked different from that morning when she'd appeared on the doorstep—younger somehow, more fragile and lost. She'd bathed, washing the dark makeup from her face, and had traded her frayed shorts and tube top for oversized lounge pants and a snug top that showed a sliver of stomach whenever she reached to retrieve her ball. Savvy had to resist pulling the shirt down.

"Your brother," Savvy prompted.

"Oh, him. His name's Derek, like Dad, but we always called him Brenton. It was too confusing."

"Does he live with you?"

Lexi threw the ball out to the side, snapping her hand sharply to pull it back. "He's gone. I mean, he's at college."

"Must be dedicated if he's studying during the summer. What's his major?"

She shrugged. "I don't see him much. He has a girlfriend."

"Does he live close by you, then?"

No answer.

Savvy watched her toss the ball a few more times, almost wishing the plastic string would break. Couldn't the girl just sit down and talk? They'd been out here nearly an hour without Savvy learning anything new.

A bird flew from the shade tree, winging overhead to land on a huge palm leaf where it was apparently intent on soaking up the light cast by the sun, now hanging low in the western sky. Following its movement to the palm, Savvy had an idea. "I like palms," she said. "We don't have any in Utah. When I first moved here it was so weird to see them. It'll be strange not to have any around when I go home to visit."

Lexi's eyes flickered briefly toward the palm and then back to her ball. "I don't like them much. They're kind of ugly when the leaves are dying."

Okay, so she's not impressed, Savvy thought. *That means she could have grown up with them.*

Or not. Maybe she vacationed somewhere warm enough for palms.

"What about orange trees? I still have a hard time believing people can go outside and pick an orange whenever they want it."

Lexi made a face. "Well, you'd get sick of oranges if you had to pick them up from the ground all the time."

"Is that what you had to do?"

Lexi caught her ball and looked at Savvy, her eyes narrowing. "If I said yes, that doesn't mean I'm from somewhere that grows oranges," she said, giving Savvy a mocking half-smile. "I could have done it when I was younger. Dad did use to live in Arizona."

"I know. I was born there." Savvy crossed one leg over the other, sighing wearily. "Look, why you won't tell me where you're from? You're going to have to eventually, you know. If we can't work things out with your parents, the authorities will have to be brought in."

Chin jutting forward, Lexi drew back her arm and threw the ball with all her might. *Snap!* The plastic thread broke, sending the ball careening over the cement wall into the parking lot of the neighboring apartment complex.

"You don't care about me," Lexi muttered, dropping her hands to her side. The piece of plastic around her finger fell to the grass.

"What do you mean?" Savvy couldn't help feeling offended. "I canceled my flight home, and I'm letting you stay here—how can you say I don't care? Before today, I had no idea you even existed. It'll take time for me to get used to the idea."

"You just want to get rid of me—like my dad."

"He doesn't want you?" Savvy's heart ached; she knew that feeling only too well. First with Derek giving her up so easily and then with Tyler not returning her feelings. "Why do you say that?"

Lexi stared at the ground silently.

Savvy arose from the bench and went to stand beside her. "Lexi, I am glad to know you, and I don't want to send you away. But I do want what's best for you."

"And you think he is?" Lexi's voice wobbled as she spoke. "Your mother didn't think so."

She had a point. Tentatively, Savvy reached out to touch Lexi's shoulder. "I want to be your friend—I do. Can you trust me?"

Lexi's eyes met hers, tears glistening. "I don't know."

Savvy squeezed her shoulder, wanting to hug her as she would have hugged Camille or Rosalie if they looked like crying, but she was too unsure how Lexi would react.

"Hey!" came a call.

Savvy looked behind Lexi, spying Chris coming from her apartment building.

"Hey," Savvy answered. "Miranda get away okay?"

"Yeah." He put his hands in the pockets of his baggy shorts. "I would have been back earlier, but I had some research to drop off." Chris worked part-time for the university doing research for the astrophysics department. "So what's going on with you two? Did you decide to rent a car?"

"I'm thinking about it, but my parents want me to hold off awhile. I'm waiting for them to call back. Actually, they might have called already. I'll have to check the messages." Savvy made a face. "I wish my car were more dependable."

"I'd take you myself if I didn't have to work."

Savvy grinned. "Yeah, right. Like your car is any more dependable." His car was a gorgeous old convertible that spent more time in the shop than on the road.

"Well, if we broke down, at least we'd be together." Chris laughed, making Savvy feel warm and tingly. Next to Chris, Lexi rolled her eyes and looked away. Savvy ignored her.

"I wish my parents weren't so paranoid," she said.

Chris shrugged. "That's the price of being the oldest. I don't think my parents let my sister go anywhere alone until she was married!"

Savvy laughed again. "If I had more money, I'd have rented a car and not worried them. I think that's what I'll end up doing anyway— my parents will probably pay for it."

Lexi was still staring away from them, but now her face was flushed and her lower lip jutting out. Her left shoulder was ticking again. As Savvy watched, Lexi's hand wiped surreptitiously under her right eye. Apparently, she felt at least some remorse for causing Savvy trouble.

"Well, you guys want to grab something to eat?" Chris asked in the sudden silence. "I mean, it's late for lunch and early for dinner, but I'm always ready to eat."

Savvy shook her head, but Lexi nodded. "Are you hungry?" Savvy asked her.

"That sandwich you made me was the only food I've had all day."

Was that because she'd been traveling? Savvy wanted to ask but decided to let the subject ride for now. "You should have told me," she said instead. "I would have made you something else. Or we could have gone out." She began to walk toward the apartment.

"I didn't want to be a bother." Lexi fell into step with her. "Besides, I have money. I could even pay to rent a car, if you want."

Savvy smiled. A child's idea of having money, whether twelve or sixteen, was quite different from an adult's. When you had to worry about rent, food, and clothes, the green stuff took on a whole new meaning. Lexi certainly had no idea how much it cost to rent a car for more than a week.

"Should we go out?" Chris asked. "Or we could drive over to my parents' house. Mom always makes extra. It's a forty-five-minute drive, but it'll be worth it. I can call and let them know we're coming."

Savvy liked his parents a great deal, though lately they'd been hinting around about grandbabies in scarcely veiled attempts to discover if she and Chris were serious. But Savvy didn't want to spend time with them tonight. In fact, she didn't even want Chris there. What she wanted was to discover why Lexi had chosen now to appear in her life and why she had run away from home.

"I think I'll make something," Savvy said. "I cleaned out most of the fridge, since I was going to be gone and I have no idea when my new roommate is going to show up. But I have some hamburger in the freezer, and there's a can of tomato sauce and some spaghetti noodles in the cupboard." She had some flour and yeast, too, which could easily be mixed up for bread sticks.

"Spaghetti?" Lexi said. "That's my favorite."

Her words instantly transported Savvy to another time and place. She and Tyler were making spaghetti, Tyler's favorite dinner, at his brother's house in Sandy. Every moment with him had been pure heaven—and pure torture. That had been the day she'd made up her mind to serve a mission. She was glad she had. Her desire to serve the Lord had given her the courage to leave him behind and make something of her life.

Truthfully, she'd hoped that once she returned, something might spark between her and Tyler. After all, she'd had more fun with him than with any other man she'd ever dated. He'd always listened to her advice, gone along on her many star-watching activities, and encouraged her rigorous study habits. He'd participated in all her family parties with good grace and invited her to his family gatherings as well. Generally, he'd been the best guy friend a girl could have. But when she came home from her mission, he had another girlfriend, resembling all the other thin, blonde girls he'd dated over the years. Savvy had been left feeling large and awkward by comparison. Unwanted. She never felt that way with Chris.

No, it was just as well she had distanced herself from Tyler. Besides, now there was Lexi. Maybe she would help lead Savvy to the destiny the Lord had planned for her.

They fell into a comfortable silence as the three of them walked toward the apartment. Inside, Savvy checked her phone messages, and there was one from her mother asking her to call back, but she decided to wait until after dinner. Soon the aroma of savory meat sauce and fresh bread sticks filled the small kitchen, making Savvy's mouth water. Silently, she blessed all the cooking lessons her mother had given her over the years. Being able to make an entire meal from odd and ends was definitely a learned skill.

Chris was charming and talkative during the meal, and Savvy felt a rush of affection toward him. Could Lexi's arrival be the Lord's way of throwing her and Chris together? After all, if Lexi hadn't arrived, Savvy would be home now—likely wondering how she could face hearing about Tyler's girlfriend from Camille, who kept in touch with him. It had been almost six months since LaNae had so clearly stated her claim on Tyler, and though Savvy hadn't heard solid plans of their engagement, he was still dating her, and that was serious enough. Tyler normally didn't date any girl longer than three weeks.

"This is really good," Chris said, breaking through her thoughts. "I'm going to eat it all." They shared a laugh.

In the end it wasn't Chris who ate most of the spaghetti but Lexi. To Savvy's wonder and, yes, envy, the girl filled her plate three times, hardly chewing between bites. *Where does she put it all?* Savvy thought.

That made Savvy wonder even more about Lexi's life. Was Lexi's father—their father—abusive? Did Lexi not have enough to eat at home? This last idea Savvy discarded. Lexi was lanky and scrawny in the way of many teens, but she didn't look undernourished. Not any more than Savvy's own sister Rosalie had looked at that age. Even Savvy herself had gone through a brief thin phase in the seventh grade before puberty hit. She wistfully eyed the third bread stick Lexi was munching contentedly. Ah, well, Savvy knew she'd be happier in the long run if she didn't give in to her taste buds. Besides, she felt full.

"Would you and your sister want to catch a movie tonight?" Chris asked Savvy. He looked between them. "My treat." His gray eyes paused on Savvy. "Or do you need to call your parents?"

"That shouldn't take but a minute," Savvy said. "What do you think, Lexi?"

The girl stuffed in the last of her bread stick. "I'm tired. I didn't sleep much last night on the bus."

So it was an overnight trip, Savvy thought.

"Must have been a long ride," Chris said. "Where did you say you were from?"

Again the shoulder tick—once, twice. "Around." Lexi's face became sullen. "Is there a place to lie down?" she asked. "I'm really tired."

Lie down? thought Savvy. This was a child who had somewhere learned proper English. The difference between *lie* and *lay* had always been one of Tyler's pet peeves, and he had harped on it enough that Savvy was always careful to use the words properly.

"Sure. You can have my bed. I made it up with clean sheets this morning. I'll take Miranda's. I hope you don't mind sharing a room because it's all we've got. But if my new roommate shows up, you'll be on the couch."

Lexi left the room without a reply.

Savvy shot Chris an apologetic glance. "Teenagers," she said, shaking her head.

"That's okay. Maybe another time."

"Maybe," Savvy agreed, though there might not be another time with Lexi. How could the child stay here? Savvy could barely support herself, much less another person. If Lexi ended up staying for long, Savvy would have to get another job, or maybe even move back to Utah to work at her father's hospital software company. The third alternative was to ask her parents for money, but she wasn't ready to consider that yet. *It's too soon to plan anything,* she reminded herself. *I have no idea what's going on with Lexi's family.*

"Want me to get a video?" Chris stood from the table, taking his plate to the sink. Savvy knew his mother had ingrained that habit from childhood, just as her own had done.

Frowning, Savvy rested her chin on her hands. "I don't know anything about her," she said softly. "She won't tell me where she's from or why she ran away. I don't even know what she wants from me."

Chris turned and leaned against the counter. "Give it time."

But what if it's something I can't face? Savvy wanted to ask. *Something that involves my birth father?* She was ashamed at her lack of courage. Before Lexi arrived, Savvy had believed she had faced the two worst things she could ever face in her life: seeing a family she had grown to love on her mission refuse the gospel, and losing Tyler for good. In less than a minute her outlook had changed. There were worse things in life, and this situation might be one of them.

Sighing internally, Savvy closed her eyes. She heard Chris come back to the table, felt his hand touch her back. "Can I do anything?"

She opened her eyes. "No. Thank you, though. I appreciate the offer. What I really need to do is call home again."

"You want me to leave?"

Savvy gave him a half smile. "Do you mind terribly? I want to try to talk to her again."

"I don't mind." He grinned. "Well, I do, but I'll take a rain check. Come on, walk me to the door?"

She did as he requested. He gave her a hug and kissed her lightly on the cheek, but she felt too distracted to focus on him. She was relieved when he didn't linger.

"I'll call you tomorrow night," he said, heading for the stairs.

Dusk was falling now, lending a sinister cast to the street and surrounding areas, but Savvy could see nothing out of place. Yet at any moment Lexi's father could show up and whisk her away to wherever he had been living all these years.

Living and not even wondering about his firstborn.

Well, Savvy wouldn't let him take Lexi. Not until she discovered the truth. She'd promised to help Lexi when she first arrived, and she would do her best to fulfill that promise.

She went back inside and down the hall to her room where she expected Lexi to be in bed, only to find the girl straightening quickly by Savvy's purse. "What are you doing?" Savvy demanded. Other than a few bills, there was nothing in the purse worth stealing, but Lexi had no business nosing in her things.

Lexi shook her head. "I didn't take anything."

"Then why were you looking inside my purse?" Savvy began to have doubts about sending Chris home. After all, what did she know about Lexi? Could Savvy be in danger by letting her stay? Maybe she should call Chris and ask him to sleep on the couch.

"It's just . . . well . . ." Lexi sputtered. "I, uh, wanted to see . . ." Falling silent, she threw herself onto Savvy's single bed, delving into her backpack. She drew something out, a small plastic picture holder that had come from a wallet. "Here," she said, tossing it to Savvy.

The first picture was of a boy about the twins' age, who resembled Lexi in the shape of the face. He was her opposite in size and coloring, however—brown hair and eyes, tall with wide shoulders. *Handsome,* Savvy thought.

"That's Brenton." Lexi watched her study his face. "It's an old picture, of course. Doesn't look much like us, does he?" she added.

"No, he doesn't."

"Well, he's as much your brother as he is mine. We're both halves."

Savvy felt a sudden longing to know this boy—or rather, the man he had become. Still looking at the picture, she sat down on the bed next to Lexi's sprawled figure. "So he . . . our father got another divorce?"

"Yeah, she left him. For a while Brenton went back and forth, but when she remarried he came to live with us. He liked my mom better."

"I'm glad for you both." Savvy felt herself relax. Surely if Brenton had chosen to live with their father, he wasn't as bad as Lexi had hinted. Then again, Brenton didn't live at home anymore. Maybe things at Lexi's had changed for the worse. "Can I see the rest?" she asked.

Lexi nodded, studying her face. Savvy turned the page and saw a school picture of Lexi, looking older and tougher than she had on the porch that morning. Savvy definitely preferred how she looked now. The next picture was of a narrow-faced woman with dishwater blonde hair, blue eyes, and a nice smile. She looked like anyone's next door neighbor, a person Savvy would like to know. "Your mother?"

Lexi nodded and looked away.

Savvy wondered how Lexi's mother was feeling now. Was she worried about Lexi? Had she already called the police?

The last picture was of Derek. He was older in this one, and Savvy could see the wrinkles, though his hair was every bit as blond. His wide set eyes were bright blue, and the oval shape of them was Savvy's own. And Lexi's. Though still handsome, the lines around his eyes were haggard, as though he had not escaped his share of affliction. Obviously, life had not been as kind to him as it had been to her mother since their parting.

Savvy stared so long that she knew she would see his face even when it wasn't in front of her. This was the man who had given her up. Given her to a better life. She was glad, and yet . . .

"Thanks." She handed the pictures to Lexi, who looked through them herself.

"You got any?" Lexi asked.

"Pictures?"

Lexi's eyes went to Savvy's purse. *Ah,* Savvy thought. Could that have been what Lexi was looking for? She pushed herself off the bed and reached for her purse. "I have more in the living room, but I carry my favorites in here." She pulled out a thin mini album with a plastic yellow cover. She opened it to the first page and passed it to Lexi.

"There we all are. My mom, the twins, my sisters, my dad." She didn't pause over the word *dad* but as she said it, she realized how strange that could seem to Lexi.

"Your mom's the only one who looks like you," Lexi said. "The others look like your stepfather."

"He's not my stepfather," Savvy found herself saying. "He adopted me. He's my dad."

"I didn't know that." The skin between Lexi's eyebrows wrinkled as she concentrated. "Still, going by blood, I'm as much your sister as they are." She pointed to Rosalie and Camille. "Or even more, because I look like you."

Her words pierced Savvy's heart. Lexi was right. If blood were the only thing that counted, Lexi was as much her sister as either of the others. Of course, she shared a lifetime of memories with Rosalie and Camille. With Lexi, she had nothing. Savvy felt a swift and deep remorse that Lexi hadn't been a part of her life before now. How much had they missed?

"Your brothers are cute," Lexi said. "This one especially."

"That's Forest. The other's Gabe. They're fourteen." Though they were identical twins, there was a distinct difference in the way they dressed and in their demeanor. Savvy loved Gabriel for his responsibility and thoughtfulness and Forest for his outgoing nature. Everybody loved Forest.

Lexi flipped through the rest of the pictures, identifying cousins, aunts, uncles, grandparents, and additional photos of her family. When Lexi turned to the last page, she gave a long whistle. "Who's this? He's hot. I like the glasses."

Savvy leaned forward to see the picture of Tyler, one she hadn't looked at in months. Her breath caught in her throat. He was grinning his obnoxious smile, the one that made that adorable dimple stand out on his right cheek. And those eyes, those wonderful shining green eyes that reminded her of a cat. She could almost hear his laughter, feel him taking her arm. "He's a friend," she managed finally.

"A friend?" Lexi's gaze was mocking. The girl saw way too much. "If I had a friend like him, he certainly wouldn't be just a friend."

"Lexi!" Savvy tried to laugh, but her heart ached.

"Well, I hope I get to meet him."

Savvy reached for her album, flipping it back to the first page. "You'll get to meet all the clan."

Lexi's smile vanished. "You could have been back with them already."

"Yes," Savvy answered slowly, "but then we wouldn't have this time to get to know each other, would we? I haven't seen them for four months, but I haven't seen you for—how old did you say you were?— sixteen years. It's a fair exchange."

Lexi's eyes fell to her lap where her own pictures still lay. Her left shoulder ticked twice. "A sister," she said softly, so softly that Savvy wasn't sure she heard her correctly.

Before Savvy could speak, Lexi stretched across the bed, reaching toward her backpack. She began stuffing the pictures back inside her wallet. A laminated card fell to the bed, and Lexi scooped it up quickly, though not before Savvy recognized what it was.

"I thought you didn't have any ID." Her voice came out sharper than she'd intended.

Lexi gazed at Savvy, her demeanor turning sullen. "It's nothing."

"Give it to me."

"No."

Savvy stood and glared down at the girl. "Now. Or I'll call the police and let them get it." Savvy used the same voice she had used on her twin brothers when they were young.

Lexi's mouth pursed as though sucking on something sour. Slowly, she held the card up so Savvy could see. It was a new school identity card, the face without scratches, the edges unworn.

"Eighth grade?" Savvy asked with frustration. "So how old are you, huh? My brothers are in ninth, and they're fourteen going on fifteen. That makes you thirteen, right?"

Lexi nodded, not meeting her eyes as she put the card away.

"Why didn't you tell me the truth? No, don't answer. I think I'm too mad to care right now. If you hadn't lied, we might be in Utah right now with my family—the airline might have accepted this as ID. Instead, you've put me to a lot of trouble and expense." Savvy stomped across the room and swept up her purse. "Well, at least it's not too late to call and ask if that ID is enough to get you on a plane. Although with my luck, we'll probably need a birth certificate or a parent's signature."

"I don't want to go on a plane!" Lexi glared up at Savvy.

"Well, right now it doesn't matter what you want." Savvy left the bedroom, forcefully closing the door behind her, shutting Lexi inside.

Thirteen, the girl is only thirteen, she thought. She had known Lexi looked too young to be sixteen, but sixteen would have been old enough to decide a lot of things on her own. Thirteen made Savvy feel like a kidnapper.

In the kitchen, Savvy called her parents instead of the airline. Since they often flew places with Savvy's younger siblings, they would likely know if Lexi's school card would be adequate ID. They might also be able to give her advice about how to deal with her. The phone rang and rang, which meant that someone was on the line. But the caller ID would record her number and her parents would call back in a few minutes. Resting her head on her arms, she closed her eyes and thought about her options.

After a while it came to her that she should have confiscated Lexi's ID card. The name of a state wasn't listed, but the school had been—partially obscured by Lexi's fingers. With that information, Savvy could have quickly found out where Lexi was from. In fact, her parents could have done an Internet search while she waited on the phone. Instead, she'd let her anger cloud her reasoning. Well, it wasn't too late to rectify her mistake.

Savvy left the kitchen and went down the hall to the bedroom. The door was wide open, though Savvy had been sure she'd shut it when she left. What kind of game was Lexi playing? Maybe she didn't like closed-in spaces. Opening her mouth to ask, Savvy walked inside.

Both Lexi and her backpack were gone.

Chapter Five

Tyler spent Friday evening changing the oil in Kerrlanne's van—the only vehicle between them that was large enough to carry everyone. He also checked all the other fluid levels, the tire pressure, and filled up the gas tank. For good measure, he took it through a car wash.

When he finally arrived home, it was past dinnertime and already dark. He walked in the door, thinking of LaNae and wondering if he should call her. Muffin the Mutt met him at the door, and Tyler could hear the other occupants of his brother's house stirring, knowing that food was coming.

A zoologist, his brother loved animals. He had more pets than Tyler thought reasonable, but part of the "rent" Tyler paid was taking care of Mitch's pets while he was out of the country. Tyler wasn't overly attached to the creatures, but he knew how much little EmJay loved them, so what else could he do but agree to make sure they were waiting for her each time she returned home? Besides, the house payment was cheaper than anything else he'd come across and relatively close to his work—until he'd blown it by writing that last article.

Mitch and Cory would be home soon with EmJay, perhaps by the end of the month. Tyler hoped they'd hurry so he'd have some help with the house payments if he didn't find a paying job in the next few weeks. He was glad that with the two new bedrooms and family room they'd added to the small house last year, there would be plenty of room for all of them.

Tyler fed the turtle, the dog, all forty-two gerbils, the chinchilla, the fish, the frogs, the guinea pig, and the lizard—most of whom lived in a specially ventilated spare room. The rabbits outside should still have plenty of feed. He was grateful Mitch had gotten rid of the cranky ferrets and hadn't bought new hermit crabs when the last ones had died. "I won't miss any of you when I move out of here," he grumbled as he worked, though he knew it wasn't quite true. At least they were company. And LaNae really loved Lady, the chinchilla.

LaNae. He needed to talk to her.

The house was quiet. Even Muffin had gone outside to the backyard through his new doggie door to investigate the bushes. Tartar the turtle had crawled under the couch. The silence seemed loud.

He considered calling LaNae but decided he'd better go to her apartment in Orem instead. If she wasn't home, it would be a wasted trip, but if she was, she couldn't hang up on him again.

The drive to Orem was quick, and LaNae opened the door after he rang the bell only once. She didn't look surprised to see him. "Hi," she said. She didn't invite him inside.

"Look, I'm sorry about this afternoon." A vision of her with the new guy at her work flashed in his mind, but he pushed it away. That had been his fault.

"Did you have a nice time at lunch?" Her voice was cool but not frozen.

He wasn't even tempted to lie. His sisters always said he was too transparent. "Savvy didn't come home. There were some problems."

"Oh. So when is she coming home?"

"It's a long story—do you want to hear it? If so, you'll have to let me come inside."

She gave him a tentative smile. "I don't know if I want to hear. But you can come in anyway."

Tyler stepped inside and followed LaNae to the couch. Thankfully, no roommates were in sight—not surprising on a Friday night. In the corner of the couch sat the white stuffed bear he had given LaNae for her birthday, and she took it into her lap as she sat down. A few moments of awkward silence passed. Tyler wondered how he was ever going to tell her about his trip to California.

"Let's just forget it all, okay?" LaNae smiled at him.

They could do that—if he didn't bring up the trip. But Tyler knew that wouldn't be quite honest.

"There's still time to catch a late movie," LaNae continued, scooting closer to him. "Want to go?"

He shook his head. "I have to get up early tomorrow."

"Is it about your job? Because if so, I've been thinking. Is there any chance you could talk to your old boss and see if she might change her mind? I know you loved that job."

"Not at the moment," he said. "Chantel was pretty upset. And I don't know if the *Tribune* has an opening. I might have to freelance for a while."

"Freelance?" She wrinkled her nose.

"It might be fun. I could travel all over. I bet if I found a few really good stories, Chantel might even be impressed enough to rehire me at the paper—after this stink with the politician dies down, of course."

"Travel? Where?" LaNae's tone wasn't pleased, and Tyler knew why. She was thinking about their future, and living out of the Jeep wasn't exactly her idea of stability. His either, come to think of it, but there was enough adventure involved to make it sound somewhat attractive.

"Oh, I don't know. Arizona, Washington, California. They have all kinds of things going on in California that interest people."

"California. That's where Savvy lives." LaNae clenched her jaw and stared at him unwaveringly.

Too late, he realized that of course she would connect the state with

Savvy. "It's a big place," he rushed on. "I could sell articles to different newspapers. There are a lot of possibilities." He told himself that he hadn't thought of California only because of Savvy. He hadn't. Well, at least he wouldn't admit to it in front of LaNae.

"Why California?" she asked.

"I haven't really decided anything yet," he said, though the idea of moving to California was sounding better and better. "I'm only thinking of California because I have the opportunity to go there this weekend, and I thought I'd put in a few resumes while I'm there."

The muscles in her jaw worked, as though she was holding back words or maybe trying not to cry. "This has something to do with Savvy, doesn't it?"

"Kind of." Taking a breath, he explained the situation. "I'm just giving her and this new sister a ride back," he finished. "Kerrianne's going with me. We'll be staying at her mother-in-law's, not at Savvy's."

"I don't want you to go." LaNae's voice had become as frigid as it had been in her office that morning. "Can't Savvy find her own way back? She's an adult, after all."

"LaNae," he agonized, hating the way she stared at him, "why is there a problem? I don't understand. Savvy's been good friends with my sister for years and my whole family as well. We're bound to run into her occasionally. I know you'd really like her if you gave it a chance."

"I don't want to give it a chance." LaNae's voice was soggy now, like the bedding under the water bottle he'd filled in the gerbil cage earlier. "I want to be the first woman in your life. I want to matter more than anyone else. That's all. Do you think that's too much to ask?"

Tyler considered for a moment. He had known Savvy first, but that didn't mean anything if LaNae was his future. He could honestly say that Savvy was only a friend, and yet . . . He swallowed hard. That "and yet" had him really worried. What could he say to LaNae that would both alleviate her fears and not betray his friendship with Savvy? He'd volunteered to go to California. He couldn't go back on that now. Even if Savvy could fend for herself, Kerrianne was counting on him. To tell the truth, he didn't want to back out of the deal. He needed to get out of Utah to clear his head. "No," he said slowly, "it's not too much to ask."

"But . . ." she prompted, hearing the exception in his voice.

"But I'll only be gone a few days. Kerrianne and her children need to visit Adam's mom. I'm just helping everyone out."

"I need you here."

"Do you really?"

No answer.

"Look, California's a nice place. Wouldn't you like living there?"

"I don't know. That depends on your real reason for choosing it."

Tyler didn't know how to reassure her. How could he when he didn't know himself what his motives were? He wished desperately that he didn't have to hurt her.

"Please, LaNae. I don't know what else to say."

LaNae stood abruptly, letting the bear in her lap fall to the couch. "I want you to choose. Savvy and California or me."

"What?" Tyler gaped up at her.

"You heard me."

"LaNae, that's not reasonable!" He couldn't believe this was happening. He jumped to his feet. "You need to trust me. Savvy has nothing to do with us—nothing!"

She put her hands on her hips, making Tyler want to cringe. "I'm tired of hearing about Savvy. Don't you see? She's the only thing we really ever fight about."

That wasn't exactly true. They fought about her dad, too, because he was so controlling, and occasionally about the late hours he worked.

"I thought it would be different once she moved to California," LaNae rushed on, "but nothing's changed. You still think about her and talk about her. Well, I'm finished fighting. Go see her. Go tell her about your job and reminisce about the good old days. But don't pretend to me that you're thinking about moving to California to find a job."

"But I am!"

Her pale eyes met his. "I don't believe it."

"Even if I did end up moving to California, you'd have nothing to worry about. Savvy's only a friend!"

"A *girl* friend," LaNae retorted. "I've heard your sisters talk about how much she likes you. They think the only reason she moved to California was because you were dating me."

"That's not true!" Tyler leaned closer to LaNae. "Savvy left because she loves astronomy and Berkeley has a great program there."

"Baloney!" Her arms shot out and grabbed the white bear from the couch. In the next second, she shoved it into his arms. "I'm tired of being the driving force in our relationship. You either want a future with me or you don't. I'm not going to compete with Savvy. Now please leave." She turned her back on him.

He looked down at the bear he'd given her what seemed like a lifetime ago. Its paws held a silky red heart that proclaimed, "I love you beary much!"

He knew he should give up the idea of going to California tomorrow, that he should go around to the local newspapers and try to find a job. LaNae would be happier. She would become her soft self, the woman he thought he loved. He'd never seen this side of her before.

He let the bear fall onto the floor.

"I'm sorry," Tyler whispered. "I really am."

Not knowing what else to do, he left.

Twenty-five minutes later, his cell phone rang as he was heading off the freeway. By the time he had his hands free enough to check who it was, the ringing had stopped. LaNae always hung up if he didn't answer right away, not wanting to cause an accident when he was driving. Tyler immediately pulled over to the side of the road and called her back.

"Hi," he said when she answered. "It's me." There was comfort in the phrase; someone knew him so well that he didn't have to say his name.

"I'm sorry," she said.

"For what? For kicking me out on my ear or for me deserving it?"

She gave a half-hearted chuckle. "I think I overreacted, and I just wanted to say I'm sorry."

He could feel a "but" coming, just as she had felt his earlier.

"But I think maybe we need to date other people for a while. Until we decide what we really want."

He sucked in a breath. "Why do I get the feeling this has more to do with you than with me and California?"

"Maybe it does." She was silent a moment and then said, "Tyler, I love being with you. I enjoy everything we do, but I meant it when I say I'm the one who drives our relationship. Sometimes I wish you'd go after what you really want. Like you do with your job. I admire your drive. But where we're concerned, you drag your feet. I think . . . well, maybe you're not sure. I don't want someone who's not sure about me, so that makes me not sure about us, either."

A tear slipped down Tyler's cheek, which surprised him because he hadn't cried in a long time. He swallowed hard. "Okay," he said. "Maybe we should take a step back. Let's talk about it when I come home."

"I do care about you," LaNae said.

"Me too."

That was nice, but after nearly seven months and all they had been to each other, they should have been saying, "I love you." He could feel her slipping away. What's more, he wasn't sure he wanted to stop her—and that made him feel worse.

He hung up the phone and drove home, more tears wetting his cheeks.

Chapter Six

The warm night smelled of orange blossoms and heat, though not the same kind of summer heat Lexi loved in Colorado. California was a lot like Arizona, and she was glad she didn't live there anymore.

She ran down the deserted street, her flip-flops clacking against the blacktop. Her chest felt swollen from the inside out. She had made a mistake coming here—a big mistake—and she had no idea what to do next. What had she expected, that her sister would welcome her with open arms and immediately fall in with her plans? The woman had a life. A life that Lexi had no part in. Of course she wouldn't be happy to see a problem like Lexi appear on her doorstep. After all, Savvy already had two younger sisters.

I so wanted a sister. Lexi could say the words to herself, though she felt they were a betrayal of her brother, who had always been her idol. She'd been close to admitting the words to Savvy in those moments alone in the bedroom. *Too close,* she thought. What she should have done was maintain a distance. Use Savvy for what she wanted but not become too involved.

Involved.

She both loved and hated that word—she'd looked it up in her mini dictionary that she carried everywhere. Involved meant connected, caring. She couldn't afford either of those now.

The backpack over her shoulder weighed a ton, and her breath burned in her chest. She slowed to a walk. *What am I going to do?* She kept moving, her feet feeling slow and clumsy against the rough street. The headlights of a car made her jump onto the sidewalk. There was fear in her heart but a little hope, too. Had Savvy come looking for her?

The car sped past. Lexi continued walking, knowing an idea would come to her. She was bright, or so they always said. She'd read more books than any ten book-loving girls her age. Maybe more

After what seemed like an hour, she entered a commercial area and began looking for a pay phone. She thought about calling home and asking for her brother, but she knew that would be a mistake. She couldn't forget that he didn't live there anymore. Her heart ached at the thought. She wished he were there waiting for her.

Spying a convenience store, Lexi dug in her wallet for the calling card she'd bought before leaving Colorado. Her eyes fell on the school ID. Tears sprang to her eyes. *Stupid card,* she thought. Angrily, she whipped the card out and tossed it into the garbage container that stood a few feet from the phone. It was the only thing she had that linked her to Colorado—she hoped.

Stepping back to the pay phone, she dialed a number she knew by heart—her own cell, the one she had bought six months ago with her dad's forged signature. "Hi, it's me," she said. "Can you talk?"

"Oh my gosh, Lex, where are you?" Amber gushed in her ear. "Is everything all right? I've been worried sick!"

Lexi could picture her friend, her brown hair pulled back in a clip and dark eyes looking too big for her freckled face. "I'm fine. I got here okay. No, don't ask where here is because I won't tell you. It's safer."

"Well," Amber said, sounding irritated, "I suppose that's just as well. Your dad called yesterday looking for you."

Lexi's heart slammed against her chest. "How'd he get the number?"

"Not your cell phone, my home phone."

"Oh. What did you tell him?"

"Don't worry, I covered for you. Told him you were in the shower. But I was scared for a minute. He was really mad. I guess he didn't see the note you left about staying the night at my house."

Lexi had been afraid of that. "He'll get over it," she said. The ache in her heart was now replaced by an emotion she didn't want to examine too closely. All she knew was that the pain was worse than when she'd gotten those sixteen stitches in her left leg last year.

"Did you ask him if I could stay the weekend with you?" Lexi added.

"He said okay. But what if he finds out you're not here and like calls the police or something. Or my parents?"

"He won't. Look, tomorrow's one of his busy days, and then he'll be out of it for a day or two, resting up, so as long as you sneak over and put one of those notes I gave you on the table after school on Monday, it'll be fine."

"Should I use one of the 'Stayed after school for literary club,' or 'Have to practice late for the play'?"

"Either one, but don't forget to mess up my room a little, so he'll think I was there part of the day. Pull down the covers on the bed. Okay? Don't throw too many clothes around, though, I don't keep things that bad."

"You mean like I do. Look, I'll do it, but I don't see how long you think you're going to keep this up."

"As long as I need to." Lexi paused, unwilling to tell Amber how badly everything had gone already. At least she had money; she hadn't lied to Savvy about that. She wondered if there was a hotel nearby that would accept cash from a minor. She had high heels, sunglasses, and a fake wedding ring in her backpack but wasn't sure if the disguise would work.

"I saw Zeke today," Amber said.

Lexi's heart turned in her chest. Zeke was a boy she had a crush on at school. "You did? How'd he look?"

"Gorgeous as usual."

"He ask after me?"

"Yeah, actually, he did." Unconcealed admiration tinged Amber's voice.

Lexi felt warmth spread through the frozen part of her chest. She hadn't told anyone besides Amber about her crush on Zeke, and she would never tell anyone else. *Well, maybe I'd tell a sister who acted like a sister,* she thought. But perhaps she was expecting too much. Maybe if sisters didn't grow up together, there was never a chance of becoming close.

"Lex, I miss you," Amber said. "Why don't you just come home? We'll work things out somehow. Maybe my parents can help."

"I can't. You know my father; he won't bend. I—I . . ." Lexi trailed off. She wanted to thank Amber, to tell her that she missed her, but the words wouldn't come.

"I know," Amber said softly. "Just take care of yourself, okay?"

"I will. Bye now."

Blindly, Lexi left the pay phone, stumbling once over the sidewalk.

"You okay, girl?" a man called on his way inside the store. Lexi nodded.

Down the street a short way, she found a park next to a library. She wandered through the motionless swings, seeing herself on one as a child, her mother pushing her.

Mother!

Pain burst through Lexi's heart. But there was a bit of anger, too. If it wasn't for her mother, she wouldn't be here now.

Spying a bench next to the swings, Lexi sat down. From the depths of her backpack, she removed a thin blanket, and drawing it around herself, she curled up on the bench and closed her eyes. Tears made a trail down to her temples before splashing silently onto the dry wood.

..*.*.*

Savvy began searching the neighborhood in her old Subaru, her emotions varying from fear for Lexi to anger at her irresponsibility. *When I find her I'm going to kill her!* she thought more than once, though it wasn't in the least true. She worried about muggers, about drug dealers, about teenage boys and raging hormones. Lexi was only thirteen, and she shouldn't be wandering the dark streets alone. She should be safe at home.

Home. Where was her home? Savvy knew she hadn't tried hard enough to find out. She should have forced her to talk, maybe actually taken her to the police station and asked them to help her find the answers. But she had been too stunned at the turn of events to do anything right. Now she was afraid Lexi would become another runaway statistic.

"You didn't really want her here in the first place," she mumbled aloud to the dark. And now she was gone.

Maybe Lexi had gone home. If so, Savvy wondered if she should leave well enough alone. But no. Savvy had learned enough about Lexi to know that she didn't give up easily. She was somewhere out there regrouping and planning her next move. Savvy had to find her before she made another wrong one. Because Savvy *did* want Lexi in her life. She wanted to learn all about her, to help her. And somewhere in all that wanting were her mixed-up feelings about her birth father.

Savvy drove up and down the streets in the surrounding residential area. Nothing. When she reached the commercial area, she parked her car and began visiting the few open businesses. Finally, a clerk at a convenience store remembered a young girl making a phone call. She'd been carrying a backpack.

Savvy walked up the street, delving into the shadows with her eyes and praying as hard as she had ever prayed. She also sent out love to her sister and received a strong impression that Lexi was near. *Where would I go, if I were her?* she wondered. The problem was that she didn't know Lexi well enough to know where she might go. She knew only that Lexi was smart, independent, well-spoken, and carried a backpack heavier than a dozen thick hardbacks.

Books. Hmm. There was a library nearby, if she remembered correctly. Savvy turned in that direction. She reached a park that bordered the library and craned her neck to see if the library was still open. Most of the lights were out, and she didn't see any people. *Closed,* she thought.

She almost didn't notice the lump on the park bench. The night was dark, and the area by the bench was made even more so by the trees that blocked the street lights from shining onto the playground. But something made her look—the whisper of the Spirit that said Lexi was nearby.

Cautiously, Savvy approached the bench. What if the lump wasn't Lexi at all? Yet, she was sure it was. Did this feeling mean Lexi was supposed to be in her life? Did it mean they were destined to become something important to each other? Savvy didn't know. She only knew that she needed to find Lexi. Now. Tonight. Before it was too late.

Several feet away, she recognized the backpack. Heaving an internal sigh of relief, she quickened her pace. Crossing the last few steps to the bench, she sat down with a sigh. Lexi started, as though she'd been asleep, and pushed herself to a sitting position, blinking her eyes rapidly. Savvy didn't speak, giving her time to adjust. Now that she was close, there was enough light slanting onto the bench for Savvy to see that Lexi had been crying.

"Why are you here?" Lexi muttered. There was a catch in her voice, but her expression was fierce. Savvy pretended not to notice either. Lexi looked more than ever like a young girl—scared and alone.

Savvy's heart hurt seeing her this way. She folded her hands in her lap, praying to know what to say. "Why are you here?"

"You obviously don't want me around, so I left." Lexi's voice sounded tough now, but her left shoulder ticked twice nervously.

Savvy stared out over the playground. The swings hung motionless in the eerie dark. Shadows fell in all directions. "But I *do* want you around," she said, her voice as soft as the darkness, "and I'm really sorry if I said something to make it seem that I didn't."

She reached over to where Lexi's hand had emerged from the dark blanket she'd wrapped around herself. Lexi didn't pull away from her touch. "Look, I'm new at this. I'm not very experienced with teenagers. I'm doing the best I can. I just don't understand why you lied to me about the ID. Was it because you were afraid I would send you home if I knew you were only thirteen? Was it because you don't want to leave California? Or what? Won't you tell me? Can you see at least a little bit why I was angry?"

Lexi's breath came faster. "I can't," she muttered.

"Can't? You can't see why I was angry, or you can't tell me why you lied?" Savvy struggled to keep the frustration from her voice, but Lexi wasn't helping matters. She gently squeezed the thin hand in her own.

Lexi shook her head. "I mean, I can't fly."

"You can't . . ." Then all at once Savvy understood. "You're afraid of flying."

Lexi hiccupped, a futile attempt to stave off tears. "I can't fly. I'd rather die. I mean, I feel like if I go on a plane, I'll die." Her tearful gaze lifted to Savvy's. "My heart pounds so hard just thinking about it—like I'm going to drop dead." Her shoulder jerked convulsively. Savvy let go of Lexi's hand and put an arm around her, pulling her close.

What made this child so afraid of flying that she would run away from Savvy when she had barely arrived? Savvy knew there had to be a reason. Lexi was too young to react so violently unless there was a serious cause. Unraveling this mystery might be the first step toward solving everything.

"Lexi," she whispered, "why are you so afraid of flying?"

Lexi swallowed hard, and then with a deliberate, concentrated effort extracted herself from Savvy's embrace. She stared down at her lap, where her fingers twisted together. "Five years ago, my mother was on a plane, and it crashed. Everyone died." The words slipped from her mouth as though they had been said many times before, as though Lexi was accustomed to the taste and smell of them. They hung in the dark air like an invisible, choking cloud.

"Oh, Lexi." Savvy reached for her again, and at first Lexi resisted, but Savvy didn't give up. Lexi had been only eight when her mother died; already she had missed too many comforting hugs. Finally, Lexi allowed Savvy to pull her into an embrace. She didn't cry, though, and Savvy wondered if she had already cried out all those tears.

Somewhere a car door slammed, and Savvy was reminded that it was dark and they were alone in a park. For safety's sake, they should go home. Still, she was loath to break the mood between them. If she asked now, would Lexi tell her about her home—about their father?

Lexi shifted slightly on the bench. "I . . ." she began, so softly that Savvy struggled to hear the words. "I always wanted a sister."

"I'm here now," Savvy whispered. With one hand she stroked Lexi's bleached-out hair. "Everything's going to be okay."

As they arose together from the bench, Savvy vowed to do everything in her power to make sure she was telling Lexi the truth.

Chapter Seven

Early Saturday morning, Tyler was ready to leave for Kerrianne's when his doorbell rang. He rushed to the door, scraping his foot along the side of the turtle's shell. "Scram, Tartar," he said, pausing to move the animal out of the way. He pulled the door wide. "Manda! Good, you're just in time."

His sister wasn't alone. Amanda's foster children, Kevin and Mara, now eight and four, were with her, as was her nearly two-year-old son, Blakey, named after his father, Blake. With exuberant cries, the children threw themselves at Tyler, who tickled them until they spun away from his grasp, giggling.

"Sorry I'm a little late," Amanda said. "You wouldn't believe how long it takes to get everyone out the door. And I didn't get to do anything to myself." Her blonde hair was clipped up on her head, her face devoid of makeup. Regardless, Tyler thought she was a striking woman whose features only improved with age. Today she seemed almost glowing.

"I know how it is," he assured her. "Kids, be careful of Tartar. He was in the middle of the hall a minute ago. Don't step on him."

Amanda wrinkled her nose. "What's that smell?"

Tyler sniffed. "Well, the gerbil cages probably need to be cleaned, but I won't do that until next week." He looked closer at her. "You suddenly look green. Is everything okay?"

Without response, Amanda shoved past him on her way to the bathroom, leaving Tyler to stare after her in confusion.

Blond-haired Kevin grinned up at him, his blue eyes looking large in his small face. "Mom's going to have another baby, you know."

"She is?"

He nodded. "She told us yesterday."

"I want a girl," said Mara. "We already have two boys." As she spoke, the dark-haired, brown-eyed child gave little Blakey a hug. "I like Blakey a lot, but I want a girl to play dollies with."

Blakey babbled something that sounded remarkably intelligent, though Tyler couldn't decipher even one word.

"Blakey says that he plays with dollies," Kevin translated.

"He did?" Tyler flexed both his hands. "You got all that, huh?"

Nodding, Kevin picked up Blakey. "Can I take him to see the fish?"

"Sure, go ahead." Tyler motioned down the hall. "I'll come in a minute when your mom gets out of the bathroom."

Amanda emerged a couple minutes later, looking shaky and slightly flushed. Tyler grinned. "I hear congratulations are in order."

Amanda's hand went to her stomach. "Yeah, believe it or not. We've been trying for six months. It's a blessing, but I forgot how sick I get."

Tyler made a face. "If I'd known, I would have asked Mom to look after the animals while I'm gone."

"Oh, no." Amanda waved his concerns aside. "The kids love coming here. Honestly, I don't mind at all. Now show me the special drops you have to give Lizzy—is it just me, or is that lizard always sick?"

He shrugged. "She keeps getting out, and without her lights she gets cold."

"And didn't you have some instructions for the fish?"

"Mitch sent a new food from Australia." Tyler rolled his eyes. "I'll be glad when he gets back here to tend them himself."

Amanda's face burst into a smile. "Don't I know it."

"Come on. I'll show you where the stuff is."

"Uh, wait a second." Amanda put her hand on his arm. "Tyler, I have a big favor to ask."

Tyler suspected this was the real reason his sister had come this morning. He'd offered to leave the key under the mat, Lizzy Lizzard's antibiotic drops on top of her cage, and written instructions for the new fish food, but Amanda had insisted on coming so he could run through the animals' care with her in person. "Sure, what is it?" He hoped it had nothing to do with the paper, seeing as he didn't work there anymore.

"It's about Kevin and Mara's mother."

"Blake's cousin—Paula, right?"

"Yeah. I have the last address she gave us in San Francisco, and it doesn't seem to be too far from Kerrianne's mother-in-law's—less than an hour, I think. I was wondering, only if you had time, of course, if maybe you could stop by and see her."

"You want me to check up on her?" Tyler knew Amanda vacillated between praying for Paula to recover from her addictions and hoping she wouldn't come back for her children. Blake had raised Kevin almost from birth and Mara from the time she was eight months old. When Amanda had met and married him over three years ago, she'd fallen as hard for the children as she had for him.

"Sort of." Amanda looked away, her eyes wandering around the tiny living room, pausing on the worn couch that had been a castoff from his parents' home, its original color so faded as to be indeterminable. After a few moments of silence, she dragged her eyes back to his. "Kevin's been calling us Mom and Dad for more than two years now. We'd like to make it official. We have custody, but we'd like Paula's blessing to adopt."

"You could probably do it without her blessing," Tyler said. "She's only visited once in the past three years—that's abandonment if I ever heard of it. You could have her parental rights terminated." This wasn't the first time he'd suggested the action, but Amanda was afraid that such an attempt would bring Paula charging back into the picture.

She shrugged. "There's still the chance that she'd fight—and that would put Kevin and Mara through a lot of stress."

Tyler bristled. "Mara doesn't even know who she is!"

"I know. But Paula is their mother, and she gave us custody because she loved them."

"You mean because it was frustrating for her to take a hit with kids underfoot. We both know her motives weren't that pure."

"Maybe not completely pure," Amanda agreed, "but in the end she did love them enough to do what was right for them." She glanced behind her. They could hear the children's voices floating down the hall, fragmented by distance. "What I'm hoping, Tyler, is that you can talk to her. Feel out her thoughts on the matter. Blake and I've tried to approach her about it, but we always seem unable to follow through— he loves her too much, I think, and I'm simply too frightened. We're both feeling kind of desperate about it. I thought that you . . . well, you're so good with words and at getting people to see the real issues— that's why you're such a good reporter."

"Not as good as you think," he said. She was entrusting a great deal to him, and he wanted to be certain she knew his limitations. "I lost my job at the paper. One too many comments about a politician's parenting skills."

His sister's face showed concern. "Oh, I'm so sorry, Tyler. I had no idea." She gave herself a little shake. "But don't you see? That makes you perfect for the job. You care enough about children to do something about it. All I'm asking is for you to visit Paula, see what she's feeling, where she is in her life. In a few weeks, Kevin'll be baptized. We'd like to have things figured out by then."

Tyler nodded. "Okay, I'll do my best. Where's the address?"

She considered a moment and then snapped her fingers. "I left it in my van. You know, I think pregnancy really does something with your brain cells—temporarily, of course. Show me those lizard drops first, and then I'll get it for you. Oh, and I have a small album of pictures for you to take to Paula. That can be your surface reason for visiting her, something to get you in the door."

In less than five minutes, Tyler was in his Jeep heading toward Kerrianne's house in Pleasant Grove, leaving Amanda and her children still playing with the animals. His thoughts drifted toward Savvy. She should know by now that he was coming. He pictured her face, with those blue eyes brighter than the sky on a cloudless day. He was suddenly so anxious to see her that his chest almost hurt with the need. Would she be as happy to see him?

⋆ *⋆* *⋆*

"What!" Savvy stood by the sink gripping the phone hard in her right hand. It was Saturday morning, and she'd finally made the time to call home again, only to be told that Tyler was on his way to California to pick her up. She'd been praying for help, but that was definitely not what she had in mind. "No, I don't want him to come. I can't believe you didn't ask me first!"

"Oh, dear," her mother said. "I did try to call. I left a message asking you to call us."

"I called you back last night, but someone was on the phone."

"I know. I called you after. You didn't answer."

"I had to find Lexi."

"Where was she?"

"Never mind. I'll explain later." Savvy's hand was beginning to hurt, and she relaxed her hold on the phone. A few feet away, Lexi was seated at the table in front of a huge bowl of cornflakes, watching her curiously. "The point is that I called to tell you we were going to rent a car and ask if you'd help me out a little."

"Of course we would—but there's no sense in that now that Tyler's going to be there."

"But that'll make us get home later. We could be there by tomorrow if we left now. Counting today, I only have eleven days before I have to head back here."

"I'm afraid he already left. I talked to him last night, and he was planning to take off at five or so."

"He has a cell phone. Call him."

"But he has business there, and his sister and her family were going as well. Apparently she has family in the area they really wanted to visit."

Savvy knew the sister was Kerrianne. A year ago when Savvy had been on her mission, Kerrianne had come to visit her mother-in-law and had left Savvy a package at the mission home. Kerrianne was always sweet and thoughtful. As mad as Savvy was that Tyler had decided to rescue her when she most certainly didn't need rescuing, she wasn't prepared to disappoint Kerrianne or her children.

"Besides," her mother said, taking her silence for capitulation, "your father and I really feel better having someone with you that we know and trust. Lexi has already proven to be very resourceful for her age, and quite frankly I worry about whatever plans she might have in store."

"What, like a hijacking? Mom, I promise you, it's not like that. You'd know if you were here." Savvy would have explained further, but Lexi was still listening intently, though she was pretending to read the cereal box.

"I'm really sorry. We should have cleared it with you first. Why don't you call Tyler if you feel that strongly about it? But remember that he's trying to do you a favor. You two used to be so close—don't you think you're being a bit unreasonable?"

Savvy sighed. Her mother didn't know the feelings she had harbored for Tyler and had no idea of the pain he'd put her through. But Savvy wasn't about to explain now. "Okay," she said as calmly as she could manage, "we'll drive back with him."

"Good." Her mother was obviously relieved. "I'll see you in a few days, then. Let me know for sure when you'll be arriving. We'll be grateful for any time we have with you."

As Savvy hung up the phone, Lexi eyed her curiously. "So who's coming to pick us up?"

Savvy walked over and sat down at the table. "Tyler. The guy whose picture you saw in my album."

"The last picture?" Lexi's eyes grew wide. "Great! He's hot."

Savvy blew out a breath. She could already tell that this was going to be a long weekend.

*****

Savvy spent Saturday visiting local sites with Lexi in her junky old Subaru. They visited Fisherman's Wharf, San Francisco Bay, the Golden Gate Bridge, and Lombard Street, the crookedest street in the world. They even went on a short tour of Nob Hill. At three o'clock they stopped by a mall to grab a late bite to eat and to rest. Savvy wasn't tired, but Lexi looked the worse for wear. Savvy wondered if she'd slept at all.

Savvy had an ulterior motive for eating at the mall. She was hoping to buy Lexi a better shirt than the one she was wearing, which looked hardly big enough for a girl half her age. Maybe a longer one would hide her belly ring. Once at the mall, they spied a beauty salon, and that gave Savvy another idea.

"Hey, I've been thinking about getting my hair trimmed," she said. "What about you?" Truthfully, she'd love to see if they could do something about the bleached-out color of Lexi's hair. Her dark roots had grown out several inches and the girl obviously had no idea how bad it looked.

"You want to cut your hair?" Lexi's eyes opened wide. "Why? It's so beautiful. I've been trying to grow mine out."

"It's a bit too long, is all." Savvy ran her hand through the strands. "Haven't had much time to cut it. I like it about mid-shoulder because then it doesn't pull down so straight."

"Well, you've got the face for straight hair."

Savvy grinned. "You mean round?"

"I didn't mean it like that," Lexi said, flushing. "I think you're really pretty. I like your hair color."

"Well, thank you. You're kind of cute yourself." *Or would be,* Savvy amended silently, *if you didn't insist on wearing so much black eyeliner.* With Lexi's poorly cut, bleached hair and too-dark eyes, she resembled something from a vampire novel.

"You won't have to cut much of your length to get a trim," Savvy said. "Why don't we try it? They don't look busy. I'll pay." With her partial refund from the plane ticket and no car rental fee looming, she had more than enough money in her checking account.

"Okay. But I can pay for me. I've got money."

Savvy shook her head. "Don't worry about it. It was my idea. Hey, what color is your hair normally? I think you might look really cool with a few different shades of blonde."

"All right. But only if it's light like yours."

Inside, Savvy drew aside the hair stylist and told her she wanted Lexi to look "less fake." The woman grinned and assured her that wouldn't be a problem. Since Lexi didn't want any length taken off, the hairdresser's job would be layering and coloring. Savvy figured that anything she came up with would be an improvement on the status quo.

"I'll buy you an outfit after," she said when the hairdresser had gone in the back room for products. "But I get to help pick it out."

Lexi rolled her eyes. "I'm not wearing a dress."

"Don't worry. It won't be. I'm only wearing this skirt because it's so hot."

"Oh, I wondered if it had something to do with you being a Mormon."

"No." Savvy shook her head. "When I was on a mission I had to wear dresses, but that was different. I was teaching people every day for eighteen months."

Lexi regarded her silently for a minute. "I don't understand why you would want to be a missionary—it's such a waste of time. You had to leave your family, didn't you? And anyway, you could have finished school by now."

"I don't see it that way. I see it as saving souls. What do you think the worth of a soul is?"

Lexi shrugged. "I don't know. But saving them from what?"

The hairdresser was coming back. "From themselves, mostly," Savvy said. "Believe me, lives change when people begin to believe in Jesus."

Lexi didn't reply, and Savvy had no way of knowing what her sister believed. Once their father had been a member, but he had strayed far from the precepts of the gospel. Had he ever taught Lexi about Jesus?

After the stylist finished, Lexi's hair was remarkably changed. The top layers curved under, while the bottom ones gently curled up and out. The color was still blonde but with interspersing darker highlights that made it look more natural. The best part for Savvy was that Lexi's ears and all those tasteless, childish piercings were hidden. If she'd had only one piercing in each ear, Savvy would have offered to buy inexpensive earrings to go with the new hairdo, but as it was, she decided earrings weren't a subject she wanted to bring up right now.

"Wow," Lexi said, eying herself in the mirror while Savvy paid. "I look different. I bet if Zeke could see me now, he'd flip."

"Zeke?"

Lexi's smile vanished. "Just a guy I know."

Savvy checked her watch. "We have time to hit one store, but then we need to get back. It's nearly six, and by the time we get home, my friends from Utah might be there."

"Don't you have his number?"

"Yeah. But if I know him, he'll be coming over as soon as he gets into town." Before Lexi could ask any more questions, Savvy led her down the mall.

The store was one Savvy chose specifically for its conservatism, both in pricing and in style. Lexi cast her a flat, challenging stare but tried on a few outfits anyway. She didn't object when Savvy bought her a pair of inexpensive jeans and three modest sale tops—all for less than forty bucks.

Savvy checked her watch. "We'd probably better get back to the apartment."

They walked in silence for a few minutes while Savvy wondered if she was doing the right thing in taking Lexi back to Utah. What if they both got into trouble? But if Lexi wouldn't tell her Derek's number or where she lived, Savvy had no choice. She didn't even have Internet access to search out Derek's name unless she went over to the college. And what would she do with Lexi while she went?

As they entered the parking lot, Savvy turned to Lexi. "We really need to talk."

Lexi's eyes were immediately suspicious, and Savvy felt her stomach flop. She wished she didn't have to question Lexi, but she was the adult here. They walked past several cars before she found enough courage to say, "I need to contact your dad."

"Our dad, you mean." Lexi's chin went up, her jaw firm.

"Yes, our dad. I'll talk to him. Let him know you're okay."

Lexi stopped walking, clenching her fists at her side. Gone was the companionable young girl she had been all day, and in her place was the sullen teenager. "He won't miss me," she snarled. "Didn't I tell you that already? Why do you think I left?"

"I don't know why you left. You didn't say anything except that you wanted to meet me. My parents think I should call the police so they can find your father. Can you give me any reason why I shouldn't?"

Lexi was silent a moment, her brow furrowed. Savvy had the strange feeling that she was rehearsing her story, and yet why should she do that?

"My dad's a horrible man," Lexi said finally. "You can't send me back to him. You don't know him—he can get violent. You should have seen what he did when I tried to go out with Zeke."

"You're thirteen—you shouldn't be going out."

"Everybody does where I'm from. I tell Dad I'm not going to do anything stupid, but he just yells at me and . . . Look, if you call the police, I'll have to run away, and then I'll never see you again." She fell silent, swallowing hard, her shoulder ticking convulsively. Abruptly the rebellious teen was gone, and she was a frightened, solitary little girl. "Please, Savvy, please. Don't make me tell you where he is. Give me a few days. I need some time away from there. Please."

Savvy's heart twisted in her chest. "Lexi, does your father hurt you?"

Lexi dropped her gaze to her hands, apparently unwilling to answer.

"Does anyone else know about your father? What about your brother?"

Lexi lifted her face. A tear rolled down her cheek. "Brenton knows everything."

"He's an adult. Hasn't he tried to help you?"

Another tear. "Brenton's the best brother ever. He's everything to me. Don't get him into this."

Savvy was happy Lexi had her brother, though she also felt a twinge of jealousy. What a close relationship her two half-siblings must have—one that didn't include her. At least Brenton might be willing to testify against Lexi's father, if it ever came to that. But why hadn't he protected his sister more? "I'd like to meet him," she said. She would love to ask him what his life had been like growing up with his father and if he had known about her before this year. Maybe he could tell her more than Lexi had chosen to.

Lexi shrugged. "Maybe. He's sort of busy. College isn't easy, you know."

"Look, Lexi." Savvy grabbed her hand that wasn't occupied with her purchases. "Whatever is going on with your father, I can get help. But I need you to trust me, okay? If we don't go about this the right way, we could get into serious trouble." *Kidnapping, for one*, she thought.

Lexi nodded and tried to smile, though she appeared miserable. "Just a few days? How about until Wednesday? Then I'll tell you everything. Okay? Please, Savvy. I promise, he won't even miss me."

Savvy briefly put an arm around her sister's shoulders, wondering how it would be possible for their father not to notice Lexi's absence. Was he a drunk? She seemed to remember her mother mentioning something about his Word of Wisdom problems. Perhaps after the death of his wife, he had gone downhill, had begun to take it out on Lexi. Savvy had to admit—if only to herself—that it made her feel somewhat better thinking this way. If he had a problem with substance abuse, if he was a lying, drinking, abusive man, then of course it would follow that his abandonment of Savvy stemmed from his own problems, not from anything she had done. Not from any fault in her younger self.

Did he even remember Savvy existed? Did he ever wonder about his firstborn and whether or not she was happy? Savvy wasn't sure she wanted to know the answer. There was the very strong possibility that he didn't care at all.

Chapter Eight

A wave of fatigue settled over Savvy as she turned the Subaru into her street. If all went well, she'd be home early next week and surrounded by her family. She could really use their support and advice.

She wasn't quite sure yet what to make of Lexi, though she understood a little better what had motivated the girl to seek her out. She was obviously trying to get away from her father, but perhaps that wasn't the only reason. From what Savvy could see, Lexi had experienced no lasting female influence in her life since her mother died. Perhaps she craved a mother figure and at some level hoped to develop such a relationship with Savvy.

Yet Savvy felt strongly that there was something more than a young girl's yearning for her mother or fear of her father. Some plan, something Lexi was trying to accomplish by contacting her. Serving a mission had trained Savvy to be aware of her feelings; more often than not, they were spiritual messages sent to her from her Heavenly Father. But what could Lexi possibly be hiding?

Everything, Savvy thought with a little grimace. In fact, it was hard to tell if Lexi had ever told the truth. Savvy put on the brake harder than needed at that thought. Was Lexi's mother even dead?

She pulled up in front of the apartment, and her heart skipped a little when she recognized the blue convertible parked in front. Chris was here! She was glad to see him again before she left. As they climbed from the Subaru, Savvy barely registered the van coming down the street—until it honked.

"Who's that?" Lexi asked, pulling the bottom of her shirt down to meet the top of her shorts. Savvy hoped she'd put on one of the new modest shirts soon.

"I don't know. I don't recognize the—" She stopped as the van approached and she spied the driver. "Tyler," she breathed. Her heart leapt in her chest, and she suddenly felt like singing. "But it can't be."

It was.

Tyler jerked to a stop and jumped from the van. "Savvy!"

He looked good—no, he looked way more than good. His hair was longer than she remembered, but it was still that same sandy color she loved. His tall frame was also thinner, but he looked handsome in his jeans and in the Golden Gate T-shirt she recognized as the one she'd sent him last Christmas. His face was lean, too, with large green eyes that reminded her of water-washed emeralds. Those eyes had always been his most compelling feature—wide, nonjudgmental, and so very, very dear. Her knees felt oddly weak and her heart raced. There was something different about his face today, though she couldn't place what. She wanted to run to meet him, to throw herself into his arms. With great effort she reminded herself that she didn't want him here.

Tyler had no such reservations. He strode up the walk, sweeping her into a bear hug. "It's so good to see you!" he exclaimed. Then he squeezed tighter, taking her breath away.

"Oof!" she grunted.

"Sorry." He let her go, his face flushing slightly.

But her heart was near to bursting because of his presence, not from his hug. "That's okay."

Tyler grinned, and his right cheek dimpled. Savvy was both frightened and exhilarated that his smile still had the same effect on her heart. Not even these nearly four months away had cured her feelings for him. She wished they had—almost. The feeling was wonderful enough that she was happy to experience it at least one more time before reality set in.

"I was only too glad to come down when I heard you needed help," he said.

"You didn't have to come." Her voice sounded stilted.

"I wanted to." He paused and looked at her more closely. "Besides, I have some business here. Wait a minute. I know that look. Are you mad at me for coming?" Hurt radiated from his eyes, but Savvy couldn't deny his words. She was angry at him, though she wasn't about to tell him exactly why.

"I had it under control, that's all. I'm embarrassed that my parents made you come."

"They didn't make me. I wanted to help."

"There's really nothing to help with." *I don't need you here,* she thought.

Again the hurt look. "Savvy, I . . ."

"I'm here, too."

Savvy started at the voice. She dragged her eyes past Tyler's face to where his oldest sister stood by the van smiling. "Kerrianne!" Savvy crossed to her and found herself enveloped in another warm embrace. "It's wonderful to see you. Thank you for coming." Savvy could thank Kerrianne, where she couldn't seem to thank Tyler.

"Actually, I just tagged along," Kerrianne said. "The kids needed to visit their grandmother. We'd have been here a half hour ago, but we dropped them off before coming over."

"How are the kids? I bet Misty's quite the grownup little girl now, and the boys—"

"Never give me a minute's rest." Kerrianne smiled widely. "Of course I wouldn't have it any other way."

82

"I can't believe you drove straight through. How was it?"

Kerrianne laughed. "Much better than I expected. I read two books, and the kids either ate, slept, or watched DVDs. They don't get much TV at home, so this was their dream day. Of course, we stopped a few times to let them run around a bit. The only one who had it hard was Tyler. He insisted on doing all the driving."

"Well, I'm glad you made it safely." Savvy hugged her again, her eyes meeting Tyler's. "Hey! I know what's different about you, Tyler. What happened to your glasses?"

He grinned, the hurt gone now from his eyes. "I finally decided to get contacts."

"He hates them, though," Kerrianne said. "He did nothing but complain about them the entire trip."

Savvy stifled an odd longing for the glasses. She wished things could be how they had once been between them, or, better yet, the way she had wanted them to be. But no, she couldn't forget about the girl who'd appeared at her mission homecoming dinner, the girl she knew was back in Utah waiting for him.

"Well, you look nice," Savvy said, forcing her mind along another path. "Except you've lost weight. I bet you've been working too hard, as usual." They were alike in that—they both let their work absorb them.

"A bit." Tyler stared hard at her. "You've lost weight, too, haven't you?"

Savvy shook her head. "Nope, not an ounce. If anything, I've gained five pounds." *There, that'll fix him,* she thought. Tyler was always attracted to such skinny women, and she'd felt fat by comparison. She couldn't let herself get sucked into that again. She loved who she was now, and she wasn't about to worry about Tyler's opinion. Besides, she wasn't overweight, she was shapely—and that was nothing to be ashamed about.

"Oh, I thought . . . well, you look . . ." He seemed to swallow with difficulty. "You look really great. Really great. And I can't—" He broke off. "I mean, I've really missed you."

Savvy was unprepared for the hope his words brought surging to her heart. She felt as if spring had exploded into her soul. For long seconds she stared at him, unable to reply and praying desperately that her emotions were not etched on her face for all to see. Her heart pounded, and her breath caught in her throat. She would give anything for it to be darker right now so that her secret feelings would be safe.

"So," came a mocking voice behind them. "Isn't anyone going to introduce me?" Lexi sauntered to Savvy's side. "Hi, I'm Lexi, Savvy's, uh, sister. Who exactly are you guys?" She smiled charmingly at Tyler.

Savvy was grateful for her interruption. A second longer and she might have let slip to Tyler how much she had missed him, too—despite the efforts she'd made to put him from her mind. She touched Lexi's back lightly. "This is Tyler Huntington."

"Nice to meet you," Tyler said, offering his hand.

Lexi blushed, as though remembering how she'd called him "hot." With her new hair and some of the black eyeliner worn off during the day, she looked quite pretty.

"Tyler and his family are old friends," Savvy continued. "In fact, I've known his sister Amanda since we were teenagers."

"But you're not Amanda?" Lexi's eyes went to Kerrianne.

"No, Kerrianne, the oldest of the bunch."

"Then Manda, then Mitch, and last of all, me," Tyler put in. He grinned, and Savvy could see by the look on Lexi's face that it wasn't only Savvy whose stomach his smile affected.

"In other words, he's the baby." Savvy cast an enigmatic look at Tyler—at least she hoped it was enigmatic. A little mystery could go a long way to misdirecting his attention from her ridiculous infatuation. It wasn't as if he were the best-looking guy in the world or had some other compelling quality that caused women to line up around the block. So what was her problem?

"Nice to meet you, Lexi," Kerrianne was saying in her ever-gracious voice. "I know Savvy must be pretty excited. Finding a sister is . . . well, it must be one of the best things in the whole world."

Lexi nodded, her face pleasant, but there was a slight clenching around her lips, as if she were struggling to control her response.

"So when do you want to leave for Utah?" Tyler asked Savvy. "I have an errand I need to do tonight and a few more things on Monday."

"Whatever's convenient," Savvy said, though it was all she could do not to hurry them into the van and leave right then.

"Well, I know you only have ten or eleven days left before you have to be back here," Tyler said, "but I was thinking if we left Tuesday morning, I'd get my work done and Kerrianne would have two days with her mother-in-law."

"Are you sure that's enough time?" Savvy looked hopefully at Kerrianne.

Kerrianne considered for a moment. "I think that's exactly the right amount of time. Adam's mother isn't as healthy as she used to be, and three active children can be exhausting even when a person feels well. I'm grateful for any time to visit with her—and to get out of the house for a while."

"Okay, so now that's settled, can we eat?" Lexi asked. She looked happier, Savvy thought, as though glad the trip to Utah had been delayed.

"We can go out somewhere," Tyler suggested. "My treat. Well, actually your dad's treat, Savvy, since he forced me to take a bundle of money that more than paid for gas."

"Well . . ." Savvy glanced toward her apartment, belatedly remembering Chris. Where was he? "A friend of mine is here somewhere," she said. "Probably talking to a neighbor. I'd better check to make sure he hasn't gone to a lot of trouble planning something."

Savvy escaped up the stairs, leaving Lexi behind with Tyler and Kerrianne. Lexi didn't seem to mind. Her eyes were fixed on Tyler as he bent forward slightly to catch what she was saying. Savvy felt the old familiar sadness—not because she was worried about him being attracted to Lexi but because it reminded her of the many times she had watched him talk to other women. The girlfriends had come and gone, while Savvy stood on the sidelines, watching.

I can't let it happen again, she thought. *I won't.*

Savvy took a steadying breath. Everything would be okay. She wasn't the same person she'd been back then. She was stronger, more sure of herself and what she wanted in life.

Intent on her thoughts, Savvy didn't notice that the door to her apartment was ajar until she was halfway inside. "Who's there?" she called, a chill running up her spine. Was it Lexi's father?

"Savvy?" Chris's familiar voice called from the kitchen.

Savvy hurried in the direction of his voice, stumbling over his feet as she entered. He drew in his long limbs quickly and leaned forward in his chair to steady her, his hand feeling warm on her elbow. "Oh, Chris!" she exclaimed. "You scared me."

He leaned back and watched her with a lazy smile on his face. "You forgot you asked me to water your plants, huh?" He held up the keys she'd given him only two days before.

"Yeah, I did. I'm glad you let yourself in. Have you been waiting long?"

"Twenty minutes or so." He motioned to the newspaper in front of him. "I was looking for a movie." His muscles moved as he spoke, and Savvy couldn't help comparing his bulk to Tyler's leanness.

"I don't think tonight's good for a movie." She explained about Tyler and Kerrianne coming from Utah. "They'd like to take us out to eat. I was thinking I might show them around a bit on the way. How about another raincheck? Or you could come with us."

He smiled and shook his head. "Thanks, but I bet you have a lot of catching up to do, and some of the guys were bugging me to go with them tonight anyway." He pulled out his cell phone. "I'll tell them it's on."

Savvy was relieved that he decided not to come with her. It might be easier to maintain distance from Tyler if Chris were there, but she didn't want to use him that way. She wanted their relationship to be completely free of her former life with Tyler. Thank heaven Chris wasn't the jealous sort.

Chris talked briefly with his friends and then stood. Once again Savvy was aware of how big he was and how small she felt in comparison. She enjoyed that feeling.

"I'd like to meet your friends," Chris said.

"I just need to grab something in my room. If you wait a minute, I'll introduce you."

"I'll be in the living room."

Savvy started down the hall, ducking into the bathroom on the way. She stared in the mirror, placing her hands on either side of the small sink. She looked flushed, her blue eyes wide and alive with emotion. She ran her hands under cool water and pressed the palms against her hot cheeks. "Breathe," she advised the image in the mirror. "I am a beautiful, talented daughter of God, and I am in control of my destiny." The image stared back—the classical, sculpted features becoming calmer by the moment. Savvy smiled, relieved that her heartbeat had returned to normal.

Composed once more, Savvy left the room.

* * * * * *

Tyler immediately liked Lexi. He could tell right away that she was not an ordinary teen. When he used the word *cataclysmic* in a sentence, she replied using *dyspeptic*. Moreover, she seemed to actually understand the word. When she discovered he was a journalist, she practically oozed excitement. Tyler thought it uncanny how much the half sisters were alike; not only did Lexi have Savvy's large, oval, sky blue eyes but she had the same way of lighting an area so that all eyes gravitated toward her. Of course, she was only a child—a rather thin one at that—and despite her apparent admiration, Tyler became anxious for Savvy to come outside. What was taking her so long?

He hadn't expected her to be upset at him for coming to California, but apparently she was. Why? Didn't she think he had anything to offer in this situation? No, he didn't know much about teens, and he obviously hadn't been much of a friend to Savvy lately, but surely he could help in some way. He *wanted* to help. He wanted to prove to her that he was the same guy who had laughed with her under the stars.

Finally, Savvy came from the upstairs apartment, but she was not alone. A handsome, friendly looking man about Tyler's age was with her. Though he was only a few inches taller than Tyler, he was more solidly built in the way many women appreciated. For a moment, Tyler was reminded of the new employee who worked with LaNae.

Savvy was walking slightly ahead of the man, but her face was angled back and up to look into his eyes. She was laughing at something he'd said. Tyler felt a wave of unreasoning jealousy crash over him. What was this man to her? Did this guy mean something to her future? It was all too apparent that he admired Savvy.

And why not? Tyler thought. Savvy was a beautiful woman who had always turned heads. He'd lost track of how many guys had wanted to marry her. Ultimately, he knew her personal life had ceased to be his business when he'd begun to think about marrying LaNae.

Then why did his mind now return to years past when he and Savvy had dated? For six months they had been constant companions. What had happened to that? Had they drifted apart? He tried to remember, but no single cause came to mind. One day they were dating, and the next they were only friends. Then Savvy had decided to serve a mission.

Tyler brought his hand up to adjust his glasses, only to discover they weren't there. He raked his hand through his hair, silently sending annoyed thoughts LaNae's way. She was why he had tried contacts in the first place, and he wore them most of the time when they were together, though he still used his glasses at work. He liked his glasses. Most people did. They were a part of who he was. So why then did he not wear them today? He had a sinking feeling that he'd been trying to impress Savvy.

And apparently had failed. She hadn't seemed impressed, and he wondered what she really thought and if she'd tell him. Once she would have—might have. But now? Tyler wasn't going to hold his breath.

Savvy was already introducing Chris Davis, and Tyler nodded at the appropriate time, though he didn't catch much except the man's name. True to his looks, he was welcoming and friendly. Tyler felt his smile frozen in place. His cheeks hurt.

"Look at that sky," Chris said when the introductions were complete.

Savvy glanced to where the low-hanging sun had painted a variety of colors on the high, wispy clouds. "Beautiful," she murmured, a smile coming to her lips.

"Gorgeous," said Kerrianne.

Tyler nodded with the others, though he felt left out. Savvy, he knew, adored anything to do with astronomy as much as he adored journalism. They had always found interest in sharing their worlds. Did Chris have another world, or did he share Savvy's? Tyler wasn't sure he wanted to know.

"Doesn't look different from any other day," Lexi said with an impatient shake of her head.

Savvy cast Lexi an unreadable look, but Tyler recognized the stress in her eyes. "Look, why don't you zip inside and change into those new clothes we bought? You know, dress up a little. Please?"

Lexi looked for a moment as if she were torn between wanting to disobey and wanting to try out the clothes.

Tyler decided to help her out. He would show Savvy that it was a good thing he'd come. "New clothes?" he said. "I'd like to see them."

Nodding with a pleased smile, Lexi accepted the keys Savvy proffered and ran toward the apartment, her sack of purchases swinging from her hand.

"Do we need to change?" Kerrianne asked, glancing down at her fitted blouse and slightly rumpled blue jeans.

"No, it'll be fine," Savvy said. "I just needed to get her out of those shorts." She shook her head. "I don't know what kind of life my sister came from, but she doesn't seem to have had many good examples."

"Have you talked to her father yet?" Tyler asked.

Savvy sighed. "I don't even know where he lives. But she's promised to tell me if I give her a few days."

"Are you sure it's wise to wait? What about the police?" Tyler was surprised that she hadn't already filed a report.

"I'm not sure about anything," Savvy responded. "But she's threatened to run away if I call the police. Maybe I could trap her somehow and hold her until a policeman gets here, but from what little she's told me, there might be something suspicious going on at her house. What if they give her back to her father before they find out what's really happening? What if something terrible happens to her?"

Tyler opened his mouth to protest but then remembered that only last week he'd written up a similar story for the newspaper where the child had suffered a concussion and a broken arm after being released into his parents' custody. Sometimes children did slip through the cracks.

"There hasn't been any news of a missing girl matching her description," he said instead. "I have some friends at the paper checking on it for me. They'll call if they hear anything."

Savvy flashed him a smile that made him glad he'd thought to check. "That's good to know. I'd hate to think of someone out there worried about her."

"Yet not having someone worry is worse," Chris put in. "Nobody seems to miss her. To me that's a clear indication that something's very wrong."

Savvy nodded solemnly. "Don't worry, I'll find out where she's from soon enough—one way or the other." There was a note of determination in her voice that Tyler recognized all too clearly.

"That little girl is lucky to have a sister like you," Chris said.

"Thanks." Savvy gave him a smile equally bright as the one she'd given Tyler.

"Well, then, if you'll all excuse me," Chris said, "I think I'll go meet my friends. Have fun, Savvy. I'll see you later." There was an unmistakable promise in his voice that grated on Tyler's nerves.

"Sure."

For a moment, Tyler thought Chris was going to kiss Savvy, but he took her hand and squeezed it instead. Letting go, Chris nodded at Tyler and Kerrianne. "Nice to meet you." Tyler shook his hand and repeated the words.

They all watched Chris climb into his blue convertible and drive away.

"What do you think Lexi's scared of?" Tyler asked Savvy when he was gone. "What do you suspect?"

Savvy shook her head. "I don't really know. She won't say. But she seems to be afraid of her father, and she claims her mother died in a plane accident."

"She claims?" Tyler raised a brow.

Savvy sighed. "It's hard to know if she's telling the truth. I found out last night that she's thirteen, not sixteen. I know, I know, looking at her she couldn't possibly be sixteen, but I wanted to believe her." She bit her bottom lip. "She—we—have a half brother, too. College age, she says. Lexi seems to worship the ground he walks on. And somewhere there's a boy named Zeke."

"What about the scar on the back of her leg?" Kerrianne asked. "Couldn't miss it as she went inside."

"What scar?" Tyler realized that his attention had been too focused on Savvy's interaction with Chris.

"She has an ugly scar on her calf," Savvy said. "Looks pretty bad. I haven't asked her about it yet. There've been so many other things to talk about. But if her father caused it . . ." Savvy trailed off. Tyler didn't miss the fact that she did not refer to Lexi's father as "our" father. He wanted to asked her what she was feeling, but it wasn't the right time. Maybe they would have some time alone later.

Lexi came back down the stairs wearing crisp, belted jeans and a black top so tight that Tyler doubted it would fit his niece Misty, who would be turning eight in a few months. At least an inch of skin showed above the waist of the pants, and he was sure he caught the glint of a belly button ring. "You bought her that?" he said under his breath to Savvy.

"Not the shirt," Savvy replied, equally low. "What should I do? Make her change? I'm not her mother, Tyler. And I've only been a sister to her since yesterday."

Tyler didn't know what to say, and before he could form an opinion, Kerrianne cleared her throat. "Let her come as she is. The pants are a good start. For now let's accept her the way she feels comfortable. The rest will come. You said it yourself, Savvy, she hasn't had a good example in her life so far. How could she possibly know how tacky and cheap that shirt is?"

"You're right, you're right," Savvy said. "But this isn't going to be easy. My mom would never have allowed me to set foot outside the door in that shirt."

Kerrianne chuckled. "That's probably why you turned out as well as you did. You had a mother who wasn't afraid to put her foot down."

In a few more seconds, Lexi had sauntered over to the van where they stood. "Well?" she asked. "What are we waiting for?" Her chin was up, as though challenging Savvy, daring her to ask why she wasn't wearing one of the new shirts. Tyler saw the girl's left shoulder jerk twice and wondered if it was purposeful or if the motion was an involuntary tick that betrayed her insecurity.

"Did you lock the door?" Savvy asked.

Lexi nodded and tossed her the keys. "Well, get in the van," Savvy said.

Tyler opened the sliding door for them. As Savvy stepped inside, her eyes met his, and he was starkly reminded of the loss he'd felt when she'd left on her mission two years before.

"Savvy," he said, wanting to reach out, wanting to say something that would fill the sudden void in his chest.

"What?" She waited, her blue eyes wide and questioning.

Tyler couldn't find the words. Did they even exist?

"Nothing," he said. "Nothing." Was it his imagination, or did her eyes reveal a tiny bit of disappointment?

Chapter Nine

After a short debate, a Thai restaurant and a seafood diner were passed over for Italian cuisine at Ristorante Milano in San Francisco. Tyler and Lexi ordered spaghetti with Milanese meat sauce, Kerrianne had fettucine, and Savvy opted for grilled vegetables with shallots and balsamic dressing.

The food was great and the company even better. To Tyler it almost felt like old times with Savvy. They talked about his family, her family, mutual friends they'd known. Kerrianne looked more at ease than he'd seen her in some time. But as they finished their meal, the easiness faded, and Tyler found himself fumbling for words. Savvy, too, seemed to feel the developing strain, so much so that she asked about the weather in Utah, a sure sign that something was dreadfully wrong. How many times had they joked that only people who had nothing to say would stoop to talking about the weather? Tyler would have called her on it but was too aware that the time when they had been close enough to do so was long past. That thought caused him more sadness than he would have thought possible.

It doesn't have to be this way, he thought suddenly. *We could get it back, if we tried.* But get what part back? For no reason he could pinpoint, Tyler found himself remembering that LaNae wanted them to date other people. Was that what he wanted? To date Savvy again?

"Raining," he answered Savvy's question. "We had a nice August storm. We really needed it, too. Been too dry." He set down his glass and leaned back in his chair. "Not like here. It's hot, but there's more moisture in the air, so it doesn't feel so dry. I like it. In fact, it's so nice that I might move here. That's what I'm doing on Monday—dropping by a few newspapers to give them my resume."

Much to his disappointment, Savvy didn't leap up in excitement at the prospect. "It is nice here," she agreed. "I've considered staying on after I finish my master's, but I really miss my family, so I might move back." She laughed. "Wouldn't that be funny if we actually switched states?"

Tyler felt a moment of dizziness, as though he was standing on quicksand and couldn't find his balance. That was crazy because he was still sitting in his chair. "Well, nothing's decided yet."

Savvy stared down at her plate. Tyler wished for a moment that he could reach out and touch her face—to force her sky blue eyes to look at him.

"I think it's wonderful here," Lexi said predictably. She had been hanging on his every word since they'd entered the restaurant. "Some newspaper should have a job for you. And I bet it'd be a lot more—" Her eyes fell to her lap, where Tyler knew she was holding a miniature dictionary that she'd taken from her tiny black purse. She looked up. "It'd be a lot more, uh, riveting for you."

He smiled. "It would be, that's for sure. A lot more going on. Of course my parents wouldn't like having me so far away, and since we're so close, it's hard to abrogate their concerns."

Lexi nodded, but her eyebrows gathered in puzzlement. She looked down at her lap to find the word's meaning.

"Abrogate?" Kerrianne shook her head. "Speak English, Tyler."

"I am. It means to ignore—well, that's one of the meanings."

"You'll have to ignore a lot more than them if you move," Kerrianne said. "What would I do without you? And the kids would be heart-broken."

Tyler hated the furrow in her brow. "I'd visit a lot. Besides, I might do freelancing instead. I could do that anywhere."

"Being a reporter must be so exciting," Lexi gushed.

"It has its moments." Tyler didn't think now was the time to talk about boring city council meetings and his conservative paycheck. "Are you interested in being a reporter?"

Lexi nodded, her eyes glowing. "I'd love to be a reporter."

"It's not always fun," he admitted, thinking of his own unemployment.

"Well, maybe I'll be a writer instead. I think I could write a book."

"The Great American Novel, eh?" he said.

She shrugged with all the innocence and power of youth. "Why not?"

Why not indeed? Far be it for him to discourage her.

"Aren't you hungry, Lexi?" Kerrianne asked. "You've hardly touched your spaghetti."

"I think I ate too much bread."

Savvy laughed. "You guys should have seen her down three servings of spaghetti last night!"

"Three plates?" Tyler whistled. "Not that I blame you in the least—spaghetti is my favorite food."

"Mine too!" Lexi gazed at him so adoringly that Tyler couldn't help but feel a rush of protective emotion for her. He'd never had a younger sibling, but he bet he would have been a great big brother.

"If you ate pasta last night, maybe we should have picked a different restaurant." Kerrianne set down her fork and pushed away her plate.

"Oh, no," Lexi said. "I could eat it every day."

"Well, are we about finished here?" Savvy looked between Tyler and Lexi pointedly. For some reason Tyler couldn't define, she seemed annoyed. Surely she wouldn't mind sharing her new little sister when she had so many younger siblings at home.

He fell into step beside Savvy as they left the restaurant, while Kerrianne and Lexi, with her little dictionary tucked back into her black purse, took the lead. "Is something wrong?" he asked softly.

She gazed at him, her eyes seeming to reach inside his soul. "Crank down the charm a notch, okay? She's a little girl trying to figure out her difficult life. She doesn't need unrequited love for a grown man on top of that."

If she'd slapped him in the face, Tyler couldn't have been more surprised at her words. "I'm treating her like a little sister, that's all," he protested.

"Well, she's *my* sister, so lay off!" With that, Savvy hurried ahead of him and out the door into the dusk. By the time he'd caught up to them, Kerrianne had already opened the van and they were climbing inside.

So that's what I get for trying to make myself useful! he thought. Stifling his irritation, he went around to the driver's seat. At least Kerrianne was letting him drive so he wouldn't have to look at Savvy or join the conversation. "Which way is Berkeley?" he nearly growled.

Kerrianne pointed before Savvy could answer. Tyler wasn't surprised. Not only had Kerrianne visited the area many times but she was good with maps. "But we really should stop at Paula's before we take them back," she said. "Paula's is only maybe ten minutes from here, but if we go back to Berkeley, we'll have another thirty-five minute drive, plus the half hour back to Pleasant Hill."

Tyler checked his watch. "It's after eight, and I'm exhausted. I don't feel like talking to Paula right now." He glanced at Savvy, thinking that the brief exchange with her had been more than enough. "Maybe we should come back tomorrow."

"Well, in that case it'll be more than an hour drive each way, and you'll have to go alone because I'm not wasting two more hours plus in a car when I could be spending the day with my mother-in-law."

Kerrianne smiled sweetly as she spoke, but he knew she meant business.

"Paula?" Savvy asked. "You mean Kevin and Mara's mother?" As one of Amanda's best friends, Tyler wasn't surprised that she would recognize the name.

"Yeah, last night Manda suddenly decided that she wants me to go see her, feel her out on the custody issue," Tyler explained. "Paula moved here three or four months ago, at least according to the last communication Manda received."

"Then we'd better go now," Savvy said. "Paula's a night person from what I've heard of her, and besides, you might need another night or two to find her if she's moved."

As Tyler pulled out of the parking lot, Lexi leaned forward and put her hand on the side edge of his seat. "Uh, who is Paula? Another sister? I thought you only had two."

Tyler shook his head. "She's our sister's husband's cousin."

"Oh," Lexi replied in a voice that clearly told him she had no idea what he was talking about.

"It's like this," he began. "When our sister, Manda, met her husband, he had Paula's two kids living with him. They were four years and eight months old at the time. They went through some rough spots, but he eventually got custody right before he and Manda were married. Now she and her husband would like to adopt them."

"They took in two kids just like that?" Lexi snapped her fingers. "They didn't even care that they weren't their own? Because some people really care about that, you know."

Tyler shook his head. "Nope, their idea seems to be the more the merrier. They've had a baby of their own, and my sister's expecting again."

"What?" Kerrianne, sitting in the front passenger seat, swatted him with her hand. "When did you find this out? And why didn't you tell me? I can't believe it—we were in the car for more than ten hours today and you didn't say anything?"

He held up a hand to fend her off. "Hey, you were reading, remember? Besides, I only found out this morning before I came to pick you up. It must have slipped my mind."

"Slipped your mind," Kerrianne muttered. "Typical male. The next thing you'll tell me is that Mitch and Cory are going to have a baby and that slipped your mind as well."

He grinned. "Well, now that you mention it . . ."

"Tyler!" Kerrianne raised her hand, but he jerked toward the door to avoid her blow. "Just kidding, just kidding. As far as I know EmJay still keeps them both hopping."

Savvy chuckled at the display. "Hey, they've been married less than a year. It'll happen soon enough."

"I remember that Mitch is your brother," Lexi said to Tyler. "But who's EmJay?"

"She's the child of my brother's best friend. Mitch was her guardian, and when his friend and his wife drowned, he got custody. But her aunt fought him over it. To make a long story short, they fell in love and got married."

"So they also have a kid that's not theirs?" Lexi asked.

"Uh, yeah." He came to a stop at the light and glanced in the back seat. Lexi was looking at him, her eyes narrowed. Tyler had the odd sensation that she was sizing him up, but for what purpose, he couldn't tell.

* * * * * *

Savvy watched with irritation as Tyler interacted with Lexi. Didn't he realize how attractive he was and how readily Lexi responded to him? It was all too apparent that the girl craved his approval, even down to that stupid dictionary she'd brought along and the difficult words they'd been slinging at each other all through dinner. Yes, Savvy was pleased that he was nice to her and had refrained from mentioning her piercings and embarrassing shirt, but he didn't have to turn the charm up so high. Several times Savvy felt herself smothering . . .

wishing . . . well, that *she* was the focus of his attention! No, she would not go there.

Besides, the reality was that he was only trying to be nice. None of his comments toward Lexi could be in any way misconstrued as flirtatious. He was treating her like a favored little sister, and if Savvy admitted the truth, she was plain and simply jealous at their easy conversation and how much Lexi had opened up in his presence. He was actually doing Savvy a favor—the more comfortable Lexi felt, the more likely she would be to tell them about her father.

They drove to Paula's address, taking fifteen minutes for the trip. With the help of a map, Kerrianne smoothly guided Tyler to an area thick with small condominiums. There was a gate to enter the community, but it was open and in disrepair.

"Well, this is it," Kerrianne said, gesturing to a condo with rock and stucco siding, only partially illuminated by a single remaining street light. The other lights were broken or so dim as to barely shine at all.

Tyler brought the van to a stop, and they all stared out the windows. The small rectangle of grass in the front yard was neatly mown, but the flowerbed was overgrown with a bush that strangled several wistful clumps of yellow flowers. The condo itself was a mirror image of most of the others on the street, differing only slightly in the color of stucco and rock work.

"I'll go see if this is the right place," Tyler said to Kerrianne.

He hadn't spoken more than a few sentences to Savvy since leaving the restaurant. She knew he was angry at her. The slight tightening of his mouth and the way he avoided her eyes screamed out his displeasure, but Savvy wasn't repentant. He needed to be put in his place. Who did he think he was, Sir Galahad? Just because he'd come running to California to help her out didn't mean she was going to lose her heart again. It certainly didn't mean she owed him anything. She didn't even want him here. Moreover, she couldn't allow him to hurt Lexi—even unintentionally. Whatever her untruths, the child had been through enough.

"Can I come, too?" Lexi asked quickly. She smiled at Tyler, her shoulder ticking once.

He hesitated only a second. "Sure. But if she's here, she might be a little scary."

"I'm not afraid." Lexi pulled open her sliding door and jumped out into the night.

Savvy watched her go up the short walk with Tyler, wondering if she should intervene. "I think Lexi has a crush," she said to Kerrianne, only half joking.

"On Tyler?" Kerrianne glanced out the window. "Well, well, you're probably right. But don't worry, it'll pass. Think of it this way—it's far better for her to imagine herself in love with a good man like Tyler than some boy of questionable designs who might take advantage of her. Tyler, at least, will never hurt her. Even when she finds out about his girlfriend, he'll be kind about it. You know he will."

Savvy knew. "His girlfriend?" She tried to say the words casually, but some of her intensity must have filtered through because Kerrianne leaned over and peered around the seat.

"LaNae," she said. "You met her, I think."

"Oh, yeah. Briefly. Right after my mission."

Kerrianne reached out to touch her arm. "For what it's worth, Savvy, we—the whole family—all hoped that you and he would . . . Well, LaNae is a nice girl." She withdrew her hand from Savvy's arm.

"I hope she likes California," Savvy said. Her heart felt tight, but she ignored the feeling.

Kerrianne gave a delicate snort. "Once my mother gets wind of Tyler putting in resumes, she'll try to talk him out of it. She's having a hard enough time with Mitch being out of the country so much. Not that she complains. She can see how happy they are."

"I guess in the end, that's what matters, isn't it?" Savvy sat back in her seat. "That your children are happy." She thought of her birth father as she said this. Could it be that he had honestly cared about her welfare? After seeing Lexi, Savvy had a more difficult time believing it than before.

"Yes." Kerrianne glanced again out the window. Tyler was talking to a man who had opened the door. In less than a minute, he was hurrying back down the walk with Lexi skipping to keep up with him.

"She was staying here, but she moved to another condo," Tyler said. "Down this street, turn left, second condo on the right."

The second condo looked similar to the other, but its well-kept flowerbed sported an orderly array of bright blossoms. Savvy recognized a few—pansies, carnations, snapdragons—but there were others she didn't know.

"This is how it'll go," Tyler said as they all went up the walk together. "We'll give her the photo album Manda sent for her, talk a little to break the ice, and then I might need to talk to her alone about the kids. I don't want her to feel like we're ganging up on her."

"When it gets to that point, we'll suddenly decide to wait in the car or something." Kerrianne rang the bell. "It'll work out."

Standing between Savvy and Tyler, Lexi bounced on her heels. Her eyes were bright with excitement and curiosity. Impulsively, Savvy reached for her hand and squeezed it briefly. Lexi gave her a brilliant smile that made Savvy feel hopeful that Lexi was beginning to trust her.

The door opened and a petite woman stared at them in surprise. "Oh," she said. "You're not . . . I was expecting . . . Hello. Can I help you?"

Even if Savvy hadn't known they were going to see Paula, she would have recognized the woman because she had an uncanny resemblance to her son, Kevin. She had a lovely, childlike, heart-shaped face with large sleepy blue eyes. Her hair was blonde, but tastefully so instead of the flagrant bleach job she'd once sported. She'd grown her hair out, and it was almost as long as Savvy's. By the dim light of the porch, Savvy marveled at how young she looked at thirty-one, though by rights her face should show the ravages caused by years of drug and alcohol abuse.

"Hello," Tyler said, stepping slightly forward. "You probably don't remember me. I'm your cousin Blake's brother-in-law. I met you when you came to see Kevin in Utah about two years ago." He pointed to Savvy. "This is my friend Savvy Hergarter. She was there too. This is my sister Kerrianne, and last but not least, Lexi, Savvy's sister."

Paula was nodding delicately. "I remember you." Her eyes met Kerrianne's. "You look like your sister, Amanda, but she's blonder, if I remember. But not as white as . . . what was your name?" She was looking at Savvy now.

"Savannah, but everyone calls me Savvy."

Paula smiled, looking ethereally beautiful. "I seem to remember that now. But"—a sudden furrow marred her brow—"why are you here? Has something happened to Amanda and Blake? Or to my children?"

Savvy saw Tyler swallow hard. If Paula was still thinking of them as *her* children, would she ever give them up? "Everything's fine," he said. "We had to make a sudden trip down here, and Manda asked me to bring you some pictures." He held up the thin album.

Paula sighed with apparent relief. "How sweet. She's a nice woman, Amanda. I knew it from the moment I met her." Accepting the album, she started thumbing eagerly through the few pages.

"Do you mind if we come in for a minute?" Tyler asked after she had seen half the pictures. "Or were you about to go out?"

For the first time, Savvy's eyes slid over Paula's black sleeveless gown that was at least four inches above her knees. Though her feet were bare, she wore black fishnet nylons, and Savvy bet her heels were near the door. This was not your average stay-at-home attire; Paula must have plans.

Closing the album and holding it to her chest, Paula gave a little giggle that matched her childish face. "I'm going out to dinner, but it's early yet, and my date's not here. So come on in—for a minute at least." Opening the door wide, she waited until they were all inside before leading them into a tiny sitting room to the left of the front door.

After hearing so many negative details of Paula's background, Savvy was pleasantly surprised to find the room neat and orderly. The furniture wasn't new, but the couch, love seat, end tables, and bookcase matched and looked well together. For a heartsick moment, Savvy wondered if Paula had truly reformed. On one hand, it would be a miraculous event; but on the other, Savvy knew the despair her friend would endure if she lost the children she considered her own.

In the brighter, stark light of the small room, Paula's face lost much of its childlike quality. Despite the heavy makeup, Savvy could now see the deep lines around her eyes and mouth, lines far deeper than Kerrianne's, who was near the same age. Her sleepy eyes weren't only sleepy but might actually have some damage as a result of her life choices. She was a woman who had lived too fast and too much in a brief period of time, leaving her face old and used.

Paula didn't seem to be aware of the change the light brought to her features. "Please, sit down," she invited breathlessly. Tyler sat with Kerrianne on the couch, while Savvy and Lexi took the love seat.

After seeing to their comfort, Paula excused herself and returned with a padded kitchen chair, which she set by the doorway, the only place it would fit in the tiny room. She sat and gazed at them, her fingers caressing the photo album on her lap. "So, what brings you to California?"

Tyler and Kerrianne quickly explained the reasons for their trip. Savvy noted how Paula responded to Tyler's charisma and Kerrianne's easy manner. Savvy herself felt uptight and uneasy, knowing how much the outcome of this meeting might mean to Amanda and her family.

"So, how are things going with you?" Tyler asked when he had finished his explanation. "This looks like a nice place."

Paula regarded him a moment without replying. Then she gave a slow smile. "Things are really great. I have a job now, and I'm sharing this condo with a roommate. But she works a lot and isn't here most of the time. And"—she ducked her blonde head almost shyly—"I'm dating someone. For two months now. I think it's serious."

"That's great," Tyler said, though knowing him as she did, Savvy could see that he wasn't quite as happy as he pretended. A job, a condo, a boyfriend—all that might mean she was ready to have her children with her. Savvy saw the same worry in Kerrianne's face.

"So you think you might get married?" Savvy asked.

"Maybe." Hope lighted Paula's face with an innocence that far belied her age. The expression hurt Savvy's heart because she knew that feeling intimately. Once she'd felt that kind of hope for her and Tyler.

"What about your kids?" The words exploded from Lexi's mouth, as though they were an accusation she had been holding onto for a long time.

Savvy's heart lurched. She reached out to Lexi's arm and squeezed, warning her to be quiet. Lexi's chin went up in response, but she didn't speak further.

Paula's brow drew in puzzlement. "They're okay, aren't they?" she asked, her eyes alternating between Tyler and Kerrianne.

"They're fine," Tyler said quickly. "Great. Kevin just turned eight this month. He's excited about being baptized."

"Eight? My little boy." Paula looked confused for a moment, and Savvy wondered if that was a legacy from years of drug abuse. "Has it really been that long?"

"Yes," Kerrianne said gently. "Mara's four now—four and a half actually."

Tears welled in Paula's eyes. "When I went to visit that last time, she called Amanda 'Mom.' "

"Well, it's a natural thing," Tyler said. "Manda's taking care of her, and she didn't want her own baby calling her by her first name."

Paula ran her fingers under her eyes. "At least my boy knew me, and I think he was glad I came. I talked to him last month on the phone. He sounded happy to hear from me then." Her blue eyes pleaded with Tyler to confirm her words.

He nodded. "I know he loves you. He'll always love you."

She relaxed a little. "My boy loves peanut butter, you know. I promised to send him some peanut butter crackers and candies."

Savvy exchanged a glance with Tyler. Paula was long on promises but rarely followed through. As though perceiving their thoughts, Paula arose abruptly. "I'll get them so you can take them to him."

Tyler stood with her. "Uh, Paula?"

"Yes?" She paused in the doorway, eyes still shining with her tears.

"Kevin doesn't eat peanut butter anymore."

"What! But he's always loved it."

"Last year he had a reaction when he ate some peanut butter and crackers. Broke out in a rash. It's not life-threatening at the moment, but the doctor wants him to avoid all peanut products for a while."

Paula blanched. "Did he say why Kevin has the allergy? Was it . . . could it possibly be because he ate too much as a kid?"

Savvy knew why she asked. Peanut butter crackers and peanut butter sandwiches were about all Paula had fed him when he was in her care.

"They don't know," Tyler told her so gently that his voice was as soothing as a pat on the back. "These things are difficult to determine. But it really doesn't matter. He's okay with it."

Paula sat down in her chair, folding her small hands over the picture album. "Yes, he was always a strong boy."

Tyler sat again on the couch but only on the edge, his body angled toward her. Savvy knew the seriousness the pose represented; she had used it herself during too many missionary discussions to count. Kerrianne caught the signal as well.

"You know, I think I'd like to call my mother-in-law to check on my kids," Kerrianne said, arising smoothly. "I left my phone in the car."

"I'll go with you," Savvy said. Lexi remained sitting, but Savvy reached for her hand and pulled her up.

"You can use my phone," Paula stood from her chair, her wide eyes suddenly wary.

"Oh, no, it's long distance from here, and I'd hate to make you pay for it. But thank you for the offer." Kerrianne held out a hand. "I'm happy to have finally met you, Paula. I'm glad things are working out so well for you." She hesitated a moment before adding, "Kevin and Mara are really great kids. My children play with them a lot."

"I wish you could have brought them," Paula said softly.

"It would have been nice." Kerrianne moved toward the door.

Savvy knew Amanda would never have allowed Kevin and Mara to come without her. She was as protective as any mother Savvy had ever seen. She glanced at Tyler, trying to tell him with her eyes to go easy on Paula. For a moment, she toyed with the idea of staying, but she knew what he had to say would be better said in private.

"Come on." She pushed slightly on Lexi's reluctant back.

Outside in the van, Lexi burst into tears. "That was so sad. She's a sad old, old woman. Why doesn't she want her kids? Why would she give them to someone else when she's still alive? It doesn't make sense!"

"She did what was best for them," Savvy said. "The children were seriously neglected with her. They needed care and love."

"They needed their mother!" Lexi shouted.

Savvy knew Lexi was reacting more because of her own loss than out of any concern for Kevin and Mara. "Oh, Lexi," she said. "They have a mother now—a real mother. Amanda loves them more than Paula ever did."

Lexi refused to be comforted. She hunched over and held her stomach. "It's wrong," she muttered. "Wrong. She should fight for them. She should be there to make sure they're okay. She shouldn't give up."

"Lexi, please." Savvy reached toward her sister.

Lexi jerked away. "Leave me alone."

Savvy had no choice but to comply. She gazed at Kerrianne, who lifted her slight shoulders in a helpless gesture. "Let her cry it out," she mouthed. "Sometimes that helps."

Savvy crossed her arms over her stomach as Lexi's sobs continued to fill the van.

Chapter Ten

Tyler waited until Paula had returned to her seat before picking up the conversation. She regarded him warily, as though wondering why he had not left with the others. She had set the picture album on her bookshelf, and now her fingers twined in her lap.

"Some time ago," Tyler began, "Kevin asked Manda and Blake if he could call them Mom and Dad." Paula showed no surprise at the announcement, but he paused to let the information sink in. "Manda was really uncertain about it because she didn't want to deny your relationship with him. When she asked him why, he said he wanted to be like other kids. He wanted a mom and a dad of his own. He didn't want to be different."

Paula's chin wobbled slightly. "I guess I can understand that."

Tyler remembered the stories of how arrogant, selfish, and demanding Paula had been in past years, but she seemed to have at least learned something in the school of life. Unless this vulnerability was an act.

"It doesn't mean you're not his mom," he continued, "or that he doesn't love you. But rather it shows how much he feels a part of Blake and Manda's life."

"Well, Blake's had him as much as I did."

Tyler nodded, faintly surprised that she admitted to the fact. "Well, three and a half years have passed since you gave Blake custody, and during that time, he and my sister have been praying and hoping you'd find your way." He stopped, unsure how to continue.

"I think I have—finally," she whispered. "But are you saying . . . ? I know they've had their own baby now, but I don't know if I'm ready to . . . I don't think I can. Maybe in a while but now . . . Kurt . . . he's not ready for children . . . and I don't—Oh!" Her tears were falling rapidly, and she covered her face with her hands. "Am I such a terrible person that I could choose him over my own children?" She sobbed loudly for a long minute, and Tyler felt compassion for her. He made a sympathetic noise in his throat and waited for her to calm down.

After an interminable time, she raised her eyes, now rimmed with smeared mascara. "But it's not really that." Her eyes pleaded for him to understand. "You see, Kurt's the one who helped me get clean. It's taken me all these years. I couldn't have done it alone. But without the drugs, I'm not as tough as I used to be. I sometimes have panic attacks that leave me unable to get out of bed. And without him . . ." She couldn't finish.

He nodded. "I understand." But he didn't—not really. He knew addictions were strong and all-consuming, but having never experienced one, he didn't really *feel* how they absorbed a life, transforming it into something ugly. How they twisted a woman into a person capable of neglecting or abandoning her own children.

"Kevin and Mara are happy where they are," he said. "Blake and Manda are happy, too. They aren't asking you to take them back."

"They're not?" Paula smiled tentatively through her drying tears. "Because things might change in the future. You never know how things might change."

That, thought Tyler, *is exactly what worries Manda.* After loving and raising the children, would she be expected to give them up? After all, Mara had no idea who Paula even was anymore. Yes, there had been phone calls and the occasional birthday present, but that simply wasn't enough.

In the past three and a half years, Amanda had been terrified that if she pushed the issue of adoption, Paula would claim to be well and somehow take custody of the children, plunging them into the same neglect they had suffered before. Though it seemed hard to believe, Tyler knew his sister's fears were not completely unfounded. That very thing had happened to Blake before their marriage. Paula had gone to court, somehow convinced the judge she was clean, and taken the children from him. But she hadn't been well, and the children were in constant danger before she finally came to her senses and returned them to Blake. Blake and Amanda's position was stronger now as official custodians of the children, but there was always a chance Paula would win custody.

"Blake and Manda love them as their own," he ventured, wondering how far he should probe. "You know that, don't you?"

"I guess." Paula's voice was barely audible. Once again, she was staring at her hands.

"You also know you can always visit the children as much as you want."

Again came the whisper, "Yes."

Tyler took a deep breath. "They realize there hasn't been much opportunity for you to travel to Utah—"

"That's right. I haven't had the money. It's been hard. I—" One hand rubbed at a flurry of scars on the inside of her other arm that branded her as a former drug user.

Well, it's now or never, Tyler thought. "Maybe it's time for Blake and Manda to consider adopting the children. Get them sealed to their family in the temple." There. He flexed his hands. The cards were on the table—no, his sister's dreams were on the table.

"They want me to give them up forever?" Paula's voice cracked on the last word.

He considered telling her it was only on paper, that she would still be their mother, but it wasn't so. She wasn't really their mother now. She had given them life, but Blake and Amanda had given them a home. They deserved all the blessings of the gospel, and even though Paula wasn't an active member of the Church, she understood the importance of being sealed as a family.

"It's for Kevin and Mara," he said. "They need a permanent home and a permanent family. They're growing up so fast. Before long Kevin will be driving, Mara getting married. There will always be a place for you in their hearts, but they need to know where they belong. They need to stop worrying—Kevin especially—that he won't get to be with his new baby brother. He adores that child. You should see them together." Tears came unbidden to Tyler's eyes. "Just think about it, Paula. Talk to Kurt and see what he says."

Paula looked up again, shaking her head. "No. I can't. I won't. I'll come to see them more. I'll bring Kurt. He'll love them—you'll see." Determination made the lines around her mouth more prominent.

Tyler's stomach felt ill. What had he done? Amanda had trusted him, but he'd only made things worse. Kevin had experienced nightmares for months after the last time his mother had taken him from Blake; Tyler didn't know if any of them could endure that again.

He stood. "Paula, you did a good thing when you let your children live with Blake and my sister. They've had a chance to be happy. Think about it. They deserve to stay at the only stable home they've ever known."

Her lips pressed tightly together. "But they're *my* children. I gave them to Blake so he could keep them until—"

"Until you were ready?" For the first time Tyler let impatience color his voice. Apparently nothing had really changed. This woman was still a spoiled, headstrong person who cared only for herself. "And when will that be, Paula? In two years? In five? Will you come see them before that? Or will you just show up one day when Mara is ten and try to take her from her family?"

She pointed to the door. "I think you should go." Her confidence seemed to be back, the softer, weepy woman completely vanished.

Tyler gave it one last shot. "You and Kurt can make a life together! You can have a child with him. You can start over."

She didn't say anything but opened the door and motioned him outside. Tyler had no choice but to step outside. A short, broad-shouldered man was coming up the walk, a large bouquet of red roses in his thick-fingered hands. He had well-proportioned features that were not remarkable except for a full head of wavy black hair which would have found a better place on the head of a movie actor. His nose had apparently been broken a few times, lending a hint of toughness to his face. At the sight of Tyler, his smile faded. "Paula?" he asked.

"Hi, Kurt." She slipped inside the welcoming circle of his arms, taking the flowers with a tremulous smile.

Tyler offered his hand. "Hi, I'm Tyler Huntington. I'm an uncle to Paula's children—they're living with my sister and her husband."

The man's grip was unsurprisingly firm. "Good to meet you. I'm Kurt Jackman. What brings you here?"

Tyler debated whether or not to say anything. Paula should be the one to explain, but her history of lies made him doubt that she would do anything but twist this encounter to whatever reality she desired. Still, whatever he said would probably make things worse. "Just dropping off some pictures," he said. "But I'd better get back now. I have people waiting in the van." He waved in the direction of the street. "Nice to meet you."

He started down the walk without a backward glance. To his surprise, Kurt came after him, catching up as he neared the curb. "Wait," he called.

Tyler turned, seeing Paula watching them anxiously from the small porch. "It's about them kids, isn't it?" Kurt said. "I bet they want her to take them back? But it ain't a good idea. She's only been clean a month. She still drinks too much." Kurt glanced back at Paula. "Look, I want a kid someday of our own, but she's not ready."

Tyler's instincts told him to go for it. "Blake and Amanda want to adopt Paula's children," he said. "That's all. They have custody now, and they could go to court to try to terminate Paula's parental rights, but they'd rather have Paula's blessing. She'd still be welcome to visit whenever she's able."

Kurt nodded, his face relaxing. "I'll talk to her, see what I can do. I have to warn you, though. She might go after them. She can be really stubborn."

"Thanks." Tyler handed him a card that erroneously identified him as a reporter for the *Deseret Morning News,* but at least it had his cell number listed. "Paula has my sister's number as well," he said. "Keep in touch."

"I will. Thanks."

Tyler went around the van and climbed inside. "That went well," he said dryly, watching Kurt saunter up the sidewalk to where Paula waited. She looked small compared to his bulk—but defiant.

"You don't sound like it went well," Kerrianne said.

He sighed. "Maybe I should have left well enough alone." He couldn't seem to solve the problems in his own life, much less anyone else's.

He moved to start the van when the cell phone clipped to his belt vibrated. Unhooking it, he saw that the number was LaNae's. Glancing back at Savvy, he was tempted not to answer. But he didn't want to aggravate the situation between him and LaNae.

He flipped open the phone. "Hello?"

"Hi, it's me."

"I know." He would normally tease her by saying "Hi, me," but he didn't feel like it tonight.

"How's it going?" Her voice was tight, anxious.

"We got here safely."

"That's good. I wanted to be sure."

"We've just been to see Paula."

"Paula?"

"Kevin and Mara's mom."

"Oh." LaNae didn't ask any questions, and though he would have liked to unburden himself, he was glad because Savvy's eyes were boring holes in the back of his head. "When will you be back?" she asked.

"Tuesday night."

"That's good."

"I have to drive now," he said. "Could I call you back?"

She was silent a moment, and Tyler realized he must have hurt her feelings. "Well, there's something I want to tell you," she said at last.

Tyler suddenly felt exhausted. He didn't know if he could take any more female emotions after the long day he'd had. "Is it important?"

"Yeah, but it can wait. Call me back tomorrow, though. I have to get up early for choir practice."

"Okay, talk to you then."

"Good-bye." This time he was glad she didn't say she loved him because he didn't think he could say it back. Was that because his sister and Savvy were in the van? Or was it because he didn't love her? Now that he was with Savvy, his months with LaNae didn't seem real anymore.

"Your girlfriend?" Savvy asked. There was no emotion on her face or inflection in her voice. He could only assume that either she was still upset with him and trying to hide it, or, more likely, she didn't even care. He nodded, and she looked away.

The phone back in its holder, he started the van and roared down the street, Paula and her boyfriend still staring after them.

Kerrianne tried to keep up the conversation on the drive back to Savvy's, but no one else seemed inclined to speak. Even Lexi had abandoned her attempt to impress him with her vocabulary. She slumped against the wall of the van in the seat behind him, staring at the headlights of the passing cars.

When they arrived at the apartment, it was nearly ten and Lexi's eyes were drooping, but she roused herself enough to ask him, "Can I go with you on Monday? To the newspapers, I mean."

Tyler swiveled in his seat. Savvy had the sliding door open so the overhead light was on. He could see tears streaked on Lexi's face. He had been going to refuse, but the tears stopped him. "With me?" he said, stalling for time.

She nodded. "Maybe they'll give us a tour, or at least let us go inside. If I'm going to be a reporter, I'd like to know what I'm getting into."

He tried to grin. "That's easy. Small cubbies, quick and rigid deadlines, irritable bosses." He was pleased to see a smile steal across her woeful face.

"Well, can I?" Lexi scooted across the seat and out of the van to stand next to Savvy.

Tyler thought a moment and didn't see any reason for her not to come. After all, he wasn't going for actual interviews. He likely wouldn't get past the receptionist. If he needed Lexi to get lost for a moment, she was old enough to wait outside the building or in a waiting room. Besides, if he let Lexi come, maybe Savvy would tag along. Maybe he could find some way to really talk with her. "Sure," he said, "if it's okay with Savvy."

Savvy's eyes were large and dark in the moonlight, like the color in the depths of the ocean. "Can I talk to you a moment?" she said tightly.

A sinking feeling came to Tyler's stomach. "Sure." He met her in front of the van, and they walked down the road a short way, angling toward the sidewalk.

"It's not a good idea, her going with you," Savvy said, looking ahead into the dark street.

"Look, I'm not trying to get between you two. I just want to help. You saw how she was crying. It won't hurt to let her come, will it?" Why couldn't Savvy see how hard he was trying?

Savvy sighed and turned to look at him. "Tyler, you can't encourage her. Besides, you don't have any idea what she might be capable of—neither of us do. She's hinted at abuse from her father, and I intend to get to the bottom of it. But what if I find it's not true? She's repeatedly evasive when I ask her about it. It could all be a lie." Savvy shook her head. "Don't you see, it's just not a good idea you being alone at all with her, especially since she seems to have developed a crush on you."

"I didn't even think of that." Tyler felt like an idiot. He'd written more than his share of child abuse stories, most of which had been real, but several had been false accusations that had destroyed the careers of some good people. "Better to make sure there's no question of misconduct."

"Exactly."

They had stopped walking, and now Tyler glanced back to the van. He was tempted to let Savvy tell Lexi that she couldn't go, but he was the one responsible. "I guess I'll go tell her," he said. "Unless . . . hey, why don't you go with us?"

She smiled at the invitation, but the smile didn't reach her eyes. "And hear you two slinging words at each other all day? I don't think so. Besides, I'm helping teach an undergrad class next semester, and I need to put on some finishing touches."

It was an excuse, and he knew it. "Oh, come on. I'm sure you finished that long ago."

"Really, I have stuff to do."

What could he say to that? "Okay, but you'll miss going out for ice cream."

Savvy glanced down at her figure. "Maybe that's a good thing."

He wasn't sure why she said it; she looked perfect to him tonight. But at the same time, there was a little sliver of guilt inside his heart because he had always secretly thought she was a bit too curvaceous. Then why didn't he think so anymore? All he could see now was Savvy's strength, her integrity, her loveliness—not only in her face but in her heart, where it really mattered.

He felt an overwhelming urge to tell her so, to take her in his arms and tell her how wonderful he thought she was. But that miraculous something that had always been alive and eager between them seemed to be broken at the moment, and the realization made him want to weep.

Yet maybe it wasn't too late. Tyler didn't know exactly what he was feeling toward her, but he knew that he wanted to spend time with Savvy—he needed to spend time with her.

"Savvy," he reached out and touched her arm.

She stared at him, seeming almost startled at the contact.

"I'd really like to spend some time with you before we go back. There's, well, there's . . . I've really missed you. There's so much that's happened. I mean, I didn't even get to tell you yet that I was fired from my job." He saw her eyes widen, and he plunged on. "I'd really like you to come with me on Monday. I promise it won't be too dull. Please?"

She studied him for a few more seconds. "Okay. I'll come."

He almost hugged her then, but she started walking back to the van where Lexi and Kerrianne were waiting awkwardly.

"So can I go?" Lexi asked.

Savvy looked at Lexi and smiled. "Yeah, looks like we're both going."

Smiling, Lexi gave Savvy a little hug.

"Well, good night," Savvy said, raising a hand to them. "Thanks for dinner."

"See you Monday," Lexi added.

As he climbed back into the van, Tyler watched them go up the stairs. A dim light was glowing outside most of the apartments, and he could see the classic outline of Savvy's face.

"Are you all right?" Kerrianne's voice was soft.

He turned to look at her. "How come I still miss her so much?"

"Maybe you're dating the wrong girl."

Tyler put the van into gear. "I was just thinking the same thing."

Chapter Eleven

Tyler spent Sunday with Kerrianne, the children, and Kerrianne's mother-in-law. They went to church and took a walk, and after dinner he drove over to UC Berkeley alone. He was tempted to call Savvy but stopped himself at the last moment, not wanting to push his luck. Was it too late for friendship? She seemed to think so. And what about LaNae? He'd called her back, but she hadn't answered her cell phone. He had the feeling something was really wrong.

He suspected it was mostly him.

There was a small student rally going on at the campus, but nothing more exciting than a protest of high tuition, certainly not something he wanted to write about. Besides, it was Sunday, and he had made it a habit not to write on Sundays. Only the rare breaking news had ever forced him to lump together a few sentences to e-mail to the paper.

On Monday, he drove to Savvy's apartment at eight o'clock. Lexi was waiting on the stairs for him and ran to the van as he pulled up, swinging her black purse behind her. "Hi," she said.

"All ready to go?"

She nodded. "Savvy'll be right down—she's on the phone. She almost didn't let me come today. I had a stomachache all yesterday, and she made me stay in bed. I think she was mad 'cause she didn't get to go to church."

"How's the stomach now?"

"Perfect." She patted it for emphasis. She was wearing the jeans of the night before, but her flamboyant red top was not overly tight, and it hid her stomach well. Tyler bet it was one Savvy had purchased and hoped there hadn't been too much of a fight to get Lexi to wear it.

"That outfit looks really great," he said. "The color is wild, the cut really nice, and I think you look older somehow. More mature or something."

She flushed. "Like a writer?"

"Yeah, like a writer. Except if you were staying home to write, of course. Then you'd have to wear pajamas. It's sort of a rule."

She giggled. "I'll remember that. Oh, here comes Savvy. Hope she doesn't fall in those high heels."

Savvy was coming down the stairs, looking sharp in fuchsia capri pants and a matching button-up shirt that she wore as a jacket over a white fitted top. Usually straight, her hair was curled today and swept up in a clip at the crown of her head. The curls waved loosely over the clip and spiraled down to barely graze the back of her neck. Tyler felt a flash of excitement—had she dressed up for him?

Tyler jumped out to walk her around the van. "Good morning," he said. In fact, the morning was fabulous. The sky was a brilliant blue that matched Savvy's eyes, and the day was warm and inviting—not nearly as hot as he had expected.

She nodded her agreement.

"You look great," he said.

"Thanks. Hey, any reports from your friends of a missing child?"

He felt a little deflated. She obviously wasn't thinking how great *he* looked this morning. "No, nothing."

"I guess that's good. Thanks."

Tyler was about to kick Lexi out of the front seat, when Savvy reached for the sliding door. "I'll sit here," she said. "Wouldn't want to get in the way of any flying words."

"But—" he protested.

"This is her outing." Savvy glanced toward the front seat where Lexi sat behind the closed window. "I'm just tagging along."

Tyler let her do as she wished; there was no arguing with Savvy when she made up her mind.

"So where are we going first?" Lexi asked when he was back in the van.

Tyler told them his plan to hit the *San Francisco Examiner,* the *San Francisco Chronicle,* and the *San Francisco Business Times.* There were other papers, but they were small or on-line—not what Tyler was looking for.

As Tyler navigated the traffic, he and Lexi chatted. He learned she had a friend named Amber and that she loved rock music. No surprise there. He caught a glimpse of numerous piercings in her ears and wished he could say something, but Kerrianne's warning of the night before prevented him. Sometimes caring about people meant shutting up—at least temporarily.

Savvy sat in the back, mostly listening but occasionally adding to the conversation. Tyler felt an immense peace having her in the van.

All the newspapers were located minutes apart. After briefly getting lost near the Bay, they started on Battery Street with the *Business Times* and then went to the *Examiner.* At both of these Tyler left a resume with an indifferent receptionist, while Lexi and Savvy waited near the door.

Their last stop was the *Chronicle,* which claimed to be the largest newspaper in the area.

"I like this one," Lexi said as they entered the reception area. "Feels important."

Tyler grinned. "Well, here goes," he said. Lexi gave him a thumbs-up.

He didn't think he'd be let beyond the front desk—he hadn't been at the other newspapers—but he had to try. The receptionist was young and blonde and extremely thin. She reminded him of LaNae. "I'm here from out of state," he told her. "I'd like to talk to someone about a job."

"You have experience?" she asked, eyes narrowing as they took in his face.

"Yes. One year full time. And a year part time before that."

"Where?"

"*Deseret Morning News.*"

She didn't appear to know the name.

"In Utah," he added. "Here, I've brought a resume."

"There is an opening, actually," she said. "I'll see that they get your resume. They may call you in a few days for an interview."

"I'm due back in Salt Lake tomorrow. Is there any way I could speak to someone now?"

"Oh." She frowned. "Just a minute." Punching in a few numbers on her phone, she made a call and began explaining the situation.

Tyler glanced back at Savvy and Lexi, who had settled on chairs in the waiting room. Lexi was studying her mini dictionary, while Savvy was reading a copy of the *Chronicle*. Strange how they looked so much alike, given that he had always thought Savvy to be a replica of her mother.

"You're in luck," the receptionist said, reclaiming his attention. "Mr. Childs will see you now." She handed him a clip-on badge. "If you'll wait by that door over there, he'll be here soon."

Tyler had no idea who Mr. Childs was, but he was glad he'd worn dress slacks and a button-down shirt sans tie. He wasn't dressed up, but he wasn't too casual, either.

Mr. Childs turned out to be the paper's human resources director. He was a tall, gray-haired man with weathered cheeks and a paunch that hung generously over his belt. "Good to meet you," he said, proffering a firm handshake. "Let's go back to my office."

They chatted for several minutes about Tyler's previous experience before Tyler had to tell Mr. Childs about the article and why he'd left the *Deseret Morning News*. Mr. Childs' mouth curved into a smile. "I can believe your article ruffled some feathers. But here we don't mind ruffling a few feathers. In fact, we thrive on it." He cleared his throat. "As long as it's all true. Of course, we do have to worry about our advertisers and so forth."

"Of course." Tyler was beginning to relax.

Mr. Childs flipped a button on the intercom. "Janie," he said, "would you bring us a couple coffees?"

Tyler's stomach sank. Already he would have to defend his beliefs. He'd known it would happen, but so soon? Any other job applicant could have taken up the offer, used the time to build more bridges, but Tyler knew none of that was worth denying his beliefs.

"Uh, no thanks," he said. "I don't drink coffee."

"Mormon, huh?" Mr. Childs asked.

"Yes, sir."

"I've heard of them. Have one or two who work here. Good people."

Tyler smiled and nodded.

An older woman came in with two mugs of steaming coffee. Mr. Childs waited until she was gone, then he arose and extended his hand. "It's been a pleasure to meet you, Tyler. I'll take a look at your resume and get back to you."

Tyler thanked him, hoping his smile didn't feel as pasted on as it felt. Despite his refusal of the coffee, he had to believe he was a strong candidate for whatever opening they had available. At the very least, he'd made a contact that might help him freelance a few articles. Of course, working for the *Chronicle* would be less worrisome than strictly freelancing. At least he'd have a steady income.

Lexi looked up when he reentered the lobby area. She stuffed her mini dictionary into her black purse and pulled it onto her shoulder. "Well?" she asked eagerly, not minding the interested stare of the receptionist.

Savvy stood up next to her. "In the van, okay?"

Lexi darted a glance at the desk. "Oh, yeah. Sorry."

"No problem." Tyler led the way outside. It was noon now, and his stomach was rumbling. "What do you say we get some lunch?"

"Good idea," Savvy said. "You hungry, Lexi?"

"Yeah, but what happened?"

Tyler opened Savvy's door first and then Lexi's. "Nothing much. I talked to their human resources director. Unfortunately, everything that could go wrong, did."

Tyler started the van, picked a street at random, and started down it.

"So what went wrong?" Lexi asked.

Tyler met Savvy's eyes in the rearview mirror, and they shared a smile at Lexi's eagerness. For a brief moment it was just like old times. "Well, first I told him why I was fired."

Lexi gaped. "You were fired? I didn't know that. What else?"

"He offered me coffee."

This apparently confused Lexi. "So?"

"I'm a Mormon. I don't drink coffee."

"Mormons don't drink coffee?"

He shrugged. "At least he knows where I stand."

Lexi's eyes gleamed. "You were unequivocal in your stance."

"You could say that." Tyler tilted back his head and laughed.

Lexi's face scrunched in worry. "Did I use it right?"

"Yes. Exactly right. Now where do you want to eat? McDonald's?"

"Mickey D's? Are you kidding? I want to go to In-N-Out."

"That's a restaurant?" At her nod, he said, "Okay, In-N-Out it is."

Lexi grinned. "But you're going the wrong way. In-N-Out is back there. I saw it when we were looking for the first newspaper."

"Then why didn't you say so?" Tyler blew out a breath. Women! They sure started young learning how to annoy a man.

"You didn't ask." Lexi blinked her eyes innocently.

From the back seat Savvy laughed. "Good thing you saw it. I've never been to the one here. It's a whole chain of restaurants, you know."

Lexi nodded. "Amber eats there all time when she comes here on vacation."

"They don't have them where you're from?" Savvy asked.

Lexi's smile faded. "Maybe."

"Come on," Tyler urged, "there's a lot of places that don't have any. I've never seen one in Utah."

"Okay, then. No, we don't. But I'm not going to tell you anything more." Lexi folded her arms and fell silent.

After a while Tyler said, "You afraid we'd put you on the next plane home if we knew where you were from?"

"Tyler—" Savvy leaned forward, her hand on the seat. Her tone told him he had said something wrong.

Lexi's face became so pale it was translucent. "Savvy wouldn't put me on a plane."

Tyler glanced back at Savvy. "Later," she mouthed.

"Hey, forget I said anything," he told Lexi. "Why don't you look up the word *penultimate*? I bet that's one you've never heard."

To his relief, the tense moment passed as Lexi fell willingly to her dictionary.

₊ *₊* *₊*

Lexi was having a good day. Yes, it would be better if Tyler and Savvy didn't constantly try to trick her into talking about her home, but the rest was still really good. She felt grown up hanging out with Tyler and Savvy. Especially with Tyler. He was much more polite than the boys she knew at school. He opened doors for her, asked her what she wanted to hear on the radio, and actually seemed to listen to what she had to say. If only her father would listen to her more.

At In-N-Out they ordered cheeseburgers, fries, and strawberry shakes and sat down to eat, chatting about books and plays and movies they'd seen. Lexi decided that Tyler was one of the smartest people she knew.

And the cutest.

No, he was beyond cute. He was a man, after all, and cute wasn't exactly manly. He was tall and strong, though a little on the lean side. She liked the thick frames on his glasses and the way he flexed his hands when he was thinking. She also liked how his sandy hair was long on top and sort of messy. He had an adorable dimple on his right cheek that threw Lexi's heart into a rapid beating when he smiled. Which he did a lot. Tyler was a happy person.

Too bad he had a girlfriend. But that was almost hard to believe because yesterday he'd stared at Savvy with an odd look in his eyes, a look that would have done funny things to Lexi's stomach if he had been staring at *her* that way. He was doing it again today, but Savvy didn't seem to notice. In fact, she was more quiet than usual—at least from what Lexi knew of her these past few days. Savvy certainly hadn't been this quiet with Chris.

When they were finishing up their burgers and fries, Savvy excused herself to use the restroom. Lexi watched her go, wondering about her and Tyler. Her attention was diverted by a woman at the counter with short black hair. She wore skimpy clothing, heavy makeup, and had more body piercings than Lexi had ever seen, even in California. A large tattoo of a black and orange tiger splayed over one bare shoulder. Half in awe, Lexi watched the woman place her order.

Sensing her interest, Tyler glanced around at the woman. He turned back almost immediately, his head shaking. His expression was far from admiring but rather saddened and a little, well, disgusted. Lexi thought it odd that he wouldn't be at least attracted to the woman's figure—which was rather extraordinary—but he only averted his eyes and frowned.

Lexi felt uncomfortable, remembering that she herself had nearly chosen a similar outfit that morning. Wanting to impress Tyler, she had put on a halter top, a ruffled mini skirt, and high heels. Savvy had taken one look at her outfit and said flatly, "No way. If you don't change, you won't go."

"I'll go anyway!" Lexi had insisted. "You can't stop me."

Savvy arched a brow. "You think Tyler will take you if I say you can't go? Believe me, he won't."

"Why?" Lexi retorted. "Because you think he's in love with you?"

An inexplicable hurt showed on Savvy's face. On her sister's face— the sister she'd longed for. Lexi felt bad, but she tried to squelch the feeling.

"No," Savvy said quietly. "Because he's my friend and a good man. Besides, you'd embarrass him if you dressed like that—especially if he's job hunting."

Lexi had stomped back to the bedroom, angered and helpless. No one except her father had challenged her clothing choices for a long time, and she resented it—especially from Savvy. What right did she have to try to control her? After all, until a few days ago Savvy hadn't even known Lexi existed. She hadn't cared to find out if she had other siblings. She had never even tried to visit her *real* father.

Lexi ended up changing. Savvy knew Tyler better than she did, after all, and more than anything at that moment, Lexi didn't want to embarrass or annoy him.

Now, seeing Tyler's obvious disapproval and pity for the woman at the counter, Lexi was glad Savvy had forced her to wear her new red shirt. If not, Tyler might have given *her* that sort of look, instead of the compliments he'd offered earlier.

Even so Lexi felt compelled to challenge his reaction. "Why do you hate that woman?" she asked him, motioning with her chin.

He looked surprised. "I don't hate her." Wadding his hamburger wrapper, he tossed it next to Savvy's uneaten fries. "I feel sorry for her, that's all. I wish I could go over and tell her who she really is."

"She's herself, that's all."

"No, Lexi, she's a child of God—like we are."

Like we are. The phrase entered Lexi's heart with arrow-like swiftness, causing her breath to catch in her throat. She swallowed hard. Her mother had talked like that, she remembered. Right before the accident.

Pushing the thought aside, Lexi stole a peek at the woman, who was taking her tray of food. "She doesn't look like a child of—" She stopped. She was being as judgmental as everyone was of her lately!

He grinned. "See what I mean?"

Savvy returned at that moment, immediately diverting Tyler's attention. Lexi tried not to feel slighted, reminding herself that the two of them had been friends long before she came into the picture.

The woman with the tattoo was joined by two guys who wore black, baggy clothes trimmed with chains. Both had their ears and noses pierced, and one was wearing makeup. Their laughter could be heard all over the restaurant. Once Lexi would have thought they looked exciting and daring, but now they seemed lost and alone—like Lexi so often felt. *Like they really don't know who they are or where they belong,* she thought.

While it wasn't exactly something she would admit to her friends back home, she was infinitely glad to be with Tyler and Savvy instead of with them.

As they left the restaurant, a man was coming inside—a very familiar man. At the sight of him Lexi stopped walking. Her heart jerked. *Dad!* she thought.

But the man pushed past her with scarcely a look in her direction.

No, he wasn't her father. He was about the same height as her father and he moved like him but his hair was white, not blond, and the many wrinkles on his face told her he was much older.

"Did you leave something?" Tyler asked.

"No," Lexi managed.

Savvy looked at her with concern. "Are you okay?

Lexi nodded, but she wasn't okay. There was a hole opening in her heart—a huge one large enough to swallow the entire world. Suddenly she wanted to put her hand in Tyler's. She wanted him to hug her like a father would a favored daughter.

No, she thought, *I don't want him. I want my dad.* The hole in her heart grew until her whole chest hurt and she was fighting tears.

"Come on," Savvy said. Lexi felt Savvy's arm around her, gently leading her to the van. Tyler jogged ahead to open the door.

When they reached the van, Lexi said, "Would it be okay if I sat in the back? Maybe stretch out on the seats?"

"Do you want me to sit with you?" Savvy's voice was kind, provoking even more tears.

"No, I'm all right." Lexi was feeling better now. It had just been such a shock, seeing that man who so resembled her father.

Lexi lay down on the middle seat, facing the back to hide her face from Savvy and Tyler. She wrapped her skinny arms around her body.

Much later, she turned over. Tyler and Savvy were talking and didn't notice her movements. Then Tyler's phone rang. He glanced at the number and he handed it to Savvy. "It's Kerrianne," he said. "Would you talk to her? I've got to find that freeway exit."

Savvy took the phone. Lexi wasn't sure, but it seemed as though she was careful not to touch Tyler's hand.

"Hello? No, it's Savvy. Yeah, pretty well. He got an interview. I guess we'll see. What?" She paused, listening. "Okay, I'll tell him. Thanks." Closing the phone, Savvy looked at Tyler. "She wants to know if you'll remember to stop at the store and get those DVDs for tomorrow's drive home."

Tyler laughed and said something Lexi didn't catch. She was too busy watching Savvy set Tyler's phone down in the catchall between the two seats.

Slowly, ever so slowly, Lexi reached out until the phone was in her hand. She turned around again, hiding it from view. In less than a minute, she figured out how to turn off the ringer. Then she closed the thin, silver case and slipped it into her purse.

Chapter Twelve

The day had been awkward at first, but it ended up much better than Savvy had expected. Tyler seemed to be going out of his way to help her with Lexi—not only to encourage good behavior but in probing into her secrets as well. He'd learned about the friend Amber and that Lexi liked to ski and fish. That seemed to rule out Arizona, at least.

With all his support, Savvy could *almost* forget what happened two years ago, the last time Tyler had deserted her for a skinny slip of a thing in one of his journalism classes. He'd dated the girl all of three weeks, she remembered. Three long, lonely weeks. Savvy had despised herself during those weeks, despised her dependence on him. For some reason, losing his attention then was worse than all the other times it had happened. Maybe because most of her close friends were engaged or married. Or maybe because she'd finally realized how hopeless her feelings were.

Not that she'd sat home waiting for his call. She'd gone out with two returned missionaries, both nice guys, but her heart hadn't been in it, not even when both asked her out again. It had been then she'd decided she was through with men and school; she was going on a mission.

That decision had been the right one. She knew she could never repay the countless blessings the Lord had bestowed on her through her service. Not only had she learned much about the gospel but serving in California had eventually guided her to Berkeley, to Chris, and a regaining of her love for astronomy. It had brought her to this quiet apartment where Lexi had found her. And the discovery of Lexi was the crowning glory of all.

Savvy already loved Lexi, and she would fight to be a part of her life. Even if Lexi's father didn't want anything to do with her personally, she and Lexi could develop a close relationship. They could be true sisters.

Of course, there were still so many unanswered questions. The biggest one being Lexi's home life. What was Derek like now? The question haunted Savvy. Why didn't he care that Lexi wasn't home?

They pulled up in front of Savvy's apartment and piled out of the van. Savvy was relieved to see that Lexi was feeling better. "Well," Savvy said, feeling awkward as she stood across the sidewalk from Tyler. "Thanks for lunch."

"You're welcome." Tyler seemed equally uneasy. "I had a good time."

"It was fun. Except for the burger. I probably gained ten pounds." Savvy winced inwardly as she said the words. Why did she have to keep bringing his attention back to her size?

"It's worth every bite." He grinned, and her heart lurched.

She felt the sudden urge to run fast and far. His closeness brought back too many memories, reminded her of old dreams best left forgotten. They could never be the friends they had once been. She wasn't willing to settle for a sideline relationship. He had a girlfriend now—a thin, blonde, pretty, smart girlfriend, but one not obsessed with astronomy and math. No, not a girl like Savvy at all.

Well, at least in a few days her proximity to Tyler would be behind her. She would be with her family and could concentrate on finding Lexi's home. She would finally, after all these years, meet her birth father. Of course, with the way things were shaping up, that meeting wasn't likely to go smoothly.

With a sigh, Savvy stepped away from Tyler. "I'd better get going. I need to pack some things for tomorrow, and I think I know where a suitcase is for Lexi."

"Hey, look!" Lexi pointed down the road where an ice cream truck was stopping in front of a group of teens. "Didn't you promise me ice cream?" She gave Tyler a pleading grin.

"Sure, why not?" Tyler looked at Savvy. "What kind do you want?"

She shook her head. "None, thanks. But you two go ahead."

Tyler's brow wrinkled and he looked about to protest, but Lexi grabbed his hand and pulled him down the sidewalk. Savvy took the opportunity to slip away.

Inside her apartment, the temperature was stifling. She turned on the cooler and went to the front closet where she remembered stashing an old suitcase she'd used on her mission. She didn't need it for her visit home, so Lexi might as well get some use from it. Her already bulging backpack wouldn't fit a hairbrush, much less the new clothes Savvy had bought for her. Much of the backpack's contents were now strewn across their room—Lexi's handiwork that morning as she had fought with Savvy over what to wear for her outing with Tyler. Savvy might as well pack it for her.

In the bedroom, Savvy folded Lexi's clothes neatly into the small suitcase. Some of the clothes were fit only for a fire, but Savvy couldn't throw them away—not yet. Until she knew how things would work out with Lexi's father, she would have to let her keep the clothing.

When the clothes were organized, Savvy hefted the backpack, tempted to dump out the rest and pack it as well. But she didn't want Lexi to think she was going through her things. The pack was heavy, extraordinarily so, and was still more than halfway full. *Books,* Savvy guessed, tracing the outline. But what kind? Romance novels? Mysteries? Classics? She didn't know Lexi well enough to be sure.

Glancing at her watch, Savvy saw that it was after one. *Where are they?* Sighing, she tossed the pack onto her bed with a little more force than necessary. With a loud *riiiip*, the backpack burst, spilling out a book: *Little Women.*

Savvy smiled. *No wonder she came to find me. That book would make anyone want a sister.* There was no way she could sew up the hole before Lexi came inside, but she could at least put the book into the suitcase. As Savvy approached the bed, reaching for the book, something protruding from the rip in the backpack drew her attention. Sucking in a deep breath, she shook her head. *It can't be.* Her hand went out, almost as though it possessed a mind of its own.

The wad of green bills was real. Savvy pulled it from the pack, gaping. The half-inch stack was made up of twenty dollar bills, secured with a rubber band that looked as though it had come from a newspaper. Lexi had mentioned money, but Savvy had no idea she had *this* kind of money. Her jaw clenched until it ached.

Warily, she eyed the backpack, knowing she had to look inside. She could wait for Lexi, but then she might learn nothing. Holding her breath, she unzipped the backpack and upended it, hoping it contained only books.

There were more books—*Anne of Green Gables,* the entire *Narnia* set, *The Secret Garden, Ella Enchanted*—but among the books sat more short stacks of the offending green. Stacks of tens, fives, ones, and another one of twenties. Without actually counting, Savvy estimated that there were several thousand dollars—maybe more. What was Lexi doing with this kind of money?

"Savvy! Savvy! Are you here? We're back!"

Savvy started at Lexi's voice and braced herself for what was to come.

Lexi practically flew into the room, her face bright and excited. "Savvy, you should have tried one of the—" She broke off as she spied the contents of her backpack on the bed and a wad of bills in Savvy's hand. She went from excited to furious instantly. "What are you doing!" she screamed, diving for the money. "You just couldn't wait to start snooping! I can't believe you!"

More words tumbled from her mouth, some of them not repeatable in good company, as she lunged at the books and money, shoving them back inside the pack. When she jerked it toward her, two books and a wad of money fell from the rip onto the floor. She stared at them for a second before glaring angrily at Savvy.

"If you're quite finished," Savvy said.

"You're horrible!" Lexi shouted. "I hate you!"

Savvy forced down her hurt at the stinging words and tried to stay calm. "Well, that's okay. You're entitled to feel any way you want. But for your information, I didn't plan to go through your things. I was packing the clothes you'd left all over, and when I moved the back-pack, it ripped and the money came out. Only then did I dump it all out."

Lexi had clasped the backpack against her chest. "You still had no right!" she cried, her face red from fury.

"I had every right!" Savvy raised her voice only slightly. "You're thir-teen years old, walking around with thousands of dollars in a back-pack. What did you do—rob a store?" Savvy's heart jumped. Maybe Lexi's father was a fugitive and that's why he hadn't reported his daugh-ter missing.

"No! It's mine. I swear! All of it. I have more, a lot more, but I didn't bring it all."

Savvy didn't see how the money could be hers, but she didn't want to show how little she trusted Lexi. "Do you know how dangerous that is? Not only could the money have been stolen, but you could have been hurt by someone who wanted it. Haven't you ever heard of a bank?"

"I didn't know how much I would need." Some of the flush had begun to fade from Lexi's face. "How else could I use it? I don't have a checkbook."

Of course not! Savvy had forgotten her age. Her legs felt suddenly weak, and she sat on the bed. "I didn't get my first checkbook until I was seventeen," she mused aloud, "and my mother had to co-sign."

Lexi bent to sweep up the books and the wad of bills. Her chin still jutted out defiantly, but she was calmer now. After a long silence, she also sat rigidly on the bed. The quiet of the room was heavy and oppressing.

"So where'd you get the money?" Savvy asked when she couldn't stand it any longer.

Lexi didn't look at her. "Mostly from the airline. They paid it to us after the . . . the plane crash. My dad put it into a savings account for me. I can only get out a certain amount each week."

The notion of her birth father opening an account for Lexi was difficult to merge with the other ideas Savvy had of him. Surely an abusive father would have kept the money for himself. Of course, the law might not have allowed that. But if the law was involved, the money would probably have been in a trust fund for Lexi, not a regular savings account.

"And the rest?" Savvy prompted.

"My school shopping money."

That surprised Savvy even more. If Lexi was given money to shop for a new school wardrobe, then someone was obviously caring for her.

Savvy shook her head, abandoning the attempt to reconcile the contrasting views of her father. "I'm sorry if you feel I violated your privacy, but when I saw the money, I felt responsible to find out what was going on. To tell the truth, I'm glad it was only money, and not something more dangerous."

"Like drugs? Alcohol?" Lexi snorted. "I'm not stupid. Besides, Dad drinks enough for both of us." Before Savvy could respond, Lexi added, "You still shouldn't have looked. It's mine."

Savvy scooted across the bed. "If you'll trust me, I'll put that money in the bank—or most of it. Then when things are settled, I'll help you open a personal account."

"I already have an account," Lexi said, twisting slightly so she could look Savvy in the eye. "But I didn't know how to get the money out unless I went to the bank."

"We'll figure something out."

"What if I need it?"

"You shouldn't need it—yet."

"But what if I do?"

"Then ask and it's yours."

"Promise?"

"Promise." Savvy offered a tentative smile. "Truce?"

"You promise not to go through my things again?"

Savvy considered for a moment. It was one thing to promise to give the money back if Lexi asked for it but quite another to promise never to snoop again. Finally, she shook her head. "I don't know. If there seems to be a reason, I think I would have to, right? I mean, if one of my brothers started acting strange—getting bad grades, acting out, being depressed—I know my mother would search his room for clues. It means she cares, that's all."

Lexi pursed her lips. "Or it means she's controlling."

"Lexi, when people care, they sometimes have to insist on knowing what's going on. If you think about it, you'll see that I'm right."

"Well then, no snooping unless there's a reason. A *real* reason."

"Like the money?"

"I guess."

Savvy would have to be satisfied with that reluctant agreement. "So what about the money?" she said. "We can go to the bank now."

Lexi began taking out the stacks and handing them to Savvy. "I'm keeping this one," she said, waving a stack of twenties.

Savvy had no choice but to agree.

"Oh, no!" Suddenly Lexi threw her stack of twenties onto the bed.

"Tyler! I left him waiting outside. It's been like forever. Hope he's not too mad."

Savvy dropped the bills in her hand on the bed and started for the door. "He'll be fine."

As they moved down the hall, Savvy envisioned Tyler's face as she told him about the cash. Maybe she'd ask him to drive them to the bank. A part of her rejected the idea—why prolong her agony? But the other part, the part that still cared, craved to spend more time with him.

When they opened the front door, there was no van out front. Tyler was gone.

*　*　*　*

"So how's it going?" Lexi kept her voice to a whisper so that Savvy couldn't hear her as she made dinner in the kitchen. The last thing Lexi wanted was to be discovered talking to herself in the bathroom. Or worse, talking to Amber on Tyler's cell phone.

"Fine. He didn't call or anything on the weekend, and today I left the note like you asked," Amber said. "But won't he expect to see you sometime tonight or tomorrow morning?"

"It depends how he's feeling." Lexi was sitting on the closed lid of the toilet seat. She pulled her legs up and hugged them to her chest. "Sometimes when it's bad, he sleeps all day." She paused and then asked, "So did you see him?"

"Yeah, he came home when I was putting out the note today. I heard the car and got out the back door. Then I hid in the bushes. He's lost a lot of weight since last summer, hasn't he?"

Last summer. The memories flooded her of camping near the lake, of swimming in the cool, clean mountain water while the sun warmed their arms and heads. Things had been pretty good then. Lexi never would have guessed how horribly their lives would change. She barely recognized him now.

"Lexi, are you there? I said, he's lost a lot of weight."

"Yeah. I know. But other than that?"

"He was whistling."

Whistling was a good sign. It meant he didn't know what she had done—yet. Lexi swallowed hard. She would have to tell Savvy soon.

"When are you coming back?" Amber whispered. "I can't believe he'll keep accepting notes."

"You don't know how bad it is watching him get worse," Lexi told her. "You don't live with him."

"I know. And I'm sorry. It's just that all this sneaking around . . . My parents found your phone, you know. I said you'd left it."

"I did. I left it with you. Look, Amber, I'm trying, but I don't know when I'll get back. There's stuff I have to do here first. I have to make sure she likes me enough to keep me when she finds out."

"You are coming back, though, aren't you?"

Lexi almost wished she didn't have to. As insecure as she felt at the moment, anything was better than the heartache she endured at home. "Yeah, but I don't know if my"—she swallowed hard—"my sister will go along with everything. She doesn't like my dad."

"Well, neither do you right now. Still, Minnesota can't be all that bad. You might like living there."

"I'm not going to Minnesota. Not ever!" Lexi couldn't even think of that. Minnesota would mean that her father was lost to her forever. "Please, Amber. Could you put another note on the table tomorrow? Use the kitchen door. The key I gave you works there, too. Look in the window first to make sure he's not there. Please?"

"Okay, okay. But if my parents ever find out, I'm going to be grounded until I go to college. Of course I might get grounded anyway since you aren't around to help me with English. Sheesh, why do teachers have to make it so hard?"

"I'll help you when I get back." Lexi was gripping Tyler's phone so tightly that her fingers were numb.

"I'll see you then," Amber said, her voice full of doubt and anxiety.

Lexi wished she could have done this without her friend's help, but she'd seen no other way.

The connection broken, Lexi sat on the toilet lid and stared at the silver phone in her hand. It was vibrating. She didn't recognize the number and didn't dare answer it. Let Tyler's voice mail pick it up. After the phone stopped vibrating, she poked around it for a long time, trying to find a way to delete the evidence that she had used the phone. The only thing she succeeded in doing was running down the battery.

Well, I'll just have to hope Tyler won't notice my call until I'm ready for them to find out where I live. Besides, the number she'd called was a cell phone. She didn't think that was easily traceable.

Now all she had to do was find a way to slip the phone back to Tyler without his realizing she'd ever had it.

Chapter Thirteen

Savvy and Lexi were waiting outside when Tyler and Kerrianne drove up to the apartment early Tuesday morning. Savvy smoothed her lightweight summer skirt and tried to think if there was anything she hadn't taken care of. She'd seen Chris last night and promised to keep in touch. She'd also talked to her co-teacher at the college, and he'd agreed to teach their first two classes alone if she'd do him a similar favor around Thanksgiving. This meant Savvy could extend her vacation another week. Her own classes would be easily made up so early in the semester when class changes were still going on.

Tyler jumped from the van to collect their luggage, greeting them with a warm smile that showed no anger at their neglect of him the previous day. Savvy's stomach clenched at his easy manner. Did he feel nothing for their ruined friendship?

Before she could dwell further on that, the sliding door to the van opened and three children burst from the interior. "Savvy! Savvy!" they called.

The oldest, Misty, reached her first. Savvy caught the white-haired, blue-eyed girl in a tight hug. "Why, Misty, you're so grown up!" The little girl looked more like a porcelain doll than ever, with her hair in ringlets and her pale skin smooth and unblemished.

Caleb and Benjamin had reached her now, but they didn't hurl themselves into her arms as they once had when she had lived in Utah. Savvy knelt down to their level. "Hey, guys, don't you remember me?" Benjamin nodded; Caleb shook his head. Benjamin shyly leaned forward to give Savvy a hug. "Well, you'll know me better soon enough," she said. "We'll have lots of fun on the drive to Utah."

"We're going to watch cartoons!" Benjamin said.

"How fun! Hey, there's someone really special I want you to meet." Savvy stood and turned, motioning for Lexi to approach. "This is my new sister. Her name is Lexi."

"Uncle Tyler told us." Misty looked up at Lexi, taking in the cut-off shorts and tight, stretch T-shirt without remark.

Benjamin wasn't so polite. "How come your belly is showing? You're not supposed to show your belly. Only boys can do that when they're swimming."

"Come on now, to the van," Tyler interrupted. "Quick, let's see who gets there first." That was all he needed to say. The three children sprinted toward the van as though their lives depended on reaching it.

"I won!" Benjamin shouted.

"No, I did!" Misty protested.

As Kerrianne began buckling Caleb into his seat, Savvy put her arm around Lexi, propelling her gently to the van. "They're little kids," she said softly. "They don't think before they speak."

"I don't care what they say." But Lexi's belligerent tone showed clearly that she did care.

"Well, for what it's worth, they're right. Are you sure you don't want to change before we go? I bet Kerrianne would rather not have to explain your belly button ring to her children today."

Lexi stopped walking and shrugged off Savvy's arm. "I don't want to change," she said tightly. "And for your information, I'm not wearing my belly ring."

"Great," Savvy said with a smile. "Let's get in, then. Looks like we're in the middle seat."

Lexi didn't return the smile but climbed into the van without comment. She set her small black purse on the floor by her feet. Within minutes they were on their way to Utah, watching a Disney DVD on the van's built-in screen.

"What time will we get back?" Savvy asked Tyler.

"Let's see. It takes about ten hours, plus an hour for the time difference and another hour or so for stops. We'll probably be there sometime around eight tonight, give or take."

"I should call my mom to let her know. Could I use your phone?"

Tyler frowned. "I seem to have lost it. I remember having it yesterday when you talked to Kerrianne—I was going to ask you if you'd accidentally stuck it in your purse."

"No. I set it between the seats."

"Well, it'll turn up. I hope."

"Is this your phone?" Lexi reached under the driver's seat and pulled out a silver object.

Tyler reached for it, keeping an eye on the road. "Thanks, Lexi! I looked all over last night but must have missed it. Since I had it on vibrate, it's hard to hear when I call my number."

Lexi smiled and said nothing. Savvy thought there was something odd about her expression but couldn't quite decipher the look. Tyler handed the phone to Savvy. "Thanks," she said. "Your battery looks about dead, but I think it'll make the call." She dialed her mother's number, pushing thoughts of Lexi from her mind.

⋆⋆*⋆*

The trip back to Utah was uneventful, if tiring. Halfway through, Savvy traded Kerrianne places when the images on the screen threatened to cause her car sickness. Once in the front, Savvy made small talk with Tyler, covering mundane things she could have discussed with a pure stranger.

She wished she could tell him how worried she was about Lexi, of how she suspected her birth father of abuse. She also wanted to tell Tyler of her own trepidation at her impending meeting with her birth father. What would she say to Derek Roathe? What would he say? Yet even if she and Tyler had been back on their old terms, they wouldn't have been able to talk openly in front of Lexi, who was watching the DVD screen with interest but whose eyes Savvy often felt resting on her own face.

Upon reaching Utah Valley, Tyler stopped first at Kerrianne's house in Pleasant Grove to let her and the children out. Then they headed for American Fork. Savvy was stricken by the bone-familiar lines of the roads and buildings, of her neighborhood, her own yard. Home.

She was choked with tears as her mother enfolded her in her arms, her siblings crowding around waiting for their turn. They were all so changed, yet so familiar, and so much a part of her that Savvy wondered how she'd survived without them. Tears streamed down her mother's face, and Camille and Rosalie cried with her. Even the twins had tears in their eyes. The only missing piece was Savvy's father, who was still in Japan.

Lexi hung back during the initial hugging, and when she was introduced, her face was carefully neutral, though she was greeted with warmth and enthusiasm. "We're very glad to meet you after all these years," said Savvy's mother. She hugged Lexi with almost as much enthusiasm as she had Savvy. "We're looking forward to getting to know you."

Lexi accepted Brionney's hug stoically but didn't speak. Savvy had thought she would at least talk to her brothers, who were only a year older, but Lexi blushed and looked away whenever they glanced in her direction.

"Come inside, Savannah," her mother said, hugging Savvy again. She wiped her wet face with her hands. "I'm sure you're all hungry after your long trip."

"And tired, too," Savvy agreed, letting her mother propel her toward the house.

Tyler turned to leave. "Well, I'll see you guys around."

Brionney shook her head. "Oh, no, you don't. You have to come in. You're part of this, Tyler Huntington. I made enough food for all of us."

Tyler shrugged. "Okay, but I need to get this van back to my sister soon."

Savvy felt almost resentful toward him for accepting her mother's invitation. This was *her* family, and she wanted to relax with them without having to constantly guard against her mixed feelings for Tyler. But as they went into the house, she saw Lexi clinging to his arm, as though to stop herself from drowning. Her heart softened. Lexi needed him.

Dinner was her favorite crockpot roast, with potatoes, onions, celery, and carrots. Savvy ate and talked until her tongue felt weary. After dinner, her mother left the cleaning up to Camille and Rosalie while she drew Savvy into the room Savvy had used growing up, the one Rosalie had recently deserted when she moved onto the BYU campus for her first year of college.

"I'll put you two in here," Brionney said. "I had the boys bring in the rollaway. I know it's a tight fit, but I didn't want to push Gabe out of the bigger room for such a short time."

"It's perfect."

Brionney smiled and hugged Savvy again. "Oh, baby, I'm so glad you're home. I've missed you so much."

Savvy blinked away her tears. "Me too, Mom." They held onto each other for a long moment before breaking apart.

"Mom," Savvy said, sinking onto the bed. "What am I going to do about Lexi?"

Brionney shook her head. "Do you know how long she wants to stay?"

"Truthfully, I don't know if she can go back at all. I couldn't tell you much with her always listening when we were on the phone, but there's something serious going on." She took a deep breath before adding, "It might be abuse. She might need to stay with me."

"You have to call the police."

"She threatened to run if I do. I know it might be the wrong thing, but I gave her until tomorrow to tell me where she lives. If she doesn't tell me, I'll contact the police then." She spread her hands. "It's the best I can do."

"It's good enough," Brionney said, sitting beside her. "Remember that we're here to help. Dad talked to his lawyer once, and when he gets home he can call again. Meanwhile, we might be able to find something on the Internet."

"Yeah, I was going to try that." Savvy was silent a moment, staring down at her hands. Then she looked up. "Mom, was Derek that way? Abusive, I mean?"

Her mother thought for a long moment. "He never hit me—ever. In the end, he wasn't treating me well, but that was because he wanted to be out of the relationship. Still, a marriage doesn't ever end without some kind of abuse. So if you're asking if he's capable of abuse, yes. But I would be surprised if it was physical abuse." She hesitated a moment. "He could also be kind. I loved him very much . . . once."

Savvy had never really given that much consideration. Her mother had loved Derek enough to marry him in the temple, and that meant she'd planned to spend an eternity with him. While her dreams of eternity had not been realized—at least with Derek—she'd obviously seen something of value in the man. "When Lexi gives me the information, I'll guess I'll have to talk to, uh, Derek," Savvy said. "I don't really want to but . . ."

"But you're curious."

Savvy looked down at her hands again. "I guess I am," she said quietly.

"That's not a bad thing, honey." Brionney's voice held the slightest hint of amusement. "Do you want me to talk to him?"

Savvy shook her head, reaching out to her mother. "No, I can do it. It's really my job. She's my sister."

Brionney gave her a wistful smile. "It seems so strange you having siblings that aren't my children."

"I know. It's really strange. But I have to admit, despite all her earrings and her very different upbringing, I feel a bond with her. It's weird, but—"

"Not really. There's a lot of your father in both of you. He was a handsome man." Brionney gazed at Savvy, but her eyes looked as though they focused on something else entirely. "I don't regret my marriage to him," Brionney added. "Without him, there would be no you."

Savvy hugged her mother again, fiercely. "I love you, Mom. And I'm so grateful to you. You've been the best mom, and you gave me Dad. He may not be my biological father, but he's the best dad in the world."

Brionney chuckled softly. "Now *that* I know. And he loves you very much."

They pulled away slowly, awkwardly, despite the abundance of love. "I guess we'd better go back out there." Savvy started for the door.

In the family room, Savvy took a glass of white grape juice and sat at one end of the couch feeling happy but exhausted. She found herself wondering why she'd chosen to study so far from home. But she knew. She'd been running away—a lot like Lexi had done. Not from her family, but from her feelings for Tyler.

Tyler was still at the house, sitting on the love seat by an unsmiling Lexi. The girl was hunched over and staring at the floor, a drink in hand, her very posture warning people away.

At that moment, Tyler looked over at Savvy. Their gazes locked, and for an instant Savvy felt they were alone in the room. Her heart ached. He lifted his glass toward her; she nodded slightly. Together they drank.

Savvy's heart felt soothed. Tyler was there for her. Their relationship might not be the one she'd once longed for, but he was there if she needed him.

* * * * * *

Lexi felt trapped. She couldn't think clearly with Savvy's family hovering around. They spoke to her, but she didn't really hear them. They probably thought she was stupid—not that she cared what they thought. The only constant in the room for her was Tyler. He stayed by her side, and for that Lexi was grateful.

Savvy was the center of attention. Her siblings and her mother gravitated toward her, seemingly vying for her attention. She was so busy with everyone that she didn't have time for Lexi. A sadness crept into Lexi's heart. She had come so far to see her sister, but her sister didn't really need her.

I've got to get out of here, Lexi thought. Desperation welled up inside, a tight, horrible feeling. A feeling she knew intimately from her life with her father. Everything seemed to be pressing in on her. She felt dizzy and close to tears.

Lexi leapt up from the couch and headed through the family room toward the kitchen, eyes focused on the opening that led to the entry-way. She careened into someone. *One of the twins,* she realized, gazing momentarily into startled brown eyes. *Just my luck,* she thought, holding her hand out to ward off the dizziness. She hadn't been able to exchange two words with them. Back home she wasn't this awkward—even around boys.

She brushed past the twin—was it Gabe or Forest?—and walked steadily through the entryway and out the front door. The night air hit her in the face, feeling good on her flushed face. The light on the porch flicked on as she sank to the top stair on the porch and rested her head against the railing.

"Are you all right?"

Lexi held her breath. Was it the twin? What should she say? She wanted to talk to him, but she couldn't. She'd probably burst into tears. Her muscles bunched in preparation to flee. Maybe she could hide in Kerrianne's van until this ordeal was over. Was it unlocked?

"Lexi?"

Turning her head slightly, she caught sight of Tyler. Not the twin after all. Her muscles began to relax. "Tyler," she said. Then to her mortification, she gave a little sob.

He sat down on the step beside her. "Gabe told me you came out here. He seemed worried about you."

"I'm fine," she managed.

"It can be hard when you don't know anyone."

She shrugged.

"Savvy's family's really close," Tyler continued. "Everyone really misses her."

"She doesn't even remember I'm here." Lexi hated how pouting her voice sounded, but she couldn't help herself.

"Sure she does. You wait and see. She'll come looking for you."

Lexi doubted it. "She doesn't need me. She has enough family."

"You can never have enough family. And you're her sister. That's special."

"She already has two sisters." Sisters who dressed the way Savvy did and who had been with Savvy from the beginning of their lives. There was no place for Lexi.

"You can never have too many sisters."

Lexi felt marginally better at Tyler's words. But that didn't mean she had to stick around. "I don't want to stay here," she said, looking over at him. "Can I go with you—please?"

He studied her for a moment. "I don't think that's a good idea."

"Why not? Please?"

"Lexi, young girls can't stay with guys who aren't related to them. That's just the way it is."

Lexi wondered if he was making up excuses.

"Otherwise, I'd love to have you," he continued. "I kind of like having you around."

Warmth flooded Lexi's body, the kind that made her want to cry—

the good kind of crying. She took a deep breath. The pressure and dizziness she'd felt were slipping away. "Thanks," she said softly.

Tyler smiled and nodded but didn't reply. He looked up into the sky. "Savvy would love this sky. Look at all those stars."

"It's like back home." Lexi's stomach gave a lurch of homesickness.

They sat in silence for long moments. Lexi was beginning to feel awkward sitting on the porch because her T-shirt wouldn't stay down over her lower back.

"Cold?" he asked.

She shook her head. No way would she confess that she was embarrassed by her clothes. Still, he was nice to ask. If his family was half as nice, she could understand why they'd taken in so many abandoned children.

The door behind them opened, spilling light and a myriad of voices onto the porch. "Ah, here you are," Savvy said. The door shut, cutting out both the bright light and the sound. "I was worried."

She came! Lexi thought. Did that mean she cared?

"We're looking at the stars," Tyler said. "But our eyes are having trouble staying open—at least mine are."

Savvy smiled. "Mine too."

"Have a seat." Tyler moved down a few stairs and Savvy took his place on the top stair next to Lexi.

Savvy yawned and stretched her arms. "You can turn in if you want, Lexi. We'll be staying together in my old room. You can have either the bed or the cot."

"I'm not staying," Lexi said.

"What? Of course you're staying."

Lexi lifted her chin. "I don't want to stay here. I want to go with Tyler."

"Lexi, we already talked about this," Tyler said. "I told you that won't work." He exchanged a glance with Savvy, but Lexi couldn't decipher what it meant.

"Why don't you want to stay here?" Savvy asked, surprising Lexi.

She'd expected Savvy to ask why she wanted to go with Tyler. Then again, maybe it was the same question.

"I don't fit in." Lexi felt miserable saying the words and stared at the ground instead of into her sister's eyes. "They're not my family, and I don't belong. Your mother divorced my dad. She can't want me around."

Savvy shifted her position on the porch. "Actually," she said, "from what I understand, your father divorced her, though it hardly matters now. But you are welcome here. My family is glad to meet you."

Lexi had a hard time believing that. "I want to stay with Tyler. Please, Savvy."

Savvy shook her head. "I'm sorry, Lexi, but it isn't appropriate. You're thirteen, a young lady now, and Tyler's not even related. What would your father say?"

"He'd probably beat me and ground me for a year." Lexi didn't mean it, but she liked to see Savvy's eyes widen. "Fine, I won't go. But I'll need my money, then."

"Your money?"

"Yes. For a hotel. You promised you'd give it to me when I needed it. If I can't stay with Tyler, I'm getting a hotel."

Savvy blew out a long sigh. Lexi almost grinned because she knew she'd won. Savvy had promised, and unless she wanted to prove herself a liar, she'd have to do what Lexi wanted.

"Oh, Lexi, that's such a huge waste of money," Savvy said. "Can't you please stay here?"

Lexi shook her head and averted her face from Savvy's pleading eyes.

"Well, I'm certainly not letting you go off alone."

Lexi stiffened. Was Savvy saying she would go with her, or was she hinting at calling the police? She opened her mouth to invite Savvy to the hotel, but Tyler intervened.

"Hey, I may have a solution," he said.

Lexi and Savvy turned toward him. "What?" Savvy asked.

"Why don't you both stay at my house for a few days until every-thing is resolved? Mitch isn't due back for a while, as far as I know, and I can crash out at Kerrianne's. There are a few things I've been wanting to fix around her house anyway—the back fence, for one. Since I'm not employed, now would be a good time to get it all done. You'd have to feed his animals, though."

"His animals?" Savvy groaned, but there was an underlying laugh-ter to her voice. Lexi thought that was a good sign.

"I'll feed them!" Lexi said, jumping to her feet. "I like animals. Well, I never actually had any pets, but I would have if my father had let me. Please, Savvy. Let's do that. It'd be just us. We could get to know each other!" Lexi hadn't meant to let the last few sentences slip, but if Savvy's expression was any indication, it was a good thing she had.

Savvy glanced at Lexi and then back at Tyler. "Are you sure?" she asked him. "We could go to a hotel for a night or two."

"Like you said, a hotel would be a waste of money," Tyler said. "And I'll even come and feed the animals. I know how much you love them." Lexi thought his grin was mocking.

"Not!" Savvy exclaimed.

Tyler laughed, and Savvy joined him. Lexi suddenly felt happy. They weren't going to stay here where she felt so out of place—like a hillbilly among nobility.

Savvy shook her head and stood. "Well," she said, "I'd better ask Mom if she minds me borrowing her car. Or maybe one of my sisters'. That way you won't have to go with us."

"I have some things to pick up, anyway," he said. "And I'll want to show you where to sleep."

"You sure Mitch won't mind?"

"Are you kidding? Of course not. You know him. Besides, it's only for a few days."

"Okay then. But I'm still borrowing a car. We'll need some wheels of our own." Savvy stepped backward in the direction of the door. "I'd better go break the news to my mother." She shook her head and sighed, causing Lexi to feel a tiny qualm about her actions. Was she being selfish? Well, it really didn't matter; she simply couldn't stay here.

"I'll put the luggage back into the van and then call Kerrianne," Tyler said as Savvy opened the front door. Savvy nodded and disappeared.

When she was gone, Lexi turned to Tyler. "Thanks so much!" Impulsively, she launched herself into his arms for a hug.

"Not a problem," he said with a grin that made his cheek dimple. "I told you she'd come looking for you. She cares about you a lot, Lexi. Don't you forget that."

Lexi wouldn't. Savvy was choosing to go with her instead of staying with her family. That was something special. That was real. Suddenly there was a lump in Lexi's throat that was impossible to swallow.

Was her plan to live with Savvy going to work? She had to believe that it was. *If only,* she thought, *we didn't have to face my father.*

Chapter Fourteen

The summer night was warm, and Tyler was glad for the light breeze. He and Lexi waited in the van for Savvy to say good-bye to her family. Tyler turned on the radio for some music.

"Ugh," Lexi said. "That's old people music." She turned the dial until she found something more to her liking.

Tyler smiled. "Good choice. I like that." The previous station had been the one Kerrianne listened to. His own tastes ran closer to Lexi's.

At last Savvy came from the house, carrying a box. Behind her one of the twins—probably Gabe—was also carrying a box. They went to the silver Oldsmobile Alero in the driveway and put the boxes in the trunk. Then Savvy came over to the driver's side of the van.

She looked ethereal and feminine in her slim skirt and matching fitted T-shirt, and the way she rested her arms on the open window rewound time for Tyler to years ago when they had been close. "Mom sent along food and stuff so we don't have to shop right away," she said. "I'm taking her car—she says she can share Rosalie's. So what did Kerrianne say?"

"She's fine with it," he said. "She already bought the screws and the paint for the fence last week."

"Sounds like Kerrianne." Savvy was so close he caught the scent of flowers which clung to her. Her hair was shorter than she used to wear it but long enough to lie across her shoulders and halfway down her back like a living shawl that captured every particle of light from the night sky. He wanted to reach out and feel the glowing strands between his fingers.

"How far is your house?" Lexi asked, leaning over from the front passenger seat to peer at Savvy.

"About twenty minutes," Tyler told her. "Not far."

She settled back in the seat. "Good. I'm sick of driving."

So was Tyler, but the reprieve at Savvy's had been a good one. He enjoyed being with her family. It reminded him of his own in some deep and familiar ways—particularly in the love they shared for each other and the gospel. He found it hard to contemplate what kind of life Lexi must have known without that kind of support. She had been so acutely uncomfortable around Savvy's family that she had radiated a standoffish attitude that chased off almost everyone. Except for him, of course. And Savvy.

Savvy removed her arms from the window opening. "And you're sure there's enough room? The last time I was at that house, it was pretty tiny."

"Plenty of room. You'll be staying in the new addition. There's even a hot tub out back you can use." He grinned. "I put that in."

"Yes!" Lexi said.

"Okay, I guess we'd better get started. I'll follow you over." Savvy gave him a smile that made his heart ache. How could he not have noticed before now how beautiful she was? *No, I knew it,* he thought. *But I never really saw.*

He wished Savvy were driving with him in the van. He wanted a chance to fix whatever it was that had broken between them. But maybe that wasn't necessary. Since their silent toast in her family room, Tyler felt altered somehow—as though he'd finally found a piece of what they'd once shared. Maybe it wasn't too late for them.

Too late for what?

But he knew what. Deep down he knew exactly what. *I've been such a fool!* If his brother Mitch were around, Tyler knew he'd agree.

The drive to Sandy went quickly, with Tyler frequently checking his mirror to assure himself that Savvy was still following them. Once they arrived, Tyler carried Lexi's suitcase from the van to the porch, and then hurried to help Savvy with her boxes. He didn't notice the aqua Mini Cooper until there was a movement from it. He stopped and stared, Savvy's box in his hands.

LaNae.

She ran toward him, her steps faltering as she got a closer look at Savvy and Lexi. Had she thought they were his sisters? "Tyler?" she asked, a touch of asperity in her voice.

"LaNae," he said. "Hi. I didn't expect to see you tonight." Checking his watch, he saw that it was already after ten.

"I came to surprise you. We've been playing phone tag all weekend, and I still really have to talk to you." Her eyes drifted to Savvy, who stood by the trunk of her mother's car watching them, her eyes dark and veiled.

"LaNae," Tyler said, "this is Savvy. Savvy, LaNae."

LaNae stepped forward, offering her hand. Had she always been so thin? "I remember you from the restaurant," LaNae said. "Nice to see you again. I've been hearing a lot about you."

"You have?" There was a mischievous glint in Savvy's eyes that didn't bode well for Tyler. "That's funny, I haven't heard anything about you—at least not from Tyler."

Tyler nearly dropped Savvy's box. Well, yes, it was true, but she didn't need to spell it out like that!

"The only thing I know is that you're his girlfriend," Savvy continued. Her smile was genuine, but there was something about her expression that bothered Tyler. It was familiar to him, but he couldn't place when he'd seen that exact expression on her face.

"I thought I was." LaNae gave him a dire glance. "But maybe I'm the only one who thought that."

"LaNae," he groaned. "Can we talk about this later?"

Her face flamed, but before she could respond, Savvy took the box from Tyler. "Don't mind us," she said. "We'll just take these things inside. You unlocked the door, didn't you?"

He nodded mutely.

"Come on, Lexi." Savvy went up the walk without so much as a backward glance.

Lexi lagged behind, casting mournful looks in Tyler's direction. Clearly, she did not appreciate LaNae's claim on him. Tyler wished he could call out to Lexi and make her stay, but he knew that would be cowardly. When they opened the door, Muffin came tearing outside and over to Tyler for an excited welcome home. Tyler bent to pet him.

"What is going on?" LaNae asked when Savvy and Lexi were in the house.

"They needed a place, so I let them stay here."

"You let them stay here?" Her voice rose an octave.

"Don't worry. I'll be at Kerrianne's."

"Why should I worry?" Her voice dripped sarcasm. "I mean you're only friends, right? It's not as if you feel for her as much as you feel for me." The last sentence ended in more of a question than a statement.

"Savvy's a friend."

"Maybe." LaNae put her hands on her practically nonexistent hips, causing Tyler to heave an internal sigh. "Look, Tyler, I came here tonight because I wanted to tell you why I didn't answer my cell on Sunday when you called. I was going to tell you Monday night, but then you didn't answer your phone. Now I think it's just as well because this is something I really should say in person." She hesitated an instant before adding, "I was with Rob on Sunday."

"With Rob?" Tyler was surprised, but he felt more relieved than jealous. "You mean, like on a date?"

LaNae nodded, tears glittering in her eyes. "I really like him. I've been so uncertain this weekend about my feelings for you, wavering from one side to the next. But on Sunday when Rob and I went to that fireside, I loved being with him. And now that I'm here and I see you with your friend . . . well, I know I was right to go with him. I still care for you, Tyler—a lot—but I can't take any more uncertainty. I don't want to pressure or force our relationship just because we've been dating so many months. Rob asked me out again, and I said yes."

Tyler's heart beat heavily. "I see." What else could he say? That he was glad they were breaking up? That she had been right all along about Savvy?

"I'd better go." LaNae cast a glance toward the house.

Tyler reached out and put a hand on her arm. "I'm sorry if I hurt you, LaNae. I never wanted to hurt you."

A faint smile touched her lips. "I know. Maybe that's what hurts the most. You're such a nice guy." Her voice became low and full of unshed tears. "But you were always holding back. Always. Maybe it's time to ask yourself why."

She was right about all of it. The only thing he wanted at this moment worse than not hurting her was to be with Savvy.

"I'm sorry I pushed so hard when Savvy came off her mission," LaNae added. "I should have given you some space. All Sunday I kept thinking that if I had, you might have worked out your feelings for her—one way or the other—and then we wouldn't be in this mess."

He doubted it. Stupidity seemed to flow in his veins of late. "We've made a lot of good memories," he reminded her.

"I know. It's been fun." She hugged him then, and he returned her hug. When she drew away her eyes were bright, but still no tears fell. "Good-bye," she whispered. With that, she spun from him and ran to her car.

Tyler stared after her with admiration. There went a woman who knew what she wanted and was going after it. What about him? What did he want? Did he have the courage to follow his heart?

He'd watched Savvy walk away from his life twice—once when she left on a mission and once when she'd moved to California. The bereft feelings he had experienced at those times had threatened to overwhelm him. Why hadn't he remembered that until now? Or understood what it meant to his heart?

Tyler glanced toward the house. "Savvy," he whispered. She had been a real part of him since the day Amanda had introduced them. Even when she had been away, there was a portion of his soul that held her close. But he'd never realized how much he loved her.

Worse was the knowledge that if he didn't change things between them soon, he would have to watch her walk away again.

"Savvy," he said again. There was a light on in the top new section of the house. A shadowy figure approached the window.

He felt hope come alive in his chest. Yes, he was a fool, but even fools could learn. With determination, he strode toward the house.

* * * * * * *

"Stop pulling me," Lexi whispered. "If I don't stay here I can't hear what they're saying."

"That's the point." Savvy tugged at Lexi's shirt again. Maybe if she tugged hard enough it would stretch enough to actually fit.

Lexi snorted. "Like you don't care."

"I don't," Savvy made herself say. "Tyler's been making a fool of himself over skinny, blonde women for years. I suppose he'll marry one someday. Why not her?"

"I don't like her," Lexi retorted.

Savvy laughed. "Since when do you have any say in it? Come on, let's explore the house."

"Well, they're hugging," Lexi reported, peeking out the crack she'd left in the door.

Firmly grabbing Lexi's arm, Savvy pulled her through the small living room to the equally modest kitchen. Immediately, she could see the changes in the house. The back wall of the kitchen had been cut away for a new family room. Stairs disappeared up one wall. "The new rooms have to be up there." Savvy made her way up the stairs, trying not to think too deeply about whatever drama was playing out in front of the house.

Sure enough, two nice-sized bedrooms waited for their approval. "This front bedroom has the small bed," Lexi said of the room located above the kitchen. "Must be mine." She lay down on the bed and sighed.

"Better see if it has sheets." Savvy found herself drawn toward the window, both wanting and not wanting to see what might be happening. She told herself it didn't matter, that she couldn't possibly hold any hopes of a relationship with Tyler, but she was relieved to see LaNae's car speed off into the night. When Tyler stared up at the window, Savvy slowly backed away.

"No sheets," Lexi reported, setting her backpack on the floor. "Just a bedspread."

"There's probably a linen closet somewhere." Savvy went into the hall. "Oh, look, they put in a bathroom up here. That's handy."

"It's almost like a separate apartment, except there's no kitchen." Lexi opened a cupboard. "Hey, I found some sheets. Oops, this one's too big. Probably for the big bed in the other room. Here are some smaller ones. Cool. I love this sky blue color."

Savvy smiled at her enthusiasm. "You go ahead and put them on, okay? I'll see if I can get the stuff from the van."

"Okay." Lexi went into her room and shut the door.

Savvy met Tyler coming up the stairs with both her suitcases, and she backed up to let him go by. He set them inside the door of the larger bedroom. "I see you found the new addition," he said.

His green eyes fixed on her face so intently, so appealingly, that Savvy knelt to open a suitcase—anything to distract his attention. "I had no idea they'd added this much."

He shrugged. "It was Cory's idea. She wanted to have a nice place to come home to, a place where EmJay could have her own room."

"It's nice."

They fell into silence. "Well," he said, "I guess I'll get the other things from the van."

"Uh, Tyler," Savvy said, following him into the hall as he headed for the stairs. "How'd it go with, uh, what's-her-face? I can talk to her if you want."

"What, and get me out of the hole I dug for myself?" His voice was mocking, but his expression was soft.

Savvy made no protest. Despite how much she loved Tyler, she knew too well his weaknesses. She'd called him a jerk several times in the past—and meant it. He'd been careless, blind, and insensitive way too often. But perhaps now he'd finally found a woman whom he loved enough to actually change his ways.

"Thanks for the offer," he said, "but I think I can handle it. I think I finally know what I want."

Savvy tried to feel happy for him. She'd always known he had a core of strength; he only had to find a way to tap it. "Good," she said. Turning from him, she went into the bedroom, blinking rapidly to hold back tears she thought she had already cried out years ago.

"Savvy?" He was in the hall, looking through the door at her.

Taking a calming breath, she faced him. "What?"

He crooked a finger, as though hesitant to enter the room. She took a step toward him, then another and another, until she stood in the doorway. He was grinning, the frustrating dimple in his right cheek looking more attractive than ever. She suddenly felt very nervous.

He shook his head, reached out his arms, and pulled her into a bear hug. Savvy resisted an instant, but his arms remained firm, and with a little sigh, she let herself relax into his embrace. Tears stung her eyes, and she closed them, breathing in his familiar scent, a mixture of cologne and laundry detergent. Her heart pounded a million beats per second. She wished he would hold her forever and was glad when he didn't let go immediately. Her knees felt like water, and she would look pretty silly falling to the floor in a mindless puddle.

Be strong, she warned herself, bringing to her mind a picture of the skinny LaNae. Hadn't he been hugging her a few minutes ago? Strength rushed through her—and just in time. Giving a final squeeze, Tyler drew away, leaving her feeling disoriented.

"I've been wanting to do that all night," he said, his voice low and husky. "Welcome home, Savvy. I'm glad you're back."

"It's good to be back." And it was—if she discounted the crazy emotions in her chest.

Again he gave her his dimpled smile. She wanted to reach out and trace the indentation with her finger. Instead, she crossed her hands over her stomach.

"You know," he said, "when I was fired at the paper, I kept thinking that I needed to talk to you about it all. I knew you would understand why I wrote what I did."

"What did you write?"

He leaned against the door frame. "Well, a certain politician's daughter has been making a few headlines with her escapades, the latest of which is an unwed pregnancy. She's only sixteen, and everyone knows that her parents basically let her do whatever she wants. I felt I should place the blame where it belonged—squarely on the parents. The dad especially. If he'd made and enforced rules, it might not have happened. And if he can't raise his own family in a respectable way, how on earth could he guide a whole group of people?"

Savvy nodded sympathetically. "I can certainly see why you wrote it, but do you really know he's so terrible? I mean, a lot of good parents have kids that go astray."

"Are you telling me I was wrong?" He grimaced slightly. "Though I guess that's highly possible. It seems I've been wrong about a lot of things lately."

Savvy didn't dare pursue that last statement. What other things had he been wrong about—going to California to get her? Not proposing to his girlfriend sooner?

"Not wrong exactly," she responded. "You're probably right about the mistakes that politician made. Hopefully, he's learned. But now that they're made, where does he go from here?" Savvy had been asking her-self that about Lexi since the moment she arrived on her doorstep.

Tyler blew out a sigh. "He loves her just as she is."

"Still trying, of course, to make up for his mistakes."

"Right."

"And just because you're a bad parent doesn't necessarily mean you're a bad political leader. I mean, it could mean that, but not always."

"I should have talked to the guy."

"Probably."

Tyler was quiet a moment, his head tilted. They could hear Lexi singing behind her shut door. "It is harder than I thought," he said, his voice low. "Yesterday, at the restaurant when you went to the restroom, I tried to make Lexi understand a few things that I'm not sure she has even a basic knowledge of. I hardly knew where to begin. She certainly has her own ideas, doesn't she?"

"I'll say." Savvy chuckled softly. "She made a plan and traveled to find me. I don't know if I would have had that much courage at her age."

Tyler's smile vanished. "Is it courage or fear? We have to find out what's going on."

"I know." Savvy felt warm at his concern. He really seemed to care.

Lexi's door opened and she came out into the hall. With a smile at her, Tyler pushed off from the wall. "Well, I'd better get the rest of your things. Then I'll check the animals, grab some stuff from my room, and head back to Kerrianne's."

Lexi's eyes lit up. "Can I see the animals?"

"Sure, come on."

Savvy watched the two of them go, her eyes falling on Lexi's calf where the long, ugly scar marred the otherwise smooth flesh. "Lexi," she called.

Lexi's head turned back toward her. "Yes?"

"How did you get that scar?" Savvy was almost afraid to ask but felt compelled.

With her head still turned, Lexi looked down at her leg. Bending, she ran a finger over the puckered flesh. She met Savvy's eyes. "My father made me . . ." She stopped, her shoulder twitching several times in rapid succession. "It was my fault."

"What do you mean?" Tyler asked. Savvy was glad he did. Her voice had suddenly deserted her.

"Nothing. I just got hurt." With that, Lexi turned and clumped past Tyler down the stairs.

Tyler made a noise in his throat. Savvy knew that he wanted to run after Lexi and force her to tell him what happened. She herself wanted to do the same thing.

And yet they couldn't.

Tyler met her eyes. "It's way harder than I thought, this teenager thing. Man, I think you're right. I made a big mistake with that article."

She gave him a sympathetic grin. He smiled back, causing her chest to tighten. *I'm in trouble,* she thought when he was gone. Her heart felt heavy. Her birth father was turning out to be worse than she'd ever expected, Lexi still wouldn't confide in her, and Tyler was only a friend. At the moment all she wanted was her *real* father, the man who had raised her, to enfold her in his arms and tell her everything would be all right.

Somehow things would have to work out with Lexi and Derek. But what could she do about Tyler? She could continue to bury herself in university life, teaching and earning her master's. She could let herself become serious with Chris. But what if Tyler moved to California?

Why, oh, why did that thought make her want to shout for joy?

Think of Chris, she told herself. Solid, dependable, handsome Chris. He was the one she should be thinking about. If she gave him more encouragement, she knew their relationship would progress quickly.

Shaking her head, Savvy went to make up her bed.

⋆⋆*⋆*

After finishing with the luggage, Tyler took Lexi to the especially ventilated room on the main floor where most of Mitch's animals had their permanent residence. He was glad Lexi was so enthusiastic because Savvy certainly wasn't fond of them—particularly of Lizzy Lizard. The first time she'd met his brother, Mitch, he'd had Lizzy in his pocket and somehow the creature had ended up tangled in Savvy's long hair. Tyler had been on his mission then, but the event was part of family legend now, and with each telling the store grew. In some versions, the lizard bit Savvy, in others Savvy's hair was chomped off. In another telling, Lizzy had made a mess that required special shampoo in order to remove the smell. This was Tyler's favorite version. Savvy had once told him that his preference showed his internal age, which she figured to be about seven.

Tyler showed Lexi how to feed the lizard, the frogs, and the fish. Then he let her hold a gerbil. "Saturday is cage-cleaning day," he said. "But I missed it, so it'll have to be done tomorrow."

"Eeeeww." Lexi wrinkled her nose. "I don't want to do that."

"Don't worry. I'll be back in the morning. But I'd love some help."

"Only if I don't have to touch their poop."

Tyler grinned. "You won't, I promise." He gave her the scout salute.

"Do you watch *Star Trek*?" she asked, puzzled.

"Yeah, all the time. Why?"

"I knew it. That hand thing you were doing is from *Star Trek*, right?"

Tyler groaned. "Uh, no. It's from Boy Scouts. Wasn't your brother a scout?"

"I don't know." Lexi shrugged. Her face had suddenly closed down again, as though she were trying to shut out memories and emotions.

"You miss your brother, don't you?" Tyler silently prided himself on the observation. Maybe he could get some information from her that would help them locate her family.

She nodded slowly. "I do miss him. He's the best brother in the world." Her chin lifted. "And you know what? He would never marry a twit like that girl who was here. Are you really going to marry her?"

Tyler blinked. *Okay, so much for getting information from her.* "Well, actually, no."

"You're not?"

"No. But she's not a twit. She's a very nice person. A good person."

Lexi rolled her eyes. "Then why aren't you marrying her?"

"Things change, that's all."

"I wish things would never change." Her expression now appeared old to Tyler—as if she were thirty instead of thirteen.

He put a hand on her shoulder. "I know it's sometimes hard, Lexi, when things change, but if they didn't, we might get a little bored, don't you think?"

It was the wrong thing to say. She jerked away from him. "No! I'd never be bored. Never! I don't care what you say. You don't know anything!" She shoved the gerbil at him and ran from the room.

Tyler blinked in amazement, his jaw dropping. For a long moment he stared at the empty doorway. Yep, this parenting thing was much harder than it looked. Lucky for him—and probably for her—he wasn't Lexi's parent.

⋆⋆⋆⋆⋆⋆

Savvy searched out Tyler in the animal room. "What happened?" She thumbed toward the ceiling. "Lexi ran past me in a huff. She was crying."

He shook his head, looking bewildered. "I'm not sure. She said something about how she wished things could always stay the same, and I told her it would get boring, and she freaked out."

"Oh, Tyler," Savvy said with a sigh. "You know she lost her mother in that plane accident. That was a pretty terrible change for her."

He groaned. "I'd better tell her I'm sorry."

They went upstairs, but Lexi was in her room with the door shut and the light out. "Lexi?" Savvy asked.

No answer.

Savvy opened the door enough for them to see Lexi in bed with the covers over her head. "Go away," Lexi muttered. "I want to sleep."

"Hey, Lexi, I'm sorry," Tyler said. "I didn't mean to make you sad."

Lexi didn't reply.

Savvy pulled Tyler back and shut the door. "We'd better leave her alone. I'm sure she'll feel better tomorrow."

Tyler nodded, but he looked miserable. "I'm sorry, Savvy."

"It's been a long day for all of us. Just go to Kerrianne's and rest, okay?"

"I'll see you tomorrow."

"What about your girlfriend? Maybe you shouldn't upset her any more. In a few days, things should be resolved with Lexi, or I might be able to convince her to go to my parents'. We won't have to stay here long."

Tyler took her face between his hands. His fingers felt firm against her skin, and his touch made her heart race. She told herself to pull away, but her traitorous body didn't obey. His eyes dug into hers. "LaNae and I broke up, Savvy. She's dating another guy. There's no reason you shouldn't stay here for as long as you need."

That was the last thing she wanted to hear. No LaNae meant the same old routine with Tyler. It meant spending time with him, falling for him again—only to have him pull away. *No way,* she thought. *I'm not going back there.* "But," she began, searching for the right words to tell him.

He shook his head, stopping her words as surely as if he had put a finger on her lips. His hands still cupped her cheeks gently. He was close, too close for Savvy's comfort. "It's okay," he said. Lowering his head, he kissed her lips, ever so briefly, and yet Savvy's heart thundered in her ears.

Tyler dropped his hand from her face. "I'll lock the door on my way out." He wouldn't meet her gaze.

"But," she began again. The word barely escaped her mouth, yet without enough force to be heard. A sense of urgency filled her. She had to tell him not to come over—that her heart wasn't strong enough yet. Of course, she couldn't say it like that, and no other words would come. She kept feeling his lips against hers, as soft as a whisper.

"Good-bye." With a wave, Tyler disappeared down the stairs.

She sat down on the stairs. Never in all their time together had Tyler kissed her lips. When they'd dated those six months, he'd come close, kissing her cheek or her hand but never her lips. Even with all his girlfriends, she knew he wasn't a man who kissed anyone lightly. What did it mean?

A single tear rolled down Savvy's cheek. She wouldn't let it mean anything. She couldn't.

Or could she?

Wiping away the tear with the back of her hand, Savvy stood and backtracked the few steps to Lexi's door and opened it quietly. She could hear soft sobs coming from the bed.

"Lexi?"

The sobs stopped, but as Savvy's eyes adjusted to the gloom, she could see that the bed covers were still shaking. *What should I do?* she wondered. If it were one of her sisters, Camille or Rosalie, the choice would be easy.

So what's the difference? she asked herself. *She's my sister all the same.*

"He's gone," she said.

No reply.

Walking to the bed, Savvy sat down and pulled back the blanket to expose Lexi's face. Lexi stiffened but didn't resist as Savvy lay next to her and put an arm over her consolingly.

"It's okay," she whispered. "I'm here. Your sister is here."

Chapter Fifteen

The sound of the doorbell sliced through Savvy's dream. She blinked open her eyes, feeling disoriented. *Where am I?* She was lying on the floor, her head on a pillow and a bedspread over her. She was still wearing her skirt from the previous night. Three of the walls around her were painted a light green with a dark green trim, and the farthest wall was papered with a scene from what looked like the Amazon jungle. Furnishings in the room included a small oak dresser, a bookshelf, a miniature table and chairs, and a toy chest.

Memories of the night before flooded her memory. This was EmJay's room, now being used by Lexi, and Savvy vaguely remembered moving to the floor when her sister had stopping crying and fallen asleep. Stretching, Savvy looked toward the single bed where Lexi was snoring softly. She looked younger than thirteen, despite the many earrings in her exposed ear. One hand rested on her check; the other had disappeared under her pillow. There were no signs of last night's tears.

Yawning, Savvy picked herself up stiffly from the floor and stumbled down the stairs. Someone was knocking on the door now. *Could it be Tyler?* She knew he wasn't likely to enter the house with his key if he thought they might be sleeping. Savvy's lips tingled where he had kissed her the night before, and she had to force down a wave of tenderness. She combed a hand twice through her hair before reminding herself that she didn't care to impress him.

"Hi, Savvy." A grinning Amanda Huntington Simmons stood on the porch, a small boy in her arms and two other children at her side.

"Amanda!" Savvy launched herself at her friend, hugging her around the bulk of the toddler. "And there's little Blakey. Oh, he's grown so much! Come to me, Blakey?" The toddler hid his face in his mother's shoulder. Savvy grinned. "Well, that's okay. I have these two to play with." She hunched down to greet Kevin and Mara.

"Can we go see the animals?" Kevin asked after greeting her.

Savvy looked at Amanda. "I don't know—can they?"

"Yes," she said with a nod. "Kevin knows what they can and cannot touch." With happy shouts the children ran down the hall. Little Blakey struggled from his mother's arms and went after them.

Savvy hugged Amanda again. "It's so good to see you!"

"I would have come over last night, but I was so sick I couldn't drag myself out to the car."

"I heard about your new baby. Congratulations!"

Amanda's green eyes sparkled, reminding Savvy acutely of Tyler. "We're terribly excited, especially Mara. She wants a sister."

"Of course she does." Savvy reached past Amanda and shut the door. "How did you know I was here?"

"I talked to Kerrianne and Tyler this morning and decided to drive out." She laughed and Savvy felt warmth spread through her.

"I've missed you so much," Savvy said.

"We've missed you." Amanda made a face. "And not just for us. Tyler's been different since you left. It's not that we didn't like LaNae, but we think you and Tyler—"

Savvy shook her head. "Don't go there. Tyler and I are friends. I did meet a guy, though, in California. I'm thinking I'd like to see where that relationship takes me."

"Really? What's he like?" Amanda grabbed her hands and pulled her two steps into the living room so they could sit on the old couch.

"Nice, smart, tall. Handsome, too. And he loves astronomy." She didn't add that with Chris she felt small and protected. She never worried if he thought she was too fat.

Amanda grinned. "That's all well and good. But does he make your heart race? Do your knees feel weak? Do you think about him all the time?"

Savvy swallowed hard. She'd felt the reactions Amanda described, though not in relation to Chris. Forcing a cheery laugh, she said, "Well, I haven't known him long, but I am always eager to see him. And"—she leaned forward conspiratorially—"he drives a blue convertible."

"Cool!" Amanda slung an arm around her shoulder and squeezed. "But don't forget the heart-racing stuff. That's important."

Before Amanda could question her further, Savvy stood. "You need to meet Lexi. I'm sure you've heard about her."

Amanda also came to her feet. "It's so amazing to get a new sister like that. I'm glad Tyler went down to help you out. I heard you went with him to Paula's." Her smile abruptly vanished.

"Uh-oh. Did something happen?"

"She called me Monday night. Said she was coming to visit soon and that she wanted to see the children more. She wanted to discuss sharing custody." Amanda stopped talking and held her hand tightly to her chest. "I tried to call Tyler right away when she called, but he didn't answer his phone. Just my luck. The one time I really need to talk to him, and it's the first time he ever loses his phone."

Savvy felt numb at Amanda's news. Paula was the children's mother, of course, but she wasn't a fit mother. Not yet. The pain in Amanda's eyes cut Savvy to the core of her being. "I'm so sorry, Amanda. I don't know what to say."

"I know Tyler tried his best, but . . ." Amanda took a deep breath, letting her hand drop. "Blake and I should have approached her ourselves. We shouldn't have been so afraid. Not that I blame Tyler, of course. I shouldn't have put him in that position."

"I know it doesn't help for me to say this," Savvy said, "but I'd do anything to help you. I saw Paula, and she's not ready to take care of those kids. I'm not sure she'll ever be ready."

Amanda heaved a sigh. "We've made an appointment with our lawyer for tomorrow morning, and we're praying about what to do. If Paula's serious, if she's really changed, then maybe she should be in their lives—even if it's only for supervised visits."

Savvy didn't know what to say to that. If she were in Amanda's place, she certainly wouldn't be so magnanimous. *Maybe that's what love means,* she thought. *Being willing to face the future with an open mind. To forgive the past.* But she didn't want to examine that last thought too closely. Her feelings for Tyler were still very much alive—but she wasn't falling into that trap again.

"Come on," she said, touching Amanda's arm. "Let's go meet Lexi. Be aware, she's had a different upraising from ours."

Amanda grinned. "I heard about the belly shirts. Better not let her wear one of those to church."

"Oh, that reminds me. She doesn't even have a skirt for church. Anything of mine'll be too big. Before I go shopping, I'd better see if Rosalie has anything nice that she's outgrown." Making a mental note to ask her mother later, Savvy led Amanda first to check on the children and then up the stairs to the new addition.

Savvy peeked into Lexi's room. She was awake now, though still lying down. "Good morning, sleepyhead," she said.

Lexi smiled and stretched her arms above her head. "Hi."

"There's someone here I'd like you to meet." Savvy glanced toward Amanda, who was in the hall out of Lexi's view. "She's my very best friend. Do you mind if we come in?"

Lexi shook her head, pushing herself into a seated position.

Savvy went to stand next to the bed. "This is Amanda."

"Hi, Lexi," Amanda said. "Nice to meet you."

"You, too." Lexi stared up at her. "Hey, you're Tyler's sister. You have the same green eyes."

"Yep. Guilty as charged."

Lexi nodded. "You must be the lady with the two kids whose mother is in California. She was really weird. I don't think you should let them go see her alone."

Amanda tried to smile, but it looked more like a grimace to Savvy. "She'll work things out," Savvy said smoothly. "Just like we will with your dad."

Lexi's brow furrowed. Savvy wondered if she remembered that she'd promised to tell the whereabouts of her father today. Lexi's next words showed she did. "But we barely got here. Can't I wait until tonight before I tell you where he is? Please? Pretty please with sugar on top? Tonight will still be Wednesday."

Savvy didn't have the heart to refuse. "Fine, tonight. Before bedtime," she said. "Meanwhile, we need to get up and get moved in." She pointed at Lexi's suitcase, which lay open under the window. "The dressers are empty and waiting. Even if we're only here a few days, it'll be worth unpacking. You didn't bring much."

Lexi groaned but pulled herself from the bed and walked toward the window. "Hey, wait!" All traces of reluctance fell from her face. "Tyler's here! I bet he's going to clean the animal cages." She flew across the room and disappeared.

"Lexi has a crush," Savvy explained.

Amanda grinned. "That's to be understood. My brother's quite the catch—if you get what I mean."

"Huh?" Savvy plastered an innocent expression onto her face. "I'd better go see that Lexi gets some breakfast." Forgetting her uncombed hair, Savvy went into the hall and down the stairs, where Tyler was already wrestling with Kevin and Mara in the living room. Again she remembered his whisper-soft kiss. Had he really said he was through with LaNae?

"Hi, Savvy." Tyler beamed a smile in her direction. The annoying dimple in his cheek seemed to mock her. "You're just in time to help us with the cages."

She shook her head. "Not a chance. I will, however, supervise from afar. From way afar."

So she did, enjoying a piece of toast with Amanda on the back patio swing. Kevin and Lexi helped Tyler clean the cages, while the smaller children romped on the grass, taking the opportunity whenever possible to stick their hands in the water from the hose Lexi was spraying into the gerbil aquariums.

Savvy felt peace steal over her. Whatever was or wasn't going on between her and Tyler, she loved being here with him. She loved the way he looked up at her every so often, smiling or gesturing for her to join him. If she were completely honest, she would admit that her heart raced when their eyes met. *Thank heaven the others are here, too,* she thought. Lexi and Amanda's presence kept her from losing perspective. This was all temporary. With Tyler it was always temporary.

Glancing at Amanda to make a comment, Savvy was startled into silence by the naked longing on her friend's face. At first Savvy thought she was watching her son, little Blakey, but her eyes followed first Kevin and then Mara as they roamed around the yard. Pity mixed with sadness filled Savvy's heart. She was not the only one who longed for something just out of reach.

Chapter Sixteen

H ow would you like to go to an activity tonight for kids your age?" Savvy said as they sat in the kitchen making an early dinner on Wednesday evening.

Lexi dropped the carrot she was peeling into the sink. Despite Savvy's agreement to give her until later that evening, Lexi kept expecting her to bring up their father. Was this some roundabout way of discovering the truth?

"You could wear one of those new skirts." After cleaning the animal cages, they had gone over to Savvy's parents' house, where her mother had been only too happy to pass on a bag of outgrown clothing. Lexi actually liked many of the items, though some needed adjusting.

"What kind of activity?" Lexi held her breath for the answer. All day she'd felt something terrible poised and waiting to happen. Was this it? *It's only a matter of time before something bad happens,* she thought. *Everything here is too good to be true.* She'd better not grow too comfortable.

"It's at the church. My brothers will be going. They're having a special program that's supposed to be really cool. Then they'll have refreshments. You might find some friends there." Savvy finished washing the lettuce and reached for Lexi's abandoned carrot.

Lexi slowly let out her breath. She'd really liked seeing the twins today, especially Forest, who was both handsome and funny. Her tongue had even loosened enough to say a few words to him. "Will you be there?" she asked.

Savvy nodded. "My mom's in charge of a class. I thought I'd help her out."

"Why do I have to wear a skirt?"

"Well, usually they don't dress up, but tonight is special."

"That sounds dumb." Lexi couldn't let Savvy think she was looking forward to it.

"It won't be."

"Well, okay, I guess." Lexi set down her peeler and began scooping the peelings into the trash. She stopped, remembering something. "Oh, wait. I told Tyler I'd go to a movie with him tonight. I practically begged him to take me." Disappointment flooded Lexi's body. If she went with Tyler she wouldn't see Forest, and he was as cute as Zeke— in a clean-cut sort of way.

"What?" Savvy's face flushed. "Why did you do that? Lexi, you have to realize that while you're staying with me, you can't make plans without asking permission."

"But I always make my own plans. Besides, I thought you'd come along." Lexi knew that was probably why Tyler had agreed to take her in the first place. He seemed to make any excuse to be close to Savvy. Lexi wondered what his girlfriend thought about that. Tyler had said he wasn't marrying LaNae, but that certainly didn't mean she'd be happy that he was getting so close to another woman.

"Well, don't worry. Tyler can take a raincheck." Savvy pulled on hotpads. "I think our chicken wraps are done. You are going to love these."

Later, Lexi dressed in her room, taking her sweet time. Savvy was waiting for her, but Lexi felt funny leaving without telling Tyler where they were going. What would he think of her when he arrived and she wasn't there? She put on dark brown eye shadow, drew a thick line of black around her eyes, and added two more coats of mascara. Lastly, she smoothed on brownish black lipstick. Well, she was ready, and there was no use in delaying further. She wanted to make a statement tonight, but she didn't want to miss the activity entirely.

She hurried downstairs and into the living room where Savvy was waiting.

"You've got to be kidding!" Savvy gaped at her in disbelief. "That top wouldn't fit a five-year-old. And what did you do to that beautiful skirt?"

Lexi looked down. The black skirt with the dark pink roses had reached down to her ankle, but a few snips of her scissors had brought it to five inches above her knee. "I cut it off."

"You what?" Savvy's voice rose to a screech.

Lexi felt herself cringing, but she forced herself to stand tall. "Hey, I made a hem. I brought a sewing kit with me. I'd think you'd be proud that I didn't need help."

Savvy bit her lip, her eyes running the length of Lexi's body. Lexi was suddenly aware that three inches of her stomach showed and that her belly ring glinted prominently in the light. *So what?* she thought. *This is what kids wear. I don't want to be out of place.*

Savvy took a deep breath, expelling it slowly. "Believe me, you won't feel comfortable dressed like that."

"I know what I'm doing." Lexi's shoulder ticked several times rapidly. "You want me to go to this activity; I'm going. But I want to go how I feel comfortable. That's all."

"And those stilettos are comfortable?"

Lexi looked down at her heels and shrugged.

"At least change the shirt."

Lexi thought about it. She guessed she could change into the new pink shirt Savvy had given her. It wasn't as tight as those most of the girls wore these days, but it was still stylish. "Fine," she agreed. "But that's all." She ran up the stairs.

When she came back down, Savvy led her to the front door with the air of someone who dreaded her destination. Lexi wobbled after her, feeling towering and powerful in her high heels.

They had reached the silver car when Tyler pulled up outside. "Hey," he said, jumping from his green Jeep. "Where're you going? The movie doesn't start for a half hour."

"We're not going to a movie," Savvy snapped. "We're going to a Mutual activity. In the future, I'd appreciate you telling me before you make plans with Lexi."

"Sorry. I thought she'd cleared it with you." Tyler looked intently at Savvy. "You look fabulous."

Lexi saw that Savvy had combed her hair smooth and changed into a blue shirt with a matching blue-and-white-flowered skirt that complemented her nice figure. Even Lexi thought she looked great. *But not in style—at least not my style.*

Savvy's irritation faded. "Thanks."

Lexi hated how they acted as if she weren't even there. "Let's go already," she said.

Tyler's face whipped toward her, starting noticeably as he took in her outfit. "You, uh, well. You look . . . uh . . . nice shirt. I like the color."

Lexi turned to Savvy triumphantly. "See? Tyler thinks I look fine."

"Fine?" Savvy shook her head as she looked at Tyler, hands on her hips. "Fine? Is that what you really think, Tyler? Would you let your child dress this way?"

He swallowed hard. "Not a chance." He looked sheepishly at Lexi. "Maybe you should change to another skirt."

"No! This is who I am. But I'm fine with staying home, if that's what you want." Lexi didn't want to look like a child—not even Tyler's child. And she was annoyed with the way he was going along with Savvy.

"You can go in your pajamas for all I care," Savvy said, fists clenching at her sides. "Come on."

Savvy went around to the driver's side of the car, but Tyler hurried up to her and grabbed her arm. "You're not really letting her go like that, are you?" he whispered urgently. His words stung Lexi, but she climbed inside the passenger door and pretended not to hear.

She sat blinking back tears in the front seat, glad she couldn't hear the rest of their conversation. What was wrong with her clothes? No, they weren't anything like what Savvy was wearing, or even like what Amber wore, but most kids she knew did dress this way.

They'll see, she said, folding her arms in her lap. *They'll have to admit I was right.*

Finally, Savvy slipped into her seat and started the engine. They drove away, leaving Tyler standing in the drive looking after them.

* * *

Everyone in the chapel was staring at her. Lexi could feel their eyes weighing on her, pressing against her until she could barely take a breath. She had felt this way before, on that other day when she'd heard about the plane crash. Air had been difficult to find then, too. There hadn't been enough to even cry—until later when she had heard her father's sobs coming through the heater vent in their house. His crying had somehow helped her find the air she needed. Of course, it had also made her cry. She'd crept to Brenton's room, crawled into his empty bed, and wept. The sheets had smelled like him, and she'd been comforted.

There was nothing similar about this situation, so why did the same symptoms come to mind? These were simply strangers who didn't like her. They weren't family members trapped in a burning plane. Well, all but Savvy. She was family, at least, plane or no.

Why didn't I listen to her? Savvy had been right about the skirt and shoes. Not only were they completely out of place but they were also uncomfortable. These kids weren't like the kids at school back home.

Not at all. She wished the ground could open wide enough for her to sink out of sight. Thank heaven Savvy had made her change her top. Even though the shirt was tighter than what most of the girls were wearing, it was at least long enough that she could pull her skirt down a bit to cover more of her thighs.

The first meeting didn't last long, but it was interminably painful to Lexi. After it was over, Lexi clutched at the fake plane ticket someone handed her, and then Savvy took her to a room full of girls and boys. Lexi was glad to see Savvy's twin brothers in the class. They stared at her like all the others had during the first meeting, but Gabe smiled.

"This is my sister, Lexi Roathe," Savvy told the woman teacher.

"Your sister?" The teacher's brow rose in surprise.

"My birth father's daughter," Savvy explained. This last bit made Lexi feel small and inconsequential.

"How nice," said the teacher, obviously puzzled.

Lexi bet she'd never heard that Savvy had a father other than the man who'd raised her. "It's good to have you, Lexi." The teacher smiled as though she meant it, but her eyes studiously avoided Lexi's skirt.

Unlike their teacher, the other kids stared at her. None of them wore black makeup, Lexi noticed. A few smiled, but Lexi couldn't smile back. Her attention was fixed on two girls in the back whose heads were together. She couldn't hear what they whispered, but she thought they looked at her and giggled. Lexi's face flamed. She wanted to cover herself with her hands and run out the door, but she felt Savvy's presence, her eyes as heavy on her as those of the girls in the back. So Lexi held her head up and walked into the classroom, taking the first open chair. No one sat next to her, not even Forest and Gabe, who sat in the back with the other boys.

Savvy smiled at her and left. The teacher began to talk, but Lexi didn't hear a word. She kept her face still, trying not to cry. Trying to breathe.

Mom, her heart cried silently.

Ten minutes were up, and they went on to the next station. This time someone sat by her because there weren't any empty chairs, and Lexi could almost imagine herself leaning over to the nice-looking girl and asking a question, maybe laughing at something with her. But the girl's eyes lingered on Lexi's short skirt and never reached her face. Lexi had no idea what the teacher said.

The next station was run by Savvy's mother. Lexi went farther back by the boys, and Gabe sat in the chair next to her. His smile gave her the courage to stay, though the two whispering girls darted looks at her that made her feel hot all over.

Lexi felt her shoulder jerking, but she couldn't stop the movement. *It's all Savvy's fault,* Lexi thought. *She shouldn't have made me come.* But that wasn't exactly true. Savvy had tried to warn her. In the end, she had allowed Lexi to exercise her agency.

Agency. What a peculiar concept. Savvy's mother was talking about agency now. For a few moments, Lexi forgot about the mocking stares as she listened. According to Brionney, Lexi was responsible for her choices. Not anyone else. Didn't that mean she shouldn't have to go to Minnesota if she didn't want to?

That night she was supposed to tell Savvy where her dad was living. What would happen then? Would Savvy take her home, glad to be rid of her, or would she call the police to put her father in jail? Lexi couldn't allow that. She swallowed hard and clenched her jaw. Somehow she had to make it through this day.

✦✧✦✧✦✧✦

"So how was it?" Savvy asked cheerfully as they climbed into the car.

Lexi gave her a dark stare. "I'm never going back."

Savvy backed out of the parking place but then let the car idle. "I'm sorry, Lexi." She heaved a long sigh. "I'm really, really sorry. I guess I shouldn't have let you go dressed like that. I'm new at this, remember? But, honestly, with that shirt, the outfit looks much better."

"It was horrible. Horrible!" Tears began in Lexi's eyes at her sister's attempted kindness. "Everybody was staring."

"Honey, it's because you were new. Everyone was curious, that's all."

Lexi knew Savvy was wrong. No one else had been wearing such a short skirt—or dark makeup. She'd been completely out of place. "They hated me! Not one person talked to me except Gabe and Forest."

"I promise, it'll be better next time."

"That's a lie," Lexi muttered.

Savvy shook her head. "I don't lie, Lexi." When Lexi didn't answer, Savvy started moving the car forward. "Look, we'll talk about this later. Why don't we go get some ice cream? I know a nice place that you'll love. Tyler and I used to go there all the time."

Lexi opened her mouth to tell Savvy she didn't want anything from her, but that was when the Suburban they were passing began to roll backwards, its rear lights glowing like two red eyes. "Sav—" she began, but she was too late.

There was a sickening crunch as the Suburban collided with Savvy's side of the car. Lexi screamed as the door and window buckled in, making contact with Savvy's head. She bounced off like some kind of plastic doll. The airbags deployed, stopping Savvy's movement almost immediately. Lexi could see blood seeping onto the white material.

"Savvy!" she screamed.

"I'm okay," Savvy murmured, but her eyes were unfocused and blood gushed from the hand she'd brought to her head.

People gathered around the car. Someone moved the Suburban, but Savvy's door wouldn't open. Lexi felt herself pulled out of the car. "Help her," she cried. "She's bleeding!"

Lexi couldn't believe this was happening. Savvy was her last chance, she was all she had left, and now—

"She'll be okay," a voice said beside her. Gabe.

Lexi tried to smile at him but couldn't. "I saw the car backing up, but I was too late to tell her."

"It was Cali. She was driving her mother's Suburban. She didn't look carefully." He pointed to a white-faced teen who was crying in her mother's arms.

They had extracted Savvy from the car now, and her mother was with her. "I'm all right," Savvy insisted. Then she swayed, nearly collapsing. Her mother and another woman carried her over to the grass. Someone had a towel pressed to Savvy's head. It seemed to Lexi there was a lot of blood.

"You're going to need stitches," a woman said, "but it's not as bad as it looks. Head wounds always bleed a lot."

"Should I call an ambulance?" someone asked.

"No, I'll take her," Savvy's mother said. "We're only a few minutes from the hospital. Just help me get her to the van."

"Wait." Savvy tugged at her mother's arm. "Where's Lexi? Lexi? Where are you?"

"She's here," Gabe said. Lexi flashed him a grateful smile.

Satisfied, Savvy let them take her to the car. Lexi didn't know what to do. Should she go with her?

"Come on," Gabe said.

Lexi and Gabe went with Savvy's mother to drive Savvy to the hospital, where she was taken in for stitches.

Lexi sat in a chair in the waiting room. She was having a hard time breathing again. Savvy was going to be okay, but what if she hadn't been? What if she'd been killed? Fear tumbled onto Lexi like a pile of dirt that threatened to bury her alive.

There were no guarantees. She'd learned that lesson only too well. In fact, given her bad luck, Savvy probably would die in the near future. Everyone connected with Lexi seemed to have some sort of taint.

Lexi could bear no more. When Gabe was getting a drink, she walked out of the hospital and into the night. She didn't know where she was going, but she knew she'd made a serious mistake searching out Savvy. Lexi didn't want to live with her anymore. She didn't want to start caring about her and then lose her. She simply couldn't.

Numbly, she walked down the sidewalk, losing first one shoe and then the other. Who cared? The stilettos were stupid anyway. Tears rolled out of her eyes. It was time for a new plan, but she didn't know what.

"Lexi!"

She looked over and saw Tyler coming toward her. She felt a rush of gratitude at seeing him.

"Are you okay?" he asked.

"Yeah. I didn't get hurt. Just Savvy." Her voice broke on Savvy's name, but he didn't appear to notice.

"I'm sorry."

"She called you?"

"She asked her mother to. Thought you might want to hang out with me for a while."

"Thanks."

"Shall we pull up some grass?"

Smiling despite herself, Lexi stepped onto the grass. She sat down, tugging her skirt down to cover her legs as much as possible. *Why did I ever cut this stupid skirt?* she thought. But it was too late now. Some things couldn't be fixed. She was glad it was dark outside.

"She's going to be fine, you know."

"I know."

"So did you have a nice time tonight?" He pulled out a piece of grass.

Lexi shrugged. "Not really."

They were quiet a long moment and then he said, "What about your dad? Did Savvy talk to him yet?"

"No."

He groaned. "You have to go back—you know that, don't you?"

Lexi's eyes met his. "Why?"

"Because you're a minor. And because problems don't go away until we face them."

An idea came to Lexi suddenly, like a bright light. "I could live with you." This new idea made a lot of sense. She and Tyler had a lot in common. They both loved words and books and gazing at puffy clouds in the sky. They both liked to fish and ski.

Did Savvy like those things, too?

It didn't matter, not if she were setting her sights on Tyler for a guardian. Now that she thought about it, his family was perfect. She would have grandparents, aunts and uncles, and cousins, but they wouldn't really be related, so if things didn't work out, or if someone died, it wouldn't make much difference. Her heart wouldn't have another hole.

"Live with me?" He studied her as though trying to gauge her motives. "Why would you think of that?"

"Your brother and sister took in kids, so why not you? I wouldn't be a lot of trouble." She leaned forward, pleading with her eyes. "I can cook, I can do laundry, and I know how to get myself to school. I'm never sick—well, almost never."

"What about your father?"

"He won't be a problem. Not when . . . well, I'll find a way."

"What about Savvy? Did you think of her?"

Lexi dropped her eyes to the ground. She couldn't tell him her real reason for not wanting to live with Savvy because he would tell her it was silly and that Savvy wasn't going to die. But how could he promise that? "She's going to make me go back."

"Not if your father's abusive. She'll help you—I promise you that."

"Do you always keep your promises?"

Tyler thought it a strange question from this young girl. "Yes," he said quietly. "I do my best."

"And Savvy?"

"Always."

Too bad Savvy couldn't promise her the one thing she wanted.

A few seconds passed in silence. "Come on. Let's go see what's happening," Tyler said. "They should be finished in there by now. I'll give you both a ride back to Sandy."

₊₊*₊*₊*

Later that night, Lexi lay in her bed curled in a tight ball. The youth activity had been awful and the accident even worse. After Tyler had driven them home, she'd run up to her room to change, wadding up the black skirt and throwing it under the bed. She would have chopped it to bits with her scissors, but she was too tired. At least Savvy hadn't tried to get her father's information from her.

When Savvy knocked at the door to ask if she wanted a snack since they'd eaten dinner so early, Lexi pretended to be asleep. She had fallen asleep for real soon after, and when she awoke it was dark. Her stomach grumbled from lack of food, but she didn't want to eat. She felt sick. The day's memories were too clear, too awful. Maybe she was dying from some terrible stomach disease. It was entirely possible.

Her face felt hot. She climbed from the bed and stood at the window, pushing it open to feel if there was a breeze. There was, and the cool air felt good against her burning skin. Her stomach grumbled again.

After a while, she tiptoed downstairs to the kitchen, stopping on the way to make sure Savvy's even breathing came from the other upstairs room. By the light weaving through the kitchen window above the sink, she could see Muffin lying by the back door, curled up close to the turtle. Lexi would have laughed at the sight, if she hadn't felt so despondent. The dog and turtle knew where they belonged better than she did.

In the kitchen she found leftover chicken wraps from dinner. By the light of the open refrigerator, she downed two cold, straight from the pan with her fingers. Her stomach felt almost immediately better. Maybe she wasn't dying after all.

Lexi wiped her hand on a rag in the sink and reached for the phone on the counter. She quickly dialed the number of the cell phone she'd left with Amber.

"Hello?" the answering voice was scarcely a whisper. "Why are you calling so late? My parents might hear! Never mind. I'm just glad you called."

A lump rose in Lexi's throat. She missed Amber dreadfully. Amber loved her no matter what she wore. "Is everything okay?" Lexi asked.

"So far. But I've been wondering—what about school? I bet they've been calling your house. It's only a matter of time before they talk to your dad or he gets a message."

Lexi hadn't thought of that. "You'll have to write a note for them."

"Me? Lex, I could get expelled! I thought you were coming back. What about your dad?"

"Not yet," Lexi said. Silent tears began down her cheeks. "I think I might have made a mistake. Maybe I don't belong here, either." As she said the words, she understood why she had felt the impending doom today and why she hadn't been able to breathe at church. Not because of the stares, not because of the whispering and giggles, but because of Savvy. Lexi was going to lose Savvy—she could feel it. No matter what, Savvy would be gone. It was only a matter of time. That was why she had to convince Tyler to let her stay with him.

Amber was quiet a long moment. "Are you okay, Lex? Maybe we should tell my mom. I bet she'd help. Please, Lex—you're scaring me."

"I'm fine." Lexi wiped the tears from her face. "But I'm not coming back. Not yet. I need to see if they really want me. I mean . . ." Lexi shut her eyes. She didn't know if she could bear to have come this far only to end up in Minnesota after all, away from all that she loved.

"I'm sorry," Amber said. "Really sorry. I'll do what I can, okay?"

"Thanks. You're the only person I can trust. I can't tell you how awful the kids here are." A creaking noise made Lexi fall silent, her heart thundering in her ears. But it was only the house settling, or maybe the dog by the door. "Well," she said. "I'd better go."

"Okay, but call again soon." With a soft click, Amber was gone.

Lexi replaced the phone. She felt alone in the dark kitchen. Not like last night when Savvy—her sister—had comforted her. What would it have been like to grow up with Savvy? Or what if Brenton had been a girl? What if he were with her now?

Tears were coming faster now. *Brenton,* she thought, *I need you.*

But he was far away. Too far for him to care anymore what she thought or felt. Her stomach began aching again.

With a little whine, Muffin left his place by the turtle. He stretched briefly, his mouth opening in a funny-looking yawn that brought a tiny smile to Lexi's face. He rubbed against her, inviting her to touch his fur, and Lexi scratched him vigorously. His eyes rolled in his head with doggy bliss.

"Okay, that's enough," she said at last, but he followed her upstairs and jumped into her bed as though he belonged. Lexi curled her hands in his fur and closed her eyes to sleep.

Chapter Seventeen

On Thursday, Tyler knocked on the front door of his brother's house in Sandy. He knew he should probably wait for Savvy to call, but he couldn't seem to stay away from her. He had been surprised and grateful that she had asked her mother to call him last night after the accident, even if it was only to be with Lexi—probably to make sure she didn't take off. Of course, there had been no time for private talk with Savvy, but at least he'd shown that he was willing to be there for her when she needed him.

But what excuse can I use for coming this morning? he thought. *Hmm, I could use their help with Kerrianne's fence, if they're not doing anything. That should keep Lexi out of trouble.*

Of course Savvy and Lexi probably had other, more important plans. Like talking to Savvy's birth father. Knowing her as he did, Tyler knew she had to be torn up inside about what might happen at that meeting. Well, he was going to be there for her, whether she liked it or not.

No one came to the door. After the third time ringing the doorbell, Tyler began to wonder where they were. Savvy didn't have a car since her mother's had to be repaired, so where could they be? Had one of her sisters come and picked her up? He couldn't just enter the house with his spare key. What if they were there but not dressed? Finally, he went around to the side gate and let himself into the backyard. Almost immediately he heard raised voices.

"You promised," Savvy was saying as he rounded the house. She wore jeans and a light pink top that emphasized the flushed color of her cheeks. "I gave you until yesterday, and that is long over."

"I changed my mind." Lexi's voice was sullen and angry. The girl was still in pajamas—oversized pants and a snug T-shirt.

"Well, I'm sorry, but you can't change your mind. We have to clear this up. It's already gone on too long. You can't keep running away."

"I'm not running away!"

"Oh, then why do you want all that money?"

"You promised you'd give it to me whenever I asked!"

"Lexi, talk to me!"

"My father is horrible!" Lexi shouted. "You don't know how he is. You don't know what he does to me!"

"Because you won't tell me! But if he's as horrible as you say, we have to tell someone."

"I want my money."

Savvy blew out a frustrated breath. "Fine, we'll go get it—right after we stop by the police station."

"You wouldn't!"

"You leave me no choice."

"Just give me my money. I'll go back home by myself."

Savvy frowned, her smooth forehead wrinkling. "So," she said, her voice deceptively calm, "you show up on my doorstep, turn my life upside down, not to mention all the hinting around about the way your father treats you, and now you expect that I'll just let you walk away and forget you ever existed?" She folded her arms over her chest, a sure sign she was sticking her ground. "I'm sorry, Lexi, but it's gone too far for that—way too far. I may not be what you expected, but like it or not, I'm your sister, and I care about you. I'm not letting you leave alone. You're only thirteen."

"I can take care of myself!" Lexi retorted. "Been doing it a long time before I met you."

"But you don't have to do it alone anymore."

"I don't need you!"

Tears filled Savvy's eyes, and her fists clenched tight at the ends of her folded arms. "I'm going to help you even if you don't want me to. Now," she said, her voice still measured but showing strain, "you'd better get dressed. We've got a long day ahead of us."

Lexi stalked to the door, mumbling under her breath. When she was gone, Savvy sat at the picnic table and put her head in her hands. Tyler approached with slow steps, clearing his throat softly to make her aware of his presence. She looked up, and for a brief, unguarded instant, Tyler saw that she was happy to see him. Then her mask fell back in place, the mask that severed him from her heart as surely as with a cleaver.

"Hi." Her voice was soft and her eyes bright, bluer than the sky above. "What's up?"

"Huh?" He was having a hard time hearing past the sudden pounding in his ears as his heart reacted to her closeness.

A smile played around her lips. "I said, 'what's up?' "

He gave a quick shake of his head. "I came to see how—I heard what happened with Lexi."

Savvy's smile vanished. "I don't know what I can do if she won't give me details about her father's whereabouts. I've been planning to take her to the police, but . . ." She chewed on her bottom lip and sighed. "I wish my father were home from Japan. He has connections. I wonder if I could hire someone to track Derek down."

"Your mother might have a number to reach your dad in Japan." Tyler sat down with her. "I have a few researching skills myself. It's one of the first things you learn as a reporter. Have you tried the Internet?"

She nodded. "I used your computer to do a general search on the white pages. Nothing so far that looks like it could match, though there are a few Roathes with an initial D. I guess I'll have to contact them all. I wish I knew who she'd called that first night in California."

"Has she tried to use the phone here?"

"No. We've been together most of the time. I can't imagine when she might have used it."

"That's too bad. If she had, we could check the phone records." As he said the words, something touched at the edges of his mind like a whisper he couldn't quite hear. He recognized it as belonging to his gut instinct, one that had led him to more than a few juicy stories. He let his mind trail after the whisper. It was almost clear . . .

"Well, I'm going around to the front," Savvy said, standing abruptly. "I've learned that Lexi tends to run away when things don't go her way." She brushed invisible dust from the legs of her jeans.

"Give me a few hours before you call your dad," he said, following her around the side of the house. "I'll see what I can do. In fact, I was thinking maybe you and Lexi could come over to Kerrianne's to help me paint. Or at least Lexi could help, if you don't want to. I could get her started and then can make a few calls to some friends, get a few searches going. Painting will keep her busy while I nose around a bit."

Savvy thought for a moment. "That'll work. I can help paint."

"Are you sure you're feeling up to it? With the stitches and all, I mean."

Her fingers went to her head, gingerly touching a spot just above her ear. Her long hair covered the four stitches, but he knew they were there. She gave a self-deprecating laugh. "Frankly, painting sounds a lot better than making a decision right now."

"Is that because of your birth father or Lexi?" he asked.

She shrugged delicately, but her step faltered.

"Tell me," he urged.

She shook her head. "It's stupid, really."

"Try me."

They had come to the front of the house, and she sat down on the steps while he stood on the walk, partially leaning on the wrought iron railing. "While I was growing up, I'd think of him," she said, her voice so low he had to strain to hear. "I wondered why he gave me up, why he didn't at least call. My mom tried to explain that he'd done it for me, but I didn't really believe her. I wanted to know what was so wrong with me that he couldn't love me, that he gave me away."

The familiar expression on her face was back, the one he'd recognized before but couldn't put a name to. Suddenly, he understood. Fear of rejection. She had been rejected by her birth father once before, and she feared it would happen again. Yet, the other night she'd had that same expression when there had only been the two of them—they hadn't even been discussing her father at the time. His mind traveled to the inevitable end of the trail. Perhaps it wasn't only her father's rejection she feared but Tyler's.

The realization was unthinkable. Never in a million years had he wanted to cause Savvy pain. *I've been so blind!* "I'm sorry," he said, though the words were less than adequate.

"I had the best father in the world," she replied. "Whatever else happened, Derek Roathe gave me that."

"No, I meant . . ." He squatted on the walk until his head was even with hers. "Okay, let's go back to him for a moment. He didn't reject you. It had nothing to do with you."

"It had *everything* to do with me. He and Mom got divorced, yes, but he didn't have to give *me* up. He chose to do that. He had other children who replaced me. I know I had a better life because of it—Lexi's proof of that—but it still hurts. And guess what? I don't know if I even want to see him after all these years." She let her eyes drop to his shoes. "Well, that's not exactly true. Honestly, I think maybe I'm glad this has all happened because deep down, I'm still curious about him. I hate it, but I am."

"That's natural. And I think it's something you have to follow through on. Especially now, for Lexi."

"Maybe you're right." She smiled, though she kept her gaze lowered.

He could see the shadow of her lashes on her cheeks, the moistness of her lips. He moved closer, and she looked up startled. Belatedly, Tyler realized he had been going to kiss her. What was he thinking? She was too vulnerable; even he could see that.

"What are you doing?" she whispered.

He drew away slowly, his eyes never leaving her face. "I'm sorry. I— I . . . Savvy, I know this is a difficult time for you, but I want you to know that I'm here for you. And after all this is over, I still want to be in your life—and not just as a friend."

She started at him as if he had suddenly grown horns.

"I'm serious," he added.

"Maybe today, right now." She shook her head, her eyes dark with emotion. "There was a time when I would have loved to hear you say that. But now, well, I love you, Tyler—but as a friend. That's all we have."

He heard her words loud and clear, but she wasn't looking at him like a friend. He knew her well enough to see that. She cared for him as much as she ever had, maybe more. The discovery made his heart soar. It made him want to shout in triumph. It made him want to weep. For the first time he understood why Mitch had started acting so strangely after he met Cory. Tyler had never felt this way before; it could only be love. But how to convince Savvy that this time he was for real?

"Savvy, I—"

Then he stopped. What if he was wrong. What if Savvy really *didn't* love him anymore? What if he had ruined things between them forever? In one brief, brilliant moment of understanding, everything was different. Now *he* was the one who risked rejection, *he* was the one whose heart might be broken. The thought of losing Savvy was almost more than he could bear.

"Savvy, please—"

The door opened behind her, cutting off whatever crazy words might have spilled from his lips. He was keenly disappointed.

"Ooooo!" Lexi glared at Savvy. Tyler heard her suitcase drop to the floor. Savvy gave Tyler an I-told-you-so glance.

"Ready, Lexi?" Tyler asked, deciding to defuse matters himself before they killed each other.

"For what?" the girl growled, though her gaze softened when it touched him.

"To help paint Kerrianne's fence." He smiled at her in what he hoped was a disarming manner. "Unless you'd like me to talk to your father first. You know, arrange a time for us to have a chat with him."

Lexi lifted her chin. "I am feeling quite bereft today," she said in what he knew was her best adult voice. "I don't want to paint *or* talk to my father."

Tyler stifled a grin, but Savvy said, "We're not asking, Lexi. We're telling."

Lexi placed her hands on her hips, glaring at them, looking every bit as intimidating as any woman did with her hands in that position. Tyler was ready to back down and offer to take her to a library instead to bone up on her vocabulary, but Savvy didn't seem in the least bothered by the hands-on-the-hips thing. "We're going," she said.

Tyler knew he had to support her as she had him, though doing so unnerved him when Lexi seemed so adamant. Maybe this was how the politician had felt with his daughter. Tyler began to feel a real pity for the man.

"Come on," he said. "I have some old painting clothes you two can borrow. I wouldn't want Lexi to ruin that outfit. Is that one of the shirts you bought for her, Savvy? I like it." Bypassing Savvy on the stairs, he led the way into the house, feeling two pairs of eyes digging into his back.

*★ *★ *★ *★*

At Kerrianne's Tyler began organizing the painting party. Kerrianne was watching Amanda's children while she was at her lawyer's, so there were a lot of so-called helpers. He and Kerrianne decided that the older children—Kevin, Misty, and Benjamin—would have their own brushes and sections of fence to paint. The younger children—Mara, Caleb, and Blakey—would be allowed to help one at a time with adult supervision.

Things were going smoothly, and Tyler was considering stealing into the house to make the calls he'd promised Savvy when Amanda arrived, looking businesslike in a fitted suit that hid all signs of her pregnancy. Blakey, who was "helping" his aunt paint at the moment, waved to his mother.

Tyler's cell phone rang. He glanced at the unfamiliar number. "I wonder who that is?" he murmured. The area code was from out of state, but he didn't think it was from the newspaper in California as he'd first hoped. "Hello?"

Silence.

"Is anyone there?" He thought he heard breathing on the other end of the line before whoever it was hung up.

The instinct he'd felt earlier at the house in Sandy kicked in. The call might have been a wrong number, but it might also mean something more. He checked his recent calls. Sure enough, his phone had placed a call to that same number the night it had supposedly gone missing.

He started toward the house. "Who was it?" Lexi asked, an odd look on her face that fueled his purpose. She had something to hide— something regarding his phone.

"Someone I have to call back," he said. "I'll be out in a minute."

Amanda followed him inside. "What's up?" she asked as Tyler found a pad of paper in the drawer beside Kerrianne's phone.

He sat at the kitchen table inside the sliding glass door. "I think Lexi took my phone and then pretended to find it."

"I knew it was odd when you said you lost your phone," Amanda said. "Mitch can never find his, but you've never misplaced yours." She opened the phone book and leaned over to look at the number he was writing on the paper.

"I can't believe she took it," Tyler said. "She looked so happy when she found it for me."

Amanda clicked her tongue. "Honey, you have a lot to learn about children. Look, I found the area codes." She pointed to a page in the phone book. "Let's see . . . it's in Colorado. I bet she lives there."

"Well, we've got a phone number." He grinned at his sister. "Why don't we use it?"

Amanda returned his grin. "Oh, let me, please!"

Tyler handed her his phone. If they were lucky, they might momentarily fool the person on the other end into giving them information.

"No, let's call from Kerrianne's phone." She set his phone on the table. "Whoever called knows you have the phone again and that Lexi won't be using it any time soon. But Lexi might call them from another phone, if the call was a signal of some sort."

"Good idea. And that way we can both be on the phone." Tyler ran upstairs for the portable extension in Kerrianne's bedroom. In less than a minute he was back at the table as Amanda dialed the number, her green eyes sparkling.

"Hello?" came a hesitant voice.

"Hi." Amanda's voice sounded breathy and remarkably young.

"Lex? Thank heaven! I'm sorry for calling on that phone, but I didn't know how else to reach you. I tried the other phone you called from, too, but no one answered. I thought if I called, you might be around and realize I was trying to reach you. Anyway, your dad was at the school today. He looked mad—furious! The police were there, too. They know, and they're looking for you. I left right away and came home." The girl's voice trembled. "Oh, Lex, it's only a matter of time before they come for me. Everyone knows we're best friends. They'll make me tell about the phone, and I'll get in trouble for the notes. My parents are going to kill me, simply kill me!" Her voice raised in a wail.

Tyler met Amanda's eyes. Her grin had faded at the earnest fear in the girl's voice. "Listen," she said, "everything is going to be okay."

"Hey, you're not Lex! How did you get this number? Oh, it must have been . . . I'm hanging up now."

"No!" The word burst from Tyler. He tried to remember the name of the friend Lexi had talked about. "Look, are you Amber? Do *not* hang up, young lady, or you will be in much deeper trouble than you already are!"

"We're trying to help," Amanda put in. "Please don't hang up. We're Lexi's friends and we care about her. We're going to work this out with her dad, I promise. That's what we're trying to do. You know Lexi's in over her head, don't you? Please let us help. If not, we'll have to call the police."

"Lexi's dad already did. He found out she was gone. I know he's coming here next. I'm going to hide until my mom gets home."

"Give us his number," Tyler urged. "Come on. I promise this is for the best. And we'll keep you out of it as much as possible."

"I don't care about that." The girl hesitated. "Well, not *only* that. I want Lex to be happy and safe. You won't let him take her to Minnesota? She'd really hate it there. She never liked those people, not since her mother . . ."

"The number?" Amanda reminded her gently.

"Okay." The girl was remarkably helpful after that first concession. She gave them not only Derek Roathe's number and address in Brighton, Colorado, but also the name of the junior high where Lexi attended school.

"So I guess now we have to call Derek." Tyler hefted the portable phone in his hand.

Amanda grimaced. "Don't look at me. I'm not going to be the one to tell this man we have his missing daughter. I have my own problems with birth parents."

Tyler searched her face. "That's right, you were at your attorney's this morning. I was going to ask you how it went when I got that call."

"Well, it all looks very good—in our favor, that is. Except . . ."

"Except what?"

She shut her eyes for several seconds. When she opened them, he was almost startled by the intensity of the tear-washed emerald color. "Blake and I've been praying . . . and we feel, well, that we're supposed to do nothing."

"Nothing?"

She nodded. "We've felt that before. Remember? Right before Savvy went on her mission and Paula came to visit. We were going to approach Paula then about custody, but in the end Blake couldn't bring himself to do it." She heaved a long sigh. "Doing nothing then was the right thing—look at the wonderful two years we've had with the kids. So as much as I want to do something now, to end all this uncertainty, I think the Lord wants us to wait."

"I see." Tyler shook his head. "You have a lot of faith, Manda. More than I do. You're an example to me, you know that?"

"Maybe." She snorted lightly and gave him a twisted grin. "Or maybe I'm just afraid."

"You? Never."

She pointed to the phone in his hand. "Nevertheless, you're making the call to Lexi's father."

"I'd better check with Savvy first."

"I'll wander out there and send her in. No use in getting Lexi suspicious."

"Stay out there and watch Lexi, okay? Just in case."

"Will do."

In a few minutes Savvy came in through the sliding door. He met her gaze and a bond as thick and strong as it ever had been sprang between them.

"You found him, didn't you?" she said.

Tyler nodded. Her face was speckled with paint, as were her hands, but he wished he could hold her. "I talked to her friend Amber. She says Derek found out Lexi wasn't at school and called the police."

She sighed. "Where's his number?"

"I'll call for you." He didn't like how pale her face was or how her hand clung to the top of the chair.

"I can do it." She sat at the table.

He admired her strength, but her expression made his heart squeeze. He wanted more than anything to protect her. "Savvy, please, let me break the news, let him blow off a little steam. Then I'll hand the phone to you."

After regarding him mutely for a few seconds, she nodded.

In the end neither of them had to talk to Derek Roathe. He didn't answer his phone. After checking with information for the number, Tyler called Lexi's junior high, thinking Derek might still be there with the police. Instead, he learned that Derek had collapsed at the school and been taken to the hospital in an ambulance.

Tyler's third call was to the Brighton police.

* * * * *

The painting crew was washing up for a lunch break when Tyler and Savvy opened the glass door and strode out onto the patio.

"Lexi, we need to talk to you." Savvy motioned her over.

Lexi approached them, her narrow face alert and waiting. Did she guess that they had important news? Savvy looked at Tyler, nodding for him to begin.

"I've been on the phone to your school in Colorado," he told Lexi.

She gasped. "How did you—"

"Never mind," Savvy said. "Tell her the rest."

Tyler kept his eyes on Lexi. "Apparently, learning that you've been gone for a week was too much of a shock for your dad. He collapsed at the school."

Lexi gasped. "Is he all right?" Tears welled up in her eyes as she stared at Tyler.

Savvy put an arm around Lexi. "Tyler talked to a detective. He said

Derek was all right but that the hospital was keeping him overnight for observation. He should be home tomorrow."

Tyler wanted to point out that Derek's hospitalization was Lexi's fault, but her face was so pale that he worried she might faint. The recriminating words died in his throat.

"We'll go see him as soon as possible," Savvy continued. Her face was full of the doubts about her birth father that she'd confessed to Tyler that morning, and his protective feeling grew stronger. He couldn't let her do this alone. She needed support. Would she accept his?

Lexi leaned into Savvy. "Okay," she said in a small and hollow voice. She looked defeated now, not a sign remaining of the truculent child who had argued with Savvy only a few hours before. The skin around her eyes was wet with tears.

Tyler was surprised to find his own vision moist, and he blinked his eyes behind his glasses, hoping no one noticed.

"What about your brother?" Savvy asked Lexi. "Should we call him?"

Lexi shook her head. "Dad will. Or somebody else—the hospital maybe. I don't have his number."

"Do you have any idea how long it will take to drive to Colorado?" Savvy asked Tyler. "What city did you say it was?"

"Brighton. It's north of Denver." Amanda came onto the patio and bent to wipe Blakey's hands with a damp rag. "But it shouldn't take long if you're flying. Blake can take you to the airport later tonight or tomorrow morning. Or, better yet, you can leave the Jeep at the airport."

"Jeep?" Savvy questioned at the same time Tyler said, "Flying's out."

Amanda smiled at them a moment, shaking her head. "Okay, no flying. I'm sure you have a reason." When no one rushed to explain Lexi's fear, she shrugged. "And I said Jeep, Savvy, because I just assumed Tyler would go with you, especially with your mother's car in the shop."

Savvy shook her head. "I can't expect—"

"Oh, would you go with us?" Lexi had come out of her trance and gazed at Tyler so hopefully that he forgave her everything.

"Sure." He grinned at Savvy. "See? I've been invited."

Savvy's smile made his stomach twist in knots. "Thanks, I appreciate it. Let's go tomorrow morning so we don't have to drive at night. And that way Derek will have time to leave the hospital before we barge in on him."

That she gave in so easily told Tyler how nervous she was to face her birth father.

"There, it's settled," Amanda clapped her hands, her expression smug.

But it was far from settled. Watching Savvy's face, Tyler knew she was fighting the urge to run. His fearless Savvy who had always faced her demons head on. He reached out to touch her shoulder, to let her know he was there, but she stepped away, averting her gaze and shaking her head slightly. She still didn't trust him. Not yet.

But you will, he vowed. *I'm in this for good—if you'll only let me. I promise.*

Chapter Eighteen

Savvy couldn't believe the direction her life was taking. Last week she'd been in California with no thoughts other than school and her relationship with Chris. And making sure she stayed over Tyler, of course. Now, less than a week later, she was living in uncertainty, a new sister shadowing her every move, and a father she'd never seen awaiting her arrival the next day—a father who had given her away. To complicate matters further, there was Tyler, acting like the romantic character he'd once played in her old, girlish dreams.

The phone rang, and Savvy went down to the kitchen to answer it. She hoped it was her father, who was due home from his business trip to Japan. "Hello?"

"Hey, Savvy, it's me."

Her first thought was Tyler, but it didn't sound quite like him. But who—"Chris! Hi."

"I called your parents' and your mother gave me your number. She mentioned you'd found Lexi's father but said to ask you for the details."

"We found him in Colorado. A city named Brighton."

"Never heard of it."

"Me neither. It's north of Denver. Take us about eight hours to drive there. We're leaving in the morning."

He made a sympathetic sound. "Not exactly the vacation with your family you envisioned."

"You can say that again." Yet, Lexi was family.

"Is there anything I can do?"

Savvy smiled at his willingness, at the tenderness in his voice. She could picture him as she'd seen him in her kitchen, his tall, muscled frame sprawled in the chair. She had no fear of not measuring up in his eyes; there was no history of watching from the sidelines as he dated other women while her heart was silently breaking. Whatever relationship she had with Chris would start now, with no past to obscure their future.

Thankfulness flooded her body. Chris was a choice person sent to her by a loving Father in Heaven. He knew her troubles and her worries about Tyler, and here was a way out, a way to a life free of the old insecurities—if she wanted it. And if not with Chris, then perhaps someone like him. Someone who was as solid and dependable as Chris but who made her heart race as much as Tyler did. The path was hers to choose.

But would there be someone out there she could love as much as she had loved Tyler? There had to be! And who was to say she couldn't grow to feel that way about Chris?

Savvy continued her conversation with Chris as she prepared the next day's snacks. She and Lexi had been shopping, but, unfortunately, neither had felt like eating, so they hadn't ended up with much. Maybe Tyler's pantry had something they could take with them. In a cupboard she discovered a huge three-pound bag of milk chocolate M&Ms. She grinned, knowing this would lift Lexi's spirits better than any medicine she could give her; she'd never met a child who didn't love the candies. And Tyler loved M&Ms more than he loved spaghetti—which was saying a lot.

She'd barely hung up the phone with Chris when the doorbell

rang. Her heart thumped inside her chest. *Oh, Tyler,* she thought. *Not tonight.* She was feeling too good to dredge up her feelings for him. Yes, they'd have to be faced but not until after tomorrow—after she discovered the truth about her birth father.

Taking a breath, she thrust open the door, hoping Lexi was so involved in her TV show in the family room that she wouldn't hear the bell. Her eyes widened. "Dad! Oh, you're home!" In the next minute she was enveloped in his strong arms. "I was waiting for you to call."

"Call? No way. I had to see my girl."

Happy tears pricked Savvy's eyes, and the burden on her soul lightened. She noticed his rumpled suit, how his dark hair looked mussed, and the tightening around his brown eyes that betrayed his exhaustion. "You came straight from the airport, didn't you?"

For answer, he hugged her again. Jesse Hergarter wasn't tall, but he was still a good head taller than Savvy. In his arms, with his familiar scent flooding over her, she felt like a little girl again—warm, protected, loved. And most importantly, wanted. "I've missed you so much," he murmured.

"Daddy," she whispered, her voice catching in her throat.

He held her tighter. "I know all about it. Your mom told me. I have to admit, it's been a big a shock for me, as I suspect it's been for you. I'd almost forgotten he existed. You're mine, you know that, right?"

"I know. I wish I didn't have to—"

"But you do, and I know that. What's more, I always knew that one day you would." He drew away, holding her out as though scanning her face for changes. "You've grown only more beautiful these past months, you know that? You remind me so much of your mother."

"Thanks, Dad."

"I mean it. But you look like him, too. Mostly in the shape of your eyes." Jesse seemed more weary as he said it, and a little sad. For the first time, Savvy noticed the white peppering his dark hair, gathering in bunches at his temples.

"Dad, about tomorrow . . ."

He shook his head. "Whatever he is to you, you're *my* little girl. Forever and ever. We are tied together through your mother, our memories, and our love."

Savvy blinked at the tears spilling from her eyes. "I know that. I really do." And suddenly she saw it. The sealing that binds families together for eternity was not so much a line as a web, branching out and connecting loved ones forever. She might be sealed to her mother and birth father, but she belonged to Jesse's family now through her mother.

"I must be the luckiest girl in the whole world," she said.

He chuckled. "Are you going to invite me in? I could sit for a while."

"Oh! I'm sorry." She backed into the room and shut the door behind him. "Let's sit, but not here. Come into the family room. You have to meet Lexi."

"I'm looking forward to it. But what's all this about Tyler going with you to Colorado? Your mother loves that boy, you know. If she were twenty years younger, she'd probably marry him herself."

"He's coming because Lexi wants him."

"I could go, if you want."

Savvy shook her head. "No. You'll have a lot of work to catch up on after being out of the office so long. Besides, this is something I need to do on my own." Tyler didn't count, of course. He was only a friend, not family.

"Okay, but remember, I'm only a phone call away."

"I'll remember." Savvy led him through the kitchen and into the family room. "Hey, Lexi, I have a surprise. This is my dad."

★ ★ ★ ★

Lexi's stomach felt as though she'd eaten too many sour grapes, but she'd scarcely picked at the pancakes Savvy had made that morning. She was too worried about what would happen in Colorado. The

Internet map they'd printed said they had eight hours before they arrived in Brighton. Eight hours before she would face her dad.

As she hefted her suitcase, she was torn between wanting to run away and wanting to hurry home to make sure he was all right. Was he really out of the hospital as the detective had said he would be? She hoped so. She even said a prayer like the ones she'd heard at Savvy's church. For some reason she felt better afterwards—not that she really gave much thought to that churchy stuff. Savvy had already talked her ears off enough about Joseph Smith and his vision. Lexi had her own Book of Mormon now, a gift from Tyler, who, she decided, probably bought the books by the case—if she could believe the stories he told about others he'd given books to.

Outside, Savvy was loading a suitcase into Tyler's Jeep. It struck Lexi how different Savvy looked from Jesse Hergarter, the man she'd called father all these years. Last night, Lexi had been surprised at his visit, but she immediately liked the man. Which was funny, since she'd been prepared to hate him. After all, he was the man who'd kept Savvy from searching for Lexi and for Savvy's real father. If he'd been a horrible father or even a smidgeon less attentive, maybe, just maybe, Savvy would have come looking for her instead of the other way around.

Meeting Jesse, Lexi understood why Savvy hadn't felt the need for another father; he was everything a father should be. He certainly wasn't a man who would throw his child away and give up. *Not in a million, trillion years*, she thought. A longing sprang up inside her chest. She wanted a father like that. A father who not only loved her but would *fight* for her. A father like she knew Tyler could be.

Living with Tyler continued to be Lexi's new plan. *It's my agency*, she thought. *My choice.* Somehow she had to convince Tyler that it was for the best—and her father.

On the drive to Colorado, Savvy let Lexi sit in the front seat, claiming she had some work to do. Lexi knew it couldn't be real work, because she'd overheard Savvy talking with her father about finishing everything for her upcoming classes.

Lexi was far more interested in Tyler's plans. She hoped he'd get that job in California, so she could at least see Savvy now and then—not that she *needed* to see her, or anything. She also had to make sure Tyler wiped that stupid look off his face whenever he gazed at Savvy. What was it with guys, anyway? It would put a serious crimp in Lexi's new plans if Savvy and Tyler somehow ended up together. Lexi didn't think she could prevent herself from loving Savvy too much if she had to live with her every day. Loving her too much and then somehow losing her.

Hmm, I'll have to do something about that, she thought to herself.

The trip was more pleasurable than Lexi expected. For long minutes she forgot her dread of the pending confrontation as she exchanged words with Tyler. She tried out *paradigm, perfidy,* and *pernicious* (she had reached the Ps in her dictionary), and he retaliated with *archetype, dissimulation,* and *injurious,* which, when she looked them up in her dictionary, were linked to her own words. She was amazed that he knew so many without having to study them out. The game was pure bliss.

That bliss ended abruptly when Savvy leaned forward with the directions in her hands. "We'll need to get off the freeway at the next exit. We're almost there."

* ★ * ★ * ★ *

Savvy didn't know what to expect in Brighton, and Lexi was characteristically silent about what they might find. In fact, Lexi seemed happy to sit in the front seat and pretend that they weren't heading for her home—and also that Savvy didn't exist. Savvy tried not to mind that her sister ignored her. After all, she'd made the choice to sit in the backseat where she wouldn't run the constant risk of meeting Tyler's intense green stare and wonder if he might try to kiss her again. Above all, she needed to keep a clear head. Her stomach was in a turmoil already, wondering how she would be received by the father who had given her away.

What was wrong with me? Surely she hadn't been too fat, too crabby, or too irritating.

Stop it, she told herself.

She looked ahead and saw Tyler staring at her, their eyes meeting in the rearview mirror, as they had far too many times today. His green eyes were bright and compelling, his expression tender. Had he ever looked at her that way before? Savvy stifled the urge to glance behind her to see if someone else was there—someone thinner, of course. Instead, she held his gaze as long as politeness demanded, gave him a half smile, and then stared out the window.

Savvy had pumped her mother for information about her birth father but had learned little more than she already knew. At the time her mother had been married to him, Derek Roathe was an advertising manager in the company where he worked, on the fast track to success. Now he probably owned a big house and expensive cars. Would he think she wanted money from him? She'd have to make sure he knew that her adoptive father was a successful businessman and that with only a few more classes, she would have her own degree and her future well in hand.

"Down there, at the end. Corner house." Lexi pointed, her face tight with what Savvy guessed was excitement layered with fear. The girl had worn black eyeliner today and navy blue eye shadow, and the colors made her face appear pale and fragile.

They pulled up at the house, one every bit as small as Tyler's brother's house in Sandy before the additions. The house matched its neighbors in size, though it possessed an air of abandonment the others on the block didn't share. The yellow siding was stained, and the tiny single garage gaped open, revealing a jumble of odds and ends that families accumulate over the years. The lawn was brown from lack of water, and the small front flowerbed was overgrown by weeds. The narrow porch had no railing, and the three cement stairs leading to the front door were flaking. By comparison, Savvy's parents' comfortable house was a mansion.

This certainly wasn't the house of a worldly man who had left his wife to pursue his own dreams. This was the home of a careless man who saw nothing in his future. The only thing of beauty was a huge shade tree that would offer protection from the hot summer sun but which also created a sense of darkness and gloom.

Biting her lip, Savvy followed Lexi up the walk, passing a nondescript brown sedan and a dull metal mailbox that looked like every other mailbox on the street. Lexi opened the door, and Savvy's step faltered. She would have stopped altogether if she hadn't felt Tyler's hand at the small of her back, gently propelling her forward. She could feel the heat of his touch through her shirt, though reason told her that was purely imagination. She wished she could grab his hand and hold it tightly.

If the house surprised her, Savvy was even more shocked by the wasted figure of the man seated in an easy chair by the front window. He was thin to the point of gauntness, his once-handsome features jutting from his face as though tacked on as an afterthought. His fingers curled over the padded arm rests and the jeans he wore couldn't mask the bony legs. Only the bright blue color of his sunken eyes resembled the charismatic man in the picture Savvy had brought with her from her mother's photo album. Pity rose in her chest. This was Derek Roathe, the man Lexi was afraid of? The man she herself had dreaded meeting? Savvy found it difficult to believe.

Derek had eyes only for Lexi. "Where have you been?" he said, turning off the TV with the remote.

She hung her head and remained silent. Somewhere in the house dinner was cooking, but the smell wasn't appetizing, increasing Savvy's queasy feeling at the pending confrontation.

"Come here." His voice was firm but not cruel.

Lexi dragged her feet across the gold-colored carpet to his chair, her body slightly hunched and her left shoulder jerking nervously.

"They tell me you haven't been to school at all except the first day."

His deep voice showed no trace of weakness. "That's a whole week you've missed. All the notes, all the lies—why, Lexi?"

Lexi's shoulder ticked again, a helpless, exaggerated movement noticeable to everyone in the room. An emotion flickered over the man's face, but Savvy didn't know him well enough to decipher what it might mean. Disgust? Anger? Compassion?

"I'm not going to Minnesota!" The words spilled from Lexi in a single burst.

Derek's jaw clenched, and he gave a sharp shake of his head. "Go to your room. We'll talk about this later . . . alone." He glanced at Tyler, who had stepped farther into the room than Savvy. Her hand was in his, though she didn't remember how that happened. The pressure of his fingers was reassuring, but with it also came an awareness of him that made her want to cry.

"Thanks for bringing my daughter home," Derek said. "I'll take it from here."

Savvy's heart felt like it was beating in her throat. She tried to step forward, but her feet wouldn't move. This wasn't how she envisioned the meeting. They would have introduced themselves properly. They would have exchanged small talk, maybe even touched briefly on the past before getting into the reasons Lexi ran away. But there was no chance of that now. Savvy made her voice as hard as his. "No," she said. "We're not leaving. We have to talk. There's been a few . . . accusations." She thought he might look at her then, but his gaze shifted back to Lexi.

"Accusations?"

"Like how she got that scar on her leg." Tyler shifted his weight to his other foot. Savvy was glad he didn't let go of her hand.

All the sharpness seemed to leak from his face. "Lexi," Derek said in a soft, sad voice, "what have you been telling them?"

Lexi stared at the carpet and didn't speak.

Shaking his head, Derek looked toward Savvy and Tyler. "There's nothing to tell. I can explain—" His voice broke off as his bright eyes rested on Savvy. "I, uh . . . Brionney?" He shook his head. "No, you must be . . ." He glanced at Lexi, who had lifted her eyes from the carpet. She gave a tiny nod, and Derek's head whipped back toward Savvy, all traces of color gone from his thin face.

"I'm sorry, sir," Tyler said. "I thought the detective would have told you who was bringing Lexi home. Or the hospital. I did call last night. They said you couldn't talk right then."

Derek dipped his head, acknowledging the comment, but his eyes didn't leave Savvy's face. "Savannah," he breathed. "You look just like your mother."

Hope blossomed in Savvy's heart. Maybe now this meeting would get back to how it should have been.

Then Derek's head began to shake back and forth, slowly at first and then more violently. He leapt to his feet. "No!" he said. "No!" His face flushed a deep red as he jabbed a finger toward the door. "Go! Leave now. I don't want you here! Go!"

Savvy's mouth gaped in shock. Of all the negative scenarios she had contemplated, his rejection of her had never been so forceful, so complete.

"But—" she began.

"Out!" He pointed at the door again. The veins in his neck bulged. "You're not wanted here."

With a shattered cry, Savvy opened the door, pulled her hand from Tyler's, and escaped from the house.

Chapter Nineteen

Tyler stood in front of the open door, stunned. He wanted more than anything to follow Savvy out of the house, but he worried also for Lexi's safety in the clutches of this apparently insane man. Flexing his hands, Tyler had to stop himself from cracking his fist into the man's face.

"Oh, Daddy, how could you!" Lexi glared at her father, tears rolling down her face. "Why did you do that? I can't believe it. I know you've wondered about her, but now you're driving her away—throwing her away. Oh, but you're good at that, aren't you!"

"Lexi, go to your room!"

"No! I won't, and you can't make me. I hate you, Daddy. I hate you!" With that, Lexi darted past Tyler and ran out the door. Tyler went after her onto the front porch, but she ran down the street past a group of children on bicycles and disappeared around a neighbor's house.

No use in following her at the moment, Tyler thought. *She knows her way around. She'll be safe.* Better that he concentrate on finding Savvy. But even as he made the decision, he spied Savvy sitting in the backseat of the Jeep. Relief washed through him. He should have known. She wasn't a child like Lexi who would run off irresponsibly.

Tyler turned back to Derek Roathe. The man's pale face was hard as rock, his eyes rimmed in iron. "I can handle my daughter," he said. "I don't need your help, and I don't need anyone checking up on me."

Hair rose on Tyler's neck at the man's audacity. "We're not leaving without Lexi," he retorted. "You aren't getting rid of us that easily. Savvy and I care about Lexi, and we're not about to allow you to treat her that way."

Derek's nostrils flared. "I'm doing the best I know how."

"Well, that's pretty lousy, if you ask me." Tyler was tempted to say more, but his heart was urging him to go to Savvy. Besides, he'd learned a lot in the past days with Lexi. Maybe everything wasn't as it appeared between Lexi and Derek. Shaking his head, Tyler turned to leave.

"Wait."

Blinking once in surprise, Tyler hesitated. "What?" he asked. "Haven't you hurt enough people today? Have you any idea what you did just now?" When the older man didn't respond, Tyler continued. "All her life, Savvy's wondered about you, wondered why you gave her up. Wondered why she never received so much as a card or letter. It's something that has affected her whole life, though she never let most people know how she felt. We've been friends for years, but only recently did she admit that she always suspected that you gave her away because something was wrong with her. And now she finally has the opportunity—and yes, courage—to face you, and you reject her. How dare you act this way! How dare you?" Tyler's vehemence was meant as much for himself as for Derek. How had he himself rejected Savvy all these years? "You're a blind, bitter fool," he added. *And so am I.*

With a snort of disgust, Tyler went down the steps. Quicker than he thought possible, the man caught up to him and touched his elbow. "Please," he said. All the gruffness was gone from his voice, replaced by pleading. "I didn't mean to hurt her. But she really shouldn't have come. She has no idea what she's getting into here. Believe me when I say it's better that she leaves. Better that she doesn't know me."

"Why?" Tyler shook off his hand. "Because it's easier for you? Are you afraid of what the police will find when we call them?"

"I've never abused my daughter. Never."

"You're telling this to the wrong person."

Derek glanced toward the Jeep, the muscles in his jaw flexing. If Tyler hadn't witnessed the man's callous behavior before, he might think that he was fighting tears. Derek swung his gaze back to Tyler. "Then you'll leave? Promise? I'll explain everything to your satisfaction, but then you take her away. Deal?"

Tyler considered for a moment. He knew Savvy wouldn't leave without Lexi, unless she was sure she'd be safe, but he also didn't like the risk of exposing Savvy further to Derek. He wanted to protect her. Yet ultimately, the choice would have to be Savvy's. "I'll talk to her," he said. "But no more theatrics. You explain—nicely. If not, I won't wait for any explanation. I'll call the police immediately."

"Okay then." Derek glanced again toward the Jeep. "You want me to talk to her now?"

Was it Tyler's imagination or was there an eagerness in his haggard face? "Not on your life," he said. "You go back inside and wait."

Derek nodded. He took the first step before asking, "What are you to her anyway? Her boyfriend?"

Tyler's heart lurched. He wanted to be so much more than that, if Savvy would only let him. He shook his head. "We're just friends."

The first signs of a smile touched Derek's face. "I see," he said. "I see."

Tyler knew he didn't see anything. He didn't know all the years between him and Savvy. Derek couldn't possibly understand his yearning for her now.

Without responding, Tyler stalked to the Jeep. Savvy didn't look up as he opened the door and climbed inside next to her. He reached out and to his relief, she let him pull her toward him.

With a little sigh, she rested her head on his chest as he leaned back against the seat. "I'm so sorry," he ventured. He smoothed her hair, as soft as silk against his fingers. Having her close this way was satisfying, and he wished it wasn't because she'd been hurt so deeply. But she had been, and if he was any kind of a friend, he wouldn't try to take advantage of the situation.

"I'm sorry," he said again.

She blinked, and a tear escaped her left eye and slid down her cheek, curving into the side of her lip. Gently, he touched the tear, rubbing it out as he wished he could erase her pain.

"For what it's worth," he started again, "we took him by surprise."

"He doesn't want me here." Her voice was calmer than he expected. Had his presence steadied her? He hoped so.

"Maybe not for the reasons you think."

She lifted her head and stared at him, her eyes luminous. "Because of Lexi?"

He shrugged. "I don't know. She didn't act afraid of him after you left. She yelled at him—said she hated him—and ran out the door. But *something's* not right here."

She drew away from him and leaned sideways into the back of the seat. "I'm not leaving without Lexi. Or until I know for sure. It doesn't matter what he feels for me."

But it did matter. Tyler could see how much it mattered.

"Don't look at me like that," she said.

"Like what?"

"Like I'm not worth anything because my own . . . my birth father doesn't want me."

He grabbed her hand, his eyes never leaving hers. "I'm not looking at you like that, Savvy. I'm looking at you and wondering how he could be so utterly stupid. You're beautiful, smart . . . funny . . . kind . . . thoughtful . . . loyal." Tears stung his eyes.

A faint smile came to her lips. "You forgot obedient, trustworthy, and thrifty."

"And brave and clean and reverent. Yes, you're all that. And that's amazing because you were never even a Boy Scout."

Savvy's smile grew wider. "Ah, you always did know just what to say to a girl."

"Not to you," he said.

"Yes, to me, too." Her lips pursed slightly, and Tyler knew she was thinking of the past. Didn't she see how he'd changed?

"Savvy, I—"

"I'm not leaving." She glanced up at the house, whose windows stared back at them blankly.

"I told him that. He wants to talk to you and explain."

She gave a soft snort. "He should have thought of that before."

"We surprised him, remember?"

Her brows drew together. "So you don't think we should call the police?"

"Not yet."

"What if Lexi doesn't come back?"

"She'll come back. She seemed genuinely worried about her father on the way here . . . and about you a few minutes ago."

"I don't know," she said, staring down the street. "She's pulling away from me. She's barely talked to me in the past two days—unless we're fighting. The only time she acted like she didn't hate me was right after we found out that Derek was in the hospital. I don't know what I did to make her turn on me."

"She's a kid, that's all. Maybe her father can shed some light on it."

Savvy glanced back at the house, and two more tears spilled from her eyes. "I'd thought . . . I'd hoped he'd . . . Oh, Tyler, I wish I never had to come."

"Me, too. But let's hear him out."

Nodding, Savvy ran her fingers under her eyes, wiping the tears.

"You missed a spot," he said. Reaching out, he rubbed a shiny place near her chin.

"Thanks." Her voice was low.

"Hey, I need the salt." He made a show of pretending to lick his thumb.

"I mean, for being here."

He sobered. "I meant what I said back in Utah. I want to be here for you. And after it's over I want—"

"Don't." She put a finger against his lips. "Please. Not now."

He had no choice but to acquiesce. "Come on, then." He opened the door and helped her out. She stopped briefly to look in the side mirror and rub her fingers under her eyes again. Then she fluffed her hair. Tyler didn't know why she bothered; she was already the most beautiful woman in the world.

"Remember," he said as they went up the walk, "he's an idiot. Okay? That's probably the reason Lexi ran away in the first place."

He took her hand, though she didn't ask him to. *Derek Roathe had better be nice,* he thought with determination. *Or I won't be.*

* * * * * *

When Derek Roathe let them in, there was no trace of anger in his face. Savvy couldn't believe this was the man who had so recently yelled at her to leave. *What is he playing at?* she wondered. If he thought she would be fooled by his abrupt attitude change, he would be surprised—again. She hadn't needed him while she was growing up, and she certainly didn't need his approval now.

"Come here, child," Derek said, settling back into his easy chair.

A warmth radiated from him. Savvy imagined it running over the gold carpet and up through her toes, legs, stomach, and chest until it erupted on her face. She was so hot that she couldn't breathe. She let go of Tyler's hand and stepped forward.

Derek's eyes ran over her face. "So you're Savannah."

"Yes, I'm Savannah. Or Savvy, rather."

"Savvy." He experimented with the word. "He gave you that name, your . . . your mother's husband. We always called you Savannah."

Savvy knew this was true—her dad had told her the story years ago. Now only her mother still called her Savannah.

Derek rubbed a thin hand over his prominent nose and down the side of his face. Savvy could see he wasn't as thin as she'd first assumed; muscles still rippled under the skin of his arm. "Come closer, would you?"

Savvy had paused several feet from him, but now she stepped over to the couch next to his chair and sat down. Her hand clutched the strap of her purse.

"So many years," Derek mumbled. "I never thought you'd—I never thought I'd see you again."

"Lexi came to me." Savvy glanced at Tyler, who walked to the end of the couch but didn't sit. His arms were folded over his chest. Savvy knew he was watching out for her, though it hardly seemed necessary. Derek might be a rude, grouchy old man, but she didn't think they were in danger. Of course, she could be wrong.

Derek narrowed his eyes. "I wonder how she found you."

"She says your son wrote to my mom some months ago and asked for the address," Savvy said. "But Mom said the only letter she got was supposedly from an old friend of mine. I think Brenton must have pretended to be that old friend and that Lexi got the address from him."

"Impossible." Derek shook his head. "If there was a letter to your mom, Lexi wrote it herself."

There was a sound from the hallway, and they all looked up. Savvy thought she caught a movement but couldn't be sure.

"Lexi? Is that you?" Derek looked at Savvy. "She must have sneaked back in through the kitchen. Come here, Lexi."

Lexi stepped out from the cover of the wall. Her body was hunched, looking forlorn and dejected, but her eyes were bright with curiosity. Savvy motioned with a slight hand movement and was pleased when Lexi came to sit by her.

"Tell them, Lexi. Who wrote that letter?"

Lexi quailed briefly under her father's stare. Then she lifted her chin in a way that had become familiar to Savvy. "So what if I did? I wanted to meet her. Brenton would have if . . . if . . ." She stopped. "You should have called her yourself, Daddy! She's your kid!"

Savvy's own feelings echoed Lexi's. She crossed her arms over her lap, experiencing a sudden chill.

Derek's nostrils flared. "Should?" He shook his head. "I gave up that right when I let her be adopted."

"And how could you *do* that?" Lexi jumped to her feet, hands curling into fists at her sides. "How could you just give her away? Didn't you love her?" The force with which she spoke hinted that there was more to her question than appeared on the surface.

But what? Savvy wondered.

Derek met Lexi's eyes. "Sometimes love doesn't mean what you think it does."

"Well, what about what *I* want?" Lexi demanded. "Savvy's my sister, and I have the right to know her. But I might never have even known I had a sister if I hadn't found those pictures last year! How fair is that?"

The muscles worked in Derek's jaw. "Life is not fair, Lexi. You should know that by now."

"For some people it is! Like with Savvy. Turns out that you giving her up was the best thing that ever happened to her. I met her new dad and guess what? He's really great. And you know why? Because he fought to get her as a daughter, didn't he? He didn't let you whisk her away from him."

"You know nothing about what happened!" Derek thundered, coming to his feet. He was as tall as Tyler, but his indignation made him seem taller, threatening. "Savvy's adoptive father was willing to do whatever it took to make her happy. That's love. Don't you see? He helped me understand that if I loved her I had to do what was best for her—as he was willing to do. And I knew for darn sure that she'd have a better life with them than being torn between homes. My second wife, Melinda, was no kind of a mother, and I wasn't ready to be a father." His voice softened, becoming almost pleading. A glance at Savvy made her understand that he was talking as much to her as to Lexi. "Imagine if Savvy'd had to grow up with that? I had to protect her—especially from Melinda. You saw what happened to Brenton over

217

the years he had to go to her house. He never knew where he belonged."

"Well, that makes two of us!" Lexi was flushed now. "But I guess that doesn't matter, does it? Soon, I'll just be another child you threw away." With that, Lexi turned and stalked from the room, every line of her thin body rigid with fury.

Savvy blinked as Lexi disappeared down the hallway. What had just happened here? Her father had affirmed what her mother had told her all along, that he had loved her—loved!—but had given her up to what he deemed a better life. And to be fair, it had been a very, very good one. She'd had wonderful parents who loved her and raised her in the gospel; she'd been surrounded by siblings and a loving extended family; she had been given every educational opportunity and endless support. The only thing that had been missing was him, and if she were truthful, her dreams of him, her yearning to know him, had leant a healthy romantic air to her otherwise ordinary life.

Derek looked down at her, his wiry body taut. "You have been happy, haven't you?" His voice was gruff, betraying deep emotion.

"Yes," she answered simply, honestly. "I've had the best life anyone could ever have." Then, lest she had hurt his feelings, she added, "But I have wanted to meet you."

He sat again in his easy chair, a wistful smile coming to his face. "I know you've had a happy life. I can tell by looking at you. You have a certain air." He shook his head. "And you are every bit as beautiful as your mother was when I married her."

"Thank you." Savvy felt stunned at this new side of him. What had caused him to be so awful when she'd first arrived?

Maybe it's all a show. Savvy wanted to push the thoughts aside, but how could she? He might be faking everything, and there were still many unanswered questions. Whatever happened, she wasn't ready to trust this man. "I should go check on Lexi," she said to cover her confusion.

Derek shook his head. "Give her time to calm down. She needs that, like her mother always did. Besides, there are things we should talk about before you leave. It'll be better if she's not here. We can start with that cut on her leg." His brusque manner was back, his emotions hidden.

Savvy sat up straighter on the couch. "She as much as told me you were responsible."

"In a way, I was." Derek cleared his throat, but that led to a coughing fit. "Sorry," he said when it eased. "I've been ill."

That's right, Savvy thought. *He collapsed when he was looking for Lexi.* But if he wasn't going to say it, neither would she.

"Let's see, where were we? Ah, yes. Last summer I sent Lexi away to camp. I admit that it was more for me than for her." He rubbed the side of his nose. "I, uh, needed some time to myself. She didn't want to go. We fought, but in the end, she went to please me. One day she was out hiking and she fell. Hurt her leg pretty badly. Had sixteen stitches and came home early. To be honest, I was glad. I'd missed her."

Savvy guessed he believed what he was saying, but that didn't mean she did. "She's been gone a whole week, Derek." Savvy stumbled over the unfamiliar use of his name, but she could hardly call him Dad. Jesse would always be her real dad. "Lexi was gone an entire week before you noticed. Frankly, I don't see how that could happen."

His frown sliced two deep lines in his cheeks. "I know it sounds bad, but you don't understand Lexi. In the summer, she's a busy kid, and when school starts, she's never around. She's in drama and choir and on the yearbook committee. She has a friend she's hardly ever without. She was supposed to be at her house from Thursday through the weekend. The kid is from a good family, and I like them to be together. It's better than hanging out with some of those kids nowadays. Especially this boy she likes—Zeke. She actually wanted to go out with him. At her age! I had to forbid her to see him.

"Then there were notes on the table in her handwriting, and her room looked like someone had been there. I knew she was mad at me, so as long as I knew where she was—or thought I did—I wasn't going to push it. When I got a message from the school, though, I went down to see what was going on. That's when I realized she wasn't just avoiding me. She'd taken off."

Derek paused, studying Savvy's expression. "You don't believe me, do you? Well, I'm telling the truth. There are other things that you know nothing about, and quite frankly, I'm not sure they're any of your business."

Savvy keep her gaze steady. "My sister is my business."

"I know what I'm doing." He lifted his chin exactly as Lexi had done, making Savvy almost want to smile.

"What about your son?" Tyler sat on the couch in the place Lexi had vacated, his knee brushing against Savvy's. "You said before he couldn't have written that letter to Savvy's mother. Why?"

Derek rubbed his chin for several long seconds without answering. Savvy wondered if she imagined the light draining from his eyes—blue eyes that reminded her so much of Lexi's . . . and her own. When he spoke, Savvy had to strain to hear the words. "Brenton is dead. He died in the same plane accident that took Lexi's mother five years ago."

Savvy's mouth opened in a silent gasp, followed quickly by a devastating sense of loss. Lexi's beloved, perfect brother was dead. Never in this lifetime would Savvy have the chance to meet her half brother. They wouldn't be able to compare life experiences. She would never be able to ask him how her father had been when he was younger and what kind of life he'd had with Derek and Melinda. She couldn't ask if he had known about her or what their father had told him about her adoption.

Tears filled her eyes. For a week she had looked forward to meeting Brenton, her desire further driven by Lexi's obvious worship of her big brother. She'd had no idea that she was five years too late.

But Derek's next words filled her with even more shock. "Lexi believes she's responsible for his death," he said. "And in a way, she's right."

Chapter Twenty

I'd no idea," Savvy said when she could speak again. "None at all. Lexi talks about him as if he were still alive."

Yet now as she thought about it, there had been clues—the way Lexi had come running to Savvy instead of to her beloved Brenton, how Lexi hadn't known what he was studying in college, how she occasionally talked about him in the past tense.

Was everything Lexi had led her to believe a lie?

"I'm sorry," Tyler said. Savvy wondered if he noticed the gray tinge that had come over Derek's face.

Savvy waited, hoping Derek would explain further but unable to ask it of him. At last he nodded, his eyes resting softly on her. "Losing your mother was the worst thing that ever happened to me. My second wife was a mistake, but it took me four years to learn that. When she left me, I wasn't surprised. I was even glad, though I swear I tried everything to keep us together for Brenton's sake."

"How old was he when you divorced?" Savvy asked, trying to organize a mental picture of her missing brother.

"Let's see, about three and a half by then. We had joint custody, but he was mostly with me. It was hard work, taking care of him, but it got easier after I met Juli—that's Lexi's mom. She was the best thing that had happened to me in a long time." He sighed and shook his head. "But I hadn't learned yet how important family was. I know, I know, I'm a slow learner. We'd been married nine years when Juli left one day when I was at work. Went to Minnesota where she has a sister. It was a real wakeup call."

"So you were separated?"

"Yes." He leaned forward. "But you have to understand, we were working things out. Losing her like that would have been the second worst thing in my life. I really loved Juli. Still do."

Savvy believed him. His feelings transformed his face, giving her a glimpse of the handsome man he'd once been. The man who had loved and wooed her mother.

"She took Lexi?" she prompted, wanting to hear more. With each passing moment, she felt she knew him better. Was his pain the reason he had reacted so violently to her appearance? Or did he still wish that she'd never come?

He shook his head. "No. She went alone. You might think that sounds bad, a woman leaving her children, but it was only a visit, at least in the beginning. Lexi had barely started third grade and loved her teacher. Brenton wasn't going to his mom's anymore—hadn't been for a few years. It was almost as if we were a regular family. Juli knew how much I loved the kids and how afraid I was to let them go." His gaze locked with Savvy's, and warmth spread through her. All at once she understood why he'd been reluctant to let Lexi and Brenton go. He'd already lost one child: Savvy.

"Besides," he added, "Juli was feeling confused, maybe battling depression. She needed to get away from everything for a while. I think that's why she ended up staying so long."

Savvy made herself ask, "So how long did she stay?"

"Well, two weeks turned into four weeks, and then several months." He tapped his fingers on the arm of his chair. "Not that I blame her. She needed to be sure what she wanted. And she called all the time and talked to the children—she was more a mother to Brenton than his own ever was. She found a job, got her act together, and after about six months came back to give me an ultimatum—counseling, more time at home, the whole bit, or she'd file for divorce. I agreed to everything." He shrugged. "I'd learned by then that I wasn't happy without her. None of us were."

"So that's when the plane went down?" Tyler asked. "On the way back?"

Derek shook his head. "No, later. She came here for a visit, and when she realized I was serious about us, she decided to go back to Minnesota, quit her job, get her things, and come back. She wanted to take Lexi with her, but Lexi was furious at her for leaving in the first place. She didn't see why Juli had to go back at all, and she threw a fit. Even at eight, that child could hold a grudge. But Brenton, he was easier. He loved Juli and wasn't afraid to show it. Other fifteen-year-olds were unhappy about having their mothers around, but he wasn't like that with Juli. He saw how hurt her feelings were when Lexi refused, so he went with her instead. They were there two weeks." Derek gave a brief laugh that held no mirth. "She even got baptized into the Church. That was one of the things she went back for, and one of the conditions of us getting back together—that I take her to church."

"She was a member?" Savvy couldn't hold back her surprise. "I didn't know that. Lexi never said."

"It was a long time ago." Derek leaned forward again, both feet flat on the carpet, elbows resting on his knees. "Juli heard the gospel from some missionaries her sister set her up with in Minnesota. Brenton was even baptized. Had to call me for permission. The next day they flew home. They never made it." The words seemed to come without effort, but Derek's eyes glistened with tears, and he was so pale Savvy worried that he might have a relapse of whatever had put him in the hospital.

"I'm so sorry," she whispered. Tentatively, she stretched out her hand toward him. Would he reject her again? Would he jab his finger at the door and order her to leave? It didn't matter. Savvy knew she had to try. As her hand touched the arm of his chair, his fingers wrapped around hers, holding on as though he would never let go.

"It could have been worse," Derek said in a low voice. "Lexi could have been with them."

"Thank heaven," Savvy breathed, biting her bottom lip to stop herself from crying.

Derek's mouth twitched upward at the comment, but he shook his head. "She's never forgotten that she was supposed to be on that plane instead of Brenton."

Savvy took a swift breath as she made the connection. So that was why Lexi blamed herself for her brother's death. "Oh, no."

Derek nodded. "It's been difficult for her, but I thought she was going to be all right. But now that she needs to go to Minnesota, it's all cropped up again."

"Why Minnesota if she's so set against it?" Tyler asked. Savvy glanced at him gratefully. Already she was too involved in this man's life to think objectively. "I mean, if it's a matter of jobs, you could find another one, right?"

Derek looked at Tyler for a few seconds without replying. Savvy had the feeling that the move to Minnesota was more important than a job. There was something more, something deeper. Something Lexi would rather run from than face.

Was it the same something that had caused Derek to react so violently at first seeing Savvy? For that there was still no explanation, though he showed no trace of that horrible man now. Savvy could almost believe it hadn't happened.

Whatever his reasons might be—for either the move or his actions—Derek didn't seem ready to share. His gaze dropped briefly to the armrest where he clutched Savvy's outstretched hand. He patted it softly before letting it go and rising to his feet. "Maybe you're right. Maybe I can find another solution. But right now I think it's time I check on Lexi. She's probably calmed down now. Afterward, maybe we can have dinner."

"I can make something." Savvy practically leapt to her feet. "Or better yet, we'll go out."

"How about take-out?" Tyler suggested, rising from the couch. He caught her gaze and looked purposefully at Derek. "We could pick up something while you talk to Lexi."

Savvy followed his gaze, studying the man who had helped give her life. What did Tyler want her to see? Derek looked much older than her own parents, more fragile, though his hair was still full and blond, and his grip strong. But he'd had a collapse and been in the hospital. Tyler was right; he was in no condition to go to a restaurant.

"Take-out sounds good," she offered. "What do you feel like?"

"Anything's fine." Derek appeared relieved.

"Lexi likes Mexican food. Is there a restaurant nearby?"

After Derek gave them directions, Savvy followed Tyler out to the Jeep. "Will she be okay, do you think?" she asked as he started the engine.

"Yeah. I think so." Tyler's smile was gone now, and he looked sad.

"What is it?" She bumped his elbow so he would look at her instead of the house.

He shook his head. "I don't know. It's just . . . Lexi has lied about so many, many things. Yet, now that I hear what happened, I understand why. I feel sorry for her."

"Me too. Living with all that guilt about her mother and Brenton. I can't imagine that." Again, Savvy felt a rush of remorse at never knowing her half brother. "At least it doesn't look like Derek's been physically abusing her."

"I don't think so either," Tyler agreed. "Still, she was gone a whole week, and he didn't know."

"I won't let that happen again." Savvy sat back in her seat. "Whether she admits it or not, she needs me." Then she added more quietly, "They both do."

"No way," Tyler said, shaking his head. "Not him. He doesn't need you. Savvy, you barely know this man. You can't let yourself get wrapped up in his life. You saw the way he yelled at you when we first got here. You heard what he said."

"I heard what he said about my adoption, too. I heard what he said about Lexi's mother. He loved her."

"Well, he made his choices; you can't change that."

"I know, but I can at least try to have a relationship with him. I want to. Tyler, I know he's not really my father anymore, but he is a part of me. Try to understand that."

"I do. Or at least I think I do. But how do you know he wants the same thing?"

"I—I guess I don't."

Tyler took both her hands, and Savvy felt a jolt of shock run up her arms. She tried to pull away, but he held on. "Look, Savvy, I didn't want to tell you, but before, when you were in here in the Jeep, he said he'd explain everything to us, but only if I promised to take you away afterward."

"Take me away?" Savvy's heart ached.

"Of course, whatever happens here is your choice. I'm not going to drag you away. Still, I don't think you should stay here."

"I'm not planning on staying—at least not long."

"Good. I don't want to see you throw away your dreams at the whim of an old man."

That made her smile, despite the ache in her heart. "He's not an old man. Goodness, Tyler. He can't be older than his late forties. Stop worrying. I'm thinking maybe I can help him and Lexi work out whatever problems they have, that's all." Even as she said it, Savvy wondered what would happen when everything was resolved. Would her relationship with Lexi be limited to e-mailing her in Minnesota? And what about Derek?

"Except . . ." She trailed off.

"What?"

She shrugged. "I don't know. I've sort of gotten used to having Lexi around. And I'm really worried about her. Guilt can eat you inside out."

"Tell me about it." The way he said it made her look at him more closely. His hair was longer than he usually wore it, and his eyes under his glasses were slightly bloodshot, though that was easily explained by their long drive. Other than that, he seemed like the old Tyler. Except maybe, just maybe, there was something different in those green eyes, something that made a shock go up her arms when he touched her hands.

"What do you know about guilt?" she asked.

He gave her an enigmatic stare. "Believe me, I know." With that he put the Jeep in gear and drove away.

*　*　*　*

Lexi waited in her bedroom on the edge of her twin bed. She knew he was coming; he always did when she made a scene. While her chest was still tight, there was also a strange sort of relief. The time had come to make her plea openly, to assert her agency. But would her father listen?

Her eyes wandered around the room. Her dresser, her fan-backed wicker chair, her cedar chest were all strewn with clothing, her various treasures, and schoolbooks—all much messier than she would have left it. *Amber must have had herself a good time,* Lexi thought with a smile.

Her favorite piece of furniture was the tall bookshelf, packed so full of books that she'd had to double up on some rows, making them stick out kind of funny. Her dad had been worried about it tipping over, so he'd attached it to the wall with fasteners.

Besides the mess, everything was the same as she'd left it, except smaller somehow. After being at Savvy's parents' house in American Fork and in the new room in Sandy, she'd realized that her house was rather small and rather dingy. Not that it mattered since she wasn't going to be here long. Long enough to pack and clear away a week's worth of dust.

Lexi's chest tightened almost unbearably. Maybe she was having a heart attack. Did teenagers even have heart attacks?

Her door opened at last, and her dad stood there regarding her gravely. He'd looked old and frail in the living room, but he was tall and strong now. "We need to talk, Pumpkin."

She nodded, allowing her heart to warm the tiniest bit at the sight of him. He was using her nickname. That was a good sign that he wasn't angry anymore. "Okay."

He sat in her wicker chair, moving a pair of faded jeans to the floor. He pulled the chair closer. "Well?"

She shrugged. He didn't normally ask her to start their conversations, so she wondered if he could tell that she was older than last week, well able to take care of herself. Maybe that would make all the difference.

"So you don't want to go to Minnesota," he said.

"I told you before. She's old. I don't want to go there."

"I'm old." He smiled, and it made Lexi mad.

"Not as old as she is," she retorted. "All her kids are gone. She's old and mean, and she hates me." Lexi looked down at her hands.

"Your aunt doesn't hate you. She's your mother's sister—why would she hate you? And you have to go there so she can take care of you."

"Did you tell Savvy and Tyler you're giving me away?" Lexi lifted her eyes to glare at him.

"I'm not giving you away!"

"Oh?" Lexi put on her best sarcastic face. "So you're going with me?"

He didn't reply, but there was a hurt in his eyes that reprimanded her more thoroughly than words ever could. Wishing she could take back the words, Lexi stood up from her bed and climbed onto his lap. He gave a little sigh and nestled his chin in her hair in the way that told her he loved her best and most of all. Tears stung her eyes. Why did it all have to be so complicated? She put her arms around his neck. "I love you, Daddy."

His arms tightened, making her feel warm and safe. "I love you too, Pumpkin."

Now's the time, she thought. Aloud she said, "I have a plan."

He choked out something that faintly resembled a laugh. "Oh? Like the one that took you to California?"

"Not that far." She took an arm from his neck and hit him on the shoulder.

"How far."

"Just to Utah. I want Tyler to take care of me."

"Tyler?"

Lexi smiled. She'd surprised him. "Tyler's family takes in orphaned children. Or abandoned ones," she added softly.

His lips tightened. "You are not abandoned."

Not yet, she thought.

"What about Savannah—Savvy?" he prompted.

Lexi knew he wanted to know why she didn't want to live with Savvy, but she purposely misunderstood his question. "You were rude when you yelled at her."

"I didn't want to drag her into all this. It's tough enough for us. But now that I've talked to her some, I think I might have reacted too quickly. She's . . . well, special. I can see why you brought her all this way."

Lexi rolled her eyes. "Actually, she brought me."

"Either way. I'm surprised you didn't ask to live with her."

She couldn't avoid the issue any longer. She had to convince him. "She's okay, but Tyler's used to a lot of kids. His family likes to have them around."

"So you think he'd make a good guardian?"

She nodded, daring to let herself hope. "If I have to go some-where"—she glanced at him to see if he might change his mind, but his jaw was firm—"then I'd rather go to Utah than to California where Savvy lives or to Minnesota." Of course, there still was the matter of getting Tyler to back off from Savvy, especially if he ended up moving to California, but she had an idea for that.

"I don't know, Lexi."

"At least try to get to know him. You'll see that I'm right."

"Well, I guess I can promise that much."

She hugged him hard. "Thanks, Daddy."

"No, thank you," he said. "I've wanted so much to . . ." His voice became hoarse, and he couldn't continue.

"To see what she was like?"

He nodded. "I've wondered about her. I thought I'd never get to see her. But here she is. Thanks to you." Lexi felt a gladness in her heart that she could do this much for him.

"Did you tell her?" she asked. "Then she'd understand why you yelled."

He swallowed hard as tears gathered in his eyes. "How could I? I could barely tell you."

For the first time Lexi caught a glimpse of what her father must be going through—and she felt frightened.

She hugged him hard. "It's going to be okay, Daddy. It's going to be okay."

If only she could believe her own words.

Chapter Twenty-One

Savvy was feeling anxious by the time she and Tyler returned to the house. What if things hadn't gone well between Lexi and Derek? What if Lexi had run away again? She scanned the street for any sign of her sister. But she saw only trees, cars, houses, and two children playing ball in a front yard.

Tyler put his hand on hers. "Relax, okay? It'll be all right."

"You know, I don't think Lexi would run away because her dad told her she couldn't date a boy or because she doesn't want to move. I mean, she'd understand if he had to move for his job. So what's the deal?"

He shrugged. "We'll get to the bottom of it."

"We have to help her. I promised." Savvy felt warmth at his support, yet at the same time she was leery. Tyler liked to solve problems. He liked to research things and discover secrets. But what happened when there were no more secrets?

Savvy pulled her hand out from under his. There was a question in his eyes, but she ignored it. She would have to deal with Tyler later. Now was for Lexi and their father. Father. The word didn't fit him—at least for herself. He would never really be her father. But maybe they could be friends.

Unless he ordered her to leave again.

Savvy sighed and tried not to think about it. Better to focus on the positive things she'd learned. "Come on," she said, exiting the Jeep.

Lexi answered their knock. "What took you so long?" she asked. "Dad and I loaded the dishwasher already and washed some plates." She wrinkled her nose. "He let things pile up while I was gone."

"You do dishes?" Tyler faked surprise. "I'll have to remember that."

"Of course I do dishes." Lexi grabbed the two large take-out bags from his hands. "Yum! I love Mexican."

Savvy arched a brow. "You're looking rather happy all of a sudden. Did your father decide not to move to Minnesota?"

Lexi's expression froze and her body slumped, as though a tremendous weight had dropped back onto her shoulders. Savvy felt immediately guilty. Why hadn't she left well enough alone?

"I'm glad to be home," Lexi said in a small voice. "That's all."

Savvy glanced past Lexi to be sure they couldn't be overheard. "So everything you said about your father—is it true? Or was it all to delay us from coming here?"

"It's not true," Lexi whispered. "Well, he won't let me hang out with Zeke and some of the others, and he doesn't really take care of the house . . . or me anymore. But that's not really his fault. He doesn't . . . you know . . . hurt me." Her shoulder ticked twice.

Frustration built inside Savvy's chest. "Then why say he did, Lexi? And what made you run away in the first place? Was it because you didn't want to move?" Savvy tried to hide her disappointment, but she knew Lexi could feel it by the way the girl avoided her gaze.

Lexi backed away from them, stumbling on the rug, and would have lost her balance if Tyler hadn't grabbed her arms. "Whoa. Are you okay, Lexi?"

She nodded, though she clutched the food bags to her chest as if she were in pain. "I'm sorry I lied about Daddy," she said with a sob.

"But I do have a reason. I mean . . . if only . . . I . . . oh!" She jerked from Tyler's grasp and darted away from them. They followed her to the kitchen where she tossed the food onto the table and flew into her father's arms, her tears bursting into full-fledged sobs.

"Lexi?" Savvy asked, approaching them. She reached out a hand, longing to touch her sister's hair and soothe her as Derek was doing. "I'm sorry if I upset you. I know you had a reason. Can't you tell me?"

Lexi's response was to bury her face into her father's chest. "Daddy," she whimpered.

Derek held onto Lexi as though she were the only thing keeping him standing. He looked firmly at Savvy, and for a moment she was sure he was going to shout at her to leave. Her heart pounded in her chest like a drum in a funeral march, each beat painfully slow and filled with torment.

Instead, he sighed, loud and long. "I need to tell you something, Savvy. I didn't want to, but it looks like I have no choice. There's no easy way to do it, so I guess I'll say it straight out." Derek swallowed hard, and in his arms Lexi gave another whimper. "I'm dying."

Savvy blinked several times, thinking at first she must have heard wrong. Dying? Well, so what?—everyone in the world was slowly heading toward the grave. But that wasn't what he meant, of course. Derek was *dying*. She saw it clearly now, as she had perhaps seen it all along.

"Of what?" she finally managed to ask, her stomach twisting. She reached out to the wall for support but instead found Tyler there. He held her fingers, rubbing them with his own.

"I have cardiomyopathy," Derek said. Savvy blinked again and waited for him to continue. "Basically, my heart is enlarged, and its ability to pump has diminished. The valves don't close properly, either, which causes leaks and other problems."

"When did you—how did you find out?" Tyler asked. He put an arm around Savvy, and she leaned back into him, afraid her knees would give out.

"I had a small stroke last year. Blood from my heart leaked and caused a clot. I was having other symptoms, too—couldn't catch my breath, tiring easily. I got over the stroke pretty well, but the rest . . ." He shrugged and his hand on Lexi's hair stopped moving.

"What about surgery?" Savvy asked.

Derek shook his head. "There's really nothing they can do for me. I have a pacemaker, I'm on the list for a heart transplant, but my liver's sort of wasted, so I'm not a great candidate for that. I've been having other symptoms that show I'm deteriorating more quickly than I'd hoped."

Lexi lifted her face and turned toward them, tears glistening on her cheeks and in her eyes. "Most people with this disease die within five years. Five years! And who knows how long it's been bad. He doesn't take care of himself."

"I do," Derek protested. "I'm trying, honey. I'm doing the diet, and I'm getting the rest. I stopped drinking."

Lexi shook her head and sniffed hard. "You say that, but you're sending me away to Minnesota so you can die. You're giving me away so you can die here all alone."

"Lexi!" Derek's voice was sharp but tinged by something else Savvy didn't recognize. Was it fear?

"It's true. You're giving me away, just like you did Savvy. I bet you wouldn't do that if I was Brenton. You're still mad at me—aren't you?—for making him die!"

"You didn't make him die!" Derek pulled her back toward him. "And as for Minnesota. I only want you to be taken care of."

"I want to be with you! I keep telling you, but you never listen!" Lexi's words were muffled as she again sobbed into her father's chest. Derek stood there, confusion on his face. Savvy didn't blame him. How could any of them comfort her? She'd already lost so much.

"Do they know what caused it?" Tyler asked.

Always the researcher, Savvy thought. Yet she found herself straining to hear the answer.

Relieved at the distraction, Derek looked at Tyler. "No. It can be hereditary, but mine's not. Drinking can be a factor, but it would have to be heavier drinking than I've done. My doctor thinks my condition was caused by a virus of some kind. No idea when."

"I wish it was hereditary," Lexi muttered. "Then I could get it."

"Aw, Pumpkin, you don't mean that." Derek rubbed a hand over her back. "Please, Lexi. What about your plan? I thought you were feeling better about everything."

Lexi sniffed again and didn't reply.

Derek sighed. "Look, the food is getting cold, and I'm starved."

"You can't have it." Lexi lifted her head and glared at him, eyes rimmed with red. "Remember? It's not low fat."

"I'll have something else, then. I was making some cracked wheat earlier. It might still be edible." He made a face as he glanced at a pot on one of the stove's back burners.

"I did get a low-fat order," Savvy offered. She'd bought it for herself, a vision of Tyler's skinny girlfriends in her mind, but she wouldn't mind sacrificing it for Derek. In fact, she'd lost her appetite altogether.

"See, Pumpkin? Come on." Derek led Lexi to the table. He sank into a seat wearily. Savvy noticed how gray he appeared and how his chest rose with effort for each breath.

He was dying. Even as she looked at him, he was dying.

It explained a lot—his reaction when he first saw her that evening, why he planned to take Lexi to Minnesota, and most of all why Lexi ran away.

Poor, Lexi, she thought. *I want to run away, too.*

Of course, she didn't. Taking a deep breath, she walked to the table and sat down.

Chapter Twenty-Two

The food disappeared, though Savvy didn't remember eating any of it. *How odd,* she thought. *I'm sitting here calmly eating at this small table when I've just learned my birth father is dying.* Wasn't there something more important they should be doing? Shouldn't they be working out their relationship or maybe discussing plans for Lexi? But the food continued to disappear, Lexi downing most of it.

When the shrill ring of the phone burst through the silence, Lexi leapt to her feet and dived to the counter. "Hello?" she asked. Immediately, a smile spread across her face. "Amber! Yeah, I'm home. No, that's okay. You did the right thing. Uh-huh." She walked to the back door, stepping outside for privacy, but in a few minutes she was back again.

"No, I'll come and see you. Let me ask." She covered the bottom of the receiver. "Dad, can I go to Amber's, please? I really need to see her."

"Not now, Pumpkin."

"Please, Daddy?"

Derek's face softened as he regarded Lexi's pleading eyes. Her face was flushed and her blue eyes bright. "It's a long way," he said, and Savvy could tell he was weakening.

"I'll drive her," Tyler offered. "And bring her back." He cast a glance at Savvy that was all too obvious. She knew exactly why he volunteered—to make sure Lexi didn't disappear again. Or was he trying to give Savvy time alone with Derek?

"Okay, then." Derek nodded. As Lexi spoke excitedly into the phone, his gaze shifted to Savvy. "You going, too?"

"No. I'll stay here with you." Then she hurried to add, "If that's okay."

He nodded. *He knows,* Savvy thought. *He knows there are things we need to say. He knows I'm afraid to leave him because there may not be another time.* The shock of his announcement had begun to wear off, and now Savvy felt like weeping. How could this be happening? Maybe it was all a dream, and she'd wake up in California, a day of school and teaching ahead of her.

"Are you sure?" Tyler looked at her with concern clearly etched on his features.

Savvy shook her head. "No. I really want to stay here."

"But—"

Derek snorted. "I'm not going to hurt her or anything."

"Of course he won't!" Lexi appeared shocked at the suggestion.

Tyler frowned at Lexi, pushing up his glasses. "Well, if you remember, he wasn't exactly welcoming when we arrived."

Savvy wished he'd stop talking and leave. "I'll be okay. If he acts up, I'll wrestle him to the ground." She tried to smile with the words, but Derek's pallor and his apparent weakness made the words hit too close to home.

"He's not going to do anything." Lexi kissed her father's cheek and then tugged on Tyler's hand. "Come on. Amber's waiting."

Tyler's eyes didn't leave hers as Lexi dragged him from the room.

"Kind of overprotective, isn't he?" Derek commented.

She shrugged. "He likes to be in control."

"Well. Where do we go from here?" Derek folded his arms on the table and studied her face. Savvy had the acute feeling that he was trying to see the baby she'd once been. Her eyes ran over his face as well. He was foreign to her, a complete stranger. And yet his eyes, his mannerisms . . . somehow she knew him. Too late, of course. There would be no future in which to build any sort of a relationship.

Savvy felt a swift and sudden wave of gratitude that her *real* father, Jesse Hergarter, was back in Utah, strong and healthy. What would she do if she ever lost him? *No wonder Lexi's such a mess.* Savvy's compassion for her sister increased. *How horrible for her to lose everyone.*

No, not everyone, Savvy thought. *I'm here now.*

Derek began gathering up the discarded food wrappers, and Savvy jumped up to help. "Sit down and relax," she ordered. "Let me do it."

He smiled. "I'm not going to drop dead this moment."

She didn't return the smile. "But you could, couldn't you?" she said softly. If she understood the disease correctly, that was exactly what would happen—exactly what could have happened yesterday at Lexi's school. Savvy might have never had the opportunity to meet him.

Like Brenton. Her throat felt painfully dry.

Derek shook his head, eyes holding hers. "Just like your mother. She always called things like they were. Tell me, how is she? Is she happy? I mean, really happy?"

"Yes. She is. Very." Savvy gathered the used plates into a stack as she spoke. "She has four other children, you know. I have two more sisters and twin brothers a year older than Lexi."

"Ah, good. Brionney always wanted twins. She used to date this French guy who was a twin."

"Yeah, she told me." Savvy threw away the napkins and rinsed the plates in the sink. Derek simply sat, watching her.

"I never thought we'd have this chance," he said when she returned to the table and sat down. "I know it was ultimately my choice, everything that happened then, but I've sometimes wondered what would have happened if I hadn't made that choice." His voice had grown gravelly, and he cleared his throat, but the hoarseness continued. "You can't know how many, many times I've thought that. I was a jerk to your mother, and I knew Melinda was a mistake. But there was a point when I knew there was no going back. Believe me, I sure wanted to." He scrubbed a hand over his scalp. "Oh, how I wanted to. But later there was Brenton, and if not for Melinda, he wouldn't have existed. After losing you, I couldn't imagine life without him."

"And then he died." Tears pricked Savvy eyes.

Derek paused for a moment, his face frozen, as though he could spare himself the pain by not moving. "Yes. But before he died, Juli came along. When she gave me Lexi, I felt I'd finally been forgiven for my sins toward you and your mother."

"But you never came back to the Church."

He shook his head. "I should have. I would have. But at the time I was still too prideful. Then after the accident, it was all we could do to live one day at a time, much less think about eternity."

Savvy felt a deep sadness at his words. Didn't he understand that while the gospel didn't prevent bad things, it did help a person make sense of them?

"Then I got sick with this disease . . ." He held his hands wide as though to show her his wasted body. "It was like the accident all over again. Only worse because this time there would be no one to take care of my little girl."

"And on top of everything, I show up."

He nodded, eyes filled with tears. "Until today I felt nothing but despair. There was nothing left inside me but pain, and seeing you after all these years, knowing I have no more time, knowing I'd have to tell you—it would be like losing you all over again. I didn't want to face that. I didn't want *either* of us to face that."

It was painful—he was right about that, but Savvy wouldn't change her decision to meet him. "Do you still want me to leave?" she asked, the question coming without her volition.

He shook his head. "I'm starting to believe the Lord sent Lexi to you. I'm glad you came. Please forgive me for how I acted earlier." His face crumpling, he covered his mouth with a hand, a hand that was far too thin for a man his size. For long moments, he struggled for control. Finally, he dropped his hand. "I'm sorry. So very sorry. I have no excuse except that I'm an idiot."

And that you're dying, she thought, forgiving him everything.

"I have only one wish now," he added, "and that's to see my two girls happy and taken care of."

"We are—will be."

Silence fell for a minute, and then he said, "Well, maybe I have another wish. I'd like to see Juli and Brenton again. I have repenting to do, but I've done a lot already."

Savvy could believe that. There was nothing like facing death to put things in perspective. But there was one thing she didn't understand. "You're not planning to move to Minnesota. You're sending Lexi away. Why?"

"My condition is worsening." He looked away from her as he spoke, his eyes lingering on the curtained kitchen window. "I can't work. I spend most of my days sleeping or watching TV. On days I have to leave the house, I collapse the minute I get home. I can't take care of Lexi, and she certainly shouldn't waste her life taking care of me. I don't want her to see me waste away. Or worse."

"Worse?" Savvy couldn't imagine anything worse, except being sent away.

His gaze swung to meet hers, his blue eyes piercing. "Can you imagine it? Her coming home from school one day and finding me lying in here dead? Who would be there to help her face that? No. Sending her to live with her aunt in Minnesota is for her own good."

More pieces of the puzzle clicked into place for Savvy. This was why Lexi had reacted so strongly to Paula giving up her children to Amanda without a fight. *She should fight for them,* she'd said. *She should be there to make sure they're okay. She shouldn't give up.* Now it all made sense.

"You're right," Savvy said slowly, "but you're also wrong. Really wrong. You can't send her away."

He studied her. "Oh? Give me one good reason."

"Me," she said. "I'm proof that sending her away is worse than letting her stay."

"Why?" His voice was scarcely a whisper.

She sat up a little straighter. "I didn't lie about having a good life, but there was one thing that could have made it better. One thing that only you could have done." Her eyes filled again with unbidden tears. "A phone call, a visit, a call, a card, a note, anything to tell me you might be thinking about me. That you"—she swallowed the impossible lump that had risen in her throat—"you cared. I always wondered, you know. Worried what was so wrong with me that you had to give me away."

"But—"

She held up a hand to still his words. "Oh, I know it wasn't me. Logically. But a little voice, the child part of me, still wondered. I mean, it wasn't as though you and Mom were teenagers. You were married; you lived together with me. You'd seen and held me." She shook her head. "Regardless, sending Lexi away . . . you simply can't do it. It's not like giving a baby to a good family, a baby who will never remember you. She's a teenager, and you're her whole world. She needs everything you can offer for as long as you're here."

"That might not be long."

"It doesn't matter." Savvy lifted both shoulders for emphasis. She had to work to make her voice remain steady. "And you know what? I think she's right. You *are* giving up. You are abandoning her."

Again the silence, but this time so deep that it felt smothering. "What else can I do?" he said. "I don't want her to see me this way. She's suffered enough."

Savvy shook her head, folding her arms between her stomach and the table. "That's not for you to say. It's *her* choice. She's the one who has to live with the fact that you sent her away. She's the one who'll have to imagine you dying here all alone. And believe me, imagination can be much worse than reality—I know that from all the years I've wondered about you. Lexi'll dream up all sorts of horrors and feel that she failed you by not being here at the end. Please, Derek, think about it. She's lost everyone else. She blames herself for Brenton's death. How can you heap more guilt onto the terrible load she's already carrying?"

Derek put his elbows on the table and rested his chin heavily on his hands. "I didn't realize," he said in a wondering, aching voice that threatened to break the fragile hold Savvy had on her emotions. "I didn't know."

"Perhaps that's why I'm here." She extended a hand toward him.

He smiled and placed a hand over hers. "Thank you for coming . . . my little Savannah." With the fingertips of his free hand he blotted tears seeping from his left eye.

"I'm here, and I'm not going anywhere. I won't leave Lexi to face this alone. Somehow we'll work things out."

"She wants to go to Utah instead of Minnesota."

Savvy didn't hide her surprise. "Utah? But I live in California. She's welcome to live with me . . . you know, when it's needed." Of course, they couldn't leave Derek, no matter how he insisted. Would he be willing to move to California? Probably not. The move itself might be deadly for him. Yet if she gave up her teaching with so little notice and stayed here instead, she doubted that she'd be allowed back. Was she willing to give up her new life there?

Derek shook his head. "It's not you she's talking about living with— it's Tyler. She says his family takes in all kinds of children and that she'd fit right in."

"But—but . . . we're family!" Savvy sputtered. She and Lexi hadn't been getting along well since that night at the church, but why would she choose Tyler instead of her?

Derek's eyes focused on a point beyond Savvy's shoulders. "Unfortunately, family isn't always the best choice when it comes to raising children. Sometimes a person has to give up what they want for the child's good."

"Like you did with me." Savvy kept her voice carefully neutral.

"Like I did with you." He sighed heavily. "It was the right thing to do, Savannah. But there hasn't been a day of my life that I haven't regretted not being able to know you."

Tears clogged Savvy's throat. "Would you actually consider signing Lexi over to Tyler? It's completely inappropriate, don't you think?"

"I agree." A ghost of a smile tugged at his lips. "But I have a sneaking suspicion that no matter who I gave custody to, she'd end up at the same place."

What was he saying? That Tyler wouldn't be able to handle Lexi and he'd give her back? Or was Derek somehow implying that she and Tyler would end up together? Had he misinterpreted things when Savvy had held onto Tyler's hand? Savvy searched his eyes for the answer.

"We're just friends," she said.

"Are you really?"

"Uh, of course." But she stumbled over the words. At the moment she had to admit that she didn't know what they were. Tyler had said he wanted more, but could she trust him?

Derek shook his head. "He's come a long way for a simple friend. I've seen that look in a man's eyes before. It might be love."

The words were like an arrow piercing her heart. "So? You said it yourself, Derek; sometimes love doesn't mean what you think it does."

"Yes." He nodded gravely. "Then again, sometimes it means much, much more."

Chapter Twenty-Three

Tyler chatted with Amber's parents as Lexi and her friend sat in a corner, heads together, whispering and exchanging giggles. Amber's parents were shocked at the role their daughter had played in Lexi's absence and apologized repeatedly.

"Believe me, we're glad Lexi has a friend like Amber," Tyler said for at least the third time.

The father was a tall, wide, slow-speaking man with a full head of light brown hair. His dark-haired wife was tall, thin, and birdlike in her movements and speech. Their language showed them to be educated, and their manners were impeccable. But Tyler was even more impressed with Lexi's choice in friends. Amber was a tiny, brown-haired little thing, whose nervous movements mirrored her mother's, yet it was clear from looking at her that she was a good kid. She didn't wear too much makeup or immodest clothing, and Tyler doubted she sported a belly button ring. He gave a silent prayer of thanks that somehow these two girls had connected.

His thoughts wandered to Savvy. How was she getting along with Derek? She had turned so pale at Derek's announcement of his disease that Tyler had worried she'd faint. She hadn't, though, and her courage at dinner had impressed him. She had taken charge, and all the awkwardness had vanished. Why hadn't he remembered how courageous she was? She'd always been that way—seeing what was needed and taking care of it. Lighting up the room and easing the feelings of others.

He loved her. He loved her deeply and strongly—more with each passing day. Somehow he had to convince her that she loved him too. Didn't she?

His focus was dragged back to the conversation when Amber's mother, whose name Tyler couldn't remember, sighed loudly and said, "We thought yesterday was the end. I stopped by the hospital when I heard. He looked near death."

Tyler looked around for Lexi, but she and Amber had disappeared. "Has this happened before?"

"Well, he's been hospitalized at least four times that I know of. Lexi always stays the night here."

"Thank you for all you've done," Tyler said.

"We don't mind," the woman said. "Though we feel better when Lexi leaves off all that black makeup like she did today. She's prettier without it."

Tyler didn't tell them that she'd started out with her black makeup on in the morning but had cried it off at her house.

Amber's father folded his hands over his ample stomach. "I know you're friends with Lexi's sister, but Lexi told Amber something on the phone earlier about Lexi going to live with you?"

Tyler opened his mouth to deny the claim when Lexi and Amber came into the room, having apparently overhead the last statement. "Yep," Lexi said. "My dad was going to send me to Minnesota to live with my aunt, but now he's thinking about sending me to Utah to live with Tyler instead."

"Really?" Amber's mother looked surprised, but no more surprised than Tyler himself. There was no way Derek could be considering such a move. Lexi must have misunderstood—or she was telling another one of her stories. Still, he didn't want to make Lexi out to be a liar in front of her friends, so he stifled his shock.

"Derek and Savvy are still working things out," he said, standing. "I guess we should get back to the house. They'll be wondering where we are."

"We need to call your fiancée," Lexi said. Before he could protest that he didn't have a fiancée, she rushed on. "She won't mind that I'm coming to live with you, will she? We can tell her I'll help out in the house. I know the rest of your family won't mind me staying with you." She turned to Amber. "You should see his family. They've got a lot of kids that weren't even born to them. It's cool."

"I think it's wonderful." Amber turned her adoring gaze Tyler's way. She sighed and batted her dark eyes.

Whatever, he thought. Aloud he said, "Come on, Lexi. It's getting late. I still don't know where we're staying tonight."

"At my house, of course. You can sleep on the couch. Savvy can stay in my room with me."

Tyler bade farewell to Amber's family and went out to his Jeep. Darkness had fallen in earnest, and the green paint of the Jeep glistened black. He turned on the engine but didn't begin to drive. Instead, he turned to Lexi. "What was *that* all about?"

She looked at him innocently. "What do you mean?"

"Your father didn't say anything about you coming to live with me."

"He will. You'll see. I can't wait to meet your brother when he comes back from Australia, and your parents. I never really knew any of my own grandparents." She was so confident that Tyler was starting to get nervous. He liked Lexi a lot, but taking care of her seemed a rather daunting task. Besides, Savvy wouldn't like it. He'd seen the way she watched Lexi—with the same protective expression his sisters had when looking at their children. No way he wanted to get in the way of that.

"What about Savvy?" he asked.

She shook her head. "I don't want to live with her."

"Why?"

Lexi's mouth squeezed into a tight line. "I just don't."

"You're shutting down on me."

"No, I'm not."

"Yes, you are."

"Am not."

"Are too."

Lexi rolled her eyes. "That's so adult of you, isn't it? Arguing with a kid."

"Hey, you did it, too."

"But I'm the kid!" Lexi gazed at the window. "So are we going home, or what?"

Tyler blew out a sigh. "Whatever, but this isn't over."

Lexi sat with folded arms all the way back to her house. When he pulled up to the curb, she reached over and grabbed his cell phone off his belt.

"Hey!"

"You need to call her. That girl. Ask her if it's okay."

He grabbed the phone back. "There is no girl."

"Yes, there is. I saw her."

"Yeah, but that doesn't mean—" He stopped, suddenly understanding. "You're really serious about this, aren't you?"

"Of course I am." Lexi's shoulder jerked once. "Don't you want me to live with you?"

Her eyes pleaded with him, and he couldn't say no. Not while her father seemed to be trying so hard to send her away. "Look, I'm sure your father will work something out for you. He'll want to see what Savvy thinks."

"I don't care what Savvy thinks!" Lexi shoved the door open and jumped from the car, slamming the door behind her. Without waiting for him, she ran up the steps to the porch.

Tyler wanted to run after her, to explain that Savvy's wishes were more important to him than life. That he loved Savvy and wanted to make her happy. "You idiot," he said to himself, chuckling. "She's not the one you should be telling."

Whistling to himself, he went up the walk.

⋆ *⋆* *⋆*

"We have to talk." Savvy sat cross-legged at the end of the makeshift bed on the floor of Lexi's room.

Lexi wished she could cover her ears but suspected that might be going too far. "What?" she said, sitting down on her own bed and looking down on Savvy.

"Well, first off, I talked to your dad."

"He's your dad, too."

Savvy was quiet a moment. "Lexi, my father is the man who raised me."

"So I suppose I'm not really your sister, either." Lexi raised her chin a notch.

"Of course you're my sister, but I won't be calling Derek my dad. That's all."

"Fine." Lexi laid an arm against her stomach. She did understand, especially after meeting Savvy's father in Utah. He was nice. On the other hand, she had to steel herself against liking Savvy too much. That would be a mistake.

Savvy shifted her position until she was on her knees, sitting back on her heels. She was almost level with Lexi's eyes. "Anyway, I talked to Derek, and he's agreed not to send you to Minnesota. In fact, he's agreed not to send you away at all until . . . he's gone."

Lexi drew in a quick breath, suddenly struggling for air. She blinked rapidly, but the tears came anyway. "You did that? You made him keep me?" The urge to throw her arms around Savvy was overpowering.

"I did nothing of the kind. He *always* wanted to keep you. But he also wanted to protect you. The only thing I did was to make him see that your place was here with him."

Lexi could hold in her emotions no longer. She launched herself at Savvy. "Thank you, thank you," she murmured. "I was so afraid he'd go, and I wouldn't be here to hold his hand." Her soft sobs filled the room, coming quickly before each word. "He needs me. He's just too stubborn to know it."

"Sounds like a family trait." Savvy gave her a squeeze.

Lexi blinked and drew back. "What?"

"Never mind."

"How long do you think, well, that he has left?"

"I don't know." Savvy glanced toward the door, but it was closed and held no answers. "But I'm going to be here to help. At least as much as possible. And later, well, we'll go back to California, okay? Start over."

Lexi shook her head. "I'm going to live with Tyler. He said I could. You won't have to worry about me."

"I *want* to worry about you." Savvy reached toward her, but Lexi scrambled backwards over the bed. "And there's no way your dad's going to let you live with a single man, not even Tyler."

Lexi knew that now was the time she'd been waiting for—the time to water the seeds of doubt Savvy always carried in regards to Tyler. "Well, that doesn't matter because Tyler won't be single long. You said yourself that he was bound to end up with someone like that girl who came to the house."

"But they broke up." Savvy arose slowly, uncertainty radiating from her eyes. "Unless . . . Lexi, do you know something I don't?"

Lexi shrugged. "They've been talking on the phone. I think he still likes her."

Savvy's eyes opened wide, and for a moment Lexi wished she could take back the words. But if she did all her efforts would be in vain. Unable to bear the look in her sister's eyes a second longer, Lexi burrowed under her covers and put her pillow over her head.

After a long minute, she heard Savvy get up and turn off the light.

✦ ✦ ✦ ✦ ✦

Tyler decided that the Roathes had the hardest, lumpiest couch in the history of hard, lumpy couches. He had slept on Kerrianne's couch, Amanda's couch, Mitch's couch, the couch at his parents', and numerous other couches during his time in college. Never once did he have a problem falling—and staying—asleep. If something wasn't poking him in the back, it was scratching his leg, or digging into his stomach. He had awakened at least five times and lay there listening to the silence in the house. Once, he'd heard Derek's hacking cough coming from the bathroom.

Somewhere in the early morning hours, he rolled onto the floor and slept more soundly, though his dreams were dark and filled with odd scenes—his editor at the *Deseret Morning News* pointing an accusing finger at him, Savvy linking arms with a handsome blond man, Derek collapsing in his arms, and LaNae chasing him with a wedding ring while Lexi shook a bell in her hands.

"Tyler!" The voice came to him from far away. "Tyler, wake up! Your phone is ringing."

"Uhhhh," he groaned.

"Tyler, wake up!"

He knew the voice now. Savvy. She needed him. With effort, he fought his way to consciousness. "Savvy?" he said, opening his eyes.

"Your phone is ringing." Savvy stood over him, though he couldn't see much of her face because he didn't have his glasses on. She was framed by the light spilling in from the front window, her hair looking like a halo.

Blinking at the brightness, he felt for his phone, but it wasn't on his belt where he normally kept it. In fact, he wasn't wearing a belt but his sweat pants. "Oh, well," he mumbled. "I have voice mail."

"What if it's your girlfriend?" she asked. There was a sharpness to her voice that surprised him.

"My what?" He shook his head. "I told you she and I are—"

"Or maybe it's someone asking you to come for a job interview."

That galvanized his sleep-deprived brain into action. Launching himself toward the couch, he fumbled between the cushions. He found nothing but his glasses, which he gratefully put on.

Savvy stood watching him, hands on her hips. Tyler stifled the desire to sigh. Why was she upset? And why did women always put their hands on their hips when they were angry? Why couldn't they choose another body part—like their calves or something? Then he'd be too busy laughing to be nervous.

She was already dressed, he noticed, in faded jeans and a fitted button-up blouse that exactly matched her blue eyes. Blue eyes he wanted to drown in. Her skin looked soft and smooth, her lips full and inviting. He wondered what she would do if he tried to kiss her.

With a swift motion, she bent over and fished out his phone from beneath the couch. He reached for it just as the ringing stopped. "See?" he said. "They'll leave a message." He saw that he'd already missed two calls.

"Why aren't you up, anyway? It's almost ten."

"Ten?" He found that hard to believe.

"Yes. Even Lexi's already up and gone somewhere with Amber."

Tyler plopped to the couch, his feet twisting up in his blanket. Freeing himself with a kick, he said, "Savvy, we need to talk." He patted the seat beside him, but she didn't sit. Her hands were once again on her hips. *What did I do to make her so mad?* he wondered.

"You bet we do," she said. "What do you mean telling Lexi she can live with you?"

"Whoa, wait a minute. I didn't tell her anything. That was her idea."

"Oh? She said you'd agreed."

"No. I think I'd remember that."

Savvy's jaw clenched. "You have no claim here, Tyler."

"Claim? You think I *want* to take her away from you?" Tyler was fully awake now and ready to defend himself. He stood, wanting the advantage that height would give him.

"Oh, no you don't," Savvy said, pushing him back onto the couch. "I'm the one who—aaah!" She screamed as Tyler pulled her down with him. She moved hastily away from him to the far end of the couch.

Tyler didn't release her hand. "Look," he said, scooting closer. "I'm sorry that Lexi's trying to put me into the middle of this, but I'm not the problem here. Did it ever occur to you to wonder why Lexi doesn't want to live with you?" The reporter in him knew there had to be an explanation.

Savvy looked stricken. "No," she whispered. After several moments she added, "Am I that bad? Why doesn't she want me?"

The words ate into Tyler's heart. He had the distinct feeling that Savvy's question ran much deeper than it appeared on the surface. Was it somehow connected to him?

Savvy tried again to pull her hand away and this time succeeded. "She's lost everything. I'm the only close relative she has left. I mean, besides Derek, and when he . . ." Tears gathered in her eyes, making them large and luminous. "Well, I'd think she'd want to do everything she could to be with me."

Tyler tried to put himself in Lexi's place. What reason could she have for not wanting to be with Savvy? It didn't make sense unless— "Maybe she's afraid . . . afraid of losing you."

As he said the words everything fell into place. Fell into place because he felt the same way—terrified of losing Savvy. For a long moment Tyler couldn't speak. His throat felt clogged and his heart full. *I have to tell her how I feel,* he thought. *I have to help her believe in me before it's too late for us.*

"Afraid?" Savvy's eyes grew wide, the hurt fading. "Oh, Tyler," she whispered, "you're right! She didn't start acting like this until that girl hit my mom's car. All this time I kept wondering if Lexi was still mad at me for making her go to church, but that isn't it at all."

"She's probably thinking you could have been killed."

"Poor Lexi. I have to make her see that I'm not going anywhere. But it's not as though I can promise nothing will ever happen. I mean, look at her family." Savvy's voice broke. Tyler thought she might turn to him for comfort as she had yesterday in the Jeep, but she lurched off the couch, averting her face from him. What had changed?

Tyler wished he could comfort her. He wanted to take her in his arms and promise to love her forever. He jumped to his feet, hoping to find the right words.

At that moment, Derek came into the room, blocking Savvy's passage. He took one look at her tearful face and opened his arms. She met him in a hug. "Savannah," he murmured, smoothing her hair. "It's going to be all right."

She sniffed, fighting tears. "I'm sorry. I—I just wish . . . I . . ." She hugged Derek again. "I'm so glad I got to meet you." Pulling away, she added, "I'll be ready in a minute to get those things you wanted at the store. Meanwhile, will you tell Tyler here that you are not giving Lexi to him?" She shot a pointed glance at Tyler. "You have to stop encouraging her." Without another word she left the room.

Derek watched her go before turning to Tyler. "Didn't go well, huh?" His mouth twitched in a half grin.

Tyler flexed his hands. "Not well at all."

Derek sat heavily on the couch, bending over to rub his ankles. "Darn legs keep swelling. Hope the doctor can give me something for the fluid retention. I have an appointment on Monday." He sat up straight and looked into Tyler's face. "She can't read your mind, you know."

Tyler started. "What do mean?"

"Seems to me you have some serious convincing to do."

"I know." Tyler stared in the direction Savvy had gone. He swung his gaze back to Derek. "What should I do?" He felt stupid asking this man who had failed so much in his own life, but given that emotional display between them, Derek did seem to have some connection to Savvy's heart.

"You should probably try to talk to her."

Tyler nodded, feeling irritated. Even he knew that much.

Savvy reentered the living room as Tyler's phone began ringing again. "Better hurry," she said. "You wouldn't want to make your girl-friend wait."

"I keep telling you—I don't have a girlfriend!"

She pulled her purse over her shoulder, opened the front door, and went out into the cloud-covered morning. Shrugging sympathetically, Derek disappeared down the hall.

Tyler jabbed at the answer button on his phone. "Hello?" he gritted darkly.

"Hi, this is Thayne Duncan from the *Salt Lake Tribune*. I received your resume this week in the mail. I know it's a weekend, and I would ordinarily wait until Monday to call, but I'm heading out of town next week. Is this a bad time?"

"No, no. Not at all." Tyler made a face. *Great, one word and I almost blew it.* "In fact, this is a great time to talk."

The phone conversation was lengthy and ended in a promise of a face-to-face interview. Tyler felt hopeful, yet at the same time, he didn't know if he wanted the job. Savvy would soon be back in California, and what would Utah hold for him then?

Chapter Twenty-Four

Come on, get up. We're going to church."

Lexi opened her eyes to find Savvy peering down at her. She was smiling, which was a relief because she had been so quiet yesterday. Not that she'd been rude to Lexi. If anything, Savvy had gone out of her way to be nice—making Lexi a nice dinner, renting her a video, inviting Amber to spend the evening with them. With each thing Savvy did for her, Lexi's load of guilt increased.

But her plan to put a wedge between Savvy and Tyler was working well. Savvy said little to Tyler, though he attempted to talk with her several times. Savvy obviously believed that he had been talking to that girl on the phone, though Lexi wasn't sure why she was so insecure. Didn't Savvy notice how Tyler drooled over her? Did Tyler know how dumb he looked? It was enough to make her sick—and maybe just a little jealous.

"Get up," Savvy repeated.

"I'm not going." Lexi put her head under her pillow.

Savvy pulled the pillow off. "Yes, you are. So's your dad. Come on. Tyler made pancakes. He's not much of a cook, though, so pretend you like them, okay?"

Though she had no intention of setting foot inside Savvy's church again, Lexi had to see Tyler cooking. She threw back the covers and followed Savvy to the kitchen.

"Whoa! You cook?" she asked Tyler, who was standing near the stove with a spatula.

He smirked. "Better than you, I bet."

Lexi saw her dad seated at the table, drinking a protein shake. "The pancakes are that bad?"

"Too much fat for my heart," he said. "All that syrup and butter."

"Oh, yeah." Lexi's stomach twisted. How could she have forgotten?

"Here." Tyler passed her a plate with a short stack of pancakes. Lexi sat down at the table and began smothering them with butter and syrup.

"Only one for me," Savvy said.

Tyler held out a plate. "You sure?"

"I've eaten your pancakes before."

"Hey, that was years ago. I've improved since then. I promise."

"We'll see." Savvy spread a thin layer of raspberry jam on the pancake.

Lexi took a big bite of pancake. Immediately, she spat it out. "Yuck! Ugh! What'd you do, use a whole cup of baking soda?"

Savvy choked on her forkful but managed to swallow it. "She's right. This is terrible."

"Worse than terrible," Lexi added.

"You guys . . ." Clearly unbelieving, Tyler took a bite of the pancake. "There's nothing wrong with—" He gagged and spit into the garbage. "Can't see what would make it so terrible. I followed the regular recipe, except that I used a bit more sugar."

"Sugar?" Derek asked, cocking his head. "What sugar? I don't think I have any—doctor's orders."

"It's right here." Tyler showed them a plastic holder containing a white granulated powder.

Derek let out a snort. "That's my vitamin C powder. Concentrated.

I put a tiny bit in my shakes every morning. If you used a cup of that—or even a half—" He chuckled.

Tyler sat down on a chair and sighed.

Lexi went to find the cornflakes.

"I'm not going with you," she said as they finished breakfast a short while later.

Savvy looked disappointed, as did her father, but Tyler grinned. "Too afraid of a repeat, huh? What, don't you have that skirt you wore last time? Maybe the kids here will like it."

"Tyler," Savvy warned.

"Hey, it's like riding a bike. She's got to get back on." He glanced at Lexi. "Come on, I dare you to go. Or are you too chicken?"

Lexi knew he was goading her and that all she had to do was run to her bedroom to get away, but she couldn't do that. She wanted to please Tyler. If she did, maybe he would agree to let her live with him.

"I'm not afraid! Fine, I'll go. But I won't like it." She tossed her head and left the kitchen, prepared for the laughter to follow. But no one laughed, and she was glad.

This time she wore a skirt that went well past her knees and a long shirt that was actually loose. She left off all but a little makeup—like Savvy usually wore—and took out half her earrings. "There, now you look like a good little sister for Savvy," she said with a sneer. The thought made her heart ache. After sticking out her tongue in the mirror, Lexi went out to wait in Tyler's Jeep.

They had barely entered the chapel when a man came to meet them. Lexi knew he was the bishop in the local ward. He'd been to the house a few times, and her father had always listened politely but then sent him away with no promises.

"Good to have you here." As the bishop shook their hands, Lexi noticed her father's face was gray and that his breathing was coming hard. Savvy noticed, too, and they quickly led him to a bench. In a few moments, his color was better, and he was able to sing a hymn.

Lexi was glad that today she didn't stand out. In fact, no one really gave her a second look—except that boy a row back who was smiling at her. Lexi returned the smile and looked away.

After the sacrament meeting, Lexi attended a Sunday School class with boys and girls. She didn't see the boy who'd smiled at her, but the other kids were nice. There was even a girl she recognized from school, who sat by her. "I didn't know you were a member," Bridget whispered.

"I'm not. My dad is. Or was."

"Are you going to be baptized?"

Lexi thought about it. She might have to if she lived with Tyler. "Maybe."

The next meeting was with girls only, and Bridget stayed with her. The lesson was on prayer. Lexi listened, experiencing the strangest feeling that she was hearing it all for a second time. Then she remembered that her mother had written things like this to her in letters before she was baptized. Lexi had been so angry at the time that she'd barely read them, but maybe she should have paid more attention.

"Do you believe in all this prayer stuff?" she asked Bridget, keeping her voice low.

"Yeah. Do you?"

"I don't know."

In her heart, Lexi wanted to believe. If she was really a daughter of God, like they said, wouldn't God want to help her? Could He heal her father? Or at least make everything work out?

"So, how'd it go?" Savvy asked as Lexi came out of the meeting, walking next to Bridget.

Lexi nodded good-bye to her friend as they moved off. "Okay, I guess."

"I see you met a friend."

"Just a girl from school."

Savvy stopped walking. "That's great! I'm glad you knew someone. Makes it easier."

Why does she have to be so nice? Lexi felt even worse about pushing

Savvy away and for lying to her about Tyler getting married, but she wouldn't give up her plan. It was too important to her future.

"Look, there's Tyler and Dad," she said. "He looks tired. We should take him home."

After a total of three nights on the hard, lumpy couch, Tyler woke up late Monday morning determined to find another place to sleep before the day was out. Having too little rest was beginning to exact its toll. Yesterday when they had taken Derek to the local ward, Tyler had nodded off in priesthood meeting. Derek had been amused, but the teacher and other members hadn't been impressed.

Grumbling to himself, Tyler stumbled to the kitchen to find some breakfast—though it was closer to lunchtime by now. The slamming of the front door called his attention away from his stomach. He'd heard Savvy leave with Derek for the doctor's less than an hour ago. Surely they couldn't be back already.

He paused, cornflakes box in hand, when Lexi appeared in the doorway. She stopped, taking in a swift breath.

"I thought you were in school," he said.

Lexi frowned. "I was, but I left."

"Why?"

"My dad's dying—remember?"

"Well, your dad's not here. He's at the doctor's—which I think you knew very well."

The defiance in her lifted chin verified his assumption.

"Come on," he said. "I'll take you back to school."

"No! Besides, it'll be lunchtime."

"So we'll stop and get something for lunch."

She nodded, though her eyes, once again rimmed with heavy black makeup, were still angry. He figured she had a lot to be angry about. *And better at me than at Savvy,* he thought. Of course, Savvy was also upset with him.

"That reminds me," he said, opening the door to his Jeep. "Did you say something to Savvy to make her mad at me?"

Lexi shrugged, but her gaze didn't quite meet his. "I told her I wanted to live with you, that's all."

"She wants you with her. I think that's for the best, too."

Lexi folded her hands over her stomach. "My dad's not even dead yet."

"You know the diagnosis."

"What about prayer? Couldn't there be a miracle? Or don't you really believe?"

Tyler hated the hope in her eyes. "Lexi," he said, "if it were the right thing to do, God would heal your father. But you have to understand that sometimes we learn more when we have to face the hard things. I think this is one of those times. No matter what happens, He will always help us. That's for sure."

"I don't want to talk about this anymore."

"We have to talk about it." Tyler couldn't help the irritation seeping into his voice. "You're not a baby. You know what's going to happen."

She glared at him. "You don't want me, do you? You'd rather I went to Minnesota."

"That's not it at all." He gave a frustrated growl. "Look, I just want to talk about this reasonably. Why don't you want to live with Savvy? Tell me. Maybe I can help." Until she was ready to admit her fear of losing Savvy, he didn't see how he could help.

Lexi stared out the window and refused to speak. After four attempts, Tyler gave up. He simply didn't understand this creature.

"Fine," he muttered. He pulled into the first fast-food restaurant he found, ordering hamburgers, fries, and shakes from the drive-up. While she ate, he drove to the grocery store on the corner.

"I know you're not talking to me," he said, "but I have to get a card to send to a certain politician. I owe him a big apology, and I'd better do it now while I still understand why."

There was a question in Lexi's eyes, but he didn't wait around to see if it would win out over her apparent vow of silence. For the moment, he needed to be away from this unpredictable child.

The ten minutes of isolation did wonders for Lexi. By the time he returned, she would at least look at him. She'd finished her food and started in on his fries. He slapped her hand away. "Hey, those are mine."

She shrugged. "They're cold."

"Where's a mail box?" He started the engine. "I'll send this note after I take you to school. I hope they let me check you in."

"Don't worry about it. I snuck out of band, and lunch isn't over yet. Just drop me off."

"You promise you'll go to class?"

She sighed. "Yes."

"Really?"

"I said yes."

"And no more leaving? You can't be a journalist if you don't get an education."

"All right, all right." She looked at him and grinned. "I will capitulate to your request. For today, at least."

He laughed. "Enough with the big words already. Which way is the school?"

When Lexi was safely inside the building, Tyler drove around until he found a mail box. Then he made a short call to discover the politician's address.

Now for a motel, he thought, as the letter dropped out of sight. *Man, I'd better get a job soon, or I'll have to hit my dad up for a loan.* Whatever happened, he didn't plan on leaving Savvy. She needed him—whether she realized it or not.

✦ ✦ ✦ ✦

Savvy was in the waiting room a long time. She tried reading several different magazines, but the words swam before her eyes. A bridal magazine on the end table was particularly disturbing because when she looked at it, the face of the male model seemed to be Tyler, or to resemble him closely enough to make her feel it was him. That caused her anger to swell again in her heart. How could she love him and be so angry at him?

I have to get away from him, she thought.

Maybe she should tell him to go back to Utah, but her heart rebelled at the idea.

She, of course, couldn't leave. Not yet. Not until she was sure Derek was stable enough to take care of Lexi. She kept telling herself she acted only for Lexi, and yet deep inside, where she didn't examine too closely, she knew it was for herself, too. She wanted to know Derek for as long as possible.

She'd called Berkeley that morning, pulling out of school and resigning her teaching assignment. The supervisor over her class hadn't been happy at the last-minute changes but was remarkably understanding about her reasons. Savvy knew her co-teacher would be able to fill in the gap—or there were plenty of other qualified replacements if he needed help. She promised to e-mail her lesson plans to smooth the transition.

Next, she'd called her apartment and left a message on the phone to let her new roommate know she had been delayed. Savvy was paid up for another month, and her lease wasn't over for eight, but she could always sell the contract, if she had to. There would be time later to decide what to do.

Savvy gingerly touched her head and felt her stitches. The swelling around the area had gone down, and only when she rolled on her side during the night or brushed her hair did she even remember that she'd been hurt.

Or when she thought about Lexi. *If only it hadn't happened,* she thought, *then Lexi wouldn't be so upset.*

Unable to bear waiting a minute longer, Savvy went to the reception desk. "Uh, is something wrong? My, uh, Derek Roathe's been back there a long time."

The pretty brunette smiled. "I'll check for you, okay?"

Savvy nodded and waited at the counter while she disappeared, grateful the doctor's office didn't appear too busy this morning.

The receptionist returned, but she wasn't alone. A tall, lean man with a warm smile and a receding hairline held out a hand. "I'm Dr. Miller, Derek's physician," he said. "Can I talk with you for a moment?"

Savvy felt pressure building in her chest. "Is he okay?"

"For now. But we need to talk."

Savvy followed Dr. Miller down a short corridor and into an empty examining room. She'd hoped he was taking her to Derek, but apparently what he had to say to her was private.

The doctor indicated for her to take a chair, while he sat on a stool by the examining table. He pursed his lips a moment, as though considering his words. "I understand that you're Derek's daughter."

"Well, yes." *Sort of*, she amended silently.

"I'm very glad to see you here. He told me about you a few minutes ago and has given me permission to talk to you about his condition."

"It's bad, isn't it?"

He nodded gravely. "Yes. Quite frankly, I'm worried. Derek's blood pressure is way too high today. I've giving him some medication to slow it enough so that he can go home, but at this point he really should be in a hospital. At least for a few days to see how things go. However, he refuses. I understand why. There's nothing we can do for him in the hospital except to see that he stays down and quiet."

"That's hard for him." Savvy had seen that he fought against playing the invalid.

"Exactly. He's the perfect type A personality. It took several serious episodes for me to get him to quit work. Unfortunately, the only thing left is a heart transplant, and he's not a good candidate for that."

Savvy took a deep breath. "How long does he have?"

"A day, a week, a year—it's impossible to say. It depends on many factors, but my best guess is probably less than a month. His heart is simply too weak."

Savvy didn't think anything more could faze her. Derek was dying. She'd known that, but having it spelled out so clearly took the hope right from her. "Thank you," she managed to say, "for being honest. Does he know?"

"I told him nearly the same thing a month ago. That he'd better make plans for his younger daughter."

And that made Lexi run off to California, Savvy thought. "Is there anything I can do?" she asked.

"I have a list." Dr. Miller took a page from the clipboard Savvy hadn't noticed he was carrying. "But as I said, things don't look good."

"I understand."

Dr. Miller checked his watch. "If his blood pressure reacts well to the medication, he should be ready to go home in ten minutes. I have a wheelchair you can use until you're able to rent one for him."

"A wheelchair?"

"Yes. He needs to relax as much as possible from here on out. That means no walking—except maybe to the bathroom."

"I see. Thank you."

Savvy made her way back to the waiting room, trying unsuccessfully to hold back the tears.

Chapter Twenty-Five

Days crept by. To Savvy's frustration—and secret joy Tyler didn't leave for Utah. He had been going to stay at a motel, until Amber's parents offered to let him crash in their spare room. He gratefully accepted, noting that he could be at the Roathes' in two minutes by car if an emergency happened.

Not that it appeared necessary. Derek flourished under the attention of his two daughters, and there was more laughter in the somber house than Savvy had thought possible. She discovered that Derek enjoyed hearing about her studies, and they spent hours staring at the sky or thumbing through the astronomy books she checked out at the local library. They treated each other like friends rather than father and daughter, but it was enough for Savvy. She made sure her conversations with Derek were interspersed with ample rest, meals, and medication breaks, which she regarded religiously.

At first Lexi went to school, but after three days of cutting class and coming home early to check on her father, everyone realized there was nothing they could do to keep her there. Savvy finally went to the junior high to work out a home study curriculum, grateful that seventh grade didn't count toward high school graduation. Tyler took on the responsibility of tutoring Lexi in English, and though his method of teaching from the newspaper wouldn't likely be approved by the district, Savvy felt the individual attention would outweigh any fault in his curriculum.

Savvy herself took over teaching Lexi math and science, which had always been her favorite. Unlike with English, Lexi was far behind her grade level in those subjects and would have needed a tutor anyway to keep up with her class. After only a few days, she showed remarkable progress, though their relationship was like a rollercoaster. One minute Lexi was warm and friendly, and the next she would ignore Savvy and treat her as though she didn't exist.

"It's like she's two different girls," Savvy said to Tyler.

"You're missing the point," he replied. "When is it that she treats you badly? Huh? I'll tell you when. Right after Derek has a coughing spell, or when he feels too weak to leave his room, even in the wheelchair. It's when she's most afraid of losing him."

Savvy tried to keep that in mind, but it still felt like rejection.

Her relationship with Tyler was at a standstill, which wasn't a real surprise because they were never alone. Savvy rarely left Derek, but the few times she did, Lexi always tagged along—although why, Savvy couldn't say. It was almost as though Lexi didn't want her to be alone with Tyler, but that seemed silly.

Tyler himself was a constant, and despite her suspicions about his possible continuing involvement with LaNae, Savvy found herself relying on him more and more. He was always willing to run to the grocery store, grab a video, fill a prescription, or help Derek to the living room or out to the backyard so they could look at the stars. He would often sit and talk with Derek while she fixed dinner, discussing world events. Tyler's eyes often met hers, causing her heart to pound furiously. She found herself anticipating his arrivals and wondering if maybe her old dreams really could come true.

Her other support was the long talks she had with her family over the phone. Their love went a long way toward soothing her heartache at the prospect of losing Derek so soon after finding him.

The next Sunday, Savvy sent a prayer of thanks heavenward when Lexi didn't balk about going to church and told her she'd invited Amber to come along. Lexi even made it a point to get up early and make the pancakes for breakfast, inviting Tyler and Amber over for the meal. In a pancake Lexi gave Tyler, she purposely sprinkled in a healthy dose of vitamin C powder, and Savvy laughed herself silly at Tyler's reaction. Later, as they pushed Derek's new wheelchair into sacrament meeting, it was all she and Lexi could do to keep from bursting into laughter every time they looked at each other.

Yet behind all the laughter and enjoyment, there was a sense of waiting. Lexi stayed at her father's side, even during the astronomy discussions, which she endured in stony silence. Savvy found herself going to any length to engage her in the conversation and to let her know how much she was loved, but try as she might, Lexi refused to participate. She was equally unwilling to talk about what would happen after Derek's death. When pressed, she only insisted that she was going to live with Tyler. Nothing anyone could do—not even Tyler—would persuade her otherwise.

On Tuesday, one week and four days after their arrival in Colorado, Lexi went over to Amber's for her English lesson. Tyler usually came to the Roathes', but he hadn't arrived yet, so Lexi had decided to go there instead. "I need to get out of the house," she said. "I'll be back by dinnertime." Noting her sallow face, Savvy let her go gladly. The walk to Amber's in the afternoon sun would do her good. Yet when neither Lexi nor Tyler appeared for dinner, Savvy began to worry.

"Give Lexi a little space," Derek said from his place on the living room couch. "She's been penned up here too much these past few days. You know she has."

Savvy stared out the front window. "I guess you're right. I'm worrying too much."

"What you should be doing is taking care of that young man of yours."

"He's not my young man. Tyler and I are friends."

Derek laughed. "Now tell me a story I can believe."

Savvy ignored him and went to reheat their cooled dinner. Derek needed to eat, Lexi or no. She was considering calling Amber's house when Lexi flounced into the kitchen. Savvy turned from the stove. "You're late. I was beginning to worry."

"Tyler's fault," Lexi said, plopping down at the table. "I had to walk back. Couldn't get him off the phone. Again. He talks on the phone more than Amber and I talk to each other."

Savvy froze at the words. She'd seen Tyler several times talking on his cell phone here, usually pacing in the backyard, but she'd hoped he was talking with his family. "Oh?" she forced herself to say, busying her hands with the plates from the cupboard. "Isn't he coming for dinner?" He hadn't missed a dinner in the entire time they'd been in Colorado.

"Got sick of hearing all that lovey-dovey stuff," Lexi continued as though Savvy hadn't spoken. "I'll be glad when he marries that girl and starts to act normal again."

Savvy had her back to the counter and now she clung to it. "He was talking to his girlfriend?"

"Uh-huh. Fiancée. They're engaged now. I told you it was going to work out. Now I can live with them. Dad's lawyer came by today, didn't he? I need to ask if he fixed the custody stuff." Lexi met her gaze for the first time. "What's wrong, Savvy? You look kind of pale."

"It's nothing. I—I'm hungry, that's all." That much was true. Savvy had lost her appetite, but her stomach still clamored to be filled.

Lexi arose and took two steps toward her. "Savvy, I know you kind of like Tyler, but you want him to be happy, don't you?"

What about my happiness? Savvy wanted to shout. *You're my sister, and you should care about my happiness!* But she wouldn't say any of that now. Not when Lexi's father was dying and Savvy was trying to win

Lexi's trust and love. Tyler didn't matter—or shouldn't. She should have known he hadn't changed. "Of course," she choked out. "Do you want to take a plate to your father?"

"Sure." Lexi gave her an anxious glance, one Savvy thought might contain at least a small bit of compassion. "I'll eat with him in the living room, if you don't mind." The last sentence was so cordial that it was a balm to Savvy's breaking heart.

I told you not to get involved, she scolded herself, as she made up a plate of dinner for Derek. *Tyler is not to be trusted—at least not with your heart.*

Lexi heaped her own plate full of the low-fat chicken casserole Savvy had made because it was her second favorite after spaghetti. Without a word of thanks, Lexi left the kitchen.

*★ * *★ * *★ *

When Tyler finally made it to the Roathes', dinner was over and he knew he'd have to forage for himself in the kitchen or go out. Savvy, deep in a conversation with Derek about the orbits of asteroids, scarcely looked his way. Lexi, however, smiled at him warmly before glancing back at her father. Tyler saw in her eyes a longing to be a part of what her father and sister shared, yet at the same time a reluctance to put her heart on the line. He knew exactly how she felt. Savvy was more open with him lately, and he knew it was time to lay *his* heart at her feet. But what if she refused his offering?

Of course, that was providing they could find time alone, without their young shadow. Savvy looked at him just then, and his heart tightened. *Now,* he told himself. *The time is now.*

Tyler tossed the newspaper he'd brought for Derek next to the couch where he was lying. "Savvy, let's go for a walk."

"Can I come?" Lexi asked eagerly, popping to her feet.

"No. Someone should stay here with Derek."

"I'm fine," Derek said. "I don't need to be baby-sat."

"I'll stay," Savvy volunteered.

"But I need to talk to you—alone." Tyler thought he saw a glint of approval in Derek's eyes. Lexi folded her arms, her face drawn in a pout.

Savvy regarded Tyler silently for a few seconds, and to his surprise the old familiar hurt was back in her eyes. "Okay," she said quietly. "I'd like to talk with you, too." She stood and walked with him to the door.

They made their way onto the porch and over the grass to the sidewalk. The lawn was greener now, and free of trash, thanks to the hours he'd spent outside working. He was thinking of pruning the tree next. The early September day was warm, and the sun shone intensely as it plunged toward the west, but the thick branches overhead cast dark, gloomy shadows, as though stalking those who lived in the house.

They walked a block in silence. Rain the day before had made the lawns green and bright, and several varieties of flowers still showed an array of blooms. But fall was almost here. He could smell it in the air.

"I just got off the phone with the *San Francisco Chronicle*," he said. "They've offered me a job." That made two job opportunities now, since he was almost positive the *Tribune* would end up making a similar offer. He'd talked twice more with them since their first call, and though they still needed a face-to-face interview, things were looking good.

Savvy gave him a half smile that made his heart pound. "Are you going to take it?"

"I think I'd rather work at the *Tribune*. Unless my situation changes." *Unless you decide you want me,* he added silently.

They walked past another house in silence. There was a comfortable familiarity between them this evening that made almost anything possible. Tyler began to believe they could finally work things out.

"Do you believe in miracles?" he asked. He'd practiced it, and this is how he'd decided to tell her how he felt—that she was his second chance at a miracle.

She gave him a sideways glance. "Of course." Then she frowned. "Not for Derek, though."

270

"I don't know. He got to meet you. That's a miracle, isn't it? And you and Lexi have each other."

She made a noise of disgust. "She still doesn't want me."

"It's just a matter of time."

"Well, we don't have a lot of time, do we?" she snapped. Looking immediately repentant, she glanced at him. "Look, Tyler. I really appreciate you coming to Colorado with me. You've gone above and beyond the call of friendship. But you should go back to Utah. I know you have your own life to live—including that new job."

"So do you. Have a life to live, I mean."

She shook her head. "For now, this is where I'm supposed to be."

"Maybe." He couldn't deny that he didn't want to leave Lexi to face this trial as much as she didn't. Or to leave Savvy, either. "I can't go," he said, his feet stopping suddenly. "I think I'm incapable of leaving." He looked at her, holding her gaze. For once, she didn't look away.

"What are you saying?"

He stepped closer. With one hand he reached out and took her arm, drawing her closer still.

"Tyler," she warned. "Don't."

"Don't what?" he asked. "Savvy, I'm here because of you. I mean Derek's a nice guy, Lexi's a great kid, but I'm here because of you. I want to be with you." He wanted to kiss her, but her next words rooted him in place.

"I'm sorry, Tyler, but I don't believe that. No, don't say anything. Hear me out." She blinked, and tears filled her eyes. "You're here with me. We're friends. You're letting this closeness cloud your mind. I think you need to go home, talk to your fiancée, and go on with your life. I want you to be happy—I really do. Besides, I'm going to be busy raising Lexi. That's going to take all my energy right now."

His hand tightened on her arm. "I don't have a fiancée!"

"Please don't say that." Her gaze dropped to the ground. "I knew it would happen. I've been expecting it."

"Expecting what?" He let go of her arm and made fists at his side. "I don't know what you're talking about. Savvy, you're the one I care about!"

Her eyes met his, filled with hurt and suspicion. "Well, that's odd because Lexi told me about you getting married. And how you're always talking to your girlfriend on the phone."

"Since when do you believe anything Lexi says?" he demanded. "She's manipulated everything from the start! You know that."

"She's confused and afraid. We have to give her room."

"To lie?" When Savvy didn't reply, Tyler went on. "If you're going to be her guardian, you can't let her control you like this."

"Well, it would be a darn sight easier if you didn't keep undermining my relationship with her!"

"What?" Tyler couldn't remember a time when he was more frustrated. "I'm not doing anything of the sort! Look, Savvy, she's obviously trying to keep us apart."

Savvy shook her head. "It doesn't matter. Tyler, I really think you should go back to Utah."

Tyler felt her slipping away as surely as if she had told him she loved another man. "Savvy, you know me. You know I would never lie to you."

"Maybe not purposely. But when I talked to Lexi earlier, I realized I can't go through it again. I won't!"

"Go through what?" Tyler took in her tearful blue eyes, the color of a clear afternoon sky, her smooth face, the delicate curve of her cheeks, the fulness of her lips. He loved her. Oh, how he loved her!

She glared at him, her brows drawn tight. "For years I've watched on the sidelines as you dated one thin supermodel after the other, never mind if they had anything in common with you or had ever cracked open a book. For years I was the standby when your dates fell through or when you really wanted to see some foreign film. And all that time I kept hoping you'd look at me, that you'd see who I really was." Tears fell down her cheeks, and the pain in her face was almost unbearable for him to see. "But you never did. I was always the best friend, the sidekick, the girl who loved you more than any of the others, but who you never looked at twice. The girl who could never be what you wanted." She clenched and unclenched her jaw. "That's what I can't go through again. I won't let you take my heart and throw it away the minute a skinny little thing crooks her finger in your direction. I just won't!"

Realization crashed over him in a terrible, life-altering way. *What have I done?* How could he ever hope to make up for such pain?

He had to try. She was everything to him.

"I didn't know," he said. "I'm sorry. So sorry. But I love you, Savvy. Whatever happened before, whatever wrongs I committed in the past, I love you now. I love you in the way that lasts for eternity. I want to wake up every morning with you by my side. I want to have children with you. I don't care what you weigh, or if you cut your hair, or if you grow old and wrinkly. None of that matters. What matters is that I love your heart. Please, give us a chance. I'll spend the rest of my life proving myself to you."

He saw that she was stunned into speechlessness. Leaning forward, he placed his hands on her arms, pulling her close to kiss her. Gently at first and then with more intensity. Savvy responded to his touch until a car drove by, and she broke away.

They walked back to the house in silence. Savvy kept her eyes on the ground, repeatedly kicking a small stone. Tyler didn't know what else to say or to do. He could only pray. The feel of her was on his lips, and his fingers tingled where they had touched her arms. He loved her so much. Couldn't she feel his love?

On the doorstep, she turned toward him. "So are you going back to Utah?"

He was tempted to say yes, to soothe his own hurt feelings. But he'd told the truth when he said he couldn't leave her. "Not unless you make me." After several heartbeats, he added quietly, "Please don't make me."

"You could lose that job."

"Better than losing you."

She watched him for a long moment, her blue eyes troubled. Tyler felt their future on the line. If she asked him to leave again, after all his confessions, what choice would he have? He couldn't force her to love him. He flexed his hands, trying to swallow the growing lump in his throat.

At last she spoke, so softly he strained to hear the words. "Go home, Tyler."

"Savvy," he begged.

"Please."

His heart breaking, Tyler left her on the porch, climbed into his Jeep, and drove away.

Chapter Twenty-Six

Tyler drove all night, arriving in Sandy at three in the morning. The house was dark and empty-looking. Stumbling with exhaustion, Tyler went up the porch stairs. He found the right key and fumbled as he tried to open the lock. Succeeding at last, he practically fell inside. Muffin was barking somewhere upstairs and soon sped into sight, shaking his tail in excited welcome.

"Sh, boy." Tyler tried to pass him, tripped, and fell. The dog yelped as Tyler's body pinned his front legs.

"Who's there?" growled a voice. Lights flooded the kitchen, pouring into the living room where Tyler had fallen.

Tyler blinked at the light and stared up into his older brother's face. He looked much the same as the last time Tyler had seen him at the airport—tall, thin, with bright blue eyes and sandy hair—except that he was wearing black pajama bottoms dotted with soccer balls and a black T-shirt. In his hands he held a baseball bat at the ready, muscles rippling with the effort. "Hey, it's only me," Tyler protested.

"Tyler?" Mitch relaxed, setting down the bat. "Whew! I was worried there for a moment. I mean, it didn't sound like Muffin was upset—until he yelped."

"I fell on him." Tyler sat up, giving Muffin an apologetic pat.

Mitch offered him a hand up, and Tyler accepted. At once, Mitch pulled him into a warm bear hug. "It's good to see you, little brother."

Tyler felt a rush of emotion. "You, too."

"Hey, aren't you supposed to be in Colorado?"

Tyler shrugged. "What about you? The last I heard you were in Australia."

"Surprise." Mitch gave him a wide grin. "Mom and Dad picked us up late last night at the airport. I had to call them before we caught our flight out from Denver. We didn't know until right before we left Australia that we would be able to get the standby tickets, and that was my first opportunity to let everyone know we were coming."

"Where's your Mustang?" Tyler asked. Mitch's ugly orange-red car would have at least given him some warning.

"Still at Dad's. It was too late to pick it up." Mitch's brow creased. "So what brings you back? I thought you were with Savvy."

Tyler bit back tears. This is what he loved about family. It didn't matter how long had passed since they'd last been together. They immediately fell into familiar routines that promised both comfort and guidance.

"I've blown it," Tyler admitted. "I've blown it big time."

Mitch sighed. "It can't be that bad. Come on. Let's sit down on this excuse for a couch and talk it out."

"You need your sleep."

Mitch waved the objection aside. "Don't worry about me, I'm on a different time zone anyway. My body's too confused to sleep."

They talked for two hours, Tyler's exhaustion vanishing as he recounted everything. At last, Mitch sat back. "You did only one thing wrong that I can see," he said.

Tyler blinked. "What?"

"You gave up too easily."

"I can't force her!"

"Did you offer her a ring? Did you ask her to marry you? No? I didn't think so."

"I wanted to!"

"Wanting to doesn't count. Think of it this way. From what I remember, Savvy held onto your relationship—such as it was—for a lot longer before she finally let go." Mitch shook his head. "Sorry to tell you, brother, but a couple weeks of devotion can't make up for that. You have to commit, and that means acting."

"Like when you chased Cory to Brazil?" Tyler was beginning to understand.

"Exactly."

Tyler smirked. "If I remember correctly, you *wanted* to go, but we talked you out of it. Savvy and I both told you to give her space. Only after Cory e-mailed you did you finally fly to Brazil." Tyler should know. He'd gone with Mitch and missed the first two weeks of his college classes, nearly blowing his scholarship. "Savvy told me to leave. How can I not respect that?"

Mitch rubbed his chin with a forefinger. "Yeah, I guess you're right." He brightened. "I know. Write her a letter and lay everything on the line. Let her know you're in there for the long haul. Then ask her to call. You can overnight the letter to her. Then the ball's in her court, but you've shown you're not giving up."

"What if she doesn't call?" The thought was very painful.

Mitch raked back his hair, which was inches longer than Tyler's. "You have to assume it's going to work, that's all."

"I won't give up."

"Good."

With new hope in his heart, Tyler tried to rise. The sooner he wrote the letter, the sooner Savvy would receive it.

But Mitch didn't let him go into the kitchen for a pen. "Oh, no," he said. "Not now. You're too tired to stand straight, much less write a letter that's going to convince a woman you're in love with her. No, it's bed for you. There's plenty of time in the morning."

Tyler let his brother lead him to his bedroom, grateful it was in the old part of the house so he wouldn't have to climb the stairs. "Thanks," he mumbled, as he fell onto the bed.

"Don't worry about it." Mitch walked back to the doorway and switched off the light.

* * * * *

Tyler slowly regained consciousness. He could feel that he was lying on his own bed, stomach down, face smashed into his pillow. Voices came to him, rising and ebbing in the distance. As he turned slightly, his head sent a warning shot of pain: *don't move.*

He groaned and brought a hand to his head. Then he heard giggles, coming from much closer. Prying open an eye and squinting valiantly, he spied three small forms hovering in his doorway. He thought it was Benjamin, Caleb, and Mara, but he wasn't sure.

"Shoo!" Amanda's voice came from the hall. The children giggled loudly.

"Aw," Benjamin said, "we just wanted to play with him."

"Go on back to Uncle Mitch. Go on, now."

The kids scattered, and Tyler let his eyes fall shut. But all at once the night came back to him. Savvy! The letter! How could he have slept at all with something so important needing to be done?

He leapt to his feet—well, at least he tried to leap. Instead, he fell back to the bed, his hands grabbing his aching head.

"That'll teach you to stay up all night," Amanda said from the doorway.

The pain was easing now. "I need a pen," he mumbled. "Some paper." He'd rather compose on the computer, but that seemed too impersonal for what he had to say.

Amanda laughed. "Okay, but first maybe you need an aspirin?"

"No. I'll be okay." He shook his head . . . and groaned. "Okay, would you get me one?"

She was back in less than a minute with a tall glass of water and the aspirin. He swallowed the pill dry and then downed the water. "Thanks," he said. "Hey, wait a minute. What are you doing here anyway?" He grabbed his glasses from the bedside table and stuck them on. There was something different about his sister today.

"We're all here, silly," she said. "Mitch and Cory are back. We're having an impromptu family reunion. The older kids even begged to stay home from school, and we shamelessly let them. We'll probably get hauled off for neglect or something, but it isn't every day Mitch comes home." She laughed, and Tyler grinned. She was right—this was a day to celebrate.

"There is other news," she said, resting her hand on her stomach. "Wonderful news."

"Better than Mitch coming home?"

"Way better."

"Must be big, then. I know he's your favorite brother."

"Would you zip it?"

His eyes went to her hand. "Are you having twins?"

Abruptly, she sat down beside him, her smile dissolving into tears. "Oh, Tyler, I got a call from Paula's boyfriend this morning. He told me that if we draw up the papers for adoption, Paula will sign them! She'll actually sign them! Can you believe it?" Tears were falling down her face, but Tyler knew they were happy tears.

"Really?" Tyler punched a fist in the air. "Oh, Manda, that's so great! No, it's absolutely wonderful!" He closed his eyes, sending a silent prayer of thanks heavenward. "I thought I really blew it in California. I'm so glad I was wrong."

"We were right to wait." Amanda's smile was back, wide and radiant. "I wanted to go to court with guns ablazing, but waiting gave Paula time to think about what was best for the children. Oh, Tyler, I'm so, so happy! Now we'll never have to wonder if they'll be taken away. We can go to the temple and be sealed." She wiped a stray tear.

Tyler's own eyes were feeling moist and his heart full. He leaned over and gave his sister a big hug. "Have you called Savvy?" he asked.

"Not yet. I didn't think to grab the number before we left this morning. If you have the number, I'll call her now."

Tyler was on the verge of volunteering to do it himself. Maybe she'd changed her mind. Maybe if he called with this good news her heart would soften toward him. Once he had her on the phone maybe he could make her see . . .

Make her see. He swallowed hard. No, it had to be her choice. This was Amanda's news, and she had the right to share it. He would write the letter.

Ten drafts later, Tyler's handwritten plea for Savvy's heart was finished. Immediately, he drove to the post office. When he arrived home, he found all his siblings—Amanda, Kerrianne, and Mitch in the kitchen. Voices and children's screams outside signaled that the rest of the family was out on the patio.

"Did you tell Savvy?" he asked Amanda.

They all looked at him knowingly, but he didn't care how much his emotions where showing. He had to know.

"Yes," Amanda said quietly.

"Did she ask about me?"

She shook her head. "I'm sorry, Tyler."

"That's okay. I'm not giving up."

"Good."

"In fact, I'm going back to Colorado."

"What! You just got here." Amanda looked around wildly at the others. "Tell him."

"We talked about this last night," Mitch said. "We agreed that it has to be her choice."

Tyler flexed his hands. "You said yourself that I have to assume it's going to work. That means when she gets that letter tomorrow, she *will* call me and when she does, I'm going to be right there on her doorstep."

"And if she doesn't?" Kerrianne's eyes showed her worry.

His heartache intensified. "I'll cross that bridge when I come to it."

"Mitch, do something," Amanda said.

Mitch shrugged. "Okay. Tyler, do you want to use my frequent flyer miles? I have a ton of them."

"Mitch!" Amanda slugged him on the shoulder. "That's not what I meant. What if it only makes things worse? Tyler's our last chance to have Savvy in this family, you know."

"There's something else to consider," Kerrianne said. "What if Derek dies? She'll need somebody then—somebody who knew him."

Tyler's stomach wrenched. Derek was dying, and he'd left Savvy there alone. Yes, he'd done as she asked, but had it been the right thing? His sisters seemed to be constantly changing their minds.

Maybe he was already too late.

Chapter Twenty-Seven

Savvy didn't know whether to be triumphant or devastated that Tyler had left Colorado. She'd begged him to go, and yet she didn't want him to leave at all. Truthfully, she wanted little more than to fall into his arms, but what if his feelings for her weren't as deep as he professed? Lexi seemed so sure that he was in love with someone else. And Tyler, with his glib tongue, had fooled her before. *But not on purpose,* she thought. *Never on purpose.*

What have I done? she thought more than once. She had the sense of somehow failing a test. But what else could she do? She loved Tyler, but trusting him was another matter entirely.

"Do you want to talk about it?" Derek asked her on Wednesday afternoon. "You look like you lost your best friend."

I did, she thought. Aloud she said, "I'm fine. What would you like for lunch?" Each day had become a challenge to entice him to eat the foods he was permitted. The choices were so limited that he'd lost much of his appetite.

"Will Tyler be coming over?" he asked. "I'd like to see the newspaper."

"He's gone back to Utah," she said. "I'll get you a subscription."

Lexi looked up from a book Savvy knew she'd already read three times. "He's gone? But he didn't say good-bye!" She glared at Savvy. "This is your fault, isn't it?" She ran from the room, and seconds later they heard her door slam.

"I'm sorry," Derek said softly.

"It doesn't matter." She arose and took a few steps toward the kitchen.

"People do change," Derek said. "I did. Maybe you should think about that."

His voice was so gentle it made Savvy want to cry. She left the room hurriedly.

She was making lunch when Amanda called with the wonderful news about Kevin and Mara. "I'm so happy for you!" Savvy said, tears coming to her eyes for what seemed like the millionth time that day. It was a miracle. Tyler was right—they still did exist! She sent a silent prayer of thanks heavenward.

She wanted to ask Amanda about Tyler. If he'd arrived safely. If he was all right. He'd been so upset. But she couldn't ask because that would be opening a door too painful to talk about. He was out of her life. Period.

But she didn't want him to be. She kept Amanda on the phone a long while, talking with her about anything she could think of. At last Amanda made a reference to Tyler, so Savvy knew he was there and safe. *Old habits die hard,* she thought.

The day dragged into night. On Thursday morning, Savvy decided to take Derek's brown sedan and find him a newspaper. He and Lexi were watching TV in the front room, with Derek lying on the couch propped up with pillows. "I'll only be a few minutes," she told them.

"Take as long as you want," Lexi muttered.

Savvy considered a moment. With Tyler gone, she would have to leave the house more often. "Maybe I'll swing by the store," she said. "Call me if you need me." She'd take the cell phone Derek had confiscated from Lexi last week.

As she drove down the street, she saw the mailman opening the neighbor's mailbox. Savvy was tempted to wait in the drive to see if her mother had sent the package she'd promised, but she was more anxious to get back to Derek. *It'll be there when I get home,* she thought.

Less than an hour later, Savvy drove back to Derek's street. She stopped at the mailbox, but it was empty, so either Lexi had picked it up, or there wasn't any mail.

She walked up to the porch. Had it only been two days ago that she'd told Tyler to leave? It seemed like a lifetime. She twisted the knob and opened the door.

She saw immediately that something was terribly wrong. Derek was lying on the floor, his head bent back at an unnatural angle as he struggled for breath. Lexi was standing over him, limbs frozen, her ashen face filled with horror.

"Savvy!" Lexi cried, her eyes wide. "Help him. Help him! Please!"

"What happened?" Savvy pushed Lexi out of the way and knelt beside Derek. She tried to adjust his head, but he struggled against her, still gasping for breath. She looked up at Lexi through her tears. "Call an ambulance!"

But Lexi was frozen to the spot, unable to do nothing but cry and mutter, "Help him. Oh, help him!" Lurching to her feet, Savvy found the phone and dialed, rushing back to Derek's side.

The next fifteen minutes were a nightmare as the ambulance arrived and whisked Derek away. Since her first outburst, Lexi hadn't spoken, the tears running down her face. Savvy put an arm around her, fearing that Lexi would push her away, but her sister sank into her embrace.

"Come on," Savvy led her to Derek's car and drove to the hospital.

Dr. Miller arrived and was already in with Derek, but he emerged before thirty minutes had passed. "I'm sorry," he said, shaking his head. "He's in heart failure. We've given him medication to lessen the symptoms and ease his suffering, but there's nothing more we can do."

Lexi let out a scream, clinging to Savvy, who tried to soothe her the best she could. Savvy's own heart felt tight and her tears close to the surface. She wished Tyler were with them; she could use his strength right then.

"You can see him," Dr. Miller added. "He's fighting really hard, but I don't know how long he'll be conscious."

Savvy practically carried Lexi into a room where they found Derek hooked up to an IV and all sorts of monitors. An oxygen tube ran up his nose. He opened his eyes as they came in. Savvy's tears fell as she saw him try to smile.

"Pumpkin," he said, his voice low and weak.

Lexi rushed to him. "I'm sorry, Daddy."

"It wasn't your fault. I was the one who insisted on getting up. I was tired of that stupid couch."

"Don't leave me," Lexi sobbed as she grasped his hand with the IV needle.

"I'm not leaving," he said. "I'm just going on ahead with your mom and Brenton. We'll save a spot for you . . . and Savvy. But you're going to have to help."

Lexi sniffed hard. "How?"

"I want you to go to church and be baptized. And someday I want you to do temple work for your mother and me so we can be sealed forever. This is very important. I wrote it down for you. Savvy can help. Be a good girl, okay?"

Lexi nodded, her face crumpling. "I will."

Derek looked toward Savvy. "You've got to give that boy a chance," he said, struggling for each breath. "I know your pride tells you not to, but he's not the same person he was when you first fell in love with him."

"Why can't he breathe?" Savvy asked Dr. Miller.

"There's fluid in his lungs. It's a symptom of the disease."

Savvy touched Derek on the arm. "Does it hurt?"

"They gave me something. I'm not even afraid." He closed his eyes for a long moment and then whispered, "Be good to each other. Be happy. I love you."

"I love you, Dad," Lexi cried. "Dad?" But Derek's eyes remained closed.

"He's lost consciousness," a nurse said, making a sympathetic noise in her throat. "He could wake up again."

Derek never did wake. They waited in the room for over an hour before the heart monitor flat-lined, sending a high-pitched, eerie beeping throughout the room. As per Derek's request, there were no heroic lifesaving measures. The nurse came in and silenced the monitor. Lexi turned into Savvy's arms and wept. Savvy held her, staring at the still face of the man who had helped give her life. *Have a good journey,* she told him. Tears fell down her face and into Lexi's hair.

Savvy was vaguely aware of Dr. Miller reentering the room. He checked Derek briefly, held a whispered conversation with the nurse, and then left the room.

When Savvy had her emotions under control, she nudged Lexi toward the door. The girl tore from her grasp and flew to the bed. She kissed her father's cheek. "Bye, Daddy!" she whispered. Then she let Savvy guide her from the room.

* * * * *

Savvy had never imagined the many decisions involved after the death of a loved one. Fortunately, the news spread fast, and the bishop of the ward was on their doorstep before they arrived home, ready to help with arrangements. His wife was with him and had thought to bring lunch in case they felt like eating. Savvy tried to eat to please her, but it was a hopeless cause. Lexi didn't even try. She went into her room and shut the door.

Later, when the bishop and his wife finally left, promising to accompany them to the funeral home the next day to pick out a casket, Savvy went into Derek's bedroom. Her mind replayed the times she had sat here with him, discussing books and life. So much crammed into such a short period of time, memories Savvy would cherish forever.

Automatically, she began tidying the room. On his dresser she discovered a folder of personal papers, including his will. After only the second paragraph, she sank down on the bed, shocked to learn that Derek had left custody of Lexi jointly to her and Tyler.

I can't believe it, she thought over and over. She felt betrayed.

In a panic, she called the attorney, who assured her that both she and Tyler could choose if they wanted to accept the appointment but that those had been Derek's wishes.

She hung up and forced herself to read the rest. The house was to be sold to settle debts and hospital bills, but there was a healthy savings for Lexi, and with the settlement from her mother's and brother's death, she wouldn't have to worry about college tuition. Derek had left his car and a fifty-thousand dollar life insurance benefit to Savvy, which generously solved her immediate problems of paying rent and tuition, but to Savvy it was a bitter recompense. The only thing she'd wanted was sole custody of Lexi—her sister. Belatedly, she realized that she should have pushed harder to become Lexi's official guardian before Derek's death. She'd fight it of course, but she knew Tyler wouldn't take Derek's trust lightly. He'd probably always want to remain in some kind of contact with Lexi and that meant running into him often.

Savvy's heart leapt in her chest. Was that what Derek had intended all along? Did he think that by forcing them to interact that Savvy would finally succumb to Tyler's charm? Or that Tyler would finally give up his thin girlfriend?

I'll never get over him this way, Savvy thought, feeling depressed. She had no idea what to do now.

She took the will to Lexi, who read it without any expression of triumph or disappointment. Her entire face was wilted, as it had been since Derek's death. Her shoulders shrank inward, and her eyes were red and swollen.

"I guess we'll have to tell Tyler," Savvy said.

Lexi's eyes riveted on hers. "You're not going to fight it?"

Ha. As if you care. "Do you want me to?" Savvy gave a weary sigh. "You've made it all too apparent that you'd rather be with him."

Lexi seemed stunned, but for a moment Savvy didn't care. She was angry at Derek for his betrayal, furious at Lexi for being so obnoxious, mad that Tyler had stuck around long enough to matter in Lexi's life, and hurt that Tyler had left when she told him to go. She knew the feelings were ridiculous, but she didn't care. She was through acting like an adult. For the past weeks, she'd been strong for Lexi. It was her turn to quietly fall apart, to mourn her losses, to lick her wounds.

Savvy went into Derek's room, shut the door, and sobbed into his pillow.

Chapter Twenty-Eight

Lexi held a hand against her heart as she listened to Savvy sobbing in the next room. A lot of Savvy's pain was her fault, she knew. But she couldn't lose someone else that she loved. She couldn't!

Yet her heart, bruised and sore from her father's passing, *was* breaking again. Not only for her father but for Savvy. *I hurt her,* she thought. *I'm making her cry.*

Guilt swept through Lexi. She closed her eyes and began to pray. God hadn't saved her father, but he had brought Savvy back home that morning when she'd prayed for help. She'd felt so useless, watching her father die. She couldn't even move to find the phone. If Savvy hadn't come home and taken over . . .

Lexi shuddered.

At the hospital her father had seemed so peaceful. *And why not,* she thought. *He's with Mom and Brenton.* Tears leaked from Lexi's eyes. *I believe,* she thought with sudden understanding. *I believe.* Wonder filled her heart. It was true! She would see them again. Another prayer answered.

"I'm sorry, Savvy," Lexi whispered, laying her palm flat against the door. Of course Savvy couldn't hear.

What to do? Lexi knew she had to make it right. There was enough pain around them without her adding to it with her lies.

After a half hour of heavy thinking, Lexi knew what she had to do.

✦ ✦ ✦ ✦ ✦ ✦ ✦

"Savvy?" Lexi called.

Savvy wanted to tell her to go away, but she simply didn't have the strength after her bout of tears. Besides, she needed her sister. They were the only ones who could mourn Derek. *Except for Tyler,* she thought. *He cared about Derek, too.*

Savvy pushed herself up with one arm to a half-sitting position. Her sister was hovering by the door, as though uncertain whether she should enter all the way. She looked lost and afraid, and immediately Savvy felt her own emotions tempering. However obnoxious Lexi had been, she was only a child and Savvy loved her.

"Can I come in?" Lexi's eyes went to where Derek's favorite blanket lay crumpled on the bed.

"Sure."

Lexi came to the bed, and Savvy watched her curl up in the blanket, wondering if she could smell her father on the material, if perhaps it made her feel more secure.

"Do you want me to leave?" Savvy asked.

"No." Lexi's voice was soft.

Savvy was gratified when the girl laid her head against Savvy's shoulder. Savvy put an arm around her and stroked her hair and her cheek. How physically changed she was from the Lexi she'd first met! It had been more than a week since Lexi had put on the dark makeup or worn immodest clothing. Her belly button ring and most of her earrings had disappeared. Savvy knew she couldn't take credit for the changes. The effort had been mutually hers, Tyler's, Derek's, and most of all, Lexi's own choice.

Lexi snuggled closer. Savvy thought she was falling asleep and was startled when Lexi's voice came without a trace of sleepiness. "Why are you still so nice to me, Savvy?"

Savvy was tempted to trivialize the question, but a tremor in Lexi's voice signaled that the question was of great importance. "Because I love you," she said simply. "And I want you to love me. I want to help you be happy again."

Lexi started to sob.

"Hey, sweetie, it's okay." Savvy embraced her sister. "I know you miss your dad, but we're going to get through this together."

"It's not that. Oh, Savvy, I've been so awful to you. I lied about Tyler getting married. I lied about how he feels about you. He hasn't been talking to any girl. I made it all up."

Savvy swallowed hard. Of course Lexi had lied! She'd known it when Tyler suggested it. Still, she'd used Lexi's lie to put distance between them. At the time it had seemed the only way to protect herself, but after Tyler's impassioned plea she wasn't so sure.

"Oh, Lexi," she murmured. "I wish you hadn't done that. I made him leave."

Lexi's whole body was shaking as she cried. "I'm sorry. I'm really, really sorry. I couldn't bear that he'd marry you and then I'd have to worry about . . . about you . . . dying."

Savvy fought down her own tears as she smoothed Lexi's hair. "I wish I could promise you that nothing will ever happen to me, to Tyler, or someone else you care about, but that's the risk that comes with love. Would you rather have not loved your dad? What about your mom or Brenton?"

"It just hurts so bad!" Lexi turned and clung to her, crying harder. "I thought if I made you go away it wouldn't hurt anymore. But I was wrong. I hurt you, and then I felt worse. I'm so sorry. I won't blame you if you and Tyler send me to Minnesota now. I've been horrible."

"You haven't been horrible." Savvy paused. "Well, maybe just a little." She forced a laugh, grateful to see a tiny smile appear on Lexi's face. "But I knew you were dealing with everything the best you could. I was willing to wait. We're sisters, aren't we?"

"I love you, Savvy. I'm so sorry."

"Sh, it's okay." Savvy pulled her closer, but Lexi drew away.

"There's something else." Lexi reached inside the blanket, pulling out a large overnight postal envelope from under her shirt. "This came for you in the mail this morning. I had to sign for it. I saw who it was from, and I hid it from you. That was before Dad . . . you know. I'm so sorry. I wish I could take it all back—"

"It's okay." Savvy cut her off, drawing her back into a tight hug. "You've given it to me now."

Lexi's face was wet, but she wasn't crying anymore. "Aren't you going to read it?"

The thin cardboard seemed to burn into Savvy's fingers, and her heart hammered in her chest. "Yes, okay." She tore it open and found a smaller sealed letter inside.

"You're shaking," Lexi said.

Savvy didn't know why Tyler would send her a letter. Had he changed his mind about his girlfriend? No, she had to stop thinking of him that way. Had she become so embittered that she couldn't find an ounce of faith in the words he'd said to her before leaving Colorado?

The words were written on a single sheet of typing paper in Tyler's bold handwriting.

Dear Savvy,

I'm so deeply, deeply sorry for all the pain I've caused you. Please believe me when I say that I love you more than I have ever loved anyone in my entire life—more than I will ever love anyone else. You are my heart, my breath, and my soul. I do not say this lightly. I want to marry you, I want to wash dishes at your side, I want to cuddle while we watch the stars at night, and I want us to have babies—lots of babies. I want to hear your laughter, touch your hair, and wake up every morning with you in my arms. I want to take you to the temple and make sacred covenants.

Please, Savvy. Will you give us a chance? Do you believe as I do that there is something special between us—that there has always been? The minute you give me the slightest hope, I'll be there. I promise. Call me.

Yours forever and truly,
Tyler

Tears ran down Savvy's face.

"He loves you, doesn't he?" Lexi asked, craning her neck in an effort to see the words.

Savvy looked at her and nodded. "I think so."

"I knew it! So what are you going to do now?"

Savvy wasn't sure. To call meant opening herself to possible pain. Not calling was safer, and yet, was she truly willing to accept a life without him, especially knowing that he was offering the one thing she'd always wanted?

Still, running away would be much less risky.

Lexi had thought so at least. She'd run from her father and then tried to run from a relationship with Savvy. All to prevent the pain of loving. Now Savvy found herself in a similar situation. If she wasn't willing to risk her feelings again, what opportunities for happiness might she miss? Would she spend her entire life wondering what could have been? Surely she could be as brave as Lexi was being by finally allowing herself to love Savvy.

"Daddy said for you to give him another chance," Lexi said. "Didn't he?"

Biting her lip, Savvy nodded. "I'm going to call him."

"Yes!" Lexi sprang from the bed. "I'll get the phone."

Savvy dialed the number she knew by heart.

"Hello?"

For a second, Savvy's breath was swept away. He sounded so near, as though she could reach out and touch him. "I got your letter," she said finally.

There was a pause before he spoke. "I've waited all day. I was so afraid you weren't going to call."

"I only got it now." She stopped and tried to take a breath, but tears were coming too fast for her to speak past them. "Tyler," she choked out, "Derek's dead. Lexi and I . . . we need you."

There were no questions. "I'll be right there."

Savvy hung up the phone, swinging her gaze to Lexi. She felt an immense relief knowing Tyler was coming, knowing he would help her face the next few days. Knowing she wouldn't have to always be strong but could sometimes lean on him.

Lexi wiped her face with Derek's blanket. "So where are we going to live?"

"I don't know. I should finish things in California, but—" There was also Tyler to consider. If things worked out between them . . .

If.

Oh, how she hated that word.

Forcing the thoughts aside, she said, "What about Minnesota? I hear it's lovely this time of year."

"Ugh!" Lexi gave a strangled laugh. "You'd better be kidding."

Savvy grinned. "So do you want dinner? I didn't think I'd ever be hungry again, but my stomach is growling like crazy."

"Me too."

"Come on, then. We'll heat up the food the bishop's wife left."

They were heating their food in the microwave when the doorbell rang. Lexi jumped up from the table. "Must be Tyler."

"Can't be." Savvy smiled at her exuberance. "Remember how long it took to drive here? Even if he flew, there's no way he could get here so fast. It's probably someone from the ward."

Yet when Lexi opened the door, there was Tyler, looking tall and handsome in the light from the setting sun. "Come in," Lexi said.

Savvy's mouth dropped open. "That was quick." She felt the urge to throw herself into his arms, but a sudden shyness overcame her.

He gave them his dimpled grin. "I flew back yesterday. Been staying at that motel down the way." He reached out a hand to both of them. "I'm so sorry about Derek. I wish I could have been here for you."

"No." Savvy shook her head. "It was all right. We were together." Lexi looked at her and smiled. Savvy's heart felt a rush of love for her sister. They *were* together now, and nothing could separate them. "Did the attorney call you about Lexi?" she asked. "Can you believe Derek wanted us to share custody?"

"Nobody called me yet," he said, "but that's a great idea."

"What?" Savvy put her hands on her hips. "Lexi should be with me!"

Tyler held up his hands, his face cracking into another wide grin. "Okay, okay, I surrender! Just don't look at me like that. And for goodness' sake, put your hands down."

Savvy didn't budge. "You'll let me have custody?" She wanted this taken care of before anything else.

"Yes. Full custody—I'll just visit when you let me." When Savvy relaxed, he added, "Still, it's a shame for all of Derek's plans to go awry."

She was confused. "What do you mean?"

"Well, it seems to me that Derek was trying to play matchmaker, don't you think? So now the question is—are we going to disappoint him?"

Savvy opened her mouth to speak, but Tyler held up a hand. "I've been a jerk in the past. I know it. But I know where my place is now—with you, Savvy. I meant everything I said to you two days ago and in that letter. I love you, and I want to spend the rest of eternity with you. But look at me here, spilling my guts when I have no idea if you called me because you want to give us a chance, or if you need help with the funeral arrangements. Tell me, I can take it. Either way, I'm sticking around for as long as you need me."

Savvy had no doubt that he would stick around. He always kept his word. Oh, she'd been so wrong! So afraid. She knew Tyler better than anyone else, and yet she hadn't permitted herself to see that he was serious—that he really loved her. And there was no way he would say he loved her unless he was sure.

Next to her, Lexi was grinning. When she caught Savvy's glance, she nodded encouragingly. Savvy squeezed her sister's arm.

Tyler took a step toward her, reaching out for her hand. "Can you give me another chance? No, actually, that's not what I want. A chance is not enough." He went down on one knee, holding tightly to her hand. "Savvy, will you marry me?"

She bit her bottom lip, her hand tingling from his touch. This was the moment of truth. The moment she had to risk everything. But hadn't she already made the decision when she'd placed that call?

Tyler's grin faltered at her hesitation. "Hey, I think it's only the proper thing, us getting married, since neither of us want to give up custody of our new daughter." He said it lightly, but she knew that he waited with everything on the line.

He wasn't safe, dependable Chris by a long shot. But Tyler was a good man, and unlike Chris, he made her heart race and her senses zing. He made her laugh at the world. He made her realize how wonderful it was to be alive.

"Well, say okay already!" Lexi danced from one foot to the next with anticipation, her eyes gleaming. "Better yet, say something like"— her face lifted to the ceiling as she struck a pose—'I acquiesce to your request.' That's much more romantic."

Taking a deep breath, Savvy turned and met Tyler's emerald gaze. "I, uh, acquiesce. Oh yes, Tyler, I'll marry you!"

He shot to his feet, and in the next instant she was in his arms. "I love you," she whispered.

He stared at her so contentedly that she felt compelled to add, "But so help me, if you even so much as look sideways at me when I regain the ten pounds I've lost these past weeks—which I fully intend to do, mind you—I'll make you wish—" Whatever she was going to say was lost as Tyler's lips met hers. Not a whisper this time but a kiss that completely stole her breath away.

Then he picked her up and spun her around. Happiness burst through her, tingling to the tips of her fingers and toes. "I love you, Savannah Hergarter," he whispered. "And I promise you, we are going to be the happiest couple in the whole world."